SHAKER

a novel by

C.C. Prestel

ISBN-13: 978-0-578-45489-4

To my father for being my biggest fan (and perhaps my only?)

Contents

ACKNOWLEDGMENTS

To Kit, thanks for your moral support and encouragement.

Special thanks to Beth Dorward for her fantastic editing.

Thanks to Eric Wilder, whose cover design turned out better than I could have imagined.

Dad, Greg, and Andy: I appreciate your taking the time to read the early versions of the manuscript and provide useful feedback.

Prologue

I have been known by several names spanning two lives, but the one of which I am the fondest is Shaker. That moniker was bestowed upon me by my comrades, the brothers and sisters who shared in my extraordinary ordeal. My precise age is uncertain. Those with an acumen for astronomy estimate it to be north of eighty years. I cannot dispute this assessment, for I feel as though I've lived for several centuries, a result of far-reaching adventures that I would have once thought inconceivable.

I am now in a position to consolidate the journals and notes that I've maintained over the years into a single narrative. I have also solicited the recollections of those comrades still with me in order to create a record of events with as much accuracy and integrity as possible. I undertake this task not to satisfy a vanity or provide entertainment. I have a higher purpose, though I am resigned to think of it as a futile endeavor. My goal is to account for the lives that disappeared so many years ago, and others that likely followed. There is no longer a wrong to be righted. I, and those still with me, seek no retribution. Instead, we trust that documents such as this might solve mysteries that have hopefully not been lost to the passing decades—or centuries.

I have laid out the scraps of paper in chronological order on the floor beneath me and realized that several pages are missing. The penciled notes on the ones I have are faded, though I am optimistic that my recollection of the events they describe has not. I stand and survey the clutter on the floor before me, wondering if the project I have undertaken might be too daunting. *Too daunting?* If I can survive the events that are on those pages, then surely I can manage to write a narrative about them.

My personal journey is fraught with regrettable missteps and careless choices that sometimes cast me in an unfavorable light. At this advanced stage of my life, I have nothing to gain from embellishing this record of my thoughts and actions. My commitment to you is to document a frank and honest account of my experiences. I shall not attempt to soften the horrors that I have witnessed, lest anyone fail to appreciate the universal nature of such atrocities and the impact they can have within any society on any world.

And yes, a part of me simply wants my story—*our* story—to be told.

1

My comrades and I divide our lives into two distinct epochs, one that occurred *before*, and the one *after*. We typically employ these standalone words when conversing among ourselves, as there is no need to further define the reference. I've never had to tell this story to anyone outside of my community and I will do my best to include the details that an outsider could not know. In this case, "before" and "after" refer to the abduction. That is, our life on Earth and our life away from it. Many of us feel as though we've lived two completely separate lives, a perception undoubtedly produced by the stark contrast between the two.

I left the planet Earth abruptly on a warm summer evening during that planet's year of 2021. I know this much because I'm certain that I was thirty-two years old. The passage of time has fogged our memories and provoked some debate about the month and date among those who were taken with me. The precise date and time are inconsequential.

Sometime during the early morning hours, I was walking on a dark, desolate road a few miles outside of St. George, Utah. I was following the road back to the cabin belonging to the family of my friend, Gary. I had been staying with him for a week or so when he invited me to accompany him to a casual poker game at the home of an acquaintance. The game was held at a house situated in the hills east of town, approximately two miles from Gary's cabin. It broke up well after midnight and I opted to walk back to the cabin rather than ride with my friend. It was a beautiful, warm night and I took advantage of the serenity and solitude to collect my thoughts. The new moon accommodated a night sky that was bursting with stars and galaxies, reminiscent of a planetarium I had once visited on a school field trip. It's fair to say that I had consumed an embarrassing amount of alcohol in the months leading up to that evening, but I was not in the least way inebriated that night.

What happened next, I can neither recall nor explain. This is not a consequence of the decades that have elapsed since the event. My memory of those days is actually quite comprehensive—a result of repeatedly swapping stories of our lives *before* with my comrades. Even in the days that immediately followed that night, I couldn't have described what transpired because I had no recollection of it whatsoever. This is made more curious by the fact that I had been so fixated on the brilliant display in the night sky, yet I was still unable to foresee what snatched me—something that must have originated from the very same sky. When one falls asleep, he has no memory of the moments just before sleep occurs, yet he knows that at some point he crossed the line from awareness to oblivion. There might have been a blinding flash of light, a transporter beam, or some other device akin to popular science fiction, but I cannot say.

Then, as if I had regained consciousness following a surgical procedure requiring a general anesthetic, I awoke with a mind as barren as a newborn baby. My body remained frozen and I struggled to catch my breath. There didn't seem to be enough oxygen to comfortably fill my lungs as I gasped for air. A hissing sound above me brought to mind steam escaping from a pipe, and I felt a cold breeze blowing down upon me. It stopped after a few seconds and my respiration became easier. With my physical survival now out of immediate danger, my brain commenced the reboot process toward complete awareness. Memories poured in and I began to take notice of my surroundings. One moment I was walking in Utah, and the next I was in a vastly different environment, feeling as though a substantial amount of time had passed, yet having nothing in my memory to fill the void. The amount of elapsed time was a mystery, though the stiffness in my joints and muscles painfully suggested that they had been immobile for days.

Where I lay was anything but a comfortable hospital bed. I slowly regained my senses to find myself in a room nearly devoid of light. I struggled to rise, only to discover that I was bound by one wrist and one ankle, confining me to the few square feet which I presently occupied. The bindings were of a material I did not recognize. I can best describe them as straps of a plastic and rubber alloy that were anchored to the wall behind me. There were no clasps or buckles attached to the loops around my wrist and ankle, as if the straps had been fused into loops after being fixed around my joints. Attempts to remove them proved futile. Instinctively, I reached for my phone and realized that all of my personal effects were gone, although I still wore the pants, shirt, and underwear from the night I was walking in Utah. My shoes and socks had been removed, leaving me barefoot.

Resembling a mime, I felt around in the dim light to ascertain my boundaries, but unlike the silent street performer, my walls were quite real. My enclosure was approximately three feet deep and three feet high, preventing me from standing erect. It was just wide enough that I could lie horizontally with my legs nearly fully extended. The rear wall, floor, and ceiling of the box were solid, but the side walls were constructed of a fencing material, with holes just large enough to stick a finger through, and they stood only about ten inches high. Above them, on both sides, was open space to another berth that seemed to resemble mine. No part of this cage was metal; its texture was that of a hard plastic, and of the strongest compound. There was no front wall. The restraining straps allowed just enough range of movement for me to stick my head beyond the front boundary of my compartment, but it was too dark to see more than a few feet in front of me.

After a few minutes spent squirming about my tiny space, my eyes had adjusted to the scarcity of light and my ears had tuned into the greater surroundings. It became obvious that I was not alone. On both sides of me, figures were stirring and emitting incoherent grumbling sounds. I detected similar noises in the distance from all directions except the wall behind me. Some were gasping for a much-needed breath of air while others seemed to be fidgeting about. A tired voice yelled from off to my left.

"Hey!"

Other voices joined the chorus until the discord filled the room. "Who's there?" "Somebody!" "Where am I?" Many of the shouts were in foreign languages, some of which spawned other questions in the same tongue. A few minutes passed before most of the inhabitants realized that none of their cries were being answered—we were simply reacting to each other's screams. Others continued to clamor for answers from the rest of us, as if we were somehow more cognizant of the purpose of our incarceration. It would provide them with a distraction of sorts, if not a small amount of comfort, to find someone more knowledgeable than they, and their questions were not merely rhetorical. These were likely people that had blindly lumbered their way through life dependent on others to provide them with whatever direction they required at any junction. We had clearly established that nobody in our presence knew more than anyone else, yet this fact did not discourage their grousing. The world needs followers too, I supposed, and we were to have our share in this group.

The cacophony of shouting revealed something interesting. Not only had I neighbors on both sides, I could hear people below me and across from me as well. Finally, a booming voice began to dominate. It originated from the enclosure to my left (as facing forward). The accent sounded Caribbean.

"Quiet! Everybody calm down!" he repeated until his voice was the only sound in the room except for a constant, faint rumbling from beyond the walls. "Now, who's in charge?" Silence. "Does anybody know what's going on or where we are?" More silence. I felt a slight sense of relief that I was not alone in my predicament nor in my inability to make heads or tails of the situation. Misery loves company, I guess.

"Well then," the voice continued, "let's find out what we *do* know." I felt comforted—as much as could be expected—by the man's calming, authoritative tone. Over the course of the next hour or so (it was impossible to accurately measure the passage of time), he led a systematic discussion, during which we ascertained the following:

There were approximately 45 to 50 of us in what we assumed at that time to be a large room. Attempts at obtaining an exact count were hampered by the inability of some inhabitants to understand English. Our group included approximately thirty-five men and fifteen women. Even as the Caribbean man moderated the primary discussion, a few secondary conversations quietly ensued in other languages. Other than English, I recognized Spanish and a language that I presumed to be Portuguese. I heard one or two other languages that were completely foreign to me.

We were stacked three people high in two rows with a long corridor in between us, like tiny berths in the sleeping car of a passenger train, or the tiny racks found in a World War II-era submarine. On that first day, I was indifferent to occupying a bunk on the top level, as it hadn't occurred to me that we might be there for some time. I would soon come to relish my premium locale as a small consolation in the face of adversity. Those on the middle and lower levels were not as fortunate. Shit flows downhill, as the saying goes. Our restraints allowed us to move about the entire space of our berth and even touch the person on either side of us. Despite the scarcity of light, the number and directions of the voices I heard indicated that I occupied a space near the middle of the room.

We hailed from at least five different countries, all of which were located in North, Central, and South America. A couple of people served as English-to-Spanish translators, which seemed to minimally accommodate everybody save for one man. He was located toward one end of the room and spoke a language that sounded somewhat primitive to me. This man talked quietly to himself, and a few others sobbed, but the majority of the inhabitants eventually participated, quite earnestly, in the Caribbean man's discussion.

For the most part, nobody could recall anything that might enlighten our predicament. A few spoke of seeing a great flash of light before blacking out, but like myself, most remembered nothing. Nobody seemed to know anybody else in the room—there were no friends, acquaintances, or family members among us. The common denominator was that we had been alone prior to our abductions. Some were driving on deserted roads, some had been out walking, and a few had been camping. Over the next several hours, I would come to learn quite a bit about the diverse characters with whom I shared this confined space. Our group comprised medical professionals, college students, soldiers, teachers, and many other everyday occupations. We even had a member of a Mexican drug cartel, though we weren't aware of that until much later.

"I wonder how long we've been here?" a man finally asked. A reply came from the berth directly across from mine. I could almost make out his face—he looked fairly young.

"Feel your face."

"Excuse me?"

"Feel your face," he repeated. "I think several weeks have passed." I heeded his instruction and was taken aback by the feel of a heavy beard, for I was clean shaven on the night of my abduction. We knew now that we had been sleeping or unconscious for a significant period of time.

The revelation suddenly made me feel famished and parched, and I wondered aloud if this might be the reason we had been awakened. The young voice across from me concurred with a surprising air of confidence.

We could only speculate about our location. An occasional vibration, a perception of motion, and a distant rumbling suggested that we might be moving. Thus, we concluded that we were on a ship. That is, we were passengers on a ship at sea or possibly an airplane, although the absence of even the slightest turbulence rendered the latter scenario unlikely. Our surroundings could certainly be explained as some sort of cargo hold.

An early consensus was that we were being held as hostages by a terrorist organization, but our circumstances did not conform neatly to that hypothesis, nor any other we could devise. How could we have been unconscious for so long? How is it that we were taken from locations that are hundreds—even thousands—of miles apart? Where are our captors? Why were so many of us taken?

Our deliberation was suddenly interrupted by the sound of a hatch opening at one end of the hold.

2

I feel as though I've jumped a bit ahead of myself. My complete story began thirty-one years before my abduction, though when I reflect upon that period of my life it seems as if it happened to someone else. I am simply repeating his tale as it was told to me countless times around a campfire or within the confines of a wooden hut. Sharing stories of our backgrounds, especially in the early days, was our primary source of entertainment and a means to ward off insanity. It seemed crucial to remind ourselves that the lives we had *before* were real, and perhaps we could return to them one day.

In the time *before*, I was known as Michael Taylor, or Mike to my friends and family. I was born just outside of Baltimore in Catonsville, Maryland. When I was a small child, my father moved the family to Richmond, Virginia, where I would grow up in a modest suburban home. I was the third of four children, with two older sisters and a younger brother. My father worked as an accountant for an aerospace company and had ascended to the position of vice president at the time of my disappearance. As a child, I never knew him to lose his temper but he was certainly not a pushover. He made his expectations clearly known and enforced them in a businesslike sort of way. I found myself in his doghouse on several occasions feeling remorse in having disappointed him.

My mother taught third grade at a local elementary school up until my little brother was born, at which time my parents agreed that she would stay home to care for her young brood. She talked of returning to teaching after we had flown the nest but had yet to do so when I left. She was significantly more animated than my father, which could be favorable or embarrassing, depending on the social setting. She had a livid temper that she held in check most of the time, though I have distinct memories of her wrath reigning down upon me—and probably deservedly so. My parents' top priority always seemed to be the well-being of their children, and I benefited from their attention and wisdom. I have no doubt that they disagreed at times, but they always presented a united front in the presence of their children.

My childhood is best described as a typical American upbringing for those days. I was a good student, a sub-par musician (in spite of countless hours spent fumbling with my sister's guitar), and a poor athlete, though not for a want of desire and determination. As a result of physically maturing a little later than my peers, I didn't participate in high school sports, other than one year of junior varsity wrestling, which I abandoned the following season in favor of the drama club. I discovered that my oratory and acting talents exceeded my physical abilities and I enjoyed being on the stage. My verbal skills carried over to ordinary high school life, which is a polite way of saying that I could be a pretty good bullshitter. This served me well when entertaining my friends in the cafeteria or negotiating with a teacher for a better grade. During my senior year I served as editor of the school newspaper, fueled not so much by a passion for journalism as a means to pad my resume for college.

An unwelcome associate to my delayed puberty was inexperience with the opposite gender. I counted numerous girl friends within my social circle but no true *girlfriends*. My gregarious, sometimes ostentatious, behavior in front of crowds masked an innocent shyness when it came to girls. I had my first date—a triple date with friends—at the age of sixteen. I had a steady girlfriend at the time of my high school graduation, though I lagged behind my friends in certain sexual experiences—compared to their boastful claims, at least.

By my freshman year in college I had sprouted to a lanky height of six feet, four inches and began to gradually fill out. Unfortunately, I suffered the curse of being unusually tall without any hand–eye coordination, dexterity, and quickness to match. Those skills would one day catch up, but they trailed a few years behind. In the meantime, I often suffered the humiliation of being chosen first in a pick-up basketball game and failing to live up to expectations. This drove me to work harder, and I spent hours refining my game on playground courts. I allowed nothing to deter me from my goal. By my college graduation I had become a respectable force on the intramural basketball scene.

Despite a larger than average size and an affinity for the game, I could never have been characterized as a tough guy on (or off) the court. I shied away from contact and relied more on my newfound quickness. I had clearly inherited my father's equanimity and my mother's affability. I always sought amicable solutions to a conflict rather than look for any paltry excuse to scuffle; being liked was more important to me than being feared. I cannot recall ever being in a physical altercation prior to my abduction, save for a few innocuous spats with my kid brother.

Returning to the subject of my university years, I attended the nearby University of Richmond and chose to study, to the slight dismay of my father, English literature. His concern was likely the combination of wishing me greater financial opportunities in life, and a higher return on his investment in my tuition, for which he was footing the bill. Still, he only passively voiced his concerns while my mother displayed her unconditional and unrestrained approval.

My success in college was attributed more to my competitive nature than a desire to learn. I focused my efforts on mastering the art of achieving a high grade, and if I happened to learn something along the way, then all the better. I've always enjoyed reading classic literature, with a nod to my mother for introducing me to her personal collection at a young age. But reading a book when it's mandated is far less enjoyable than when it's read voluntarily, even before factoring in the term papers, exams, and other classwork that is inevitably attached to it. Had I known how much I would miss those books just a decade later, I might have spent more time in the library than at keg parties. During my four years in college, I toiled through countless professor-mandated novels and thoroughly enjoyed countless unmandated novels on my own time.

I also made up for lost time in the pursuit of the fairer sex while in college. One can never be too sure how he stacks up against the competition, but I considered myself at a minimum to be an average looking guy who could make up some ground with his personality. Girlfriends would tell me that I was handsome, though I had to take that with a grain of salt, assuming they were only telling me what I wanted to hear. Still, I enjoyed my fair share of relationships. A few seemed quite serious at the time; none seemed the least bit serious in hindsight. It's easy to confuse lust for love at that age.

I had nurtured a penchant for creative writing since I first learned to form a sentence, and my career plan was noble. I would teach English and spend my summers in pursuit of writing a novel—with historical fiction being my preference. The former goal came easy to me. Upon graduation, I settled in comfortably as a high school English and literature teacher in the nearby town of Petersburg. The latter ambition was thwarted by the abundance of more leisurely summer activities that proved more enticing to a young man in his early twenties. I participated in a local basketball league and otherwise occupied those first few summers traveling, drinking beer, watching television, and not the least of all, chasing women. All of those self-involved bachelor pursuits came to an abrupt, albeit necessary, halt when I found myself with a family.

I met Lindsay at a friend's house shortly after my twenty-fourth birthday. Gary had been a friend of mine since childhood and his girlfriend at the time had graduated from the University of Virginia with Lindsay. Memorial Day was as an excuse as good as any for our circle to converge for a barbecue and beer. I soon found myself with a sufficient mixture of courage and alcohol to approach the appealing newcomer who had captured my attention from the moment she arrived. I thought she might be a little out of my league with respect to physical appearance but hoped that I might charm her into at least one evening out with me.

Something I said that day must have struck the right chord, or perhaps she didn't place as much emphasis on superficial qualities as I did, because we began seeing each other exclusively within a few weeks of the cookout. My relationship with Lindsay was far from being my first, and the comparisons intimated that my feelings for her were beyond anything I'd ever felt. I sheepishly confided to my friends that I couldn't imagine my life without her. My candidness was clearly played to the wrong audience, and my buddies rewarded it with playful ridicule, which I convinced myself to be borne out of jealousy. Undeterred, I resolved to take my future more seriously and make her my wife before she came to her senses and found a suitor with brighter prospects.

Once again, my instincts apparently led to the correct course of action, as we were married in two years, nearly to the day, after the barbecue. The celebration was met with great fanfare, as I was the first among my siblings and immediate friends to take the plunge. I felt a bit young to be married even relative to that day and age—the twenty-first century—but I had little doubt that it was the right step for me personally. My wife was continuing her education as a medical student at the University of Virginia, so I relocated to Charlottesville and found a job teaching literature and theater arts at the local community college. On a whim, I hooked up with an amateur theater group and took to the stage in community theater productions where the cast often outnumbered the audience, which mattered little to us thespians.

The next two years passed conventionally, neither exceeding nor disappointing my expectations. It would be disingenuous to portray a storybook romance here. We settled into a pleasant, albeit monotonous, routine, and I can say with certainty that I was content. I believe that Lindsay would have described our situation similarly. Our marriage had little chance of matching the dreams infused into her by a childhood filled with pop culture's movies, songs, and television shows that promised a Hollywood ending. I, too, was influenced by those and also by the great romances in novels such as *Wuthering Heights* and *The Return of the Native*. In fact, I was instructing the next generation on the virtues of those books while withholding the cynicism that I had recently amassed.

After two years of marriage I found myself envying the lifestyles of my single friends, while some of them, it seemed, envied our relationship. I presently write about this period of my life following years of reflection. At the time, I didn't think of my marriage with Lindsay quite so coolly. I'm confident that if we had met when we were more mature, older, and wiser, we might have been much happier. Forthcoming circumstances would render that impossible.

As with many young couples, the hint of any dissatisfaction quickly evaporated upon receiving news of a baby on the way. We made no attempt to postpone learning the gender of our child, and I was soon bouncing off the walls in anticipation of meeting my daughter for the first time. Only those who have become parents can describe the overwhelming feelings of receiving their firstborn child, and in turn, only they can relate to hearing that description. I'll therefore spare you the attempt on my part, except to say that nobody could have felt more joy and anxiety than I did upon becoming a father. Nothing could separate me from my little Marie in those early years of her life.

Lindsay stayed home with Marie for a few months before the demands of her internship required her full-time attention. I do not wish to discredit Lindsay; she was as devoted a parent as I, but simple logistics dictated that I had more time to dedicate to child rearing, while she focused on the long-term financial security of the family. I know that she cherished the time she spent with our daughter. I maintained my teaching position at the community college and arranged a schedule that would minimize the time Marie spent in daycare. Having two doting grandmothers living within an hour helped immensely. At that time, Marie was the only grandchild on either side of the family.

You might have already speculated that of all the family and friends I left behind upon my involuntary exit from Earth, none caused me greater distress than my daughter. Were that true, I would be forever thankful. I might have found some solace imagining her adjusting to my absence and living a long, happy, and prosperous life. Lindsay surely would have married a suitable stepfather—she would have done a wonderful job as a single parent as well. But sadly, Marie left us first, and I can devote only the minimum amount of time necessary to convey this experience, for I find that it saddens me today nearly as much as it did then. I didn't know death then as I do today, but even if I had, the familiarity would not have made the loss of my own child any more bearable.

Marie was four years old at the time of the accident with which I was very much involved. I was driving her to a birthday party a few miles away from our house on a Saturday in the early afternoon. She was seated in the rear of my sedan as we ventured out into a picture-perfect spring day. Marie had been bugging me for days to relinquish her car seat. She had just barely reached the minimum weight requirement for using a regular seatbelt, but I wasn't ready to get rid of the extra protection. It might have been my overly-cautious nature or perhaps I just didn't want her to grow up so quickly. Unfortunately, the additional protection provided by the car seat wasn't enough to save her.

I followed the car in front of me into a busy intersection after the light changed from red to green. Had I been the first car at the intersection, I would have instinctively looked in both directions to ensure that the road was clear of cross traffic. Instead, I proceeded systematically behind the lead car while stealing a glance at my daughter in the rearview mirror. The driver in the oncoming vehicle had breached his red signal by such a wide margin that he completely missed the car in front of us and broadsided my sedan directly where Marie was seated. The driver was, of course, found to be at fault, and claimed some sort of justified distraction. None of that was of any consolation to Lindsay or myself.

And so I found myself a year removed from the tragedy and still mired in a vicious cycle of grief, guilt, anger, and lethargy. The fuel which had once rekindled my marriage was suddenly depleted. Lindsay and I eventually separated and barely spoke. I couldn't help but wonder if she blamed me for the loss of our daughter. She never came anywhere close to saying as much, yet I swore that I could see it in her face. How could she resist those feelings? It was probably a manifestation of my own guilt-fueled imagination, but it was the final straw in our ill-fated relationship. We divorced amicably as soon as the state of Virginia would grant it.

Family and friends had allotted me a conventional amount of space to grieve before attempting to nudge me back into society. Their advice was appreciated but unnecessary. I knew exactly what I needed to do, yet I struggled to find the motivation to pull myself away from the television. My old friend Gary arrived at the door to my rented apartment one afternoon and refused to leave until I agreed to his proposal. We were to fly to Las Vegas on the following day, where we would rent a car and drive two hours north to his uncle's cabin in Utah. He intended to stay for a week or so, but the house was available to me for the duration of the summer. I agreed on the condition of extending the layover in Las Vegas for a couple of days. I had never been to Sin City and figured that I was ripe for the distractions it offered. It was an easy sell to Gary.

The two days in Las Vegas provided more diversions than I had prepared for, and I was happy to be making my way north following our short visit. If I had the wisdom to quit when I was ahead, I might have left the craps table with a small profit in my pocket. Instead, my fortunes turned sour and I soon reached my self-imposed limit of five hundred dollars. Luckily, the complimentary rum and cokes granted me a one-time waiver to increase the ceiling, which I did, in spite of Gary's urgings to the contrary. I relocated to a blackjack table in a strategic maneuver designed to restore my winnings and managed to lose it all. Nevertheless, a relentless hangover and the deflated feeling of losing eight hundred dollars were not enough to preclude me from marveling at the Virgin River Gorge and other scenery as Gary sped up Interstate 15 late the next morning.

The first few days at the cabin did wonders for my spirit. Maybe it was simply time to rid myself of the funk, but I'm convinced that the vacation accelerated the process. We hiked, dined (mostly on fast food and take-out), and spent the evenings playing board games—completely sans alcohol. Gary had spent many childhood summers in the St. George area where he maintained a few friendships and acquaintances. We ran into some of them one evening at a seafood restaurant and were subsequently invited to the aforementioned poker game, which was scheduled for two nights later. This was to be a tournament-style Texas Hold'em game, and the late addition of participants was welcome, especially inexperienced players such as ourselves. Gary sensed that I wanted to attend but knew that I'd be uncomfortable without him, so he postponed his return flight to Virginia. I recall faring quite well in the tournament, finishing in the top five—undoubtedly due to beginner's luck. I was likely relishing my victory as much as I was admiring the night sky while strolling back to the cabin.

I hope that my family didn't dwell long on my disappearance, though I suppose it highly improbable they did not. I also fear that Gary harbored some guilt of responsibility. Friends and family likely wasted considerable time and money searching for evidence of my fate that would never be found. I couldn't help but feel responsible for their frustration, sorrow, and bewilderment. Yet I was somewhat luckier, for lack of a better word, than the others confined with me in that cargo hold. Many of them had left behind wives, husbands, and children. In the early days we held out hope—even assumed—that we would be reunited with our loved ones one day. As the gravity of our plight unfolded, the impact on the others was much greater. I had no dependents—not even a pet goldfish. It's curious that we found the time to anguish over the suffering of those left behind in spite of our own predicament. It illustrates how little we understood what lay ahead.

For a long while I attempted to form mental images of my daughter, my family, and close friends, but they became very blurred over the passage of so many years. I feared that the pictures I managed to create in my head were woefully inaccurate without the aid of a single photograph. A few years after my capture, I was inspired by the success of others to sketch likenesses of those who were once close to me, but I was thwarted by a fading memory and lack of artistic talent.

3

Over those first few hours upon awaking in the hold, our deliberations had yielded far more questions than answers. My vision in the darkness was limited to the ghostly figures in the compartments on my sides and across the narrow passage. On my left was our self-imposed leader, the man with the Caribbean accent whom we would come to know as Charles. From the few words she spoke, I knew that the person on my right was a Latina woman. The person across from me on the top level sounded like a young American man.

The strap affixed to my wrist was much longer than the one attached to my ankle. This arrangement enabled me to position myself quite freely within my compartment but prevented me from moving beyond it. In spite of the darkness, I soon became quite familiar with my confined space and its limited features. Facets of those "amenities" were shared among the inhabitants as they were discovered.

"I'm thirsty," groaned someone from one end of the hold.

"There's a faucet on your back wall. Feel for the button above it," came a distant reply. I quickly ran my hands across the smooth wall. Sure enough, I came upon a small spigot toward the bottom corner and felt two square buttons above it. The floor directly beneath the spigot was indented several inches, forming a small sink. A third voice contributed to the revelation of our plumbing systems.

"The other button is for the drain," she said. Pressing one button caused a small flow of water to come out of the spigot for a few seconds, not unlike a public restroom. Pressing the other button produced a more interesting effect. The entire bottom of the indented bowl opened inward, flushing the water that I had just placed into it. Finding no other such sources of water and drainage, we dreadfully concluded that this built-in basin was intended for all forms of waste—human and otherwise. Our fears were later confirmed, yet the awkwardness of our exposure diminished over time as we adjusted to our situation and reverted to a more primitive human condition. The adaptability of humans is not to be underestimated.

Our theories on abduction were reinforced by mutual consensus within the hold. We were certain that we had been taken as hostages. Our inabilities to recall the moments of captures were explained by the drugs that were likely administered on the scene. They might have rendered our brains unable to store those few moments of memory prior to being captured. We concluded that we were on a ship at sea, probably circling within international waters or headed to a safe haven for pirates and thugs. Our families and governments were assuredly working around the clock to secure our freedom. Given the large number of us, this incident was certainly garnering international attention. I speculated that U.S. Navy Seals were close at hand. It was reasonable to imagine that somebody had witnessed the moment of at least one of our abductions. We began to feel a little more at ease when the hatch suddenly began to open.

The group fell immediately silent, only to gasp when lights came on inside the hold. In an instant, our space was revealed to us, thanks to a series of lights that ran along the ceiling in the middle of the corridor. The lighting was not particularly bright but it was sufficient to momentarily blind me, for my eyes had become accustomed to the darkness. I shielded them with my forearm and attempted to survey my surroundings while waiting for someone to emerge through the hatch. I quickly noticed that my neighbors didn't quite conform to the mental images I had conjured for them in the darkness.

There was Charles, with a large frame and of African descent. His hairline had receded beyond the midpoint of his crown, revealing a shiny brown dome that was flanked by salt-and-pepper patches of hair above his ears. A short curly beard of similar colors engulfed his entire face and neck. In spite of the intermittent gray, he appeared to be in his mid- to late forties. He was dressed in dark, pinstriped slacks and a white button-down shirt. I surmised that they were the remnants of a business suit that he was wearing at the time of this abduction. On my other side was a woman with medium-length dark hair. I couldn't see her face, for she lay on her back and covered her eyes with her hands. From my perspective, she appeared of average height and build. She was practically motionless and seemed to be in no hurry to remove her hands from her face. Across from me was the young American man. He was slender, Caucasian, and could not have been older than twenty-five.

My spartan compartment was true to the mental image I had forged in the darkness. There were no additional accessories to be discovered. The spigot, two buttons, and indented sink in the floor completed the space. I turned my eyes back toward the young man across the corridor who squinted back at me with a puzzling expression. He was about to speak when something entered through the hatch. I craned into the maximum forward position allowed by my restraints and stuck my head into the corridor. Looking left toward the hatch I saw approximately twenty-five other heads in a similar position. To my right were twenty more. Under lighter circumstances I might have snickered at the illusion of forty-plus detached heads floating in the air, stacked three high.

I fully expected to encounter a rugged, international terrorist dressed in paramilitary garb and sporting a beard that would have made Fidel Castro proud. Instead, what I saw spawned even greater mysteries than we had encountered upon waking just a few hours earlier. The spectacle cast a large shadow of doubt on most of the conclusions we had drawn up to that moment. The young man across from me dropped his lower jaw and cast a bewildered look toward Charles and me.

The machine was robotic in nature and moderately humanoid in appearance, yet it would never have been mistaken for an actual human. It had three lower appendages. Two were used in the way we use our legs for walking; the third attached in the back and appeared to have no function. (I learned later that it facilitated high-speed lateral and forward movement when necessary.) An arm-like, quadruple-jointed appendage extended from each side. At the moment, the end of each arm contained two opposing digits, similar to a thumb and forefinger, but of equal size. On the top of the torso rested a futuristic-looking, oval-shaped head, complete with two electronic eyes facing forward and various other appurtenances that appeared to be sensors of some kind. There was no visible mouth, yet the being was capable of generating sounds that emanated from its head. The entire being, other than the sensory attachments, appeared to be constructed of the same material. Its texture was smooth but with more of a plastic complexion than metallic. It had a dull grayish color that was darker in the joints. Standing nearly seven feet high, it barely cleared the corridor ceiling.

"Food," said the android in English. The voice was easy to understand yet its machine-like quality made it seem unnatural compared to human language. It made no attempt to sound pleasant but likewise did not seem intent on frightening us. It pushed a four-wheeled cart in front of it. The cart appeared custom-made to fit the corridor, like a larger version of an airplane beverage cart. It contained several large bowls and softball-sized wads of a cotton-like material which the android began handing to each of us using its clawed appendages as it moved up the corridor from the left. "Food," it repeated over and over, though the vocal accompaniment to its presentation was superfluous. It was obvious even to those who did not understand English that it was meal time, and we had grown even hungrier since awakening. My fellow captives bombarded the android with questions as it slowly progressed in its task to feed us.

"Where are we?"

"Why are we here?"

"Where are we going?"

The thing began to alternate a response of "no questions" in with its proclamations of "food." It looked toward each inhabitant with an odd, human-like demeanor as it distributed the food bowls. I guessed that it was using its electronic eyes to make an assessment of our individual conditions. I observed that some of us were in a much better physical and mental state than others. When it approached my area, the young man across from me demanded to know the identity of the person responsible for our plight.

"Who's in charge here?" I'm sure that he, like myself, expected no reply from the android. The machine exceeded our expectations.

"I am in charge of you," it replied. Its near-monotone delivery conveyed a modest arrogance, but I was not yet ready to ascribe a personality to this being. It dispensed our bowls and moved on.

"Well then, who are you?" pressed my young neighbor. The android, now servicing the Latina woman next to me, reverted to its earlier position.

"No questions."

I set the wad of cotton aside and carefully examined the sustenance in my bowl, still hesitant in spite of the increasing hunger inspired by the thought of eating. The contents reminded me of the dry cereals I ate as a child. They most resembled corn flakes, but paler in color and with no odor. I lifted my nose from my bowl and met the eyes of the young man across from me. He was scrutinizing his own bowl with a look of misgiving on his face.

"What do you think this is?" I asked.

"I have no idea," he responded. "I'm Nicholas, by the way."

"I'm Mike." Noticing that Charles and the occupants of the stalls below Nicholas were already devouring their cereal, I concluded that it was probably safe to eat.

"If they wanted to kill us, we would already be dead," I wondered aloud. I added some water to my bowl, which was quickly absorbed by the dry cereal. Overcoming the lack of utensils, I scooped a handful of the bland paste into my mouth and swallowed—no chewing was required. My taste buds were surprisingly satisfied and my hunger was appeased. I had never been difficult to please when it came to dining.

"Yes, most likely," replied Nicholas. His delivery sounded highly educated, a supposition supported by the stereotypical slight build, a plain haircut, and a short-sleeved button-down shirt. The juxtaposition of seeing him and Charles in their respective compartments made the former appear feebler and the latter appear stockier than they likely were. Our captors had seen fit to allow Nicholas to retain his thick eyeglasses. Only his beard belied his nerdy appearance, but even that was incomplete in some patches, which had the effect of making him appear even more youthful. Being my nature to find a morsel of humor in the dourest of situations, I asked him if he had been abducted directly from a library. I think he appreciated my levity but couldn't bring himself to smile.

As we ate, Nicholas told his story to me and Charles. It turned out that my library quip was not far from reality. He was a graduate student at the University of California Berkeley, studying astronomy. (The fortuitous advantages of his knowledge I would not appreciate until later.) He spent the evening of his abduction with a group of fellow students and an array of telescopes in the deserted hills above Berkeley. Living up to his reputation as an over-zealous scholar, he remained behind when his peers decided to call it a night. The last thing he remembered was observing Venus in the early morning sky before waking up here. Nicholas left behind his parents and a sister in Reading,

California. He made no mention of a significant other.

During the conversation with Charles and Nicholas, I couldn't help but notice that the middle-aged woman with shoulder-length dark hair on my right wasn't eating. She seemed oblivious to the buzz that had filled our room, first with its illumination, followed by the baffling appearance of the android creature. When Nicholas had finished his story, I turned to her and asked her name. After asking a third time, she slowly raised her head.

"Valeria," she muttered. English was clearly not her first language, so I summoned my three years of high school Spanish in an attempt to further the discourse. Using a combination of hand gestures and imprecise conjugations, I suggested that she needed to eat. She took a few bites then slid the bowl away and sat back against the wall behind her. She repeatedly asked me, in Spanish, where we were and the whereabouts of someone called Sofia, who I assumed to be her daughter or some other close relative. Her tears were so despairing that the empathy they engendered caused me to momentarily forget that I was in the same predicament as she. I wished that I could help her.

I tore off a small piece of the cotton-like wad and wiped down the surface of my cage. I saved most of the wad for later on a hunch that I might need it for other bodily functions. Then, without warning, the lights went out. The android had departed our hold several minutes earlier and the powers that be must have determined that mealtime had concluded. I shoved my bowl away and sighed.

4

We began to measure days as the interval between our feedings. It felt, according to what remained of our biological clocks, to be a close approximation of a circadian cycle. We didn't suspect that we would eventually count these days well above sixty. The regular feeding schedule helped to promote a consistent, albeit artificial, day-night-sleep routine to which most of us adhered, in spite of the scarcity and discordance of our lighting. There were exceptions, of course—especially in the beginning. A few of the inmates refused to accept their new habitat and spent most their time sleeping and sulking.

Two android custodians governed our cargo hold. The second was distinguishable from the first in that it appeared to be an older model and much more worn. One of its electronic eyes was blackened over, and we debated its functionality. Otherwise, it was similarly constructed, but with a paler hue than the one we first encountered. We referred to them using male pronouns due to the low pitch of their computerized voices and went so far as to assign each of them a name. We didn't shy from calling them by name directly once we learned that they didn't seem to mind. Whether they were capable of minding or experiencing any form of emotion was a still a mystery to us. They were quite adept at ignoring us.

There was some discussion with respect to naming our android keepers. "Thing One" and "Thing Two," an homage to Dr. Seuss, eventually stuck, winning out over several other candidates, including "Bart and Homer," "Batman and Robin," and "Starsky and Hutch." The antiquated model was known as Thing One. Thing Two was also known to us as Thing One's "little brother," and we often referred to the pair as the "Things." The extent of their English vocabulary was adequate, as was their command of Spanish and the one or two other widely-used languages spoken among our group. However, they chose to use English almost exclusively, thus forcing everyone in the hold to learn it, which might have been their objective. Those of us English speakers spent many hours teaching the other inhabitants the language. (I use the term "hours" liberally, of course. Other than our definition of days, we could only guess at the passage of time.) With so much idle time, nearly everyone became proficient speakers of American English, with one notable exception.

The challenge of ascertaining the level of artificial intelligence within the robots seemed trivial to the questions raised by their mere presence. The appearance of the android on that first day of consciousness fueled our imaginations and widened the aperture of explanations for our abductions. It was Nicholas who first suggested that we had left the confines of Earth. I have always ascribed to a philosophy of accepting the most simple and logical explanation to be true until it can be disproved, rather than jumping to a fantastic, more exciting theory, which humans seem so inclined to do. The alleged vast government conspiracies of faking the lunar landing in 1969 or staging the 9-11 attacks in 2001 make for a fascinating discussion, but they lack the plausibility of the more obvious explanations: America really did land on the moon and terrorists really did hijack planes and crash them into buildings.

Even with my skepticism fully intact, Nicholas presented a compelling case. I had trouble forming a more logical explanation than his spaceship hypothesis. From a mathematical standpoint, there had to be alien civilizations in the universe, many of which could be far more advanced than we were. Two thousand years is a miniscule fraction of time compared to the age of the universe. It's reasonable to assume that an alien race that is only that much further advanced than humans could have overcome the barriers to traveling great distances in space.

Of one thing we were certain—we were moving. The occasional jolts, rumblings, and vibrations approximated a ride on a commercial jet. If we were traveling in a ship at sea or in the air, we would have surely reached our destination by now. Were we circling aimlessly in the ocean while waiting for a ransom to be paid? Will we stop to refuel? Could someone on Earth have constructed these robots? They seemed quite advanced.

There were arguments to be made against Nicholas' theory. In fact, Nicholas himself posited some of them. He had a peculiar way of debating with himself, continually second-guessing his theories and rarely reaching a conclusion. Our accommodations resembled the timeworn hold of a cargo ship at sea more than anything I had seen of a spaceship in science fiction movies. But we were clearly not precious cargo; other areas of the ship might appear very futuristic. If only we could meet our captors. If they *are* aliens, what do they want from us? The presence of a couple of robots wasn't enough to convince me that we had left our planet. Until proved otherwise, we were hidden away somewhere awaiting ransom payments, a diplomatic solution, or a military rescue. Nicholas' ideas were captivating, but they were obviously biased toward his area of expertise.

"It's just like a neurologist would diagnose an ailment as being caused by a neurological issue and a psychiatrist would claim the same ailment is a mental disorder," Charles reasoned to me. This subject preoccupied much of our discussions, but we found time for lighter subjects as well.

On that first day of awakening, I had detected two languages that I could not remotely place. Both emanated from the left end of the corridor. Through the expertise of our Caribbean occupants, the former was identified as Papiamento, a native language from the island of Curacao. Fortunately, the woman owning this voice also possessed a very strong command of both Dutch and English, and she easily switched over to the common language of our group. Her name was Leesheh. Her compartment was several down from me, and I couldn't see her very well. Her voice sounded young and cheerful—a welcome respite in light of our circumstances.

Things were more complicated with the occupants past Leesheh on the very end of the corridor near the hatch. The problem of identifying the mysterious language was exacerbated by the general dysfunctionality of the personnel occupying that area of the hold. After several days, we still had not learned much about the "hatch people." This is what we in the center of the hold called the six or seven inhabitants at that end of the corridor. Information relayed from that area was less accurate than it would have been coming from thirty children playing a game of "telephone."

Although the rest of the hold became quite organized over time, those few people on the left might as well had been miles away. Our analysis of the information that made its way to Charles, our de facto leader, was that a native South American occupied the cubicle closest to the hatch, on the bottom row, and on the same side as mine. From what we could tell, he was faring generally better than many of the occupants, perhaps due to an increased sense of oblivion. He rarely made any attempt to communicate with anyone else and passed most of his time quietly meditating. We named him Monte, short for Montezuma. (Adherence to political correctness was not a priority in our situation.)

We looked forward to our visits from the Things, chiefly because it meant that the lights would be turned on, if only for a moment. We concluded that their eyes functioned only slightly better than ours in the dark, or they provided light during the feedings in order to reduce our sloppiness while eating. Nicholas asserted that they must have an infrared capability, yet they rarely visited us in the dark. Conversely, our eyes became more effective in the dark as we adapted to spending most of our time in a near blackout.

Thing One made his first visit to our cabin on the second day following our awakening and stopped at the first group of three captives stacked opposite Monte. He contracted his two-fingered claw into his wrist, then extended it again, but his hand was now replaced by an odd-looking contraption. He used this device to unfasten the straps attached to the uppermost inhabitant and guided him down to the floor of the corridor. He repeated the process for the other two captives in the column, then led all three out of the room via the hatch, saying only, "Come with me."

This action spawned a lively discussion surrounding the fate of the departed. It certainly did not bode well for the rest of us if they failed to return. After forty to fifty minutes, our fears of impending doom were assuaged when Thing One returned the three people to their pens and re-affixed their straps. Craning my neck to see, I concluded that they looked no worse for the wear. Thing One then repeated the process with Monte and his two vertical companions. Monte was practically naked, wearing nothing but a thong-like loincloth that barely covered his crotch. He offered no physical resistance but he broke his silence and began chanting to the android while waving his hands around its head. We supposed that it was either an admonishment or a hex. We could never know for sure.

Thing One worked his way up the corridor throughout the day and eventually reached my rack. By this time, I knew exactly what was in store for me. The hatch people had failed to articulate what they encountered on that first excursion, but the subsequent captives had passed adequate details up the chain. I would be taken to a small room immediately adjacent to this one and given an opportunity to move around. The woman below me and the gentleman below her would accompany me. All of this would occur under the watchful electronic eye of Thing One.

The prospect of standing vertically was as enticing to me as the chance to finally see my neighbors from below. I had been able to stretch my legs horizontally in my cubicle but I was unable to place much weight on them, and I feared the onset of atrophy. Thing One removed our straps using one of his many swiss-army-knife attachments. I stretched my arms to the ceiling while he freed the other two inhabitants. It felt as if I had been bedridden for days, which I had, and my muscles and joints appreciated the change to a vertical orientation. Charles bid us a pleasant farewell, having recently returned from his own stint in what we would come to call "the yard."

"Enjoy," he said, as Thing One led us down the corridor. I tried to soak in as much visual input as possible, looking left and right at my fellow captives as I walked past their compartments. This was my first look at many of them, though I would have many more opportunities in the weeks to come.

The yard was an empty room that resembled our hold except that it was much smaller and devoid of anything except for us. There was a hatch on the wall opposite the one from which we entered, but it was closed and provided no hint of what might be on the other side. I canvassed the small room—maybe two hundred square feet in all—for buttons, handles, levers, or anything else that one might expect to find on the walls of a spaceship. I was disappointed to have found nothing, yet not surprised in the least. Thing One got the party started.

"Exercise," he said. I couldn't discern whether it was an order or just a suggestion, but I was happy to oblige. First, I intended to meet my neighbors. I turned to the woman and extended my hand. She already knew my name but it seemed to be an appropriate ice breaker.

"I'm Mike."

She accepted my hand and replied, "Susan. So, what the hell is going on here?"

I already knew that she hailed from Springfield, Illinois and was the mother of three children. The man also shook my hand. His name was Pablo and he was from the island of Cozumel in Mexico. English was not his first language but he spoke it fairly well. We knew that our time in the room was short, so we moved around and swapped stories about our lives and kidnappings.

Susan was extracted while out for a midnight jog in her suburban neighborhood. With three young children, a husband, and a full-time job in sales demanding most of her day time, workouts were relegated to the night. Her attractive, athletic physique supported her backstory. She was making the most of her first day in the yard, with plenty of yoga and stretching. She was dressed for the part too, having been abducted in capri leggings and a tight-fitting tank top. I guessed that her light brown hair was probably short and stylish prior to her abduction. Now it was a little tousled and extended well below her ears, not that she seemed to mind.

Unlike most of us, Pablo was snatched during the day, under a bright afternoon sun in the Gulf of Mexico. He was enjoying a few days off with a solo fishing trip in his small boat. He last remembered falling asleep in a deck chair before waking up here. Pablo was a tall tour guide who ferried busloads of cruise ship tourists to and from the Chichen Itza Maya Ruins in Yucatan. His otherwise spindly frame supported a paunchy midsection, making him appear fat and skinny simultaneously. He told us that he was forty-six years old, divorced, and had one adult daughter. We were too polite to ask Susan her age, which I estimated to be thirty-two or thirty-three.

The luxury of spending time away from our cages was granted to each of us approximately every other day. I always shared my stint in the yard with Susan and Pablo, and we soon became close. Over time, I came to feel as if I had known many of my fellow occupants in the hold for a lifetime, but my bonds with those in the closest physical proximity were the tightest. Valeria, my neighbor on the right, was no exception. She rarely spoke and never participated in group enterprises, but each night, without saying a word, she crawled over to the half-wall separating us and placed her head on my shoulder. This was not a romantic gesture—just a primordial need for human contact, one which I was happy to oblige. Likewise, I felt no physical attraction toward her. I was concerned for her well-being and grateful for the physical communion. We were confronting a crisis unlike anything we could have ever imagined, but we weren't facing it alone.

Not long after the first day, someone came up with the idea of measuring how much time we were allotted in the yard. It was not as if that particular factoid was required for anything other than providing an occupation for our undernourished minds. Among us was Mario, a postman from Venezuela who moonlighted as a drummer in a pop music cover band. We asked him to beat a rhythm at a rate of sixty beats per minute. He gladly flipped over his bowl and tapped his best approximation of the desired tempo on his makeshift bongo. A few others joined in, and before long, the correct tempo (according to Mario) was firmly rooted in our rhythm section. A group of five, including myself, alternated counting sets of sixty beats and calling out the cumulative total of minutes at the end of each. Thus, our method for measuring time in the form of minutes and hours was born. Assuming that we were always fed at the same time each day (which was reasonable considering that we were governed by machines), we could approximate the amount of time that had elapsed from that point. All we needed were drummers and counters willing to participate, and an ample supply was always at hand. For the record, we were allocated forty-five minutes of yard time for each group.

Another activity that stemmed from Mario's skills as a metronome was singing. It was slow to develop, as some people were reluctant to allow themselves the slightest amusement in the face of our adversity. We had individual performers, some more talented than others, who participated in karaoke-style sessions. I preferred the drum circles and group sing-alongs over the solos. My favorite song leader was Leesheh, the girl from Curacao. (If I had only known of my affinity for the Curacao Tumba prior to my abduction!) My partiality to her songs was surely influenced by her charm, effervescence, and adorable face, the latter of which I studied each time one of the Things led me past her compartment. Her perky sense of humor could even force Nicholas to smile sometimes. In the midst of despair, filth, sorrow, and gloom, I managed to develop a boyish crush on Leesheh, and I wished that my berth could be closer to hers.

I fear that my memories of this period on the ship, so long removed from the actual experience, have precipitated a description of an environment that was at least accommodating, if not congenial. It is, after all, our nature to view personal history through a nostalgic lens. To infer such comfort and complacency in the cargo hold would be a gross misconception. I have chronicled the natural adaptations we made to survive. It is accurate to say that we utilized communal activities as a means of deflecting and diminishing the stresses of our captivity, but most of our time was spent quietly missing loved ones or imagining what horrors awaited us at the end of our journey. The small victories won by conversing, singing, and laughing were few and in no way counterbalanced the hardships. Nonetheless, these small victories for the human condition were vital to our survival, and as the days wore on, we began to surmise that we were not in any immediate danger. To say that we relaxed might be an exaggeration. Most of us softened and accepted our predicament for what it was—as much as we could know and could not change.

5

As the days turned into weeks, we stopped asking questions of The Things. We knew that we couldn't wear them down or grate on nonexistent nerves. There would be no answers from them. We eventually stopped asking questions among ourselves and quit speculating about our fates. We simply existed—one artificial day at a time.

Determined to survive this ordeal, I developed my own routine to preserve what remained of my health, strength, and nerves. The temperature in the hold was warm and dry enough that I could remove my pants and shirt, rinse them, and expect them to be dry within a few hours. I discovered that dabbing my body with the cereal and water mixture helped to reduce odors. I applied it to my clothing as well. News of my remarkable discovery spread throughout the room but was somehow lost on the hatch people, who lived in outright filth.

Susan showed me stretching and strengthening exercises that I could perform within the confines of my enclosure. Having never been fond of regular exercise, I developed a love–hate relationship with the workouts. I loved that they provided routine and purpose, which I knew were vital to the sanity of prisoners. I loved that they lubricated my joints and strengthened my bones. I hated them for the same reasons anyone hates to exercise—they were difficult and often felt like a tedious homework assignment—not that I had anything better to do. If not for Susan's tough love bellowing up from below me, I might have skipped a few of those cage workouts.

Skipping training in the yard was never an option—not with Susan in our faces. My favorite exercise was the tai chi plie. A plie is similar to a squat but with a straight back, as if it's flat against an imaginary wall. Susan told us that they were great for building cardio and strength. The problem was with our lack of nutrition, and in spite of our dedication, we grew a little weaker with each passing day. Pablo was overweight coming into the ordeal and he quickly shed pounds from his gut. I was probably fifteen pounds heavier than my ideal weight and they also disappeared within a few weeks. Poor Susan had few fat cells to spare and before long, portions of her skeleton were discernible through her skin.

We exhausted hours in the yard exercising and chatting, always within the presence of Thing One or Thing Two. The androids appeared to take little interest in our activities and conversations. It was if they were in a sleep mode, returning to life and escorting us back to the hold when our forty-five-minute session had expired. We learned to ignore them as naturally as they ignored us.

The stench in our crowded hold swelled until one day we just didn't notice it anymore. The more hygienically-conscious of us begged the others to flush water through their sinks more thoroughly and more frequently. I was sensitive to my neighbors below and tried to conduct all of my hygienic activities in a fastidious manner. I carefully discharged all waste into my basin and never allowed it to overflow. Other captives didn't have such courteous neighbors living above them, as indicated by a higher rate of sickness in the lower berths. Hardly a day passed without an argument between vertical neighbors over waste disposal. These rarely escalated beyond rants, though I heard of one or two physical altercations in the yard which were quickly quelled by the Thing on duty.

The groove of relative complacency and security I had created for myself was abruptly interrupted on the twenty-first morning (as estimated by our rudimentary time keeping). I woke in the usual manner, with Valeria's head resting on my shoulder. Eager to begin my morning routine, I nudged her gently. This was our normal process, as I typically awoke first. On this day, there was no response. I touched her chin in order to lift her head and felt very cold skin. I grabbed her arm and found it to be somewhat stiff.

"Valeria, wake up." I shook her slightly, then again. I placed my hand on her throat and searched for a pulse. Adrenaline quickly cascaded through my body as I came to the realization that she was dead. Jolted by a sudden sense of horror, I shoved her away and quickly scooted to the center of my cage. At this time, death was still foreign to me. I had been spared witnessing the passing of my daughter, for she had been whisked away by paramedics at the scene of the accident while I lay in a daze. She passed away en route to the hospital. My daughter's death enveloped me in a surreal, numbing aura that clearly was not present here. Valeria had practically died in my arms, and here was her body, still next to me and completely devoid of life.

"What's going on?" asked Charles. I gathered my composure and advised him of the situation. "We'll have to call the Things in," he said. But we had no way of calling the Things in. Up to this moment, contacting them was something we had never needed, nor cared to do. We had to wait until feeding time. I spent what felt like several hours with my head between my knees, rocking in discomfort. Valeria's body sat against the back wall in peace, still in the contorted position that resulted from my shove—leaning forward and to one side. In the darkness I hoped that her hair completely covered her face, for which I would be eternally thankful. I had no desire to see her lifeless expression when the lights came on. When they finally powered up, I forced myself to look in her direction, where I was met by two large brown eyes curiously staring back at me, as if I was expected to have the answers. I had none.

"She's lucky," said a voice from the cage below her. "She got what she wanted."

"What do you mean?" asked Nicholas.

"She's free."

"She's not free," said Charles, "she's dead. I don't want to do die—do you?" The voice didn't respond.

I sure don't, I thought to myself.

We started yelling to Thing Two as soon as he entered the chamber. He paid us no attention, so we ceased after a minute or two of clamoring. When he reached Valeria's cage, a silence fell on the entire hold as heads peered toward her body from both directions. Thing Two extended a bowl and fresh wad of the cotton-like material out to her.

"She's dead," I said. Thing Two returned the bowl and wad to the cart without missing a beat and proceeded to grope and probe her body with a robotic pragmatism. After a few seconds, he resumed the feeding process for the rest of us. When the last bowl had been distributed, he pushed the empty cart back down the corridor and exited the hatch. Within seconds, he reappeared with Thing One and the two androids proceeded to Valeria's enclosure. Without communicating with each other, at least not in any mode evident to us, they removed her straps, collected her body and carried it out of the hold. Perhaps my melancholy state was playing with my imagination, but it seemed that the androids were handling her body with a degree of tenderness and respect. They took great care to prevent her corpse from contacting any of the other captives as they carried it past. I shared my observation with Charles.

"Of course," he replied. "They don't want her body to come into contact with any of us in case it's diseased." This observation yanked me back into reality. I wondered if Valeria might have died from a disease and whether I was in danger. Strangely, I wasn't worried. I was convinced that she simply had no reason or will to live, and her body consequently shut down. That night I felt more alone than ever.

As would be expected, days of monotonous persecution crept by slowly, yet strangely, the weeks seemed to pass by in a flash. Nicholas' hypothesis for this paradox had something to do with a combination of a daily routine and a lack of milestone events. Major events, such as a vacation, wedding, job change, etc., normally regulate the perception of time passage, and we had none of those. And so, it followed that within a few days of her passing, my memory of Valeria faded quickly—not that her life became devalued; her death just seemed to have occurred so long ago.

I find it difficult to describe the peculiar relationship we had with time. I suppose that only those who were plucked from modern society and kept in captivity for a long period of time can appreciate the effect it has on our biological clocks. Quantifying our days and weeks, however inaccurate our measurements might have been, was vitally important to us.

Valeria's timid and taciturn reaction to captivity, for which I cannot blame her in the least, could not have been more contradictory to my neighbor on the opposite side. From day one, Charles exhibited a position of confidence and authority. One might go so far as describing his attitude as "cautiously optimistic." What could be more advantageous than having Nicholas, the budding physicist, residing directly across from my berth? The answer is having a medical doctor in the cage next to mine, which was Charles' chosen profession.

Charles told us about the general medical practice he owned in Barbados. He traveled frequently to Washington, D.C., where he owned a second home, and where some members of his extended family resided. While on the ship, I didn't have an occasion to stand next to him, but I estimated his height to be only an inch or so less than my own. He had a large frame that carried more weight than would be considered healthy, an irony common to many physicians. He told us that he had spent most of his time sitting behind a desk, in front of a television, or on an airplane, and he made no apologies for his paunchiness. He joked that one benefit of his captivity was the cessation of a nasty smoking habit, a vice for which he exhibited a little embarrassment. His sense of humor was on par with my own. We shared a need to find humor in the wake of hardship, and he took it a step further with an infectious, baritone laugh that filled the entire hold.

Like Susan, Charles left behind a spouse and children, and incurred the added remorse associated with these losses. Both admitted to experiencing a sense of guilt for abandoning their families. Initially this sounded ridiculous to me, though I later reconciled the feeling as being similar to how I felt when my daughter died. I *knew* it wasn't my fault, yet I couldn't dismiss the feeling of culpability. I didn't share my comparison with them at the time, as I didn't want to appear to be "one-upping" them with a story of greater suffering. There would be ample time to learn the intricacies of our personal histories. Charles took some consolation in the fact that his daughters were young adults and fairly independent. They would surely look after his wife until his return—a return that we still assumed to be imminent.

From the onset of our predicament Charles assumed a leadership role for which we were grateful. He endured minor protestations from the few skeptics and misanthropes throughout our journey, but his authority was generally unopposed. The doomsayers could never offer a better idea and their opinions were usually discounted and ignored by the larger community. I would describe Charles' position as more of a facilitator and organizer than a supervisor. I also felt that he was a very good actor. His ability to suppress his own fears had a calming effect within the hold. I followed his lead and tried to exhibit a posture of equanimity to my fellow captors. I discovered that this approach, as spurious as I knew it to be, also had a positive effect on my own mood. In a way it made me feel as though I was better off than the others, although we were likely to meet identical fates.

Cliques naturally formed, determined mostly by location, though other factors also influenced the groupings. Those who leaned toward optimism and shared a determination for survival gravitated to each other while those preoccupied with anguish preferred to fraternize with others willing to share in their misery. Charles, Nicholas, Susan, and I fell into the former category and were fortunate to be within a close proximity to facilitate conversation. Pablo and the other captives near the middle of the hold participated in the discussions less frequently, yet almost always lent an ear. I could see that they were visibly buoyed by our little conferences.

I was fortunate that none of the doomsayers and whiners were in my immediate vicinity. Had there been any nearby, Charles and Susan would have probably muzzled them anyway. Leesheh was not so lucky and I wished that she could move into Valeria's empty space. One day, I went so far as to question Thing Two about the possibility of Leesheh relocating as he handed me my cereal. Surprisingly, he gave me the courtesy of a reply.

"Impossible."

Thing Two must have had enough experience dealing with humans to know that the word "impossible" implies that there is no invitation for debate. Obviously, it was *possible*—all she had to do was move from one berth to another. I could see that this was not up for discussion. I made it a point to check on her and inquire about her well-being each time I passed her berth on the way to the yard. She always replied with a spirited smile and an affirmative nod.

I benefited greatly from my serendipitous location that placed me in the vicinity of Charles, Nicholas, and Susan. I believe that I returned their favors to some degree with endless hours of philosophical discussions and storytelling. Most of my neighbors were unfamiliar with the classic novels on which I had lectured in recent years, so I had no trouble holding their attention. Albeit, I had no competition. I could have just as easily retained my audience with a recital of the Magna Carta. Nevertheless, I was pleased to contribute in my own small way.

I delivered a variety of comedies, dramas, and romances, including The Return of the Native, Rob Roy, The Idiot, Silas Marner, among others. The consensus favorite was Day of the Triffids, perhaps because the abrupt change in the world of its protagonist was not unlike our own.

I failed to remember some of the secondary plot elements of the stories, and was forced to create some composite characters, but nobody was the wiser. What I delivered was more akin to a film version. After finishing his bowl of cereal one day, Charles prodded me in his witty tone.

"And now, I'd like to hear a story from Mr. Shakespeare," he proclaimed. From that day forward, I was never again referred to as Mike. Shakespeare became my name for the remainder of the voyage. In a half-hearted protest, I pointed out to Charles that I was neither an aficionado nor a big fan of the playwright, and I had never once recounted one of his plays to the present company. "Just tell us a story, Shakespeare," he replied. "We don't have all day, man." We did, of course, have all day, and I readily obliged.

In retrospect, I'm also thankful for the relative health and sanity of those in my immediate area. Others were less fortunate. A week or so after Valeria's death, the first sounds of illness could be heard coming from the right end of the corridor. This came as no shock to us; the real surprise was that it took as long as it did for symptoms to arise within the feculent state of our quarters. The coughing increased to an incessant level and soon graduated to feverish moans, vomiting, and other evacuations which I will not describe in detail here. I once again became cognizant of the foul stench that permeated the hold. Combining data from our limited vantages on opposing sides of the corridor, Nicholas and I estimated that there were three people who were seriously ill. We asked our resident physician what, if anything, we could do to avoid the pathogen.

"The only thing we have here to combat the spread of the infection is fresh water," Charles advised. "Rub your hands frequently with water and wipe down your space as best you can." I was already a meticulous cleaner of my cell and I upped my game to another level. I was engaged in this process when Thing One practically dragged one of the poor ailing souls to the yard for his allotted exercise. I recoiled to the back wall as they passed. Charles pleaded with the android.

"He's sick. He needs medicine." Thing One did not respond to Charles, but the afflicted gentleman informed us on his return that he had been given a pill. The medical intervention was too little and too late, for the man died on the following day. The Things were met with a resounding chorus of pleas when they entered to evacuate the corpse.

"Those people are sick!" shouted someone in a thick Spanish accent.

"They need a doctor," added a woman. I tried a more logical appeal. These were, after all, computers. I presumed that we had no value to them unless we were alive.

"If it spreads, we will all die," I noted calmly, as if a more intellectual tone would garner their attention. Whether or not in response to our petitions, the androids removed one of the very sick captives from the hold later that day. She was a young woman from Baltimore whom I didn't know very well, though she seemed pleasant enough. We never saw her again and assumed that she had also expired. This particular epidemic claimed three more lives over the ensuing week. The rest of us were provided with a single orange pill in our food bowl on each of the five days that followed the young woman's death. More notably, each of us was taken individually into the yard where we were stripped and hosed down with a chemical solution. Charles' turn came before mine, so I had some idea of what to expect.

"Cover your nose and mouth, or they'll spray it directly inside," he warned. In the context of our dire situation, this small gift of hygiene was received with as much enthusiasm as a child receiving his most anticipated gift on Christmas morning. The piece de resistance was a new set of clothing. It was merely a dark gray frock, pants with a string tie (resembling pajamas), and slippers, but the change boosted our sunken morale. I had the foresight to retain my old clothes for use as cleaning rags.

Now dressed alike, I noted to my friends that we resembled the prisoners which we were. What I didn't share was the image of a Nazi concentration camp that our new apparel had conjured. That evening, unruffled by the darkness, Leesheh led the entire group in a new song that had something to do with picking fruit. We could only wonder why this disinfecting process had not been implemented sooner. Perhaps it was a sign that we were nearing our destination. At least we seemed to be free from the clutches of disease for the time being.

6

Sickness was not the only source of attrition during our time on the ship. It stands to reason that some people are better suited than others to handle adversities such as ours. This is likely determined by a combination of upbringing, lifestyle, and genetics. Some of the captives in our group simply did not have the physical constitution to survive the ordeal. Our captors evidently counted on, or at least expected, the demands of captivity to eliminate the weak among us. They probably didn't have the advantage of screening potential victims beforehand, likely having to snatch a large number of isolated people within a short window of time. They would have otherwise filled the hold with well-constructed, healthy young adults instead of the hodgepodge they wound up with. Even if they had the ability to filter out candidates lacking the requisite corporeal abilities, they would have no way to measure their psychological capacity for such trauma. This was the case with a couple of the so-called hatch people.

A few days after the illness that claimed four lives was eradicated, we began hearing shouting, moaning, and other strange noises from the hatch end of the corridor. We attributed this to an argument among a couple of the captives. We were later informed by those living closer to the scene that the origin of the sounds was a single person talking to himself. I had seen this man when walking to and from the yard and noted that he appeared to be in good physical condition. I found out later that he was, in fact, a soldier in the Columbian army. His immediate neighbors implored him to calm down but this only exacerbated his insanity. The next morning, while still howling to himself, the young soldier began to kick violently against the ceiling, floor, and side partitions of his compartment, further unnerving his neighbors above, below and beside.

"That guy has lost it," I announced to nobody in particular.

"It was bound to happened to someone," replied Susan from below. "I'm just glad it's over there."

Thing One arrived on schedule with our daily rations. The presence of the old android seemed to fuel the Columbian's anguish, and he violently swatted away the bowl that was extended toward him. The contents flew in all directions and the bowl crashed to the floor with a loud clatter. Thing One pushed the cart forward and reached out to grab the young man. In response, the soldier turned his back to the wall and began kicking Thing One with his unrestrained leg. Without hesitation, the android retracted his claw into his arm and replaced it with a probe-like appendage, approximately a foot in length. As soon as the probe physically contacted the Columbian it emitted an electrical charge that jolted him backward. He convulsed for a few seconds then fell unconscious.

The taser (which we would come to call this particular android accessory) rendered the soldier comatose for several hours, but the tranquility lasted only a short while. The consternation of witnessing the taser apparently robbed the person directly across from the soldier of his last crumb of sanity. Within an hour of the incident, he was shouting incoherent expletives and begging his unconscious friend and neighbor to wake up. The aforementioned friend, upon regaining his senses, resumed his tirade and the two fed off of each other. I slept very little that night, harassed by their rantings and the chorus of angry reactions they begat. I had never witnessed true insanity and found it to be disconcerting. I was particularly worried for Leesheh, who was firmly embedded in the chaos. I attempted to ascertain her status and provide whatever support I could by calling out to her. My calls went unanswered and I realized that I was only contributing to the ruckus.

We didn't have to wait until the following day's feeding for a resolution. The commotion was enough to prompt a rare evening visit from Thing Two. When the lights came on, all noise ceased except for the two loons, who seemed oblivious to anything except each other. I had come to think of Thing Two as the harsher of our two android overseers for reasons I cannot articulate. Something about his actions made him seem less tolerant than his older brother. Thus, his arrival was something akin to our father having to address the problem that our mother had been unable to resolve earlier. Now the kids were *really* in trouble. Thing Two wasted no time installing his taser appendage and approaching the Columbian's berth. The soldier cowered, placed his hands in front of his face, and begged the android not to proceed. It was too late. Thing Two jolted him severely and he collapsed in a silent heap. The robot then swiveled to face the soldier's compadre and swiftly administered the same punishment. I was secretly glad that the two men had been silenced by the taser and felt little sympathy for them. The notion that I might one day experience the same fate hadn't occurred to me.

Instead of leaving the two men to recuperate, Thing Two unfastened the soldier's straps, pulled him out of his cage and carried him out over his shoulder like a sack of potatoes. He returned and repeated the process with the other man. This additional step prompted a lively discussion centered upon the fate of our two fellow prisoners.

"Why wouldn't they leave them here to recover?" someone asked. The answer became increasingly obvious when two days passed and the men had not returned. They were not rendered unconscious by the taser, they were killed. Some saw this action as more drastic than necessary and interpreted it as a warning to the rest of us. Nicholas postulated that the android simply made a calculation that these men were no longer of value and beyond repair. The entire incident rattled me for days. This was partly due to the remorse I felt for the two victims. I also wondered how close *I* was to the brink of madness, and what trivial event might push me over the edge.

Fifteen more days elapsed from the time the Columbian soldier and his cohort were excised from our little society. Whereas these days passed in a less dramatic fashion, they were not without consequence. We lost two more souls—one clearly the result of a fever, while the cause of the other death was a matter for debate. Although we were somewhat distant from the location of the deceased, Charles' medical opinion was starvation. The victim was the eldest among us and an outlier of sorts, having "celebrated" his fifty-sixth birthday in the cargo hold a few days earlier. None of us who remained were older than fifty, and the vast majority were younger than thirty-five. His neighbors cited his erratic appetite, and his yard mates noted that the man rarely exercised.

His death was likely caused by a combination of several factors, and we members of the middle clique discussed the possibilities for hours on end, as we did for all of the departed. Not only did this activity occupy ample amounts of idle time, it also made us feel slightly less vulnerable. Discussing the demise of others in such a practical manner distanced us from the possibility of a similar misfortune befalling one of us. I doubt that we recognized the sociological motivation at the time; we simply behaved as humans do.

The notion of starvation was puzzling to me. There was no shortage of reasons to perish in the cargo hold but I had a difficult time accepting a lack of nourishment as a potential cause of death. Although the cereal-based mush was a little bland and lacked any hint of sweetness, it presented no reason for rebuff in favor of going hungry. It didn't taste bad—it simply had no taste at all. I for one, looked forward to my daily meal, and I find myself salivating a little as I write about it now. Moreover, I felt as though my own physical condition was actually improving following the initial weight loss.

It's reasonable to assume that the food on board would contain a vigorous mix of protein and vitamins without the sugar and saturated fats we were used to. Whether we were hostages or slaves, our captors certainly didn't want us to perish, and in the latter case, they would want us to thrive physically. Of course, the misery of our cramped and foul living conditions might suggest other motives, but we couldn't justify a scenario in which we were abducted simply to be slowly tortured and killed. We concluded that our inhospitable environment must be due to a lack of space and resources on the ship and was likely—hopefully—temporary.

I was passionately implementing Susan's recommendations for building lean muscle and improving cardiovascular health, both in the yard and in my berth. I was cognizant of the mental nourishment that the exercises provided as well. I couldn't imagine the challenges awaiting me in the near future, and I promised myself that the chances of my demise would not be multiplied by a lack of preparation. Approximately half of those in our company embraced the guidance of Susan and the other experienced health nuts in the hold. We shed pounds, gained some muscle, and boosted levels of serotonin while the other half merely shed pounds. This did not produce within us a feeling of superiority over them. Instead, we beseeched them to adopt our habits and improve their own chances for survival. We were now a team—even a family—and I wanted all of us to thrive. I was particularly concerned for my friend Pablo, who had lost much of his earlier enthusiasm for exercise. He hadn't lost any capacity for talking, and he spent much of his time in the yard engaged in conversation with Susan and me while watching us labor through our routines.

The legacy of those who lost their lives in the cargo hold was an increase of time allotted in the yard for those us who survived. This is not something for which we had to ask the Things; they took it upon themselves to distribute the extra time among those who remained. We now received yard time nearly every day, and the duration of each stint increased to more than an hour, according to our rudimentary estimation. It was during one of those sessions that Thing One gave us a surprise.

I don't know exactly what emboldened me that day. Perhaps I had been lulled into a false sense of comfort brought on by day upon day of monotonous routine. For whatever reason, I confronted Thing One with the following question:

"When will we arrive at our destination?" Thing One paused—the first time I had ever witnessed such a delay from him or his associate. We later wondered if he was obtaining permission from higher powers via a wireless communication.

"Soon," he replied. The three of us humans looked at each other in disbelief. I felt as if I had just won the lottery, so I pressed on.

"How many days?" When he failed to respond it occurred to me that the concept of days is relative to Earth and might be ambiguous to a computer, i.e., android, on a spaceship. I tried a different approach. "How many feedings do we have left here?"

"It is time for you to return."

As he escorted us back through the hatch, I continued firing questions from a variety of angles. None evoked a response. Still, the word "soon" was a remarkable breakthrough, and I shared my discovery with the entire company that evening in the darkness. Expressions of fear, anxiety, excitement, and even relief filled the hold until the last of us drifted off to sleep. We awoke the next morning and continued our deliberations.

There was a man in his early thirties residing across from me on the top level and two berths down from Nicholas, whom we had dubbed

Tex. Though lacking in originality, the nickname accurately characterized his stereotypical southwestern drawl. Early on he had protested, pointing out that he hailed from Oklahoma. He eventually acceded and embraced his new name. I don't think anyone in the hold knew his given name. Tex had been employed as a hand on a large cattle ranch and often spent days at a time isolated in the far reaches of the property. He went to sleep under the stars in the bed of his pickup truck one night and woke up with the rest of us. I didn't know Tex very well, but I ascribed a reasonable level of intelligence to him. I was thus taken aback when he made the following statement with such glee.

"See? The guverment's done fixed this. We're goin' home."

"Or they paid the ransom. Either way is fine with me," said another equally joyful voice.

I could barely see Nicholas' face in the dim light but his expression of curiosity was quite noticeable. My own countenance was marked with wide eyes and raised eyebrows in response to these statements.

"Do they really think we're going home?" I whispered to Nicholas, loud enough for the others nearby to hear.

"I guess so," he whispered back. "I think they're gonna be disappointed." Everyone in my immediate vicinity had long since accepted Nicholas' spaceship theory as fact. It hadn't occurred to us that some others might still be clinging to the theories we had dismissed weeks earlier.

"I hope they're right," said Charles quietly. We said nothing to Tex or the others about our doubts. Why dash their hopes? We only had crazy, outlandish theories with which to replace them. His comment reawakened a glimmer of hope inside me. For the first time in weeks I started thinking seriously about returning to my life on Earth.

A few days later, just when the trepidation spurred by my brief conversation with Thing One was beginning to simmer, we awoke to rumblings and vibrations that shook the hold. Before a word was spoken, we were suddenly and briefly thrust downward, as if we had been riding down an elevator that came to an abrupt halt. The rumblings gradually ceased and the hold grew eerily quiet. The steady background noise that had become a fixture in our heads was now gone. The sensation was familiar to me—like a commercial airliner shutting off its engines upon arrival at the gate.

After what we calculated to be sixty-one days of captivity plus the undetermined amount of time we spent unconscious, we had arrived.

7

Minutes after landing the lights came on. Both androids entered through the hatch and stopped at the first set of berths. Straining to look down the corridor I could make out another figure behind them. It was by all appearances, a man.

Had we never left Earth after all? Suddenly, the idea of space travel seemed so implausible that I wondered how I could have allowed myself to be so gullible. The man made his way into the hold, slipped between the Things and began addressing us loudly. He had a medium build and a weather-worn face that was intensified by his tattered clothing, which comprised an olive-colored button-down shirt, shorts, and calf-high boots. His beard was short but not well-trimmed, as was his hair—a mix of light brown and gray. I placed his age to be more than fifty, although I might have been influenced by his rugged appearance. I recognized his accent as Australian, which hastened my newly-found aspiration of going home.

"Listen up!" he bellowed. "Just do as your told and you won't be harmed." His voice had an authoritative yet calming tone. As the androids began releasing the captives near the hatch and lining them up in the corridor, the man walked toward my location. What he said next shocked me back into the reality of the past sixty-plus days.

"The gravity's a bit stronger here than what you experienced on the ship and on Earth, but don't worry—you'll get used to it." He spoke casually, as if we had already been fully-briefed on the situation in advance, and he was merely filling in a few of the minor details. His words replayed in my mind. *On Earth? Stronger gravity?* Nicholas must have been right all along. At least I was somewhat mentally prepared for this realization. I wondered what effect his comments were having on Tex and the other non-believers. The man glanced at each of us as he traversed the corridor, only stopping briefly when he encountered one of the less healthy captives.

"You okay, mate?" he asked the sickly captive while patting him on the shoulder. The prisoner mumbled something in return and the man moved on. I couldn't wait for him to reach me.

"Where are we?" I shouted. Without waiting for a reply, I continued, "What's going on?"

"All in good time, mate. Don't sweat it."

We marched single file through the room we called the yard, and for the first time into the room on the other side. It was empty and contained doors on all sides. The two side hatches were closed and the one directly in front of us was open. I followed the shuffling line of captives into the next room and found myself within another hold that was nearly identical to the one which we had just vacated. It was empty, but the litter and stench indicated that it had also been occupied by abductees.

"My god," Susan said softly behind me. She needn't have said anything more. The line progressed through the corridor and into the next room which I guessed had served as the other group's exercise space. In this room, a side door was open to the outside. Daylight flooded through the opening and I instinctively shielded my eyes upon entering. The light was not particularly bright but my pupils had not been exposed to anything more than a dim, artificial light for weeks. The others reacted similarly and we stumbled forward blindly. I put my free hand on the shoulder of the man in front of me. The Aussie stood next to the exit door and helped us step out into the new world. By the time I reached the door, half of my group was already outside.

"Step out and line up to the right," said the Aussie as he gently grabbed my elbow. I managed to open one eye just enough to see where my feet were stepping and headed to the right. Things One and Two remained on the ship but waiting for us outside were two more androids cut from the same mold. Without making a sound, they shepherded us into three rows facing back toward the ship. I stood quietly in the middle row while the rest of the group exited the ship and joined the loose formation. My eyes gradually adjusted and I lifted my head to survey the ship which had served as my prison. Its exterior was nearly as squalid as the interior cargo hold, and not at all what I had imagined. It didn't appear to be air-worthy, let alone space-worthy. Nicholas agreed.

"We're lucky to be alive," he whispered loudly from a few positions to my right. I tried to imagine the old vessel in its younger days, cleaned and sorted, and it slowly began to resemble a spacecraft more analogous to what I had seen in movies. It was long and thin, barely wider than the width of our hold. I reckoned it was metallic in structure, though it was too dirty to know for sure. It rested on four pods that extended to the ground on the ends of jointed legs. Protruding from one end of the ship were two large cylinders which I presumed to be part of the thrust mechanism. I saw no windows or lights, nor could I see anything resembling a cockpit or a bridge. What I *could* see of the ship resembled what it was—a cargo vessel. And now I surmised that the cargo of this vessel comprised freshly-recruited slaves. I could think of no other reasonable explanation.

My attention suddenly turned to Leesheh. I had forgotten about her amid the anxiety induced by our drastic change in circumstances. I quickly looked over each shoulder and spotted her standing in the row behind me. She must have sensed my concern, for she met my eyes with a smile and a small wave, as if to tell me she was okay. She looked healthy, and I daresay cut an attractive figure, even in the loose-fitting gray pajamas. Her black hair was frizzled and a bit disarranged, but it was eclipsed by her charming caramel-colored face, flawless teeth, and hazel eyes. When she waved a second time, I realized that I was staring and sheepishly turned back toward the ship.

A few more minutes of silence passed. My eyes became accustomed to the light and I took stock of my immediate environment. In addition to Leesheh, standing alongside me on that day were Charles, Nicholas, Susan, Pablo, Tex, and thirty-one others, most of whom I was seeing clearly for the first time. I counted ten deaths during our time in the hold, which meant that we had left our home world with forty-eight souls in our section of the ship.

Next to our group, closer to the front of the ship, stood another formation of about thirty people. They were equally battered, tired, and exasperated, and it was not difficult to deduce that they were the unlucky abductees that had occupied the other hold on the ship. This faction also comprised a mix of Caucasian, African, and Latino races. They, too, were likely plucked from the Americas, a premise I verified upon meeting them shortly thereafter.

I didn't have cause to mention much about Monte, the native South American, during my description of our voyage. This is because he had adjusted to captivity as well as any of us and spent his days on board keeping quietly to his self. Had I not seen him each time I went to the yard, I might have forgotten about him. Here he was now, standing on the end of the back row and staring straight ahead, like a soldier at attention.

"Poor Monte," murmured Tex. "He ain't got no idea what's happenin' to him."

"And you do?" I shot back. "It doesn't look like the government intervened." As soon as the words left my mouth, I regretted the sarcasm. I had nothing against Tex, and we were all in this frustrated mess together. I should have apologized but didn't. Instead, Tex and I bickered back and forth in a loud whisper until Charles implored us both to quiet down. I felt ashamed for a moment but soon became preoccupied by surveying my surroundings.

A couple of younger men dressed similarly to the Aussie walked among them. Unlike the Aussie, who was unarmed, each carried what appeared to be a weapon that loosely resembled a rifle. They also differed from the Aussie in that they were racially mixed, with darker hair and complexions.

I expanded my visual exploration of the physical surroundings. The temperature was pleasant to the extent that I had not even noticed a change when departing the ship. The terrain consisted mostly of dirt and rock but there were thick green trees and smaller plants at a distance in every direction. We seemed to be standing in a clearing within a forest. Other than the ship and ourselves, I saw no signs of civilization or any unnatural objects whatsoever.

Despite feeling slightly heavier, I could have otherwise been convinced that I was still on Earth without much persuasion, had it not been for one notable exception. It was such a spectacle that I couldn't fathom how it had escaped my attention until that moment. To my left, sitting low in the sky was a large orb. It was either very large, very close, or both, for it appeared to have a diameter ten times that of the sun as viewed from Earth. It was pale blue in color and bright, yet not so bright as to preclude looking directly at it. Bands varying in hue between dark blue and white circled the sphere horizontally. I called to Nicholas quietly and pointed up toward the sphere with a curious expression, as if to say, "check that out." Susan was fixated on the brilliant orb as well.

"We're not in Kansas anymore," she quipped. Nicholas nodded affirmatively and was about to provide us with a scientific explanation, but it would have to wait. The Aussie, who now stood before the two groups, began to address the ensemble. A few feet to his left stood the two young men. They couldn't have been older than twenty and appeared to be in excellent physical condition. They had lean, athletic builds—more like basketball players than football players. Their beards were merely stubble, not dapper by any stretch, but clearly attended to. I stroked my own lengthy beard and took inventory of the men in my company. I surmised that like them, I too resembled a shipwreck survivor on a deserted island. It was an odd moment to feel embarrassment and a twinge of jealousy in the company of my female cohorts, yet I did.

Although the two men wore the same tattered attire as the older gentleman, the similarities ended there. These boys resembled soldiers, with their short hair and closely-cropped beards. The Aussie appeared to be in adequate shape for his supposed age, but his best years were clearly behind him. The first young man stood with his weapon resting on his shoulder. One hand grasped the weapon while the other rested casually in the pocket of his shorts. The second man clasped his hands behind his back. His rifle rested horizontally behind him, held in place between his arms and lower back. Neither man appeared to be overly concerned about the proceedings before them.

"My name is Malcolm," the older man started, speaking loudly enough for all to hear. "You are now soldiers of the People's Resistance Front."

Soldiers? Such a notion hadn't occurred to me during all those days I spent pondering my fate within the darkness of the cargo hold. Nor had the idea crossed the minds of my cohorts. Murmurs filled the crowd as we exchanged looks of disbelief. We were not the stuff of soldiers. The only true soldier among us had perished—he'd lost his mind, in fact. We had no time for anguish at the moment. We had to reign in our imaginations and focus on Malcolm. The gravity of his words was contrasted by his informal demeanor, and a hint of empathy in his voice.

This was not a great general rousing his troops; he was simply a messenger—perhaps merely a peer. A few people shouted out the obvious questions in response to his declaration.

"There will be plenty of time for questions later," he continued in a thick Australian accent. "At the moment, we've got to get you lot down to camp. Now don't try anything silly. There's nowhere to run, and nowhere to hide. You can't survive in this world without us."

Throughout this brief discourse, the two young men exchanged whispers and smirks, and appeared to be having a conversation wholly unrelated to Malcolm's speech. I inferred that the jokes were at the expense of specific captors in our formation whom they were subtly pointing out to each other.

"Right, then," Malcolm gestured toward the men next to him, "these two men here are Sparks and Tully." Next, he nodded toward the androids resembling the Things that stood behind us. "I believe you know the sentroids and what they're capable of. The best chance you have of staying alive is to listen to me and these young gentlemen here."

They proceeded to march us in two parallel lines down a path that led into a more wooded area. Malcolm led the procession while the two so-called sentroids brought up the rear. There were a few grumblings along the way, but for the most part we remained quiet as we walked. Malcolm had issued no directive for silence; we were simply too overwhelmed by the events of the past hour to engage in anything but our own thoughts. The tense quietude was interrupted about two minutes into the march by a loud rumbling noise behind us. Everybody stopped and turned to see the large ship which had brought us there rise above the tree line. It hovered in place for a few seconds before moving—slowly at first, then quickly accelerating. A few seconds later it was out of sight. The others resumed walking while I remained frozen, staring at the empty sky.

"Shakespeare, stay with me," said Charles. I jogged up to him and rejoined the formation. I would see that ship only once more.

The trees, now much closer, looked both familiar and unfamiliar. The plants and terrain seemed both natural and foreign, as if I was visiting a lost continent on Earth that had traversed a separate evolutionary path for millions of years. The large blue orb rising in the sky behind us reminded me that we were nowhere near our home planet. Still, the Earth-like familiarity of the surroundings managed to assuage my apprehension, if only a little.

We walked a few hundred yards before entering a small clearing that revealed a camp bustling with activity. There was no fencing or any other form of defensive structure. The camp was surrounded by woods, and the camouflaged nature of the structures within suggested that its purpose was that of a hideaway more than a defensive stronghold. Malcolm halted us in front of the camp, where a small group was assembled to meet us. We pressed together into a tight mob and surveyed the ensemble standing between us and the camp beyond.

I had been nervously anticipating this moment since first seriously entertaining the notion, so many weeks ago, of having been abducted by extraterrestrials. I had prepared myself mentally to encounter the alien life forms responsible for my captivity when I disembarked the ship, only to find three human men and two android overseers. Now, only an hour or so later, the anticipation had been suppressed by the Earth-like familiarity of my surroundings. It was no longer in the forefront of mind. I suddenly stood with mouth agape in the presence of what was certainly these long-foreseen aliens.

I realize that the term "alien" is more befitting of ourselves, as the creatures that stood before us were most likely native inhabitants of this planet. However, I reserve the right to apply it in this narrative when describing anything beyond what could be found on Earth. That is, to describe anything that is alien *to me.*

And so, after walking from the landing site to the camp, we bunched together and stood quietly. I was devoid of any further anticipation, having no life experiences to prepare me for what was immediately before me, let alone for what my long-term future held. I knew only that I was earmarked to serve as a soldier in some capacity—undoubtedly a soldier with the utmost expendability. It was reasonable to conclude that the leader of the faction for which I had been conscripted to serve now stood before us with his entourage.

The two young men that had escorted us moved forward and took a position with the small party that blocked our entrance to the camp. Malcolm remained with us and stood slightly in front, as if to formally present us to the king and his court, yet he said nothing. Two humanoid creatures, ostensibly alive in every sense—clearly not machines, stood before us on small hovering platforms. These platforms had short walls on three sides that shielded the rider up to his waist. They could have been characterized as futuristic chariots—self-propelled and fully-armored.

The creatures standing within each chariot were short and slight in stature, easily less than five feet tall. Each was clothed in ornate garments, including a black hat that somewhat resembled a beret. The only portion of their flesh visible to us was the lower half of their faces. These hairless faces were pale in complexion, not unlike an albino, with a slight violet hue reflecting in the daylight provided by the large blue orb. The creatures wore tinted visors covering the area where one would expect their eyes to be. These goggles appeared to serve as something more than sunglasses, as I saw tiny lights on the sides occasionally flicker on and off. Below the visor was a wide mouth. I saw nothing in the areas where one might expect to find a nose and ears, although much of the creatures' bodies was concealed. My unscientific conclusion, based on brief and distant encounters with these creatures I would have later, was that they were either androgynous or there was no obvious distinction between genders.

In front of these chariots stood the aforementioned two young men, three other men with Asian features, two more of the so-called sentroids, and another android. The three-legged sentroids were visibly of the same class as Thing One and Thing Two. The other android appeared more spartan and timeworn, making it seem much older. Its right arm was red, a completely different color than its grayish body. It was apparently not an original part, calling to mind an old car with a replacement door. Its body was peppered with small dents, scuffs, and scratches, and it wore a utility belt around its waist that contained several pouches. It resembled a human more than the sentroids, mostly because it stood on only two legs and was approximately six feet tall. Its arms were proportionate to that of a human, and instead of a two-pronged claw, they had something comparable to a hand with fingers at the ends of them. As we approached, it broke ranks with the entourage and came forward to meet Malcolm. It moved as smoothly as a human.

Malcolm and the scruffy, human-like android engaged in quiet conversation until one of the alien creatures turned its head and pointed a gloved hand toward one of the sentroids. Some form of communication must have been exchanged between the creature and its servile robot, though I saw nothing but a brief flurry of lights on the sides of the former's visor. The sentroid began speaking in a voice identical to the Things. It addressed us for about ten minutes, entirely in

English. I wondered about the handful of captives in our company who didn't understand English very well. Little Monte stood attentively in the front of the crowd and listened to the sentroid as if he understood every word, though I knew that he didn't comprehend one iota of the speech. I made a mental note to keep an eye on him, as if I could somehow protect him.

The gist of what we were told outside of the camp that day was as follows. I should note that on this and all other occasions on which a sentroid addressed us, he used only very basic English words that I am paraphrasing here. I suppose that many terms and concepts were compromised and simplified in the translation from the native tongue to English. Furthermore, you must realize that we were surely regarded as a lower form of life, perhaps in the way that a human regards a chimpanzee. In this framework we were commodities. As such, we were told only what we needed to know in order to best serve them. Does the zookeeper discuss the zoo's finances with the chimpanzees? Does the foxhunter inform the hounds why he chose a particular location for the hunt? The gap between our intelligences was likely smaller than those examples but did our captors see it that way? I'll leave that discussion for the historians. Here's a summary of what the sentroid told us, supplemented with information that I learned in the days that followed:

We were the property of General Abasha. "Abasha" was not exactly how the sentroid pronounced his name but it's what the humans called him. General Abasha was not present in the camp. His whereabouts were not disclosed to us at that time.

General Abasha was the leader of the People's Resistance Front (PRF), which was the official governing body of Serrone, Region Seventeen. Serrone was the name of the planet on which we stood. The term "region" was analogous to a country or nation.

The portion of the PRF based in this camp was under the leadership of Captain Cheefon. (Again, liberties have been taken with pronunciations.) The sentroid gestured to one of the chariot creatures while making this statement. The humans referred to him as "the Chief."

The sentroid referred to the native subjects (or "people," for lack of a better word) of Serrone as Serrones. To quote the messenger exactly, it was their "right to freedom" for which we were now indentured to fight.

Several rebellious factions opposed the PRF. (Of course, General Abasha claimed it was the legitimate government of Serrone Region

Seventeen.) The General was committed to ridding his region (and the planet) of the unlawful, barbarous rebels.

Anyone refusing to fight would be "destroyed." Anyone deemed to be an unusable resource would also be killed.

Some of the "females" would be assigned to "reproduction duties" and others would fight alongside the males. Of all the proclamations, this one caused the greatest stir among us.

Our training would commence tomorrow and we should expect to participate in combat soon.

Replacement clothing and footwear would be provided forthwith. I hoped that "replacement" meant new, but I was to be disappointed.

There were a few other statements made by the sentroid, but this summary captures the most salient points. It wasn't exactly a welcoming speech, nor did it boost our rapidly declining morale. Upon the conclusion of the remarks, the Chief and his entourage turned away from us and entered the camp. Malcolm raised his hands in front of us as if to say "stay here." Sparks and Tully, the two men who had met us at the landing site, separated from the entourage and returned to us while whispering to each other. Something had caught their attention. They approached a young woman standing in the front.

"You," said Tully as he grabbed the woman by her arm, "and... you." He pointed to another young woman nearby, whom Sparks subsequently plucked from the crowd. I felt a sudden rush of adrenaline resulting from an epiphany. I turned my head to Charles, who was standing next to me. His eyes conveyed that he was mulling over the same concern. Leesheh stood partially behind me over my right shoulder. To her left was Susan. Looking straight ahead and keeping my torso motionless, I slowly moved my arm backward until my hand found Leesheh's waist. I gently nudged her to the left so that I would fully obstruct her from view. Charles followed my lead and adjusted his position ever so calmly such that he completely eclipsed Susan. Pablo, on my other side, recognized our intent and closed ranks beside me. Sparks and Tully identified a third woman standing near the front of the assembly and motioned for her to join them. They briefly surveyed the crowd once more then headed into the camp, apparently satisfied with the three women they had tabbed. The women offered no resistance and freely walked alongside the young men.

One of the women hailed from my cargo hold. She was Tina, a tall, attractive young student at The University of Utah. Coincidentally, she had been abducted not far from my own position. Living with her parents in St. George for the summer, she had taken the family's golden retriever for a late-night walk and was ostensibly never seen again. I didn't know Tina well, for her cage was on the lowest tier and toward the far-right end of the corridor. That didn't lessen the heartache I felt for her in that moment as she walked away. She turned around only once to see us silently watching and eventually disappeared into the camp. I hoped that my horrid notion was off the mark, but the sentroid's earlier reference to "reproduction duties" made it difficult to refute. Leesheh grabbed my hand from behind and squeezed it.

Malcolm and the tattered, two-legged android watched this brief selection process while taking no action. When it was over, Malcolm turned to face us and put his hand on the android's shoulder.

"This is Dee, your sergeant, and I'm what's called the Human in Charge for this squad, which is you lot. You can just call me Malcolm," he said. "Dee and I will see to it that you are fit for soldiering." Dee took over on cue. His voice sounded remarkably human.

"Malcolm will do his best to keep you alive."

"Why?" interrupted a voice from the middle of the group. This was clearly not a reaction to anything specific, nor could the person responsible find the words to elaborate on his question. No elaboration was necessary. That one simple word, with all of its connotations, captured it all. The implausibility of our current circumstance, juxtaposed with the lives we led some sixty-odd days earlier, had suddenly overwhelmed the petitioner as he stood patiently listening to a barrage of regulations, declarations, and instructions—from aliens, no less. These regulations, declarations, and instructions had been presented as if the subjects receiving them had fully expected to be standing on this very spot on this very day. You might suppose that his question was followed by others demanding answers, and that the crowd began to ferment with indignation, yet this was not the case. We stood in complete silence and waited for a reply.

"Look, I know you're confused," started Malcom. "I wish… I wish you weren't here… but you are, and I can't change that. You've probably guessed that I'm not from here either. My home is the same as yours. Just… just trust me. Things will become clearer later."

"Just tell us how to get home," came another unseen voice.

"You can't..." Malcolm replied empathetically, his voice nearly breaking. "It just isn't gonna happen. The sooner you come to grips with that, the better off you'll be."

I was surprised at the despair in his voice. I appreciated his candor and sincerity, though I wondered why he dared to commiserate with us in the presence of the android, Dee. Dee was obviously *not* from our home and served as the delegated representative of our oppressors. I would soon come to know that Dee was much different than his three-legged sentroid cousins, but that portion of the narrative must wait until later.

8

This is probably an appropriate place to break from the narrative and spend a few moments describing the planet which we had come to inhabit. Much of what I write here was yet to be discovered in the weeks that followed, but I'll document it at this juncture, lest you form an inaccurate visual image of the planet's geology, flora, and fauna.

You might have surmised that what we called a planet was not a planet at all. It was a moon orbiting the aforementioned large blue gaseous planet that occupied a sizeable portion of the daytime and nighttime skies. This arrangement meant that the days were never as bright as a sunny day on Earth, and the nights cycled through phases ranging from pitch darkness to continuous twilight, similar to an Alaskan summer. Most of our heat and light was provided by the parent planet, which had been named Wiyanga by the humans that preceded us. The star at the center of this solar system was distant and provided no more illumination than a full moon reflects to Earth. It had no name—we merely referred to it as the star.

The combined orbits of our moon (Serrone), our parent planet (Wiyanga), and the star precipitated numerous color and light variances in the skies. Despite these variances, the climate was represented by only two seasons—a warm dry span, followed by a cooler period dotted with heavy rainstorms. The hottest days were no less bearable than those I endured while growing up in the Mid-Atlantic region of the United States. The temperature in the cool season rarely dropped below the freezing point of water. Under different circumstances, the location of our camp might have been ideal for a vacation resort. The warm season lasted slightly longer than the cool season and we referred to the cycle of both seasons as one year.

The duration of a year on Serrone roughly measured 380 days, where a day refers to a single rotation of the moon we occupied. This was slightly longer than a day on Earth—according to the consensus opinion of the astronomers among us. For reasons that predate my arrival, the humans on Serrone tended to note the passage of time in terms of seasons rather than years. One might say that he "spent the last six seasons here," which equated to a little more than three Earth years.

In the early days, we took little notice of the nuances in gravitational force, air pressure, climate, and daylight intervals, for we had much more pressing worries to occupy our minds. By the time we might have noticed the differences, they had become our new normal.

In spite of its scientific designation as a moon, the humans on Serrone persisted in referring to it as a planet. I will honor the local vernacular and do likewise henceforth. Its geological features mirrored those of the Earth. Nicholas explained to me that this was to be expected, as the same elements produced by the mega forces of the universe (supernovas, gravity, fission, collisions, etc.), are thought to be common throughout.

The terrain of the planet included oceans, rivers, mountains, thrusts, cliffs, plains, and anything else you would expect to find on Earth, indicating that it embodied similar plate tectonics and their seismic consequences. There were a couple of notable differences. Although slightly larger than Earth, Serrone was covered by oceans in a greater proportion. Thus, the amount of inhabitable land was less than Earth. Secondly, I never witnessed a catastrophic natural weather event, such as a tornado or hurricane.

Earlier, I wrote that my first impressions of the planet invoked contradicting sensations of familiarity and unfamiliarity. The best way to describe the flora and fauna of the planet is to paraphrase a witty observation made by Susan a few days after we arrived. She said it was as though the life on this planet had been designed by someone tasked with duplicating life on Earth without the luxury of ever having visited Earth. That is, the designs were based solely on secondhand descriptions.

We could relate the animals we encountered to similar creatures on Earth, yet nothing ever matched *exactly*. There were four-legged varmints that leaned toward the mammalian end of the spectrum and scaly creatures that displayed reptilian characteristics. The most common animal in our area, and a common food source, was a large rodent-like creature we called the cappy, so named by my South American friends for its close resemblance to the capybara. There was less distinction between the creatures that could fly and those that could not, as there is between birds and non-flying animals on Earth. On this planet, some animals had wings and others did not; there were no unique features to distinguish those that flew, such as beaks and feathers.

The planet hosted its version of an arthropod population ranging from very large beetle-like critters down to microscopic organisms (presumptively). We quickly learned to avoid a particularly venomous predator that humans called a "roller." This odd creature was about the size of a man's fist and resembled what one might imagine as the hybrid of a scorpion and a salamander. The roller was so named because of its ability to move quickly by thrusting itself using its two hind legs then curling itself into a ball and rolling over terrain. A single bite almost always resulted in death, though rollers were not known to bite humans unless accidently stepped on. Still, we often found them in camp and I can recall a few deaths at their hands.

The trees, at least in our region, were neither decidedly deciduous nor coniferous. Most sported leaves but they were not dropped en masse in conjunction with a season. The trees in my area seemed to drop and generate leaves at their own discretion. Within the vicinity of our camp grew a variety of edible vegetation which we included in our diet. As with the fauna, some of the plants resembled fruit, some resembled vegetables, and most were something in between. I eventually found the native cuisine to be quite agreeable.

As would be expected on a life-sustaining planet, water was abundant. A large stream flowed through the camp, which wasn't a coincidence. To my knowledge, there was no large body of water near the camp. I would later find myself on the shores of one of the planet's immense oceans.

This respite should provide a suitable basis to form a visualization of the region of the planet which I occupied at that time, yet I feel compelled to note one final observation before resuming my story. The oddest thing about this planet was its familiarity—an overwhelming resemblance to Earth. Under more congenial circumstances, humans could have surely thrived on this planet. Nicholas once pointed out that this was perhaps a paramount reason for our abduction—our adaptability.

9

Upon entering the camp on that first day, Dee led us to a large wooden shack where buckets of food and water were provided. We were not given the grand tour per se, but he pointed out various structures and points of interest along the way. A mix of human and android sentries roamed the perimeter of the camp on the lookout for foes trying to enter and presumably, captive soldiers attempting to exit. The structures in camp mostly consisted of wooden shacks, huts, and tents that had the appearance of being hastily constructed and situated without the benefit of any master planning.

I soaked in the environment with less wonderment than you might imagine. Save for a few notable exceptions, the camp was not discordant with one you might expect to find on Earth, albeit this one resembled a guerilla compound more than a government-backed military base. I shared my analogy with Nicholas and he noted that most of the camp was probably built by humans. There was a building for latrines that contained stalls with wooden toilet seats and large wooden buckets underneath. The buckets were emptied into the wide stream that rambled along one side of the camp. The stream itself was demarcated into three sections: upstream for collecting drinking water, midstream for bathing and downstream for sewage and waste disposal. The "dining hall," as it was acerbically known, was a pavilion with wooden tables and benches. I saw no kitchen, only an open firepit littered with charred bones.

The food provided for us that day consisted entirely of native fruits and vegetables. It arrived in large baskets carried by a handful of Chinese men and women who left abruptly without saying a word. I was hesitant to sample the local cuisine and longed for my cereal mush. My hunger eventually triumphed, but only after I witnessed others take a few bites and not keel over. The food was bland at best. The flora on this planet had evolved in harmony with the native fauna; our alien taste buds had not figured into the equation. (I grew to tolerate most of the foods and acquired a taste for one fruit in particular.) Following the meal, Malcolm and Dee circulated among the tables with bowls containing what resembled large vitamin pills.

"You're gonna wanna eat one of these every day," Malcolm advised. "This'll boost your immune system." He walked over to the next table. I held up the pill in front of my face.

"What do you think, Doc?"

"What have we got to lose, Shakespeare?" replied Charles. "That man looks like he's been here a long time. I'm going to do what he says… for the time being." My tablemates carefully watched for my next move.

"Here goes nothing," I said and swallowed the pill with a swig of water.

After eating our fill, we were taken to a nearby building. Inside were various heaps of clothing strewn about in an otherwise empty room. One had assorted footwear—primarily ankle-high boots constructed of something resembling leather. Another contained shirts and still another was full of long and short pants. There was a pile of socks and even a collection of under garments.

We were instructed to remove our pajamas and find new attire, and we didn't have to be told twice. None of the clothing was new. It didn't take a Rhodes Scholar to realize that the best items would have already been claimed by the existing soldiers, and what *they* were wearing didn't appear to be fresh off the rack. Within seconds the room resembled a sale on Black Friday. Living in such close proximity on the ship had long since quelled any modesty, so nobody took notice of the half-naked men and women scurrying about the room. It occurred to me that the first priority was to secure suitable footwear before the best boots were taken. Everything else was secondary to protecting the feet. I had to shout over the ensuing racket to convey my idea to the group of friends within my vicinity.

"Feet!" I yelled while gesturing toward the pile of boots. Several of my fellow captives were already there and boots were flying in all directions. I managed to find a left boot with no holes and most of its sole intact. I placed it on my bare foot and realized that a pair of socks would have been helpful. It was too late for that. The pile of boots was now the most popular attraction in the room and shrinking fast. I procured a boot for my right foot. It was in better condition than the left boot, so I was willing to overlook the blood stain on the heel.

Rather than trying to improve on my choices, I decided to help Leesheh find a suitable pair. I held on to her provisional choices while she searched for upgrades. Working as a team, she and I moved on to selecting pants. I wanted to grab socks next, but Leesheh suggested pants, in order to have pockets into which we could stuff multiple pairs of socks. Brains *and* beauty! She continued to impress me, though admittedly, I was a bit predisposed in her favor. When the dust cleared, I was attired in olive-green, knee-length cargo shorts and a khaki shirt. One of the lower front pockets in my shorts had been torn off but the others were in decent shape. We joined up with Charles and the others to compare wardrobes. Susan had the most success, having found nearly-new, well-fitting items in every pile.

Dee next walked us to the middle of the compound under a darkening sky. Before us stood a row of five long, single-story huts with wooden walls and thatched roofs. These barracks had doors on each end and rectangular holes were cut into the sides for windows. A few men and women were watching us from the windows while a larger crowd gathered outside to look over the new conscripts. A band of about forty Chinese men and women, interspersed with a handful of Africans, emerged from the huts farthest away and joined the rest of the crowd. I counted five androids among them. They were from the same humanoid mold as Dee and shared his scruffy appearance. The crowd was silent and expressionless as Dee instructed us.

"These two buildings are empty," he said while pointing at the closest huts. "There are enough bunks there for most of you. The rest of you can find an empty bunk in that one." He shifted his mechanical finger toward the third building in the row. "Do not leave the barracks except to use the latrine. Go now. Tomorrow we train."

Both crowds dispersed—the newly enslaved and the veteran conscripts. The latter class appeared to have a longer leash as they scattered to the various reaches of the compound. I watched Malcolm make his way toward the third hut and it occurred to me that it might be advantageous to take up residence with the old guard versus stumbling blindly with the other newbies. My second priority was to keep the faction from the middle of the cargo hold together, into which I had unceremoniously drafted Leesheh. She was standing nearby talking to Susan when we were discharged. I called them over and made my case for bunking in the third hut. Charles and Nicholas had simultaneously sought my attention, and the five of us convened. We agreed on the third hut and made our way inside.

We were received somewhat coldly by a handful of circumspect men standing in front of their double bunks. The first two we encountered were the seemingly inseparable Sparks and Tully. Nicholas was the first to pass by them, and he extended his hand.

"I'm Nicholas," he said. Sparks returned the gesture with a smirk as he briefly scrutinized the lean newcomer and his thick spectacles. Tully added his own wry smile and pointed down the corridor, as if to say "move along." The two men turned away, relieving the rest of us of any potentially awkward eye contact. At the next bunk stood an older Aboriginal man, leaning back against the bed frame with his arms folded. His bright white beard markedly contrasted with his dark complexion. The old man's standoffish posture did not deter Nicholas. He extended his hand once more and told the man his name. The old man shook his head and replied in a heavy Aussie accent.

"Don't even wanna know, mate," he said. "If you're still 'ere in a few weeks we can siddown an' have a nice chat." Malcolm had been watching us closely since we entered the building. He approached Nicholas and put a hand on his shoulder.

"Don't mind ole Swag here, Nick," he said with a smile that revealed a few missing teeth. "He's just an old softy at heart."

"Friends call me Swag. You lot can call me Harold," Swag proclaimed in our general direction. Then he caught Nicholas eyeing the lower bunk, which appeared to be available. "Don't even think about it, boy."

"Sorry, Mr. Swag," said Malcolm. "All the bunks are gonna be taken. Go ahead, son."

"Just stay out of my way, boy," added Swag, then all at once he showed a crack in his hard-nosed façade. He loved the idea of presenting a rough veneer, but his heart had no trace of the cruelty required to sustain it. "You'll wanna mind those spectacles," he kindly told Nicholas. "We'll fetch ya some tape later 'an get them reinforced. Ya don't wanna wait until they break." Nicholas nodded in gratitude and tossed his spare socks onto the bed.

The double bunkbeds were made of wood. Each bed incorporated wooden cross slats covered with a sheet of plywood. On top of the plywood was a mattress made from a foamlike substance. A smaller hunk of foam served as a pillow. Malcolm looked toward the rest of us and nodded his head to the side.

"Right this way, gentleman—and ladies. There's some empty racks over here."

We passed by a few more of the veteran soldiers. Some nodded, and a few managed to utter a "hello" or "g'day." Toward the back of the hut a short, brawny woman stepped out and blocked our path. Her hair was closely cropped and nearly invisible underneath the olive-green floppy hat that she wore. Next to her stood a lean, pubescent boy that couldn't have been older than sixteen.

"I'm Jessie," she said in a gruff American voice that coincided with her appearance. She playfully ruffled the boy's hair. "And this is Ammo."

"Hey," I said while extending my hand to the boy. He smiled and nodded kindly, yet didn't respond to my outstretched hand. I didn't feel as if he was being rude. It seemed as if he had no idea how to react to my gesture. I quickly withdrew my arm in the hopes of averting any awkwardness and changed the subject. "You're American?" I asked Jessie.

"Yup. Columbus, Ohio. There's a few of us yanks here." She pointed in the direction of some of the men we had just passed. One of them gave us a slight wave and nod.

"The boy too?" I asked. She looked at me inquisitively and hesitated before responding.

"Not exactly."

We chose two sets of beds next to each other—Charles and I in one, Susan and Leesheh in the other. Leesheh and I procured the top bunks, which prompted another joke from Susan at my expense.

"Be careful with that guy sleeping above you," she said to Charles with a straight face. "I had to deal with his shit the entire time on the ship—and I mean that literally." I chuckled for a second then was suddenly overcome by a strange feeling. Why were we not gravely serious at a time like this? We could all be dead soon—we'd been told as much. I felt foolish for having let down my guard for those last few minutes and wondered if it was normal.

The sky outside was now completely dark. Somebody pushed a button near the door and lights very much like those in the cargo hold illuminated the room. I saw Malcolm sitting alone on the edge of his bunk and he became the focus of my attention. I walked over to him.

"Malcolm, can I ask you a few questions?"

"Only a few? I suppose you've got a lot on your mind." He clearly expected this moment to arrive. "Tell you what, mate. I'm a bit tired and it's late. Can we wait 'til tomorrow? I'll tell ya everything I know."

"Just a few minutes, okay?" The chances of me waiting until the next day were on par with asking a child to wait until December 26th to open his Christmas presents. I needed answers.

"Okay," Malcolm conceded, "but bring your friends over here so as I don't 'ave to repeat myself later." The others had already begun to make their way over to us, along with Jessie, Swag, and a few other old timers. I was about to speak when Dee entered the hut and sat down in a wooden chair near the door—one of two chairs in the room.

Malcolm noticed my hesitation. "It's alright, mate. Dee's one of us," he said in a voice loud enough for the android to hear. Ignoring us, Dee put his hands on his thighs and froze in fixed gaze toward the opposite wall. "He's in his power saving mode anyway," continued the Aussie.

I exchanged glances with my friends then decided that it was safe to proceed. I still lowered my voice, just in case. My mind was so saturated with questions that I couldn't figure out where to begin. With the eyes of my friends upon me, eagerly anticipating my sagacity, all I could muster was:

"Is this… is this real?"

"Yeah. It's very real." He laughed—mostly to himself. "The life you knew is over."

"But what… what…" I was clearly struggling and unable to descend below 30,000 feet into a more substantial line of questioning. "None of this makes any sense."

"It will. I'm not sayin' it'll get better, but it will soon make some sense," he told us.

I felt a little embarrassed for having wasted this precious opportunity to solicit information. On the other hand, none of my cohorts exhibited any desire to assist. Having regained a little of my footing, I posited a question for which I knew there must be a logical answer. I still needed to hear it.

"These things... Serrones—right? I don't see a lot of them around here. What's stopping us from simply overtaking them?"

Malcolm looked at me for a moment then shifted his gaze toward Sparks and Tully. They were engaged in some other activity at the front end of the hut and completely oblivious to our conversation.

"You see those two lads over there? They're not from Earth," he told us as he returned his eyes to me.

"What do you mean? Where are they from?"

"Where're they from? You're not following me, huh mate? Those two, and all those other kids you see walkin' around here lookin' hard as nails—they were born here—in captivity you might say."

"Here?"

"Not in this camp, but here on this planet. They've been the property of the PRF—or some other organization—from the day they were conceived. And most of 'em are fiercely loyal to it."

"Why?" I countered with a look of bewilderment. The notion that people would want to be there seemed preposterous.

"Because they don't know any better, now do they?" Malcolm continued. "They were raised as killers and it's the only life they know. It's not like they've been to finishing school, mate. You make a move on the Chief and they'll slit your throat before you get within ten feet of him, not to mention the sentroids." Charles finally jumped into the conversation.

"Have you not told those boys about Earth, sir? About their ancestors?" he asked in his most proper Caribbean English.

"Sure, they've heard our stories. It's all fairy tales to them. You try explaining your history to a kid with a two-hundred-word vocabulary—one hundred if you don't count the ones that have to do with killing a rebel."

"What about the robot?" continued Charles in a much softer voice, lest the android had a superior capacity for hearing.

"Dee? Oh, he's alright, I reckon," said Malcolm. "He's hardwired, you know, but not exactly for this situation 'ere." His statement came across to me as a riddle that compounded my frustration.

"I don't know. It sounds like you've given up," I said dismissively and started to walk away.

"Shakespeare," said Susan. She spoke only my name but her glare said something akin to "calm down," as only a mother could. She had undoubtedly perfected this look with her children. I knew that I had crossed a line and instantly felt regret. Malcolm rose from his bed and came to life.

"Hey! Don't you walk away from me. What is it—Shakespeare, right? How long 'ave you been here—one bloody day? Listen to me Shakespeare, and you might live one *more* day." I returned to him. He lowered his voice but remained stern. "You think I've given up, is that it? Like I'm some kinda sell-out? He pressed his finger into my chest with each question.

"I didn't mean it that way," I responded sheepishly. Recognizing my attempt to backtrack, Malcolm returned to his calm demeanor.

"Look, suppose you found a way to get outta here—away from the Chief—even the General. Then what? You're gonna catch the first space shuttle back to Earth, is that it? Well I got some news for ya. There's no goin' home for you or anybody else. This is your home now."

"But what if we could contact a legitimate government, or some other authority?" proposed Nicholas in a whisper.

"Oh, I see. Appeal to the United Nations—is that it? I'm just not gettin' through to you lot, am I?" He took in a deep breath and released it as his eyes swept across us. "This entire planet is one big shithole. This is all there is. You know what the rebels call us? Rebels. These bloody warlords are the only government this planet has left."

"I'm sorry. I shouldn't have come at you like that," I said. I realized that I had overstepped a boundary and was now in full retreat. Malcolm accepted my surrender.

"Well, it's not like you're the first rookie to come in here and try to sort things out in his first week," he replied. "You newbies just worry about surviving first. If you're still around in a few seasons, you can start focusing on changing the world. Alright mate?" He finished the speech with a pat on my shoulder. I was relieved and anxious to change the subject.

"How long have you been here?"

"Ha. You can tell me, I reckon. I'm going on about forty seasons here. What year was it when you left Earth?"

We spent a few minutes trading information and determined that Malcolm had been abducted nearly thirty years before we were, which only left us more confused, because that would have made him much older than he appeared. Nicholas attempted to explain that the theory of relativity, as applied to interstellar travel, could account for such a discrepancy.

We stayed up most of the night bringing Malcolm up to speed on the latest events from Earth. We were the first group of abductees to arrive at his camp in four seasons (two years), and the group before us consisted entirely of Chinese people. This explained the abundance of them in camp. With his need for Earth news satiated, Malcolm sat back against the wall and shook his head.

"Jesus," he said. "I can barely remember it. It's like I was never there—just read about it in a book or somethin'." His eyes welled and a single tear escaped down his cheek. "I had a wife and son, you know. Thing is, I can't remember what they look like." I felt even worse for having badgered him earlier. Who was I to question this man's logic? He continued to reminisce. "It was a lot different when I came here, you know. I was part of the first group to arrive, but that's a story for another time. You guys and gals need to get some sleep."

I realized later just how insulting my naivety must have come across to Malcolm, Swag, and Jessie. My frustration had arisen from my need of a philosophical explanation for my predicament—a big picture. If Malcolm or any of the other old timers had ever pined for the same, that candle had long been snuffed out. They had come to terms with their new world without trying to rationalize it, which is perhaps why they had survived this long. As I lay in my bunk reflecting on my gaffe, I turned toward Leesheh, only a few feet away and whispered, "I'm such an idiot."

"Yes, you are," she whispered back with a smile then added consolingly, "but otherwise you are not so bad."

Her tenderness made me feel better about my confrontation with Malcolm, yet I slept very little that night. For the first time in weeks my thoughts turned to my family. I wondered if they held out any hope of finding me alive. I began to feel sorry for myself, accepting the notion that I was probably no longer in the forefront of their minds. They had their own lives to worry about, as did I. It was the last I would think about them for a long time.

10

We were all awake long before the gaseous planet rose in the morning sky bringing forth a new extraterrestrial day. Ammo, the teenaged boy I met the previous day, carried in two buckets of fresh stream water. We newcomers stood around patiently watching the veterans begin their routine in the hopes of garnering handy knowledge of local procedures. Admittedly, we were a little intimidated by the vets and didn't wish to step on any toes. The men and women dipped a shared cup into one bucket and drank; the other was used for rinsing faces and other body parts. A couple of frayed towels were shared among them. A few took turns in front of a small mirror that I hadn't noticed the previous day. When the vets were finished, I ventured over to see my face for the first time since my abduction. The person I saw looking back at me in no way coincided with the image I had been carrying around in my head. I stood for several moments studying this mysterious personage.

"I can trim that beard for you—fix the hair too." I was so lost in my thoughts that Jessie's voice startled me. "Sorry," she continued with a laugh. "I didn't mean to scare you." I never would have taken this masculine woman to be the village hairdresser. Her offer was irresistible.

"Sure… I mean, definitely. Thanks."

"Okay. I'll do it tonight when we have time. Right now, you should get yourself ready. I think we're gonna see what you newbies are made of after chow." Her words troubled me a little, though I had already suspected that we were to be tested in one way or another. Feeling a bit intimidated, I walked over to the water buckets. They happened to be on a table next to Swag's bunk. He was sitting on his bed, lacing up his boots.

"Is it okay if I grab a drink?" I asked.

"Water's not for you, mate," he said with a very sobering expression. He couldn't maintain his charade for more than a second and suddenly burst into laughter. "Of course, have at it!" I smirked in acknowledgment of having been fooled. Swag and most of the others had begun to welcome us in their own small ways, but I was still very wary of Sparks and Tully. It was more than just the glares they occasionally shot in our direction. The way Malcolm spoke of them, and their seizure of the women before we entered camp, put me ill at ease. I was relieved that they were not presently in the hut.

Taking a drink from the communal cup, I tossed my head backward to allow every last drop to find its way into my throat. This action directed my eyes to the wall behind the table where they focused on a curious sight. Hanging on a large nail were several square pieces of paper. Handwritten on the front piece in large block letters was "Monday." No sooner had I spied this makeshift calendar when Ammo walked up to it, removed the papers, shuffled them, and replaced them onto the nail such that the front piece now displayed "Tuesday." Swag must have noticed my bewilderment.

"Tuesday it is, then," he proclaimed.

"You keep track of the days?" I asked.

"Why not? It doesn't really mean anything," he said. "We don't synchronize the weeks with the seasons or anything fancy like that. Just a little taste of home. The younger ones like it too."

"Don't the Serrones have a calendar?"

"Oh, no doubt, mate. But they're not gonna share that with us, now are they?" he said in a jovial but slightly condescending tone, as if I should be an expert on Serrone behavior after one day on the planet. Then he walked up to me and added with a smile, "But don't rely on it too much. Sometimes we forget to change the days. And the Chinese over there are usually a day ahead or a day behind."

A few minutes later, Dee called us outside. We came out to the yard in front of the huts and loosely assembled with our brethren from the ship and few of Dee's android brothers. I approached Pablo and Tex who were talking together. I still felt badly about how I spoke to Tex on the previous day and wanted to bend over backwards to show him that I was his friend. I inquired as to how they fared during the night. Pablo told me that they had the pleasure of a sentroid's company for the night, along with a couple of androids similar to Dee.

"At least for most of the night," Pablo corrected himself. "The sentroid was gone in the morning."

We sixty-plus newbies clustered into small groups to discuss yesterday's events and warily speculate on what the new day held for us. A slight commotion quickly spread and fixed everyone's attention on something that was rapidly approaching. It was a sentroid walking toward us alongside a man he was propping up with his right claw under the man's armpit. The man was barely conscious, if at all. His legs occasionally mimicked the action of walking but mostly his toes dragged in the dirt, unable to maintain the sentroid's hurried pace. His head slumped downward, as if he was studying the dirt that passed beneath him. When they reached the yard, the sentroid dropped the man at our feet, said nothing, and walked away. Dee kneeled down beside the derelict and inspected him. I recognized the man from the day before as hailing from the other cargo hold.

"I told you yesterday," Malcolm preached to the rest of us, "do as I say and you won't get hurt. You can't run, and you can't hide." Dee hoisted the man onto his shoulder like a soldier wounded in battle and carried him into the first hut in the row of barracks. He returned from the hut empty-handed.

"Time to eat," he said.

I was pleasantly surprised to find an ample supply of my trusty cereal available at the chow pavilion. After a breakfast of fruit and my beloved mush, we proceeded in a loosely-formed line through a portion of the camp we had not yet traversed. We stopped before crossing a dirt road to allow an oncoming caravan to pass. We lined the side of the road to get a glimpse of the convoy as it headed past, presumably leaving the camp. I felt as if we were villagers watching a conquering army pass through its streets. We weren't heralding them with miniature flags—just watching with curiosity.

The convoy consisted of five vehicles. At the head was a small open-air car with five occupants. The car, as well as the other vehicles, made no noise resembling a combustion engine. Its power source was something that emitted little sound and no exhaust. But that isn't to say that it was otherworldly in appearance. It didn't have a front end jutting out beneath a hood, as there was ostensibly no requirement for a large engine bay. It did have four wheels and two bench seats.

Mounted on the back of the vehicle was what appeared to be a large weapon. Its appearance suggested that there was nothing else it could have been. Sitting on a raised seat behind the weapon was an African man wearing a sleeveless shirt and a makeshift bandana around his head. He slumped back in his chair while casually resting one forearm on the muzzle of the weapon. Another African man sat in the front and was seemingly operating the vehicle, though there was no steering wheel where a person of Earth might expect to see one. His gaze was fixed on the road before him while one of his hands appeared to be manipulating some kind of control mechanism. A Chinese man and woman occupied the back seat. Long weapons, similar to those held by Sparks and Tully, were propped up next to them.

Next to the driver sat an android of the same make and model as Dee. We would soon learn that this class of android was called a "combat robot," or more colloquially a "combot."

The next three vehicles were transport trucks, about twenty feet in length, each with six large wheels. Pairs of soldiers and combots sat in each cab. Behind the cabs were flatbeds with short walls on three sides; the back was open-ended. The walls were constructed of three wooded slats with a few inches of open space between them. Within each flatbed were seven or eight soldiers—mostly Chinese. Some were sitting and paying no attention whatsoever to anything happening around them. Others were leaning over the side walls and watching us watch them. Still others sat with their legs dangling over the rear of the vehicle. Some soldiers held their weapons; others were stacked in the corners where the flatbed met the back of the cab.

The rearmost vehicle was a car similar to the first. Sitting in the rear seat was the only Serrone I detected in the entire party. His small size provided ample room for two sentroids to flank him, and I almost missed seeing him altogether. I didn't think that this Serrone was the Chief. His attire was less ornate than the two aliens that had greeted us on the previous day. His vehicle was the only one of the five being operated by a combot.

All of the soldiers in the convoy were attired similarly to the ragged gentleman manning the weapon in the lead vehicle. Some had accessorized their appearance with creative headgear made from strips of cloth. A few had smeared mud on their faces in various warrior-like patterns. The men and women that passed by us were, to a person, quiet. Absolutely none of them wore any expression that remotely hinted at fear, happiness, sadness, anxiety, or any other emotion. Nor did they acknowledge our presence other than staring blankly at us, with one exception. The very last person to pass by was a young Chinese woman who was manning the outboard weapon on top of the last vehicle. She waved at us ever so slightly. I couldn't see if she was smiling through the dust that had kicked up behind her.

The condition of the vehicles varied. None promoted the image of a spit-and-polished army heading off to battle. Like their combot occupants, they displayed battle scars in the form of dents, scratches, and even a few missing parts. Of all the oddities passing in front of me, I was most bewildered by the sight of some soldiers smoking cigarettes. Cigarettes must be as universally common as the wheel, I thought. I guess one can find something worth smoking on any inhabitable planet.

Next, we walked across the road and headed for an open patch of land. We passed within fifty yards of a pair of huts that stood near the far boundary of the camp—farthest from the entrance. The first was encircled by a wooden porch, on which a few women were sitting in chairs. Another woman leaned against the door jam, and others popped their heads out of the window openings to review us. In the latter group I caught sight of a familiar face, Tina. She walked to the doorway in order to get a better look at us, but dared not say a word. It wasn't difficult to recognize the expression of longing on her face—longing to be with her fellow captives from the ship. We, the same captives who were preparing to fight an unknown enemy for unknown causes with unknown consequences. To choose our fate over her current circumstances, I thought, does not speak well of the atrocities occurring within that hut.

The building next to it, although identical in architecture, presented a discordant image to its neighbor. That is, until I pieced together the undeniable affiliation. A few women stood on its porch as well. They were holding infants, some cradling them and others with tiny heads resting on a shoulder. Scurrying among the adults and spilling into the adjacent yard were a few barefooted toddlers clad in nothing but cloth diapers. All appeared to be in dire need of a bath. I couldn't see inside the hut very well. The sounds emanating from it indicated that there were a few more children within. I was compelled to confirm what required no confirmation, so I hastened my pace to catch up with Jessie, who was walking a few feet ahead.

"Jessie," I asked in a low voice, "what's going on over there?"

"Cathouse and nursery. You probably want to stay away from there."

"Yeah, but is that where the women are…" I struggled to finish the thought. Jessie cut me off as if she intended to end the line of questioning.

"Yes."

"But who are the…" I hesitated only for a moment when Swag, who had been eavesdropping nearby, finished my question.

"Fathers? Why they're our own heroic warriors, of course. Distinguish yourself in battle, my friend, and you will be rewarded with the privilege of breeding our next generation of great soldiers and concubines," he said facetiously, correctly suspecting that I would cringe at the notion. "As you can see," he continued acrimoniously while pointing to the second hut. "We breed little warriors for the nursery."

In a somber tone which I had yet to witness from the old man, he added, "Unfortunately, most of the little bastards won't see the age of two." I was anxious to continue the conversation but we had arrived at the open space and Dee demanded our attention.

Waiting for us at the site were three other combots and two sentroids. Standing safely behind the two sentroids in his chariot was a Serrone, whom I recalled from the previous day as our Chief, and whose identity was later confirmed to me by Jessie. Whether the Chief was there to preside over the activity, or merely observe, was unclear. There was little communication between him and the androids (or anything that I recognized as such), and his face was devoid of expression (or anything that I recognized as such). The three combots huddled for a moment then ordered the veterans over to the sidelines and began pairing the rest of us off. We were denied the courtesy of an agenda, expectations, or any other useful information that might help us to mentally prepare.

It soon became evident that the first stage of our so-called training was going to be something of a categorization process to determine who had the makings of a soldier and who was destined for other duties. I doubted that any consideration beyond proximity went into the pairings, so I quickly distanced myself from my friends, lest I be placed in the awkward position of squaring off with one of them. I visibly measured myself up to those in my company and questioned whether I had the mettle and fortitude to face off against some of the larger men. Surely my physical strength and agility were sufficient to hold my own in this group, yet I had my doubts, for I possessed no fighting instincts whatsoever. I was fairly certain, if only in that singular moment, that my safety was not in question. The looks of fear and panic on many other faces suggested that courage and confidence were in short supply.

The first two unfortunates, men whom I did not recognize, were motioned to enter a makeshift circle in the dirt and face each other. One was tall and lanky, the other short and stout, and neither appeared up to the challenge—whatever it was to be. As a pair they looked more like Laurel and Hardy than gladiators.

One of the combots broke the awkward silence and said, "Fight. Put your opponent on the ground." He pointed at the dirt between them. The stout gentleman turned to the combot and shrugged his shoulders with his palms facing upward, as if to say, "I don't understand." The taller man seized upon the opportunity. He lowered his head, rammed into his opponent with his shoulder and wrapped his arms around his waist. The stout man was caught completely off guard; we heard a gasp as his wind was knocked out of him. His sturdy frame, however, prevented a take down, and the two were now locked in a near-motionless struggle, as one might expect from two men that had never been involved in a physical altercation.

After a few moments, the stout man had regained some of his breath. He began to hammer on the lanky man's back, as if playing a large kettle drum in the finale of a symphony. The latter man, having realized the futility of his position, released his grip on the stout man's waist and backed off to square up once again. Their initial expressions of confusion and fear had been replaced by anger and determination. The experience reminded me of watching a schoolyard fight escalate from a playful contest to an anger-fueled melee in a matter of seconds. Only there was no teacher nearby to break it up. The battle continued for another minute or so before the stout man finally pushed his opponent to the ground. Both men stopped and looked to the combot for further instruction.

"Go stand over there," ordered the combot, pointing to an area near where the veterans were standing and quietly watching. The two befuddled men brushed the dirt from their clothes and obeyed the instruction. Several more pairs of men followed, each having the benefit of learning from the errors and successes of their predecessors. The contests varied from spirited, if not skillful bouts, to utter absurdity, with an emphasis on the latter. Throughout the affair, the rest of us stayed mostly silent, save for a few words of encouragement to a friend or former neighbor in the cargo hold. Then came an interesting pair, in that it included a woman and a man. Furthermore, the woman and man were none other than Susan and Tex. Susan was easily sixty pounds lighter than the ranch-hand and there was little doubt he would prevail. Still, there was some question as to how he would conduct himself against a female.

Whether to lessen his guilt or perhaps psyche him out, the ever-confident Susan said to the cowboy as they faced each other, "Don't worry about me, Tex. Do what you gotta do."

Tex grinned and began to reply when she suddenly tore into him, burying her face in his chest and pounding his ribs with her fists, like a boxer with his opponent on the ropes. Shocked into reality, Tex abandoned all chivalry and threw her to the ground. The fracas continued spiritedly but without anger for a few minutes before Tex pinned Susan to the ground. For a brief moment we forgot about our dire circumstance and cheered the worthy adversaries. The combot directed both of them to the same area as their predecessors.

Not long after, another pair comprising a man and woman stepped forward. The middle-aged man, though not overly muscular, must have weighed nearly two hundred pounds. The woman was slight and also middle-aged. Her ragged clothing could not disguise an air of docility and gentleness. I pictured her as the proud wife and mother in a family portrait enclosed with a Christmas card. Most of us cringed as the man took a step toward her, though not more than she herself cringed. She put her hands in front of her face and winced, as if her opponent had leprosy. The man picked her up, placed her on the ground ever so gently, then looked to the combot with an expression akin to "now what?"

The combot, finally surmising it to be a blatant mismatch, pointed to the man and said, "Return to the group." The man complied and returned to our ranks with a grimace of disappointment. The combot then pointed to the woman, who had risen to her feet with a helping hand from a nearby friend.

"You," he said, then guided his robotic finger from the woman to an area opposite of where the other combatants had been sent. "Go there."

The woman walked over to her designated area and stood in solitude. Soon after, a pair of young women were matched in the dirt ring. Both put forth a valiant effort but one was clearly unaccustomed to any form of physical exertion. She offered little defense to her opponent's unorthodox, yet aggressive technique. When the dust cleared, the dominant woman was relegated to stand with Susan and the other men; the defeated woman was placed with the lone woman from earlier.

The subdued body language of the two isolated women suggested that neither comprehended the implications of where they stood, though it soon came over me like a waterfall. I felt the same rush of fear-inspired adrenaline that I had known the previous day when Sparks and Tully plucked women from the crowd. I looked over to Jessie on the sidelines and waited for her eyes to catch mine. When I had captured her attention, I squinted and lowered my eyebrows inquisitively.

"Cathouse," she mouthed to me.

In the same knee-jerk manner as the previous day, I swiveled left and right in an attempt to locate Leesheh. I found her behind me, paired with none other than Pablo. I didn't know Leesheh well enough to predict how she might carry herself in this situation. It occurred to me that I knew very little about her. Furthermore, I questioned whether Pablo understood the gravity of his position. There was little chance that he would be deemed unsuitable for fighting in light of the lesser men that had ostensibly "passed" this first stage already. But Leesheh also had to prove herself equal to the challenge, and she faced far more portentous consequences if unsuccessful. Up to this point, exactly fifty percent of the women (two out of four) had been accepted as potential fighters.

Leesheh was in good physical condition yet was nonetheless slender and stood not more than five feet, five inches tall. She had beauty in her favor, but that couldn't gain her any bias from the androids (nor the Chief, I presumed). I realized on second thought, that her appearance could only work against her, and I was grateful that Sparks and Tully were not present. My racing mind contemplated every reasonable scenario, and I concluded that she depended on Pablo's cooperation in order to prevail. I was not about to put her fate into his hands. I left my assigned partner and walked back to Leesheh. The androids took no notice, for I stood near the rear of the assembly; however, my partner, a smaller man close in age to myself, lit up with worry.

"Where are you going? Stay here!" he admonished in a loud whisper. I had no time for his concerns. Without looking back at him, I extended an open hand at arm's length behind me intending to convey "don't worry about it," "not your problem," and "stay there" all in one simple gesture. The man squirmed and craned to watch my every subsequent action but did not dare to vacate his position in line. Leesheh greeted me with a conflicted expression—a simultaneous smile and frown. I gestured toward the two women standing alone.

"You know what that means, right?" I asked solemnly.

"Yes." She had a glint of hope in her puppy-dog eyes, sensing that I had a plan.

"Are you okay with that?"

"Of course not."

"You're sure?"

"Why do you ask me that? I'd rather die than go there."

"Okay—good." I looked at Pablo. "Go up there and take my place with that guy." Visibly relieved of his burden, he didn't hesitate to comply.

"Sure thing, bro," he said, and quickly walked over to my previous position. My former partner initially reacted with consternation. After sizing up Pablo and looking back to me once more, he must have concluded that he had gained a better deal. He turned around to face forward and said nothing further.

I instructed Leesheh with a commanding whisper. "Just hit me like you've never hit anything before. Don't worry about hurting me. And look like you know how to fight—look mean and angry." It then occurred to me to ask, "*Do* you know how to fight?"

"Not really. I used to wrestle with my brothers when I was a child," she answered in her island accent. I must admit that it charmed me even in that worrisome moment.

"Good. Pretend I'm your brother. Don't hold back. Growl and grunt too. Can you do that?" She nodded and grabbed my hand. I felt her hand tremble and hoped that she wouldn't detect the same sign of fear in my own hand.

We stood together silently and observed the next few pairs. One included a scrawny older man who, sadly, did not represent himself very well. I knew him as Arthur, a resident of my cargo hold. During one of the epidemics on the ship we had written him off, yet he had managed to hang on and finish the voyage. On this day, it was obvious that he had not fully recovered from the ravages of his illness, nor had he been blessed with the genetic constitution for fighting, regardless of his health. To make matters worse, his opponent was a very capable young man who showed him no mercy.

Less than a minute from the start of his contest, poor Arthur lay on the ground holding his hands up to protect his face, which was already bleeding from mouth and nose. My heart poured out to him as I watched his opponent continue to beat him. It was as if the memory of every innocent creature I had ever seen bullied or wronged poured into my head, and I shed a tear—which caught me off-guard. I quickly and covertly wiped it away in fear of Leesheh discovering my vulnerability. We all watched helplessly as the combot directed Arthur to a location separate from both the other combatants and the women presumably destined for the cathouse. Nobody was sure what this position designated, but it couldn't be good—relatively speaking.

Pablo and my former partner faced off in a nondescript contest, with the latter eventually gaining the upper hand, and with neither man having embarrassed himself in front of the android judges. I wondered if Pablo shouldn't have been more dedicated to Susan's workouts in the yard. They had certainly benefited me. At any rate, Pablo had safely advanced into the group of chosen combatants, which by now had grown quite large. Even Nicholas met the challenge with little fanfare as I held his glasses. His opponent was Mario, our resident drummer. Mario was nearly as thin as Nicholas and they matched up quite evenly. Only a few pairs remained, and before long our time had arrived.

I tried earnestly throughout our faux battle to make it look realistic. How long should it last? To what extent should she appear to hurt me? How should the ending transpire? For her part, Leesheh played her role as well as could be expected and came at me aggressively. Still, I feared that the combots might not be buying it. And what of the sentroids? And the Chief? Were they even paying close attention? I clenched Leesheh and whispered in her ear that she should hit me in the face. Then I pushed her away, as if I had merely been toying with her. She complied, although it was more of slap than a punch. I hoped it would be enough. She followed up with a roundhouse kick. I threw up my hands in defense and stepped backward, feigning surprise at her aggression.

We had reached a point where any simpleton would have discovered our ruse if we continued with the phony struggle. This woman couldn't have been expected to compete with a six-foot, four-inch, one-hundred-and-ninety-pound man. (That's what I estimated my weight to be at that time.) I grabbed her and took her to the ground, albeit all the while making it appear more difficult than it should have been. Our performance was over; her fate rested in the hands of the combot—or so I thought. For the first time that day, the presiding combot conferred with Dee and the other two combots for what seemed like ten minutes. In reality it was probably less than thirty seconds. The combot emerged from the conference and pointed to Leesheh. My pounding heart felt as if it was going to bust through my ribcage.

"Over there," he said, pointing to the large group standing near the veterans. I tried to conceal my relief so as not to betray our deception. As Leesheh walked over and stood next to Susan and the others, the combot turned to me. "You stay here."

It seems that the combots had been discussing my own behavior, not Leesheh's. They were satisfied enough with her commitment, if not her performance, but not with mine. I was immediately matched up with the man who had also been held back after facing the woman who offered no resistance. The man sized me up with an air of confidence. He seemed happy to have a go at me.

As soon as the combot gave the order to commence, the man came at me. I caught the full force of his body in my gut and fell to the ground, pulling him down on me. I summoned some freshman-year, rudimentary wrestling moves and futilely attempted to free myself. I had the will but lacked the way. He remained on top of me and began to slap at my face. I returned with a barrage of my own slaps aimed at no particular target. I caught him in the eye with a random, flailing finger which caused him to lurch backward. I seized the opportunity to squirm out from under him and jump to my feet. Having seen enough, the combot halted the match, and ordered us both to join the other soldiers. When we arrived, my opponent shook my hand and congratulated us both on a well-fought match. I mumbled something in acceptance then walked over to Leesheh, taking caution not to stand directly beside her. I gave her a wink which she returned likewise.

In light of my lopsided loss to the man, I figured there couldn't be any question of fraud concerning my match with Leesheh. I was a little embarrassed and probably the happiest guy to have ever been whipped.

The final pairing was a rather odd spectacle featuring Charles and

Monte. Both men were favorites within the company—Charles because of his benign leadership qualities and Monte because he had become something of a mascot for us. I use that term in a most respectful and endearing way; we did not treat Monte in a condescending manner. He was such a small man and so much at a disadvantage for not knowing our language that we could not help but feel protective of him. To our relief, however, this particular activity played into his wheelhouse. He seemed to fully grasp the concept of the contest, if not the repercussions of it. This was clearly not the first time Monte had faced off with an opponent, and Charles found that he had his hands full with the scrappy South American native. In the end, Charles' size won out over Monte's enthusiasm, though both men had acquitted themselves well and joined us.

Upon the conclusion of this exercise the Chief took leave of us, apparently satisfied with his crop of budding warriors that had advanced over the very low bar. We were dispatched to the nearby stream for a brief respite. That is, most of us were. The five women that had been separated from the larger group were led away by one of the sentroids in the direction of the cathouse. Two of the women verbally protested but offered no physical resistance. The other three were either resigned to, or ignorant of, their fate. Perhaps in their minds, this path represented the lesser of two harsh cruelties: certain death versus the worst kind of enslavement. Like Leesheh, I would have chosen the former.

During the evaluations, Arthur had been joined by another feeble gentleman who displayed no redeeming qualifications in the eyes of our instructors. They remained behind as we walked toward the stream. I was hopeful that they might be put to use in a supporting capacity—a bleak form of servitude perhaps, but alive. As I looked back at the two unfortunates, Swag, who was walking beside me, took notice.

"Don't worry about them," he said. "They'll go quickly. One jolt 'a lightnin' from that sentroid and they won't know what hit 'em."

"Can't they be put to work in the camp?" I asked.

"If ya can't fight and ya can't breed, you're of no use to these buggers. Hell, they're the lucky bastards, if ya ask me." We continued on toward the stream and I did my best to put the men out of my thoughts.

I was on one knee at the bank of the stream splashing water into my face and cupping water into my mouth when Malcolm crouched down beside me. His hand stirred in the water and he looked straight ahead as if locked on to something on the opposite bank. He addressed me in a low voice but continued to gaze straight ahead, as if to conceal our conversation.

"I saw what you did back there."

I was pretty sure that he was referring to my charade with Leesheh but I feigned ignorance. "What are you talking about?" I responded incredulously, while studying my reflection in the water.

"The girl. I know what you did."

"And?" I was trembling inside and barely managed to present an outward tone of defiance.

"You think you're protecting her?"

"I did what I needed to do—and it's what she wanted."

Malcolm took a drink a continued looking straight ahead. "Maybe so… maybe so. But don't think you can put one over on those robots. They were on to you. Dee told me as much."

I froze in place and tried to conceal the dread that engulfed my body once again. "So, what now?"

"Dunno exactly," the old veteran replied. "She's with us for now, I reckon."

"That's good then."

For the first time since he squatted next to me, Malcolm looked at me. I inferred from his somber countenance that he didn't think I understood the weight of my actions. "She's your responsibility now. If she dies, that's on you."

I had regained some of my composure and began to feel a bit defensive. I returned his stare. "You don't think I know that? She would rather die than go to… the alternative."

Malcolm stood up abruptly and said quietly as he turned away from me, "Right then. Enough said." True to his word, he never mentioned the subject again.

11

I had yet to learn how to interpret the relative positions of the parent planet and its own parent star in the daytime sky, but it felt like midafternoon. Baskets of fruit were brought to us at the stream, and we sat in small clusters eating and discussing the events of the morning. Watching over us now were only the three combots. I briefly entertained the notion of escaping across the stream but quickly yielded to its futility. I recalled Malcolm's warning from the previous night and concurred that the devil I knew was better than what might be lurking on the other side of the stream. But it was more than the fear of an unknown alien world that kept me in that camp. A feeling of camaraderie, seeded in the cargo hold so many weeks ago, had taken root. It was probably from this day that I began to view those in my company more as comrades rather than fellow captives or victims with a shared plight.

Dee assembled us once again into a loose formation and led us back in the direction from which we came. We passed through the patch of dirt we had utilized in the morning and once again came within close proximity of the cathouse and nursery. I saw nothing of the new inductees in the brief time I had to survey the area. We came to a small clearing where we were instructed to form a line, side-by-side and two-deep. In the open space that lay before us stood a combot holding a long weapon like those we had seen a few times previously. He handed it to Malcolm, who stood facing us.

"This weapon," said Malcolm loudly enough for all to hear, "is what we call an arc rifle, and I'm gonna teach you how to operate it effectively."

The arc rifle, or arc, resembled a conventional Earth rifle only in that it incorporated a barrel from which a projectile was fired. The barrel was shorter than most rifles I had seen, and in place of a gunstock was a small T-shaped pad. I had no experience with guns of any kind beyond skeet shooting a couple of times on my uncle's property in West Virginia. The arc rifle seemed very light compared to the shotguns I wielded there. The projectiles fired from the arc rifle were something of a mystery and apparently beyond Malcolm's comprehension. Nicholas later hypothesized them to be capsules containing a plasma gas that liquified for a fraction of a second upon contact, then solidified into a substance resembling plastic. The effect was to shower the target with tiny, misshaped fragments of solidified plasma that could penetrate metal alloys, not to mention human flesh. The weapon produced a scatter similar to a shotgun. It was unlike a shotgun in that the projectile flew through the air like a streamlined bullet and didn't scatter until contact with the target was made.

The arc projectiles were fed automatically into the weapon via disposable cartridges that attached underneath the barrel. The capacity of the cartridges varied between ten, twenty, and thirty. The arc did not incorporate a trigger. Instead, the operator fired the weapon by pressing two buttons simultaneously—one on the top of the barrel and one on the side of the T-shaped pad. The locations of the buttons allowed one to fire using a thumb and finger from the same hand. That is to say, a combot hand, which was larger than a human hand. Firing an arc was typically a two-handed operation for us humans.

Malcolm demonstrated a method for holding the arc rifle that involved continuously pressing the top button down with one hand. We fired by pressing the side button with the other hand. Consequently, we called the top button "the primer" and the side button "the terminator." He slid a cartridge into the appropriate slot and fired a single shot at a wooden target set up approximately fifty yards away. Expecting a loud bang, I was surprised to hear nothing more than a whooshing sound caused by the projectile cutting through the air. Nicholas told me that the projectile was likely propelled by a force similar to electromagnetic acceleration, as opposed to the combustion of a material such as gun powder. Sound or no sound, the projectile found its target and tore a hole through it that was easily six inches in diameter.

Over the subsequent days it became obvious that there was a shortage of arcs in our militia, surpassed only by a scarcity of cartridges. On this day, our combot instructors thought it wise not to share that factoid with us. (Were they concerned about our morale? It had already bottomed out.) They informed us that only a select few would be permitted to fire the weapon in the training session while offering no explanation for the constraint. The rest of us were to go through the motions with an empty cartridge. Positioned near the middle of the line, I was not to be one of the chosen. I watched as the first selectee stepped up and handled the weapon with the aid of Malcolm's watchful eyes and helpful hands. He fired, missed the target, and returned to his place in line. Two more followed uneventfully as the rest of us drifted into a state of complacency, if not boredom. Clearly this activity did not warrant the same anxiety as the previous one, and we felt relatively safe in the afternoon twilight.

The fourth man walked coolly up to Malcolm, took the weapon into his hands, placed the barrel into his mouth and promptly fired it.

The now familiar whooshing sound was replaced by one that was, at that time, foreign to me. The plasma projectile completed its metamorphosis instantly within the man's throat and proceeded to dismember the flesh above his neck. The sound of his skull splintering and the pulverization of the gray matter within—much of it taking flight above him—lasted for only a split second, yet I can recall it as if it happened yesterday. I witnessed the entire horrific event. Some in my company did not, their minds having wandered in light of the monotony. The collective gasp of those who saw the incident, combined with the sound of the impact, jolted the others and grabbed their attention. Some recalled later that they looked up to see a headless body standing on its own for what seemed an eternity before collapsing upon itself. For many, to include some eyewitnesses, the implausible sight was beyond explanation, and they had to be told what had happened—repeatedly.

All of this transpired within a few seconds of the man's demise, as did the rush of sentiments that came over us. All of us humans were stunned if not surprised. (I didn't chance to see the combots' reactions.) Some were envious of the man's audacity to choose his own fate and secretly wished that they could trade places with him. Most of us knew that given the opportunity, we could not pull the proverbial trigger. And we would certainly have that opportunity, if not today.

"Anyone else?" said Malcolm, breaking the eerie silence in a calm, rhetorical tone. I assumed that the remainder of the activity would be called off but the combots thought otherwise. Two of them dragged the torso by its feet over to a patch of dirt behind us and we resumed our training without live cartridges. When it was my turn, I had to avoid stepping into the fleshy remains that lay in my path, now adorned with flying alien insects. I took the arc rifle from Malcolm's outstretched arms, pointed it toward the wooden target and fired the imaginary bullet.

When we had all taken a turn with the rifle (including Monte, with whom I noticed Malcolm had shown disproportionate patience and attentiveness), Dee set us back on the path toward the barracks. We passed within visual range of the cathouse for the third time that day. The only noticeable difference was the presence of Tully standing on the porch. He leaned with his back against the wall and one leg raised, such that the sole of his boot was also pressed against the wall. One hand slowly stroked his facial stubble while the other rested on the handle of a large knife that was holstered in his belt. This was the first time I saw him without the company of his associate, Sparks. I had a hunch that Sparks was on the other side of the wall, subjugating the poor women therein. Tully eyed us carefully with an intimidating grin. He appeared to be taking a mental inventory of those who survived the day and delighting in the fact that our numbers had dwindled a little since the morning.

At one point, his eyes caught mine, which startled me a little and I quickly looked away. As I walked, I pondered why these two young men harbored such resentment for us. Were they not in our situation once? Of course, they weren't—they were never abducted. This is their home. Still, are we not on the same team? Maybe we're not. Do they understand that they're being held in captivity? Maybe they're not. My questions only begat more questions, but my attention was soon focused on something else as we neared the barracks.

The convoy from the morning had just returned. The three larger vehicles were parked in the dirt courtyard in front of the barracks, and the last of their inhabitants were piling out from the back. One man remained in the rearmost truck and handed down weapons and boxes to a few soldiers waiting with outstretched arms. Another man was greeting the troops with bottles of various shapes and sizes, which were readily accepted and eagerly swilled. Some of the bottles were metallic and others resembled glass. All were undoubtedly filled with some sort of hooch. Everybody appeared cheerful, if not ready for a complete blowout. I visibly scanned the area for evidence of wounded or dead soldiers and found nothing. For a fleeting moment I allowed myself to entertain the possibility that this war might be much ado about nothing—maybe not so dangerous after all. Many of the veterans in our group joined the festivities over by the first two huts. None of us newbies took part. We weren't in a partying mood, nor did we feel particularly invited.

As Jessie trimmed my hair and beard later that evening with a homemade pair of shears, I further debriefed her on the subject of the cathouse and nursery—so called by the humans. Sexual liaisons were forbidden in the barracks. At that early stage of my residence in camp I couldn't envision anyone engaging in such an intimate act within the open space of our barracks. Later I realized that such acts were possible when we're forced to revert to our basic human instincts. Jessie told me that if a woman not already assigned to the cathouse were to become pregnant, she would be sent to the nursery when she was no longer able to fight effectively. Following birth, she may or may not be reassigned to the barracks.

Swag had suggested earlier that men had to obtain permission to fraternize with the hapless women of the cathouse—the latter apparently having no right of refusal. Jessie indicated that the rules had relaxed in recent years, and that anyone could visit the cathouse when they were not otherwise occupied. She added that the disproportionate demand to supply, combined with old-fashioned jealousy and alcohol, often resulted in fights.

"It's not a very pleasant place to be," she noted.

"I suppose not. Did you say alcohol?"

"Yup. We call it Chinese moonshine. They discovered a way to ferment something or other, then distill it. But they're not the first moonshiners on Serrone—far from it."

She said that many of the men in camp rejected patronizing the cathouse out of respect for its victims, but others gladly embraced the barbarism. I had already seen that this group included the likes of Sparks and Tully. Women from the cathouse moved to the nursery when their situation required, then resumed duties in the cathouse following childbirth. A few very lucky women were permanently assigned to the nursery as nannies.

"Children don't stay in the camp for long," she said. "The ones that survive are shipped off to the city right about the time they learn to walk."

"The city?"

"Yeah. That's where General Abasha lives."

"What happens to them in the city?"

"Well, it depends. When the boys are old enough, they're shipped out to camps like this one. The girls… well, some are also sent out to fight. I guess they're the lucky ones. The others end up as slaves and, well, whatever else you can imagine."

Jessie told me that she visited the nursery often to help out and teach the children whatever she could. "My goal is to get them talking before they ship out."

I had detected a special bond between Jessie and the teenaged boy, Ammo, and I concluded that she was the reason he displayed a more virtuous nature than Sparks and Tully. I thoughtlessly rewarded Jessie's hospitality by prying into her personal affairs.

"What about Ammo?" I asked. "Was he sent here recently?"

She told me that Ammo had been with her his entire life. He was born in the city, during a period when Jessie was assigned to a larger army there. Children that were born there remained in the city with the army.

"Are you… his mother?"

"No, no," she replied, "but I knew her well. We were very close. She died shortly after giving birth to him. I promised her that I would protect him." She didn't seem to mind the intrusion so I pressed on.

"His father is… in the city?"

"His father? God knows. He's most likely dead, whoever he was. I was shipped out here a few seasons ago and managed to bring Ammo along. No one stopped me. He was old enough to fight."

I decided to quit while I was ahead. "Well, he seems like a good kid."

"He's a great kid," she said proudly, "and smart too—all things considered."

Leesheh and Susan entered the hut displaying freshly braided hair, as was the fashion preference for most the women in camp, in no small part due to the hairstyle's low maintenance. Those women without braids, such as Jessie, tended to keep their hair in a closely cropped cut. I commented (with slight exaggeration) on the professional quality of the dreadlocks, to which Leesheh responded that she had first braided

Susan's hair, after which the novice Susan returned the favor under Leesheh's attentive guidance. From my chair I stealthily admired Leesheh's natural beauty while my own hairstylist carefully scraped the blade of a sharpened knife down my cheek. I would have been terrified if I wasn't so preoccupied with Malcolm's warning from our conversation at the stream.

Jessie had just finished with me and started with Nicholas when Tex and Pablo popped in to see, as Tex put it, "how the other half lived." We finished the day in a somewhat pleasant mood, notwithstanding the shadow cast by the gruesome death we had witnessed firsthand, and the presumed deaths of at least two others. I felt neither relaxed nor festive and had no desire to discuss what had transpired in camp that day. In retrospect I can see this as part of my gradual acclimation to death that had begun weeks earlier on the ship. I was not unlike those professionals who become accustomed to death—policemen, paramedics, and more relevantly, soldiers. My grief would not wane, but my survival—and the survival of my comrades who were still breathing—demanded that it lessen in duration and depth.

Nobody else seemed keen on deliberating the somber events of the day either. Pablo suggested that I regale them with one of my stories, and I obliged by starting into a Cliffs Notes version of Dickens' *Great Expectations.* Many of the veterans listened in, including the young Ammo. Mr. Swag was so delighted by the fable that he took every opportunity (and a few less opportune moments) to spontaneously declare, "Shakespeare!" I suppose that this form of pastime had never before been seen at the camp. The next morning, he pulled me aside and requested a preview of Pip's forthcoming adventures.

Two more days passed without major incident. Other than a brief session covering hand signals to be employed during combat situations that required silence, we received no formal training. It became apparent that the remainder of our instruction was to be in the form of on-the-job training, plus whatever we could elicit from the veterans in our free time. Most of our time was occupied by emptying latrine buckets, procuring food, and cleaning up debris. These tasks afforded me a greater exposure to my surroundings and I formulated my own inventory of the small camp. I had no prior military experience, but I had studied twentieth-century warfare in school and seen my fair share of war movies. As for being part of a grand army that represented the lawful regional government and its citizens, I had my doubts. Nothing I saw refuted the notion I had formed upon first entering the camp—that this was little more than a guerilla outfit.

I estimated the size of the human population in the barracks to be approximately 140. The majority struck me as being from Earth, albeit some had been on Serrone for several years. I assumed the younger soldiers to have been born on Serrone and they numbered about thirty. Nearly every one of them was a genetic mix including varying degrees of Caucasian, African, and/or Asian heritage. I had not been close enough to the cathouse or nursery to obtain an accurate headcount of their residents. Based on the size of the two buildings, I estimated there to be ten to fifteen women in the cathouse and a few more in the nursery caring for a handful children.

The combots numbered twelve. It was easy to distinguish one from the other as a result of their unique colorings, scratches, dents, and replacement parts. Each wore his own utility belt that contained, at a minimum, a small weapon, a knife, and a handheld communication device. Combots each had a single-syllable name—usually three letters—though I had yet to learn all of them. I am told that the names were shortened versions of the designations assigned to them when manufactured, similar to a serial number. Ten of the combots spent their nights in the barracks, two in each hut, either sitting or standing. They alternated between their normal state and their power-saving mode. (I never discovered the source of power.) The other two combots spent their nights patrolling the camp's perimeter.

A combot known as Bar resided in our hut along with Dee. Bar's most interesting and identifiable characteristic was a replacement eye that was much darker and larger than the standard combot eye. It resembled an eye patch and gave its owner the appearance of a robot pirate. Dee appeared to outrank Bar, though this was difficult to verify, as most of the communication between combots was done without speaking. Combots had an ability to communicate with each other silently and without the aid of a device, but only at close range.

I found it interesting that they typically made eye contact when communicating. To us it seemed as if they were just staring blankly at each other. Combots said little but were not opposed to conversing with humans and sometimes initiated conversations, albeit some more than others. In as much that Dee and Malcolm had forged a bond on some level, Bar sometimes consorted with Sparks and Tully, but usually kept to himself. I found it odd that these androids might have slight personality traits. A possible explanation was revealed to me later, as I learned more of their history.

The sentroids in camp numbered only five. Their duties included patrolling the perimeter and administering discipline to the humans, but their primary responsibility was to protect the Serrone PRF officers in camp—our alien masters. The sentroids were clearly more modern and more mechanically diverse than their combot cousins. Just like our old friends Thing One and Thing Two, the sentroids in camp displayed no humanlike tendencies and treated us like inanimate objects. Naturally, as humans are wont to do (especially with our pets), we projected personalities onto them. We perceived them as being snobbish and supercilious henchmen, which made them easy for us to despise. They had no official names and no reason to identify themselves to us, but the soldiers had taken to calling them Kaiser, Chairman Mao, Adolph, Stalin, and Khan.

The Serrones whom the sentroids protected were only three, although others visited the camp from time to time. In addition to the Chief, whom we came to recognize by his ostentatious apparel, were his two lieutenants, derisively known as Ringo and Ratso. Rank in the Serrone army was somehow represented by colors—the flashier the outfit, the higher the rank. One could deduce that Ringo outranked Ratso when comparing the former's two-toned sash with the latter's monotone frock. We rarely interacted with the Serrones and never without a sentroid standing between us, and with his taser appendage on full display. The Serrones resided in a guarded area toward the center of camp of which no human was ever allowed within fifty yards.

In the back of the camp was the motor pool, although vehicles were typically scattered randomly around the camp. The running joke was that the last place anyone would search for a vehicle was the motor pool. Seven of the nine larger transport trucks were reliable enough for daily use. The other two were in a constant state of disrepair. There were three of the smaller vehicles in working condition and a fourth that lay in the motor pool with no wheels. We called the trucks "flatbeds" and smaller vehicles "jeeps" (naturally). Humans were permitted to operate vehicles except for when a Serrone was a passenger. In our camp, the vehicle maintenance and repair were performed by combots only.

The remaining buildings consisted mainly of storage sheds. There was a storeroom containing odds and ends that were available to any soldier for the taking. Needless to say, the junk in this tiny thrift store was of little value to anyone. Most of the inventory comprised threadbare articles of clothing that had already been passed over by every slave in the camp, though the scraps came in handy for patching. A few gems could be found in the storeroom, such as pencils and scraps of paper. I had no interest in writing at that time.

During the course of completing my tasks, I witnessed a few small patrol convoys leave and return without ever showing any visible evidence of casualties. We were told nothing of their purpose or result, except for one such patrol that included Malcolm and Jessie. I inquired as to the objective of their mission and learned that it and the other recent convoys were for reconnaissance. Rebel forces had been spotted traversing a road not far from our location.

12

In addition to establishing an informal inventory of the camp, I used the next few days to pick the brains of Malcolm, Jessie, and Swag in an effort to learn as much as I could about the history of the planet and the wars that preoccupied so much of it. The amount of information they provided far exceeded my expectations, and I continued to learn from them and others over the subsequent weeks. Some of what I heard was hearsay layered upon hearsay, yet undoubtedly rooted in truth. The following is my best attempt at a synopsis and editorial of the recent Serrone history preceding my arrival.

The conflict in which I participated was merely a power struggle created in the vacuous aftermath of what the Serrones called the Great War. Before that war, the planet of Serrone was a single nation and society ruled by what can be best characterized as an oligarchy. It had vast congressional assemblies that were at one time the powerplant of a great republic. Over the centuries they were gradually corrupted and transformed into the instruments of the powerful few. Over many more years those powerful few became fewer still, and control over the entire planet eventually consolidated into two factions, or regions. These regions were roughly divided into the two major land masses of the planet: one based in the northern hemisphere and one in the southern hemisphere. A cold war ensued. Each region focused scientific research on developing battlefield technology and weapons of mass destruction. Unable and unwilling to share power, the cold war eventually heated up. I don't know the specific catalyst for the war—it isn't important.

During the peaceful centuries leading up to the Great War, the Serrone people rapidly advanced in the arts, science, and technology.

They overcame the physical barriers to interstellar space travel and ventured far beyond their solar system. It was during this golden age of the Serrone civilization that their explorers studied extraterrestrial worlds—strictly as unseen observers, like zoologists studying a pride of lions in the Serengeti. One of these foreign worlds must have been our own Earth.

Before the war, the continents were dotted with large cities exhibiting the latest technological approaches to communication, transportation, and architecture. Virtually the entire Serrone population resided in these great cities, leaving the majority of the planet to the wildlife species. There was no poverty and only a negligible amount of crime. Manufacturing and agriculture had become completely automated using advanced robotics. There was little left for Serrones to do that required much physical exertion.

I listened to the stories about Serrone and the Great War in the surroundings of my primitive hut and found them to be fantastic and implausible. It was not until much later, when I beheld the remnants of that pre-war society, that I truly believed them. The Serrone that I knew seemed little more advanced than the Earth that I left—maybe by fifty or a hundred years. In some aspects it seemed more primitive than the society I left behind. But this was a war fought on a scale never seen on Earth. One might say that they bombed themselves back to their own version of a Stone Age.

Serrone had not experienced a war of any size for at least a hundred years prior to their Great War. As such, battlefield tactics had not kept pace with battlefield technologies, and the early battles resulted in millions of casualties on both sides. The abundance of Serrone soldiers at the start of the war was nearly depleted within a few years, during which no significant gains were made by either side. Both armies faced a shortage of personnel. More and more civilians were drafted into service while researchers and engineers on both sides searched for solutions to the shortage of personnel. The answer came in the form of robotics, an area in which the Serrones excelled. Various android models were prototyped, tested, and manufactured. These early generations were designed for support roles, such as truck drivers, builders, hospital orderlies, and pilots for cargo aircraft. (Fighter aircraft were generally drones.)

The war progressed far longer than any of the so-called experts predicted, reducing cities to ashes and further diminishing the population. With no end to the conflict in sight, the two regions began to repurpose androids for use in combat. The use of robots in combat had initially been rejected due to their costly expense and the depletion of natural resources required to construct them, but prolonged war has a way of adjusting priorities. New models were developed and deployed, and they gradually supplanted the Serrone warfighters on the battlefield.

Several varieties of combat robots were produced, though none was as effective and versatile as the combot model that I came to know. It was not as powerful as other models but its simple design allowed for versatility and relatively inexpensive manufacture and repair. (You might say it was the Serrone's AK-47.) This model was produced by the millions. It was also unique in that its designers programmed these androids with a capacity for loyalty and brotherhood. The theory was that these traits would make them better soldiers—willing to die to protect their comrades. The combots made effective soldiers but their creators failed in one sense. Similar to human soldiers, the loyalty component of their artificial intelligence was focused on their fellow soldiers and less so on their leaders or the greater cause of the war.

A war fought with intricate, complex technologies eventually suffers from a dearth of the resources required to build them. Natural resources—the metals and gasses—become depleted. Intellectual resources—scientists and engineers—are killed. Intellectual property—designs, formulas—is destroyed. A fateful decision was made by one side to enslave the "primitive" beings of other planets so that the androids might not be wasted filling support roles. It began as a covert experiment and developed into a major factor of the war—not necessarily a *deciding* factor, for the other side soon followed suit. Ships were dispatched to find the best candidates for slaves among the known civilizations in the galaxy. The first sentroids were subsequently built for the purpose of managing the burgeoning slave population. These specialized androids were more powerful and more expensive, and thus produced in far less quantities than the combots.

The Serrones were careful not to reveal themselves to the alien civilizations from which they pilfered. They abducted relatively small numbers of beings in order to avoid detection. This strategy was not borne out of a respect for the primitive civilizations. They simply wanted to avoid dealing with alien defiance. They didn't have the military resources that would have been required to deal with resistance on a foreign planet. This was easier when dealing with less intelligent species. Great care had to be taken to prevent the inhabitants of the more advanced planets from suspecting anything. Humans were among those early samples and were found to be excellent candidates. They adapted well to the climate and were easier to control than some of the more feral species brought to Serrone. As such, humans were captured in larger numbers. Malcolm's story begins here.

He was brought into a world that looked much different than the Serrone I found upon arrival. He was one of hundreds of enslaved humans and other creatures who traveled with a great android army that fought for the northern region. He told us that he was promised freedom and a return trip to Earth if he served them well.

His first assignment was to carry ammunition from the rear to the front lines. Unlike the sentroids, combots were not equipped with built-in weaponry. This was for economic as well as security reasons. It was cheaper to upgrade and replace handheld weapons than to maintain built-in weapons, and there was, at that time, a surplus of arc rifles that had been used by Serrone soldiers. More importantly, the Serrones were wary of bestowing too much power on their androids. Combot-to-combot communication was purposely limited to a small radius—just large enough for battlefield operations. They were not granted access to global communication networks. No androids were. This was one of the few fail-safes implemented by the otherwise shortsighted armies.

Malcolm spent five seasons serving in this capacity and watched the armies of both factions dwindle. He described epic battles to us, incorporating massive drone fleets, colossal armored vehicles (like giant tanks), hundreds of naval ships and thousands of combatants. By that time, the Serrones only occupied leadership positions in the military, yet there were still many more of them living on the planet than during my time. Androids fought the battles, but civilian cities and their inhabitants couldn't escape the weapons of mass destruction. Populations dwindled. Entire cities were evacuated or deserted.

One of the combots assigned to the unit Malcolm supported was Dee. A story surfaced around our camp from time to time about an incident in which Malcolm saved Dee's life. (Were the combots *alive*? I'll leave that for another discussion.) Neither Malcolm nor Dee ever spoke of this, nor would they confirm it if asked.

The Great War slowly reverted to a more primitive form of warfare. World-wide satellite-based communication networks had been destroyed and were too complex to repair. The war became disorganized and slowly fragmented into separate conflicts. Engineers that were trained to repair or reprogram androids became scarce. Combots possessed a basic ability to repair themselves and began to cannibalize their fallen comrades.

Serrones were seen less often. The more powerful among them employed personal security details in response to infighting among the leadership, and sentroids were ideal for this role. Truces broke out in disparate provinces as armies divided and provincial leaders emerged. During this transitional period, humans and other enslaved creatures from foreign worlds were forced into combat to fight alongside the androids. The combot programming for soldier loyalty carried over to these alien races. The Serrones recognized this development as a threat, but by this time the engineers that had created the combots were nowhere to be found. It was during this time that Malcolm met Swag. Swag had been abducted from a small town in the Australian Outback a few years after Malcolm.

Ten seasons (more than five Earth years) after Malcolm arrived on Serrone, a formal truce was brokered at the highest levels and a transitional government was formed. This government lacked the resources and political capital to bring peace and order to the planet. An immense void emerged in the wake of this powerless bureaucracy. Regions declared independence as dictators, warlords, and hoodlums stepped in and vied for their control. Serrone became little more than a scarcely populated world of thugs and scavengers.

The post-apocalyptic world was short of citizens, androids, technology, intellectual property, and weapons. Enterprising warlords realized that the most effective way to secure and hold power was to control the slave populations. The most successful of these gangsters recognized that it was easier to abduct new slaves than to spill blood trying to capture the ones already there. Thus, the handful of interstellar ships and pilots that remained in service became the ultimate prizes. More aliens, including hundreds of humans, were brought to Serrone during the first few seasons following the truce than at any other time—before or since. Jessie was abducted from Columbus and brought to Serrone about sixteen years before me. The Serrone responsible for her capture was an up-and-coming gangster named Abasha, who was engaged in a struggle for the recently established Region Seventeen.

Our own self-proclaimed *General* Abasha had served as a junior officer in the same Northern Army that enslaved Malcolm and Swag. Foreseeing the inevitable before others, he began to carve his own path, and profit from the spoils of war long before the truce. When the powers above him had dissipated, Abasha claimed his small piece of the planetary pie by effectively employing the universal techniques of betrayal, money, power, and intimidation. Ownership of Region Seventeen was his goal. Or, as Abasha communicated it through his sentroids, his goal was the "liberation" of Region Seventeen from the evil hands of despots who cared nothing for the Serrone people. He formed the Serrone People's Resistance Front for this purpose, though not very many Serrone people actually participated.

Many of the veterans and all of the combots that I met upon arrival in camp had fought in Abasha's so-called war of liberation. It seemed for a short time that Abasha had successfully exterminated the preceding dictator and eliminated all rival factions in his region. Sadly, he failed to rein in potential opposition, and new rivals emerged with their own slave armies and their own "rightful" claims to the throne. It was these rebellious factions that I was conscripted to defeat.

The Serrone I encountered was a mere shadow of the highly-advanced civilization that Malcolm had witnessed upon his arrival. Only a few examples of their technological marvels remained—anachronisms against a backdrop that bore a resemblance to mid-twentieth century Earth.

13

On the morning of the fourth day in camp, I emerged from the barracks with the others and headed for the chow pavilion. Sparks and Tully stood off to the side, about ten yards beyond the door of the hut. Tully gave me a nod as I approached, as if to get my attention. I couldn't ignore him but I was wary of getting lured into some sort of confrontation. I reciprocated with a modest nod and quickly broke eye contact. My hopes of avoiding the pair were quashed when Tully stepped into my path, faced me, and extended his hand toward my chest. It wasn't an overly aggressive gesture but I knew that I was expected to stop, and so I complied.

"Where you from, Earth-man?" he asked. Tully, like the others of his ilk, spoke as if English was a second language. His native language was a rudimentary hybrid of several Earth languages, of which English accounted for the vast majority of his narrow vocabulary.

"A place called Virginia," I replied while trying to disguise my discomfort.

"Vir-geen-ee-a," he pronounced to Sparks, then returned to me. "Is that U-S-A… like Jessie U-S-A?

"Yes."

"Ahh," Tully responded with a smile. He seemed proud of his ability to make the connection. I sensed there was more behind this conversation than just getting to know the new guy. Sparks followed up.

"Shake-a-spear… What that means, Earth-man?" He probably assumed that my name was just a compound of the three simpler words.

"Nothing. It's just my name."

"But you like to tell the story, right Shake-a-spear?" continued Sparks.

"I guess so. People like my stories." For some reason the two men found my response quite amusing and burst into laughter, making me feel like the object of an inside joke. Tully put his arm around my shoulders and we began to walk.

"We gonna have fun today, yeah Earth-man?" Tully said with his familiar grin. He paused for my reaction but I said nothing. "You come with us today, huh? We kill some rebels—you and me," he added, while patting my chest with his other hand.

"Okay…," I said hesitantly. I couldn't decide if they were testing my resolve or just having a laugh at my expense.

"Listen, Shake-a-spear. Old Malcolm, no good. Swag man, no good. Jessie no good either," added Sparks in a more serious tone. "You stay with me and Tully here. We teach you right." I had no reply.

"Okay?" pressed Tully.

"I'll do whatever I'm supposed to." The two men looked at each other curiously while trying to interpret my vague response. Then they burst into laughter again.

"Okay," proclaimed Tully, "good soldier man here." He firmly patted me on the chest once more with the palm of his hand, then the two men walked on ahead of me. I made my way to the pavilion while trying to fathom why they would single me out. I fixed myself a bowl of mushy cereal and found my inner circle seated at a nearby table.

"And what did those two gentlemen want?" asked Charles.

"Something's up today," I announced softly before taking a sloppy drink from the bowl. "I think we're going on patrol."

Clouds rolled in overhead as we walked back to the barracks. This was the first sign of any overcast since my arrival. They reflected the various shades of blue radiating from Wiyanga, which rose from the east. Nicholas was so captivated by the chromatic morning sky that he nearly walked into a tree.

"Better focus on what is happening down here, young man," Charles advised with a laugh.

We reached the courtyard in front of the barracks to find several vehicles parked in the dirt road nearby. On the ground next to them were stacks of cartridge boxes in the dirt and rows of arc rifles leaning up against the sides of the flatbed trucks. A large, round woven basket had been placed next to the cartridge boxes. A few combots were shepherding the entire company of humans into a loose formation. A combot called Cap addressed us.

"We will take a large group for an operation today," announced the combat robot. "I will select from my squad. Dee will select from his." That was the extent of our briefing. The only thing I had learned was that our camp comprised two squads. Cap proceeded to call out foreign-sounding names to which various Chinese and Africans responded by walking over toward the awaiting vehicles. Dee conferred quietly with Malcolm and the combot known as Bar. The rest of us stood quietly and succumbed to whatever horrors we could imagine. Part of me hoped to be selected so that I could face the inevitable. Reality is never as bad as what we fear, right?

I watched my comrades from the other squad prepare themselves for the patrol as if it was just another day at the office. Several of them approached the wooden basket, pulled out small handfuls of dried brown leaves and placed them into their mouths. I walked over to Swag and pointed toward the basket.

"Is that something like tobacco?"

"Ha." His white beard widened with his smile. "They chew it and smoke it like tobaka, mate, but nah… You should… uh…" He seemed to be at a crossroads.

He put his arm on my shoulder and continued. "I don't do it meself, but uh, if you're goin' out there into wild t'day, then uh… maybe ya should chew a few leaves. They call it 'catnip'. It'll put ya in a fightin' mood." His expression did not agree with his words. His face appeared to be doing whatever it could to prevent them from coming out of his mouth.

"You mean it's a stimulant?" I asked. My experiences with recreational drugs were limited to what I like to characterize as "momentary lapses in judgement" in my youth, from which I learned that a foggy mind was not agreeable to me. "No thanks," I told him. Swag's face lit up, indicating that I had responded correctly to his body language even though I had rejected his verbal suggestion.

"Good call, mate. I don't do it meself. Highly addictive, that stuff is. It's got its claws dug into some of the lads 'round here—especially the young 'uns. They won't do without it."

As if on cue, Sparks, Tully and some of the other young "natives," as the old timers called them, took their turns grabbing handfuls out of the basket. I walked back over to my friends and relayed the information.

They agreed it that it was probably not the most appropriate time to take on a drug habit. I felt no compulsion and dismissed the notion of ever indulging. I swore that I never would.

"But I wouldn't say no to one of those bottles, if offered," added Charles, referring to the rotgut we had seen around the barracks earlier. Although none of us reacted with reproach, he felt compelled to clarify. "I mean if… *when* I come back."

"Listen up!" shouted Malcolm. "We're gonna need a lotta hands on deck today. It's time for some of ya to get your feet wet." He proceeded to select about twenty of us newcomers, mostly by pointing and saying "you," as he had yet to learn most of our names. He did know the names of his bunkmates. "Shakespeare, Doc, and... Susan—you too." My anxiety lessened a little when Leesheh was not chosen.

"Sorry guys," said Nicholas.

"Don't be sorry, man. Just wish us good luck," replied Charles.

"Right—of course. Good luck." Nicholas shook our hands and looked at us as if he never expected to see us again.

"*Really* Nicholas?" quipped Susan. "You're looking at us like we're already dead."

"Sorry."

"Let's get some rebels," I said in jest—trying to alleviate the tension. I met Leesheh's eyes briefly. She nodded slightly and forced a smile. I nodded back and headed over to the vehicles where Malcolm was waiting. He called together the newbies that had been drafted for the mission.

"Now, do exactly as I say and you might live to see tomorrow," he said with a motivational skepticism that I had come to expect from him. Perhaps he thought that by lowering our expectations we might be more grateful to him for surviving, or at least we wouldn't blame him when we lay dying. He spent a few minutes teaching us how to wear a water canteen and an ammo belt, then concluded the lesson by saying that most people prefer to stuff cartridges in their pockets because the belts restrict their movement.

"So why did he tell us all that if nobody wears the belts?" I whispered to Susan.

"Maybe he's required by law," she responded without missing a beat. I also wondered why he had waited until five minutes before our departure to show us how to store cartridges when we had spent the previous few days frittering around the camp. He wrapped up without clueing us in to where we were going or what we would be doing.

"Grab a rifle and three cartridges. Stow two cartridges and load one into the rifle. Then climb into the trucks."

I briefly studied the arc rifles leaning against the nearest truck and couldn't find a reason why one might be a better choice than any other. This wasn't surprising given that I knew very little about arc rifles, having held one only once, and for not more than fifteen seconds. Nor was I surprised, although a little disappointed, to see some of my fellow newbies avail themselves of the catnip in the woven basket. My attention was suddenly brought back to the rifles when I realized that they were quickly disappearing, and there seemed to be more of us than them. I grabbed the first one I could get my hands on. When the dust cleared, three of my comrades stood unarmed.

"It's alright," Malcolm told them. "Stick close to your buddies and be ready in case one comes available." I could only think of two ways that a rifle could come available; the first was bad and the second was worse.

"The three of us should stick together," suggested Charles, bringing my focus back to the mission.

"Makes sense," I replied, and followed him to the rear of the nearest flatbed. A voice called out to me as I watched Susan climb up into the truck.

"Hey! Shake-a-spear! You come with us, yeah?" shouted Sparks while standing at the back of a vehicle parked two ahead of the one I was about to board. Not that I needed it, but a little voice in the back of my head told me that it would be a bad idea. I nodded to Sparks as if to say hello and climbed into the back of the flatbed with Charles and Susan, hoping he would think that I had misunderstood him. My plan must have worked because he shouted again, "Hey! Shake-a-spear!" I slunk down in the truck with my forehead planted against the barrel of my rifle and cringed in fear that he might come over to fetch me. He did not.

The vehicles started rolling shortly thereafter, which caught me a little by surprise, as our departure wasn't preceded by the sound of engines revving. In spite of its silence, the flatbed truck felt very powerful beneath me. I stood up to see Leesheh and Nicholas among the crowd watching our departure. I refrained from waving, as nobody else was doing anything of the sort, and it seemed like an appropriate occasion to blend in with the crowd. While standing, I surveyed the convoy in front and behind. We numbered seven flatbeds and three jeeps carrying roughly eighty soldiers, eight combots, and three sentroids who flanked the Chief and Ratso riding in the penultimate vehicle. (I cannot say whether the Chief was interested in witnessing the task at hand or if he simply felt safer wherever the majority of his troops happened to be.)

I sat back down and surveyed my comrades in the flatbed. There were five newbies in addition to Susan, Charles, and myself. Also riding with us were a Chinese man and woman sitting with their backs against the cab and facing rearward. The man looked hard as nails and the woman made the man look like a pansy. He wore an expression that made me think he was trying to figure out how he ended up in a truck full of rookies. She had no expression whatsoever and stared right through us. I don't think we newbies yet existed in her world. She wore a shirt with the sleeves cut off, full-length pants that were stuffed into her boots, and a headband that partially covered her short black hair. Around her waist was a small belt with a large sheath that carried a huge serrated knife. Also strapped to her belt were a few cannisters that I presumed to be grenades. I saw no notches on her belt but I sensed that she had earned the right to carve a few into it. She had no arc rifle; instead, a smaller weapon attached to a shoulder strap lay at her side.

The man also carried a small weapon, slightly different than the woman's, which made me wonder if the arc rifles were not the weapon of choice among the veterans. He wore a short-sleeved shirt and shorts similar to my own, yet they somehow looked better on him. He chewed catnip and occasionally spit out of the truck through the gap in between the second and third slats, narrowly missing the man to his right. I noticed he grew more fidgety as the minutes passed. The arms of both veterans were adorned with black designs that I can best describe as prison tattoos. The Chinese woman closed her eyes soon after we left camp. I don't think she was sleeping, for she continued to hold her head up, as if she was watching the vehicle behind us through her eyelids. I was drawn to her countenance but careful not to stare. I daresay that she was attractive beneath her tenacious façade, and I figured she would kill anybody who tried to tell her so.

"Does anyone here know anything about what we are going to be doing?" asked Charles, surely not expecting much in reply. To our surprise, the Chinese man did know something about our mission, and to our even greater surprise, he was happy to share it with us. The hard-boiled woman spoke not a single word the entire ride.

"Ambush," said the man in a thick accent. We waited for more but he looked as if he had told us everything we needed to know.

"I assume that *we'll* be doing the ambushing," I said quietly to Susan.

"Unless he's the world's biggest pessimist," she whispered back. Fortunately, Charles was able to coax more information from him. In his best English, which I found difficult to understand at times, the man told us how small groups of rebels had been observed using a particular road as of late. His squad had previously scouted a suitable place to ambush them, and we were going to stake it out today in the hopes of catching them off guard. One of the other rookies asked him how he thought things would go.

"Fish in a barrel," he replied with a smirk. He butchered the phrase so badly that I didn't think he understood exactly what it translated to in Chinese, only that it meant things would be easy for us. I felt a little better after this brief conversation and relaxed a little, taking more notice of the environment we traversed.

We drove for an hour or more, during which time I saw nothing out of the ordinary, save for a creature resembling an aardvark with wings, when it nearly flew into the truck. We were under no orders to remain silent but did so by choice—each in his or her own quiet reflection. At one point, seemingly out of the blue, Susan confided to me that she really missed her children. We turned a few times, each on to a narrower and less maintained road than before, until we rode upon what was little more than a rocky path.

Finally, our truck followed the one in front of it off the path and into a heavily wooded area. All of the vehicles except for one jeep turned a hundred and eighty degrees and parked facing back toward the path, so that they could make a hasty exit if needed. A combot and four veterans piled into the lone jeep and drove farther up the path and out of sight. We assembled in front of the flatbeds and were officially ordered to remain quiet. Cap conferred silently with his fellow combots, which looked more like a staring contest than a meeting. We then proceeded single-file into the brush on the side opposite of where the vehicles were parked. The sentroids and the two Serrones remained with the vehicles.

After walking for a hundred yards or so we reached the base of a small hill. It was there that we divided into groups and fanned out along the bottom of the hill in a line spanning about fifty yards. Charles, Susan, and I were part of a small crew of rookies assigned to Malcolm on the rightmost flank. On Cap's order, the entire company began traversing the hill (about twenty feet high) on our hands and knees. We came to lay at the summit of the hill where we found a road beneath us. Down to my left, near the leftmost flank of our company, the jeep that had departed us lay on its side in the middle of the road, presumably having been set in that position deliberately by its five occupants. Those same occupants were standing casually around the jeep. Upon seeing us, they moved into recumbent positions, feigning having been killed in the staged accident, and with their weapons laying conveniently nearby. A group of about twenty soldiers quickly hustled across the road and took up positions on the opposite hill. Our ambush was set.

Minutes that seemed like days slowly accumulated into hours that seemed like weeks. I was twice excused to retreat to the bottom of the hill behind me in order to relieve myself. I otherwise lay on my stomach and watched the road. I must have verified that my arc rifle was loaded more than thirty times. I was comforted a little by my position on the right flank which was likely to be farthest from the action. I assumed it was no coincidence that Malcolm had placed us there.

Just when the daylight started to fade we caught sight of something approaching on the road from the right. Malcolm signaled for us to crawl down the hill a few feet to avoid detection. My heart started racing as I crouched down and buried my face in the dirt. I could see nothing of the road from this position, but I heard the quiet hum of tires coming to a stop, followed by voices. Time came to a standstill.

I heard no official signal, yet a chorus of whooshing arc rifles instantly filled the air, accompanied by warrior cries. I inched upward to view the spectacle, forgetting to hold my rifle in a ready position. Before me was a convoy of four vehicles taking heavy fire from both sides. Bodies were already strewn about the road and inside the vehicles. Some of the soldiers had begun descending the hill to finish off the rebels at close quarters. It was as if I were watching a movie from the front row of the theater, and my panic slowly morphed into awe. I decided to raise my rifle and take a shot. I located a rebel crouched down in a vehicle, still fighting for his life. I took aim and suddenly froze. The rebel within my sights was a human! He looked like an average joe from back home. For all I knew, he could have been one of my students. I lowered my weapon and watched the poor man absorb several shots before falling dead.

Of course, we would be fighting humans. Had I not listened to anything Malcolm had told us? I don't know why it hadn't occurred to me as I lay on the hill for so many hours that we would be facing our own kind—people that, merely by chance, had been enslaved by the opposition. I looked to Charles, then to Susan, searching for the same empathy on their faces. Before any of us could speak, our attention was drawn to a commotion near the front of the convoy.

A rebel Serrone lay dead, propped up against a vehicle. In front of it stood a large android, something unlike anything I had seen during my short time on the planet. Its bottom half resembled a mechanical spider, with six gold legs sprawling in all directions. On top was a thick cylindrical body from which four arm-like appendages protruded. Each arm was firing what appeared to be small bursts of light, which had my comrades scrambling for cover in all directions. Lying dead at its feet were two of our own soldiers.

"Hell, I didn't expect to see one of those," Malcolm told us. "Keep your butts down, guys." We were content to oblige and remain spectators on the hill. The battle had dwindled into a standoff against the lone robotic enemy despite it being severely outnumbered. The action subsided for a minute or so, save for a few sporadic shots. Then all at once three grenades were lobbed toward one side of the spider android. As soon as they exploded, I saw Dee and Bar make a flanking maneuver to the opposite side of the vehicle. Without hesitation and at great risk, they jumped into the vehicle and fired point-blank shots into the rebel android from behind. Seeing that the threat was eliminated, the soldiers slowly revealed themselves, descended the hill, and traversed through the wreckage.

We came down to join the others and the inspect the carnage. I walked over to the group of soldiers that had assembled around the two dead comrades. I immediately recognized Tex. His wound looked more like a severe burn than a gunshot. The clothes around the wound were singed and small plumes of smoke rose softly from it. His eyes were half open and rolled upward, as if he was trying to see something above him. The other body belonged to another member of my cargo hold—the member of the Mexican cartel. His entire torso was severely burned and nearly torn in half.

"Spider got them," said Jessie, looking over my shoulder. "They thought it was safe to run down the hill. Before I could stop them, the spider popped out of the car."

"Clean it up," said Cap. "We cannot stay long." I watched a few soldiers drag the bodies to the side of the road while reflecting remorsefully on the time I had admonished Tex for making a foolish comment. I tried to control my breathing in an attempt to suppress the tears that were welling in my eyes. Then I heard my name.

"Shake-a-spear!" called Tully. I turned to see him standing on the other side of a rebel vehicle about twenty yards up the road. He was waving me over. "Come here!"

I walked over to find him standing over Sparks, who was sitting and holding down a rebel who lay face up with his head resting on Sparks' chest. Sparks had one hand wrapped around the man's torso while the other clutched a large knife under his chin. The young man appeared to be unscathed and very much afraid. Sparks looked up at me and smiled. He could barely contain his excitement.

"This one's alive, Shake-a-spear," he said, then continued in a lower voice, "you kill him." A thousand thoughts rushed through my head, none of which entertained the notion of me killing this person. He was either African or African American, no older than thirty, weighed no more than a hundred and fifty pounds, and wore glasses. I couldn't help but think of Nicholas. The captive clearly understood what Sparks had said, because he turned his eyes onto me. Tears emerged from them as he trembled.

"Aren't we taking him prisoner?" I asked of nobody in particular as I looked around the small crowd that had gathered. Sparks laughed heartily and Tully smiled. Nobody else made a sound.

"No prisoner. You kill him," Sparks said.

"Why me?"

Sparks looked up toward the top of the hill. "Chief wants you to do it."

I followed his eyes to the ridge where I saw the Chief standing with his favorite sentroids, Kaiser and Khan. His dark visor appeared to be looking directly at us. I had my doubts as to whether the Chief specifically requested that I kill this man. The notion was absurd and I suspected that Sparks knew I wouldn't believe it. But we both knew that the validity of his assertion was irrelevant, as I was in no position to question it. I scanned the crowd in the hopes of finding a reprieve. Malcolm was my best chance. All he gave me was a slight nod indicating that I had no choice. The inaction of the combots nearby confirmed it. In that instant I resolved to kill the poor man and knew that my best chance of following through was to act immediately without further deliberation. I raised my rifle and pointed it at the man's chest.

"No, no, no!" interjected Sparks as he pushed the barrel of my rifle away. "Can't waste bullet. Use this." He flipped his knife, caught it on the blade, and extended the handle toward me.

"I don't… I don't know how to…" I muttered.

"Like this," Tully advised, as he leaned over and ran his finger across the prisoner's neck. The entire company silently awaited my next move. I became very self-conscious of the large knife shaking in my hand. I thought of Tex, closed my eyes and thrust the knife into the man's stomach. The knife penetrated so deeply that my hand partially entered the wound. The poor man screamed in agony. I opened my eyes and stumbled backward while staring at my blood-soaked hand. A couple of soldiers caught me and prevented me from falling down.

"No, not like that, Shake-a-spear," said Tully calmly. He pulled the knife out of the man's torso and proceeded to slit his neck just as he had demonstrated with his finger. Then he walked over to me, grabbed me by the back of the neck and pulled my face into his. "Good job, Shake-a-spear! You one of us!" He pulled my numb body close to his, rubbed the back of my head and let out a yell. Some of the soldiers cheered.

I didn't feel like one of them.

I shoved Tully and walked away. In a flash his mood swung from elation to anger, as one might expect from a man-child such as he was, having been raised as a war commodity and never taught to control his raw emotions. He lunged at me aggressively but instead met the iron bar that was Dee's outstretched arm.

"Stay back," the combot told him.

"You watch yourself, Earth-man!" shouted Tully over Dee's arm. I ignored him, though his exclamation was likely intended for his fellow soldiers more than myself.

We hid seventeen rebel bodies and two of our own in a wooded area near the road—a total of eighteen humans and one enemy Serrone. I understood that we had no time to bury them but I wondered why we did not at least burn them. I soon had my answer—legions of wormlike creatures engulfed the bodies within minutes of their disposal. We commandeered the two rebel vehicles that were still serviceable. Before shoving the other two to the side and rendering them even further beyond repair, a few combots ravaged through them and salvaged vital parts for our motor pool.

I was one of a few soldiers ordered to load the spider android into one of the newly acquired vehicles. My anguish over killing the young man was briefly displaced by a fear of the powerful android bursting back to life as I held on to one of its photon-spewing arms.

There was a single combot in the rebel party and I found the treatment of it to be quite curious. Upon inspection it had been deemed to be beyond resurrection. The sentroid Khan extended a blowtorch-like tool from his appendage, decapitated the combot, and carried off its severed head. Maybe the Chief collected trophies?

The entire cleanup operation was completed in less than twenty minutes, after which we scurried back to our hidden trucks and headed for camp. I sat silently for the entire ride. My mates recounted the day's events among themselves but nobody spoke to me. It was dark when we pulled in front of the barracks. I climbed down from the flatbed and placed my arc rifle against the side of the truck.

Malcolm approached me. "Make no mistake," he told me. "That man would've killed you in a heartbeat if he had the chance." I assumed he was referring to the rebel I had killed, but perhaps not?

I looked at him for a moment. "You don't know that." I started walking over to the first hut, where the Chinese were handing out bottles. Malcolm caught up to me and grabbed my arm.

"Hey—I *do* know that. This is a war. You have to kill to survive."

"It's not *my* war," I replied, perhaps feeling as sorry for myself as I was for my victim.

"Yeah, maybe not. But ya still gotta survive, mate."

I left him and grabbed a bottle of Chinese moonshine from a table, though I had no desire to join the party. I walked over to a desolate area and sat down against a tree. The rotgut burned my throat on the first swig and its numbing effects soon kicked in. After several minutes, Leesheh approached and sat down next to me. She rested her head on my shoulder and said nothing.

14

I killed my second rebel soldier two days later. Several reconnaissance groups were dispatched to locate the rebel stronghold we suspected to be operating in the area of the ambush. The one to which I was assigned happened upon on a small enemy patrol in the early afternoon. We practically stumbled into each other in a thick wooded area and a chaotic firefight ensued. I took position behind a tree and dispatched a human rebel with my arc as he darted for cover. The entire skirmish lasted less than a minute. We eliminated their entire party of eight fighters but not without a price—the life of one of our Chinese veterans. Swag told me that the man was a distinguished warrior who had served in the company for more than ten seasons. We stood over him for a few minutes then quickly evacuated the area. We were in unknown territory and feared that a larger rebel force could be nearby.

My feelings were mixed. I was troubled by what I had done, though less so this time. I felt a bid cowardly for hiding behind a tree and shooting a man who was running away. I didn't know the person that I killed, nor did I know the Chinese man that the rebels killed. Nevertheless, I felt justified in taking the life of someone whom I considered responsible, at least by association, for the death of "one of my own." I can see now that a visceral hatred of the enemy had germinated within me. It would continue to grow unabated. What it was rooted in, I cannot not say for sure—probably a survival instinct.

Leesheh participated on her first patrols during these days and met no rebel opposition. I wasn't with her. Jessie told me that both Leesheh and Susan carried themselves well on the excursions. I could already see that Susan was adapting quickly to her warrior role and I found no reason to worry about her safety more than anyone else's. Leesheh's situation grew more vexing every day as a result of my ever-increasing fondness for her. I needed her to perform well and show value as a soldier, lest she be reassigned to the cathouse. Yet I couldn't bear to imagine her in harm's way.

On one morning around that time, Charles and I were ordered to empty the toilet buckets. By our third trip from the latrines to the stream we had sworn to never eat again. The large buckets had handles on the sides such that two people could carry them at arm's length, and with luck, dump them without having to see much of their contents. Even so, the stench was insufferable. After the final trip, we jumped into the water upstream then made our way back to the barracks by way of a more leisurely route. We happened to pass within sight of the cathouse.

"Let's go inside," suggested Charles.

"What? No—I don't want to go in there, Doc."

"Come on, just for a short while."

"We're not even allowed in there, are we?"

"Don't act like a child. Let's go."

"Knock yourself out, but I'm not going in there."

"Shakespeare, it's not what you think. I want to see how Tina and the others are doing—see if we can help them."

"Oh." Admittedly, I was very curious to see the inside of those buildings, though I was very wary of the sentroids. I didn't see any in the vicinity. "Okay, I guess."

We stepped up to the cathouse porch and I knocked on the door.

"I don't think you need to knock, Shakespeare," said Charles.

We entered into a dimly lit room with two rows of small wooden beds split by an aisle that spanned the entire length of the floor. Some of the beds were partitioned by old blankets hanging loosely from the ceiling. Ten or eleven women were inside—some sitting on beds, some trying to sleep, and one attempting to sweep dirt out the back door. They were dressed in ragged shorts and tee shirts. Most were wearing boots and a few were barefoot. There were no other men in the hut at the time. A few women looked our way for a moment to see who had entered, then quickly resumed what they had been doing, as if to avoid eye contact. I felt an urge to announce that I was not interested in having sex with anyone there. I couldn't quite find the right words, so I let it go. No one seemed happy to see us except for one young woman in the back whose face suddenly brightened up. I pointed her out to Charles, and we walked over.

"Tina!" said Charles in his booming voice. He clasped his hands on her arms, just below her shoulders, and greeted her as if she was his own daughter returning from a trip abroad. "How are you?"

"How am I?" she asked with a contorted face.

"Yes, I see," Charles said grimly. "I am so sorry for you."

"Can you get me outta here?"

"I don't think so," Charles told her. "Not today, but we'll try—I promise. We need to figure out what's going on around here first." His words were full of encouragement. I was far more skeptical and held my tongue. There was nothing we could do to help her.

A sullen expression suddenly came over her. "Wait, are you guys here to–"

"No, no!" Charles and I said in unison.

"We just came to check on you," Charles added.

"Trust me. It's as bad as it looks," she said.

We talked for a short while and managed to avoid the elephant in the room. That is, the despicable atrocities that she had likely endured since arriving and would continue to face indefinitely. She introduced us to several of the women, whom we pledged to help in any way possible. They told us that they were generally confined to the vicinity of their hut and disallowed access to the storeroom. We promised to bring them better clothing and fresh fruit when it was available.

Tina took us over to the nursery where we found the conditions to be equally deplorable. The women inside were admirably devoted to providing the two infants and four toddlers with the best care possible, but it was clearly not enough. Charles examined each child for a few minutes. One little girl looked very sick.

"How long has this child had this rash?" he asked one of the women.

"A few days now," she responded.

"She has a high fever as well. Try to keep her isolated from the other children," he told her. The woman nodded. Charles patted the woman on the shoulder empathetically and said, "Thank you." Outside the nursery I asked him what was wrong with the little girl who appeared to be so sick.

"I have no idea," he said. "I have never seen anything like it and I don't think she will live much longer."

True to our promise, Charles and I brought food and supplies to the cathouse and nursery one or two times per week when we weren't on patrol. It wasn't much, but they appreciated the gesture. We always went early in the morning to avoid being there when other men might be present. We didn't want to bear witness to such a hideous sight, and one which we were powerless to stop. Occasionally we would stumble over a soldier passed out on the floor, sleeping off a night of debauchery.

One morning, Leesheh and Susan approached us about tagging along to the cathouse and nursery. They had heard us speak about the conditions there and wanted to help. They were a little taken aback by my no-nonsense reaction.

"Absolutely not. It isn't safe for you there," I said adamantly. "We might not be able to protect you."

"It's not safe for anyone, anywhere around this place," said Susan.

"This is different. You know what happens there. You *have* to promise me that you will never set foot anywhere near there," I said sternly. Charles nodded in support of my ultimatum.

"Okay," said Leesheh. She could see that I wasn't playing around.

"Promise me."

"I promise."

"You too," I said to Susan.

"Yeah, me too," she replied.

The company continued in a pattern of small patrols and minor skirmishes for several weeks with little to show for it. Serrones seemed to measure success in terms of body count. There were no territorial boundaries—General Abasha claimed ownership of the entire region. Our job was to exterminate anyone or anything that disagreed with that notion. The rebels tended to be very mobile and usually traveled in small factions to evade detection. They might occupy a village for a few weeks before moving on. Our masters widened the radius of our patrols in search of the suspected rebel stronghold. Jessie speculated that the camp might be moving soon to facilitate the broader search. She told me that her time in the current location was the longest she had ever spent in one place.

One night I was stirred from a deep sleep by the sound of heavy rain beating on the roof. There had been no indication of an approaching storm, so I assumed it to be a fast-moving front that would pass through quickly. I was wrong. The rain continued to pour down in thick sheets for three straight days, transforming the camp into a swamp. The stream became a river, fed by a labyrinth of newly formed streams that snaked through the camp. Strange creatures took refuge in and under our barracks, including a pair of the rodent cappies that soon became our dinner. We also learned why our particular bunks had been available to us on that first day in camp. They were the ultimate destinations of the water that made its way through the leaky roof. Only Nicholas was spared, having chosen the bed beneath Swag. The rest of us newbies were forced to find dry spots on the floor and make temporary beds there.

We passed the hours away in the barracks, leaving them only for meals and patrols. The latter decreased a little during the rain but were not entirely eliminated. We swapped stories of our lives on Earth, which in hindsight I realize probably caused some resentment among the young natives who resided with us. They showed little interest in our biographies with the exception of Ammo, who always relished the memoirs of our strange, distant homeland. My storytelling talents were called upon as well, and our hut was often overfilled with visitors from the neighboring buildings when I performed. I worked my way through several more Dickens stories. I loved his characters, though my attempts at recreating them fell short of his vivid physical descriptions. Fortunately, we had very few Dickens readers in the group.

Even before the rain, Leesheh and I had been spending more and more time together. I learned that she had recently completed law school and was clerking for a small firm in Curacao's capital city of Willemstad. She was in the process of repaying a considerable student loan at the time of her abduction.

"At least I will not have to pay them back now," she joked.

"That's fine," I told her, "but I'll need you to be in good standing for my lawsuit against the planet of Serrone. I'll expect you to represent my interests."

Her parents worked in the tourism industry along with many of their countrymen. Her older brother served as the assistant manager in a branch of the central bank and her younger brother studied finance and marketing in the Netherlands. She described her home island to me in such detail that I told her it felt as if I had visited it in person. She remarked that I would someday. Though we both knew that was unlikely, I was buoyed by her ceaseless optimism and told her as much.

Having settled into the camp routine, mastered our chores, and gained some trust from our overseers, everybody found themselves with extra time. Many of my companions from the transport ship had further declined since arriving. Some had fallen into the throes of addiction, having become dependent on the daily rations of catnip or drinking themselves into a stupor whenever possible. One comrade was found hanging by his neck from a tree one morning. I cannot fault anyone for attempting to shut down the reality of our situation—temporarily or permanently—but it was not in my nature. My instinct for survival was too strong and I still nurtured hopes of returning to Earth. With each passing day, my acceptance of my circumstances increased, my hatred for the aliens responsible increased, my grudges against my enemies increased, and my feelings for Leesheh increased.

I had no doubt that she reciprocated my feelings, though we had not discussed our relationship specifically. The idea of talking about a future together seemed ridiculous in light of our situation, yet I was not about to deny myself this silver lining of happiness, however fleeting it might have been. The dread of losing her sometimes prevented me from enjoying the moments alone with her. I even contemplated if we would both be better off without this complication. Nevertheless, ending it was not an option for me, nor did it appear to be for her.

There were other couples within the company, or so it appeared. Like us, they chose to conceal their affairs for fear of castigation at the hands of the Serrones. The combots seemed apathetic to the sexual antics of their wards. I might have thought they were oblivious, yet even in those early days I knew that the combots were oblivious to nothing.

On the third day of unyielding rain that announced the semi-annual change in seasons, we were loitering in the barracks when a commotion was heard outside. It was barely audible above the pattering rain. Ammo anxiously ran to the window facing the courtyard.

"The patrol is back. They've got something," he announced over his shoulder. Amid the distraction of the rain I had not realized that a patrol had even been dispatched. The absence of Sparks, Tully, and a few of their native cohorts was not unusual. They were rarely in the barracks, as they seemingly had carte blanche access to the camp. They could typically be found near the motor pool or the cathouse. (They were scarcely missed by the rest of us.) Unbeknownst to me, as most things were in those days, they had left camp during the preceding night. They were members of a small patrol led by Bar searching for evidence of the elusive rebel faction. They returned this day with a prize—two prizes, in fact.

We gathered on the porch of our hut and endured the spraying rain to get a better view. We would soon learn that the patrol had spotted the campfire of a small band of rebels not two miles from our camp. Bar's team of native soldiers (as was his preference to employ) had quickly subdued the enemies and secured two prisoners: one Serrone and one human. The presence of any prisoners in camp was an anomaly, but a Serrone prisoner was such a prize that Ringo and Ratso, along with their sentroid entourages, braved the rain to assess the acquisition. The Chief was nowhere to be found.

Tully held the human prisoner, a young woman, up by the back of her collar. He reminded me of the deep-sea fishermen I used to watch at Virginia Beach as they proudly displayed their prize catches of the day. She was barely conscious. The marks on her face disclosed the brutal beating that she had sustained—more than likely at the hands of the man who was currently propping her up. The Serrone prisoner was tiny, even by Serrone standards. Chairman Mao, Ringo's personal sentroid guard, swooped in and took custody of the haggard alien being. From my vantage point, it looked to have one foot in Serrone heaven already. With their prisoner in hand, our Serrone masters exited the courtyard. We saw nothing of the alien prisoner again. Dee and Malcolm approached the raiding party.

"Look here!" Tully said enthusiastically as he pointed first to the battered woman then to the Serrone prisoner being whisked away. "One for us and one for them, eh Malcolm?"

Dee, Bar, and Malcolm became engaged in a conversation while the young natives inched closer to hear it. Malcolm appeared to disagree with Bar. After a few minutes, Dee gave orders to Tully, who then took the prisoner away. Malcolm walked off, visibly dissatisfied. The rest of us filed back into the hut to escape the rain. A few minutes later, Tully entered, followed by Bar, Sparks, and a few others who had participated in the raid. We all knew that the fate of the female prisoner would unfold within the cathouse, where no actionable intelligence would be attained. I'm sure that I wasn't the only one who secretly hoped that she might die before being subjected to the unspeakable horrors that awaited her. To my surprise, Charles approached Tully and broke the uneasy silence.

"Where have you taken her?" he asked.

Tully remained seated on his bunk with his eyes fixed on the floor. "Prisoner needs to be questioned," he replied nonchalantly. "Took her to the cathouse."

"That child needs medical attention," said Charles as he took a step closer to Tully's bunk. Tully, now bothered, stood up and faced the older man.

"Not your problem."

"Suppose it is," countered Charles. I had never seen him so serious and deliberate. In an instant the situation escalated. I cannot recall whether it was Tully's or Charles' mates who first came to their friend's defense. Everyone suddenly rose and squared off, as if on cue. I expected Bar to intervene but he stood to the side, silently watching. Tully put his face within an inch of Charles' nose and upped the ante.

"I can give you problem. *Big* problem."

"Tully," said Dee, who now stood as a silhouette in the doorway. "Stand down." Tully hesitated for a moment then took a step back and smiled at Charles. "Doc," continued Dee, "leave the barracks."

Charles walked past Tully as if he was invisible and proceeded out the door. Dee turned around and followed Charles outside.

Perhaps Tully felt humiliated by Dee's reproach and sought revenge, or maybe it was because I had stood beside Charles, or maybe he needed no excuse. For whatever reason, he redirected his displeasure toward me.

"Shake-a-spear," he mocked in a low voice as he moved into my personal space. "You my friend, yeah?" I held my ground and said nothing. "Hey—I asked you question," he added, pointing his finger near my chin.

I was trembling inside and convinced that Tully could read my fear. Somehow, I now found myself acting as the leader of our little group in Charles' absence. I had no choice but to stand my ground. Stuck between a rock and a hard place, I decided to bluff, and summoned my community theater skills.

"*My* friends are behind me," I responded coolly.

I did my best to appear smooth and resolute, but I was terrified—not unlike how I felt when ordered to kill the young rebel. The difference now was that I was fully committed to seeing this through. I was also energized by my supporters standing with me—Jessie, Nicholas, Swag, Susan, and Leesheh—and I felt that I couldn't let them down. I sized up my opponent. He was a tough, experienced fighter. I was bigger and possibly stronger. My foremost concern was his knife, on the handle of which his hand now rested.

"Your friends? These are your friends?" he asked rhetorically. He looked directly over my shoulder at Ammo. "You his friend, Ammo?" Jessie responded by putting her arm around the boy.

"Back off, Tully," she said sternly. Tully next found Leesheh and fixed his eyes upon her. "I don't know… maybe your girlfriend should live in the cathouse. What you think, Sparks?"

"Maybe," said Sparks. "I take good care of her." Any window I might have had for backing down was now sealed shut. My jaw tightened and my eyes flared, though I still secretly hoped that Dee would return and squelch the standoff.

"If you touch her, I'll kill you," I said through clenched teeth. "If one of your friends lays a hand on her, I'll kill him, and then I'll kill you. Do you understand?" I didn't want a fight on my hands and figured that my best chance for averting one was to double down on my resolve.

"Shakespeare, it's okay," said Leesheh softly. I appreciated that she was giving me an out, but I had to ignore her.

"*You* can kill *me*?" Tully retorted. I noticed the slightest hint of uneasiness in his voice. I doubled down once more.

"Why don't you put that knife on the floor so we can find out? Man-to-man."

Tully froze for a second then let out a nervous laugh and looked at Sparks behind him. "Shake-a-spear in a bad mood today!" Then he said to me, "I just yank your chain, Shake-a-spear," and walked over to his bunk.

To my surprise and great relief, I had won this round. My adrenaline surged as it naturally does the moment one realizes he has narrowly avoided catastrophe. I knew that it would be foolish to rub it in, so I nodded and retreated as well. Tully appeared to have fallen for my bluff, though he likely had his doubts. I knew this wasn't over.

I lay on my bunk trying to disguise my enormous relief as Swag eased tensions by engaging the young men in casual conversation. Tully and his entourage of natives left soon thereafter, presumably to visit the cathouse and its newest resident.

Before daybreak the next morning, Charles and I stole away to the cathouse to check on the prisoner. She appeared to be recovering from the torture she had sustained at the hands of the young soldiers. Like the men responsible for her beating, she was also native-born and couldn't have been older than nineteen or twenty. Her straight, jet-black hair and olive complexion suggested that one of her parents might have hailed from India or the Middle East.

We took the liberty of moving her over to the nursery, where she might enjoy a more sequestered recovery. I engaged her in conversation as Charles looked over her cuts and bruises. Her name was Saba. She told us that her mother was from a place on Earth called "Bonglidish," and that her mother had fought for the Northern Army during the Great War. Using a limited vocabulary, she described what life was like in the rebel army. Not surprisingly, it sounded very much like our own. Saba was so sweet and innocent that it was impossible not to care about her. She was the antithesis of a war prisoner. I assured her that we would check on her again.

"What happens to me?" she asked as we stood up to leave.

A blunt "I don't know" was all I could muster. It wasn't a lie. I didn't know exactly what would happen to her. I did know that it would probably come down to the cathouse, death, or both. I had no intention of telling her that. Charles and I returned to the barracks and filled the others in on the prisoner's status.

Charles predicted a full recovery but added, "only if those hooligans leave her alone." None of us thought that was very likely.

The Serrone prisoner must have yielded useful information to the sentroids, for rumors of locating a large rebel encampment soon began to spread throughout the compound.

15

A few days after the prisoners were captured, Dee was ordered to mobilize a small team to reconnoiter a village. I had yet to see a Serrone village and as a member of Dee's squad I would have the opportunity to observe one from a relatively safe distance. The party comprised eight human soldiers plus Dee. Noticeably absent were Sparks, Tully, and their native compadres. Cognizant of the growing rift within the barracks, Dee could ill afford infighting on such a vital operation and selected only old-timers—and myself. At least, that's what Malcolm told me. He made it clear that my inclusion was not to be interpreted as a vote of confidence. He and Dee had decided that I should be separated from the natives if they could not be there to babysit us. I was instructed to keep my "ass down" and my "trap shut," and otherwise stay out of the way. Swag and Jessie were on the team, as was the rugged Chinese woman with whom I had ridden on my first mission. Her presence could not help but make me feel a little safer. Swag knew why I was there and needled me about it as we rode out to the drop-off point.

"Don't sweat it, mate. We'll make a soldier outta you yet," he told me as we sat in the flatbed, then turned to the Chinese woman and said, "Isn't that right, Ying?" Ying glared at Swag and said nothing. This was more than satisfactory to Swag, who understood that any kind of acknowledgment from Ying exceeded expectations. "See, Shakespeare?" he told me. "Ying likes you."

We drove for about twenty miles then continued for several more hours on foot, loaded with packs of food, canteens of water, and extra ammunition we had accumulated from the recent skirmishes. We reached the outskirts of the village at dusk and bivouacked in a position hidden within a thick forest. In the morning I took my first look at the small village. It didn't resemble the mental image I had conjured on the journey there. I had expected to find a futuristic, suburban metropolis replete with technological advances beyond my wildest dreams. To my disappointment, what stood before me looked a lot more like our camp than Epcot Center. Buildings were little more than shacks, roads were unpaved, and strange-looking animals roamed freely. I counted about sixty Serrone civilians—the most I had ever seen in one place. My ability to interpret Serrone behavior and expressions was severely limited, but compared to my masters, these tiny beings seemed destitute and miserable. I shared my impressions with Jessie as we sat together on a rock eating a tangy yellow fruit we picked from a nearby shrub. She removed her floppy hat and wiped her brow while gathering her thoughts, then provided me with something of an explanation.

Prior to the Great War, the entire population of the planet resided in the grand cities—the ultimate achievements of the Serrone civilization. When the oligarchs decided that victory could not be achieved by winning tactical battles fought by soldiers on battlefields, they resorted to destroying cities and the citizens therein. Scores of refugees fled into the wilderness. Villages like the one before me were haphazardly constructed as temporary shelters for displaced civilians. When the war dragged on for so many more years than anyone had predicted, these villages morphed into permanent settlements, forcing their inhabitants to revert to a more primitive lifestyle. Erected somewhat randomly and remotely, records of these villages evaporated along with the civilizations that created them. Most were uncharted.

The village was not completely devoid of advanced technology. I witnessed small hovering vehicles (similar to the Chief's chariot), automatic doors on the decrepit buildings, a large antennae-like structure, and a few robots of various shapes and sizes performing domiciliary tasks. Some of the Serrone inhabitants wore visors similar to the Chief's and carried around handheld devices that resembled smartphones. Most abundant were the skeletal remains of dilapidated gadgets consigned to the junk pile or repurposed for more primitive uses, such as shelters.

A large rebel force moved freely within the village. We estimated it to include fifty human soldiers, six combots, two sentroids, and three officers. We used the term "officer" in reference to a Serrone, as we never came upon one that was merely a grunt or ever participated in any form of combat. If there had ever been any valiant Serrones, they must have been driven into extinction during the Great War. The human soldiers in the village appeared to be mostly East Indian or Middle Eastern, with a few Africans and Caucasians interspersed within.

Swag was the company's most skillful operative in covert reconnaissance operations. He wormed his way along the fringes of the village undetected while the rest of us remained in the surrounding rocks and brush, observing the traffic moving in and out. He returned to our makeshift camp late on the second night with some distressing intelligence. He had spotted at least one of the dreaded spider androids. This news prompted me to ask Malcolm why we didn't have one of those, to which he only huffed.

Dee had been instructed not to use his communication device for fear of detection, so he dispatched a messenger to inform the camp of our findings while the rest of us relocated to a rendezvous point a few miles away from the village. We spent two mostly uneventful nights waiting for the attack force to arrive. I write *mostly* uneventful because I awoke on the second morning to the sight of a roller (the scorpion–lizard hybrid) not six inches from my face and looking quite undecided as to whether it wanted to strike my nose. Not wishing to negatively influence its decision, I froze. With one side of my head pinned firmly to the ground I was unable to see if there was anybody in my vicinity.

"Guys…" I whimpered quietly. The standoff continued for an eternity—at least five seconds—before a knife blade thrust down through the torso of the animal, splattering my face with a thick, pinkish liquid. I looked up to see Dee. He extended the knife toward me with the impaled creature still quivering in the throes of death.

"Stay away from these," he advised with his combot equanimity. "They will kill you."

Gee, thanks, I thought to myself as I wiped my face with my shirt sleeve.

The balance of our attack force arrived under the cover of darkness that evening. The soldiers were crammed like sardines into the transport vehicles and looked very relieved to have arrived.

"One of the flatbeds broke down on the way over," said Charles. "We had to abandon it by the side of the road."

It seemed like the entire population of the camp was now there.

Charles told me that a very small crew was left behind to guard the compound. When I questioned why so few were left to defend it, he made an interesting observation.

"What is there to defend?" he asked. "Everything of value was brought here." His point was valid and I was happy to see that the person in whom I placed so much value was not left behind. I wanted to embrace Leesheh, but that, of course, was out of the question. Fortunately, we had learned how to interpret each other's nonverbal facial expressions. She knew that I was happy to see her.

The sentroids carried over some heavier weaponry that I had not yet seen. They began to assemble what I presumed to be small pieces of artillery—larger than a mortar yet still very mobile when carried by the robust sentroids.

I was not the only one who met with a restless night. In the morning we were fed various fruits and a nut-like kernel that was picked from nearby trees. All of the soldiers were provided with an adequate supply of cartridges, and the veterans were allowed to supplement their armament with grenades. A basket of catnip was produced and nearly emptied within minutes. I briefly contemplated artificially boosting my courage and quickly thought the better of it. The two company squads were further subdivided in two, and the four teams assembled separately for instructions. I was relieved for multiple reasons: I was under the command of Dee and Malcolm; I was with Leesheh and my friends; and Tully and Sparks had been assigned to Bar's team. My bluff in the barracks appeared to be holding but it seemed tenuous. I feared it could be challenged at any moment.

The plan was fairly simple. Two teams would attack from the east—the direction of the rising planet Wiyanga. The attack would begin with an airstrike and artillery barrage followed by a slow advance using a widespread line in order to create the illusion of a larger force. The other two teams would wait in a hidden location outside of the western end of the village and ambush soldiers if they retreated, or pinch in from behind if they held their ground. Dee's team was assigned to watch one of the western roads. Nicholas and I approached Malcolm after the briefing.

"Airstrike?" I asked. "What exactly does that mean?"

"The Abasha Air Force," he said facetiously. He told us that the PRF maintained a small squadron of aircraft that survived the Great War. The fleet consisted mostly of drones and a few transport vessels, "but the

General hasn't figured out how to properly operate the drones, so they usually get shot down."

"Transport ships? Like the one that brought us to Serrone?" asked Nicholas.

"No, mate. I'm talkin' about *aircraft*—airplanes. What you're referring to is the real prize—the starship. That's what keeps him in power—as long as he's got a supply of soldiers coming in."

"There's only one starship?" I asked.

"Abasha has one. The bloody thing can barely fly. Dunno what else is out there." He took a quick survey of the soldiers on his team. "Right—we gotta get a move on. Get yourselves ready."

Many of the soldiers smeared their faces with mud created by pouring canteen water into the dirt. Some darkened their entire face while others applied warrior stripes. I started to get the feeling that this was going to be a very serious fight. I stuck my finger in some mud and streaked it across each cheek. It made me feel a little more confident, though I might not have felt that way if I had a mirror. I probably looked silly.

The order was given to move out, which prompted a group of soldiers to mob together and begin jumping up and down while holding their weapons in the air and whipping themselves into a frenzy. Others quickly joined in to form a large mass moving up and down in unison. One African soldier led chants that were repeated by the group. I was initially taken aback by this prefight ritual, then slowly found myself drawn to the mob, jumping alongside my comrades.

It took us about an hour to reach our position. We made our way quietly up a small embankment that overlooked a dirt road and waited in tall grass for the sounds of battle. I propped myself up on my elbows and took stock of my surroundings. We had a good view of the buildings in the western half of the town. To my left lay Susan. I turned to my right and found none other than Monte. I hadn't thought much about him in recent weeks. He and I resided in different barracks and I had plenty of other concerns occupying my time. The loveable Monte was a favorite among newbies and old-timers alike; there was no shortage of benefactors watching his back. Some had made it a priority to teach him English. I decided to see how he was coming along with his studies.

"Hi Monte," I said quietly with a nod.

"Monte," was his only reply, which he delivered with a grin. The conversation ended abruptly and without resolving the question of who

Monte thought that "Monte" was. I got the impression that we were all Montes in his eyes. The brief levity was more than welcome. It was soon interrupted by the thunder and reverberations of artillery shells exploding. I covered my ears and watched the shells indiscriminately shred buildings, sending civilians and rebels alike scrambling for cover.

"So, if I understand this correctly," Susan said to me, "our job is to kill our fellow Earthlings over there with the objective of liberating those alien villagers in the name of General Abasha—the same villagers who are, as we speak, being slaughtered by our alien masters… who report to General Abasha?"

"Something like that," I added. "For me, it's about staying alive, I guess."

A minute or so after the shelling began, two egg-shaped flying objects appeared low in the sky.

"Look—there's the air force!" someone shouted over the exploding artillery. The drones hovered above the center of the village and commenced firing what appeared to be bursts of plasma that exploded on impact. They immediately attracted a lot of attention in the form of rebel gunfire, and they zipped off within thirty seconds after arriving.

"So much for that," I mumbled to myself.

The shelling eventually ceased and was replaced by the faint whooshing noises of arc rifles and the louder cracking sounds created by their plasma bullets making contact with targets, both intended and unintended. A few more minutes passed before Dee ordered us to our feet. We fanned out to arm's length and slowly crept forward. Something scurried in front of a building in our path. It was quickly put down by our guns. A vehicle suddenly came around a corner and darted toward us. We dropped to the ground and sprayed it with plasma. It slowly rolled to a halt, with all four occupants having been killed several times over. We inched forward and took cover behind the vehicle. I purposely glossed over the deceased soldiers and focused my eyes forward.

The battle rumblings from the other end of town heightened as we made our way into the village and took up positions along the outlying buildings. It seemed to me like a pretty good spot to wait for the enemy but Dee motioned us to continue forward. We began to spread out and cluster in smaller groups under the cover of various structures. I could hear the sounds of tiny skirmishes erupting nearby but could not see them. They lasted only a few seconds—a few shots here, a few shots there. I came to the side of a stone building and took cover. The only other soldiers I could see were those who had followed me to the wall: Leesheh, Susan, and Nicholas. Next to me along the wall was a closed door. Just beyond the door was a large window.

It was clear that we wouldn't be able to advance farther without coming under fire from whatever was inside the building—if anything was. We huddled against the wall and exchanged ideas by way of mouthing words to each other. It seemed as though our comrades had moved forward into the village without us, and a bizarre calmness came over our immediate surroundings. We couldn't stay where we were and I was fairly confident that the building was unoccupied. I conveyed to the others that I was going to kick in the door and jump to the side, and that they should be ready to fire upon whatever came out.

No sooner had I summoned the courage to move when the door was yanked open from the inside, and two young rebels darted off in the direction of the woods from whence we came. They took no notice of us nor did we react other than watch them disappear. After exchanging curious glances with my comrades, I walked slowly to the door with my rifle ready to fire. Inside were three Serrones crouched down behind an overturned table. For the first time, I saw the naked eyes of these creatures. Perhaps I was projecting, but in those eyes I saw despair and resignation, making me feel more like a conqueror than a liberator. I stared at them and they stared back at me. Nobody moved until I carefully retreated outside, pulling the door closed behind me, and leaving them how I found them.

We advanced past the stone hut and found the entire squad engaged in an active firefight on the edge of what looked like the village square. It was really just a large patch of dirt and boulders, with a few oddly-manicured trees, in the middle of town—perhaps the Serrone version of a city park. Pinned down in the center of the square under the cover of bombed out vehicles, were what remained of the rebel force: two combots and the aforementioned spider-android. The rest of my company was raining fire down upon the enemy from rooftops and other elevated positions on the other side of the square. The three remaining rebels put up a gallant defense yet eventually succumbed to the overwhelming numbers. Susan distinguished herself in this final stage of the battle. She played a decisive role in eliminating the spider-android, putting herself at considerable risk while executing a diversionary tactic.

Soon after the last shots in the village square were fired, adrenaline levels diminished and we slowly came back to reality, first taking stock of our own health, then taking inventory of those around us. I incorrectly assumed that every last rebel was dead. I soon learned that a group of eight had been captured on the east end of town at the start of the battle. They were marched down to the village square under the watchful eyes of combots and forced to sit with their hands clasped together on top of their heads.

"What happens to them?" I asked Swag.

"They'll be taken to the city," he said. "Probably be put to work there. Then one day they'll be soldiers again, this time for the PRF."

"They'll fight against their own army?"

"Nah, Abasha can't trust their loyalty. I 'spose they'll work 'em real hard in the city for a while. The ones that survive will join the ranks of the PRF, fightin' some other enemy of the General. Lord knows he's got plenty."

Just when I had started to relax, Cap, the lead combot, informed us that any celebration would be premature.

"Clear out every building," he ordered. The company began to disperse into several small groups. Having realized that my strategy for clearing out the stone hut earlier would have likely ended in my death, had the two rebel soldiers not decided to vacate first, I decided to watch and learn from an expert. I beckoned for Leesheh to follow and walked over to join up with Swag.

"Mind if we tag along with you?" I asked.

"Not at all, mate."

Swag led us, six in all, in and out of a few buildings. We stepped over several dead bodies—mostly rebels—and encountered no live resistance. Occasional shots and shouts were heard from other parts of the village. As we were walking back to the village square, Jessie came running up to Swag.

"Swag—Ammo's missing!" she gasped.

"Missing? How?"

"I don't know. We got separated near the square. I don't know—just help me find him." Within seconds, most of the squad was engaged in the search. After a few minutes, Nicholas emerged from behind a building and hurried toward Jessie, who had been searching with us on the other side of the village square.

"Jessie! Jessie!" he shouted. "We found him. He's back here!"

We rushed over and followed him through an alley to the building. It had the appearance of some kind of shop, with a double-sized entry door and large glass window that had been blown out. A crowd was funneling in through the door, so Jessie bypassed them by stepping through the broken window. I followed behind her. Inside, lying peacefully on his back was Ammo's lifeless body. The body of a dead rebel soldier sat in the corner with its legs outstretched and its chin buried in its chest, as if pointing us to the gaping wound that lay beneath it. Kneeling down beside Ammo was Tully, wiping clean his bloody knife on Ammo's shirt. Ammo's throat was slit ear to ear. He also had a plasma wound in the area of his left thigh. Standing behind Tully were Bar and Sparks.

"No, no... Ammo, no," sobbed Jessie as she rushed to his side and embraced him on the ground. Nicholas turned to me with a look of disbelief and seemed unable to speak. Malcolm and Dee pushed their way to the front of the crowd.

"What happened here?" asked the veteran Aussie.

"He killed him," blurted Nicholas, pointing at Tully. Tully stood up and placed his knife in its sheath.

"I did," he said placidly while staring back at Nicholas. He then turned to Dee. "He was dying. This is our rule." Next, he turned to Jessie. "You know that, right Jessie?"

I wondered if he had waited for Jessie to arrive before wiping the blood off his knife. Upon hearing her name, Jessie quietly lifted her head and turned to Malcolm while ignoring Tully's question. Dee looked at Bar.

"It is true," added Bar following a moment of hesitation. "The boy would not have survived." Jessie began sobbing again. We gently pulled her away from Ammo and helped her back into the square, where we sat her down under the shade of a tree. It was there that Nicholas pulled me and Charles aside.

"Guys, Ammo wasn't hurt that bad. He was alert—and talking."

"Tell us exactly what happened," said Charles.

"I found him inside the building with the dead rebel. He told me that he had lost Jessie and had taken cover inside. The rebel stumbled in and they shot each other. I asked him how badly he was injured and he said it wasn't too bad."

"Did it *look* bad?" asked Charles.

"I can't say, Doc. I mean, Ammo didn't seem very concerned."

Charles let out a deep breath. "Then what?"

"Then Tully came in. He looked at Ammo and told me to go find Jessie, so I did."

"Was Bar with him?" I asked.

"No."

I turned to Charles. "What are you thinking?"

"Hard to say," replied the doctor diplomatically. "We cannot be certain of anything. Even if Tully… if he–"

"If he murdered Ammo?" I interjected.

"Yes, or something like that. What can we do? These men are dangerous. This is their world, not ours."

By this time, the Chief and his Serrone lieutenants had magically appeared and assumed charge, as was their custom to wait until any threat of danger had long passed. We soon learned that Ammo was not our only casualty. Three other soldiers perished during the initial assault from the east. The bodies were brought down to the courtyard and laid out near the prisoners. I recognized one as the Chinese man who sat with us in the flatbed on my first patrol.

Somebody in the chain of command confirmed that there were no other rebels left alive, and we were ordered to begin the cleanup process. This time seemed a little less gruesome than the last time, despite there being much more carnage. For better or worse, I was acclimating to my new life.

16

The prisoners were loaded into a couple of vehicles that were salvaged from the village and sent away. Most of the company climbed into the awaiting flatbeds, but my return to camp would be delayed. I was assigned to a detail tasked with protecting the village refugees until vehicles could arrive and transport them somewhere. I assumed their destination would be the region's capital city, the proud home of the People's Resistance Front. I don't know what the Serrones called the city, nor could I pronounce it if I did. We called it Abasha City.

The village looked reparable to me yet the surviving citizens were not offered the option of remaining. They had been driven from their city by one war only to be forced back into it by another—and these were the lucky ones. Fourteen of the sixty-three villagers were lost to collateral damage. Maybe General Abasha felt it was easier to maintain his rule if he had fewer subjects *to* rule. The average Serrone citizen seemed to be nearly as expendable as we were.

Someone or something decided that it wasn't safe for the villagers to wait in their own village, so we were ordered to shepherd them to a rendezvous point several miles into the wilderness. Our commanders could spare only a few supplies for this march, and for reasons unknown, they were unable to spare any veteran fighters for the escort detail. The detail, charged with bringing forty-nine villagers and their belongings safely to the rendezvous point, consisted of one combot and ten of us newbies, including Nicholas and Pablo. To his credit, Swag volunteered for the assignment and was denied. (I'm certain that Jessie would have done the same if she was in a healthier state of mind.) Moreover, as no vehicles were made available for this effort, each soldier was assigned a heavy backpack containing the aforementioned villagers' belongings. No soldiers were left behind to hold the village for which we had spilled so much blood to liberate, as it held no strategic value.

The leader assigned to our expedition was a combot whose three-letter tag name was Mik. His selection was a bit of a surprise and added to our apprehension. Mik wasn't assigned to a squad in camp; he spent his time in the motor pool or patrolling the camp perimeter. I could not say with certainty, but he was presumably the lowest-ranking combot in our company, and we found it disconcerting that he was the only android placed in charge of sixty villagers and soldiers. The term "suicide mission" was murmured once or twice as we prepared to leave.

We humans could have made the trip in a matter of hours, but Serrones had long since evolved beyond the need, and thus the ability, to walk great distances. We left the village at a snail's pace and lost speed with each passing hour. It soon became obvious that we would not reach the designated location before nightfall, so Mik directed the caravan into a wooded area to bivouac. The consensus estimate of our progress among the soldiers was two miles. The refugees seemed more miserable than we were, which was understandable. On this day, I heard Serrones communicate verbally for the first time. It wasn't a pleasant noise, consisting mostly of high-pitched squawking and squeaking. I asked Mik what they were saying.

"They are very unhappy," was his reply. *No shit.*

They were clearly afraid of us too. As such, we were instructed to keep our distance and forbidden from addressing the Serrones in any manner. Nicholas came up with an interesting analogy that he shared with Pablo and me.

"Imagine if you were being protected by wolves that had been caught in the wild and trained to be guard dogs," he explained. "You wouldn't feel very safe around them, would you—fearing that they might revert to their feral ways and rip you to shreds? We're nothing but wild savages to these beings."

"So, we are like wolves, eh Nicky?" asked Pablo, somewhat missing the point. "Lobos—that's pretty sweet."

Curiously, I found myself sympathizing with the refugees. I had previously avowed to despise all Serrones, yet I couldn't place these poor little beings in the same category as our captors. Like us, they were unwilling participants in a senseless war and had suffered great losses at the hands of ruthless thugs. At least *my* friends and family were safe at home. Who knows how many of theirs had died during years upon years of brutal warfare? Nonetheless, I wasn't naïve enough to think that my sympathy was reciprocated. Any one of these villagers would have gladly enslaved me if given the opportunity.

I learned something else about Serrones on this excursion: they slept—*a lot*. They required about ten hours per night, in addition to an afternoon siesta. Despite being exhausted from the long day, I was much too jittery to sleep. I volunteered to take the first watch, and I volunteered Nicholas to join me. We passed the time sitting on a log, mulling over Ammo's death and what to tell Jessie about it, if anything. Charles had made it clear that he intended to leave things as they were, but I continued to waffle on the issue. Nicholas was equally ambivalent and seemed determined to argue against whatever position I was leaning toward at the moment. Just when I had resolved to tell Jessie that Ammo might have been murdered, Nicholas took it upon himself to play the devil's advocate.

"The thing is," he pondered, "Bar did confirm that Ammo was gravely wounded."

"Yeah, that's true," I conceded.

"However, I think it's possible that a combot could lie."

"Really? Androids can lie?"

"Not the sentroids. I'm just talking about the combots—and it wouldn't be lying, exactly. Look, Malcolm said that they were programmed with a level of artificial intelligence, right?"

"Right—something to do with camaraderie."

"Well, that might be a Pandora's box of sorts. They weren't given an entire conscious—I don't see how that would be possible. They were only provided with a propensity for a specific trait. Without the proper safeguards… I mean, left unchecked, this tendency for camaraderie could evolve in various directions."

"Like lying?"

"Why not? If they're wired to protect their fellow soldiers, then it might be possible. That's all I'm saying."

"But they're just computers, right?"

"Yes, but don't forget that the Serrones are far more advanced than we are—at least, they used to be." He thought for a moment then continued, "Let's assume for argument's sake that the combots do have a capacity for distorting the truth. Which combot is more likely to do it—Dee or Bar?"

"That's easy. Bar. I can't imagine Dee lying—especially not to protect a complete ass like Tully."

"See?" said Nicholas, "You've just proved my point. You have different perceptions of Dee and Bar. How did you obtain them? In your view they have personalities—varying tendencies, so to speak."

"It does *seem* like the combots have different personalities, unlike the sentroids—the sentroids are interchangeable."

"Yes, and the so-called personalities of the combots might evolve based on their experiences," lectured Nicholas, "if provided with a basic ability to habituate, such as an adaptive neural network might allow."

"I think I get it. The Serrones wouldn't hardwire one combot to be a liar and another to be brutally honest. They developed their own personalities over time." Nicholas nearly had me convinced that Bar might have lied to protect Tully, until he retreated once again.

"Yeah, but we have to assume that the Serrones programmed them with safeguards."

"Okay..."

"Then again, we should consider that the combots were designed and implemented in the context of a major war. It's possible that their designers failed to consider, or even ignored, the long-term implications of A.I. They were working under stressful conditions and time-sensitive constraints."

"You're killing me, man."

Nicholas suggested that we change the subject. "I've come up with a few constellations. Wanna see them?" He proceeded to identify some of his astrological creations through a break in the tree line while I remained fixated on the previous topic.

"Do you think they like each other?" I asked.

"Who?"

"Dee and Bar."

"I think it's a bit of a stretch to think that they're capable of liking or disliking something," said Nicholas. "That would be far more complicated than programming a bias toward soldier loyalty." He rubbed his chin. "But then again…"

"Ugh. Just show me the constellations, Nick."

I woke the next morning feeling no closer to a decision regarding

Jessie. Nicholas, Pablo, and I ate our morning rations under the shade of a large canopy tree, perched on its large roots that dove in and out of the ground like giant worms. We curiously watched the villagers suck nourishment through straws protruding from silver cannisters and speculated as to the contents. They slowly rallied and we hit the trail in the hopes of reaching our destination by the end of the day.

It was one of those odd days that never amounted to anything brighter than twilight, due to the positions of the parent planet and its star. This would prove to be a stroke of good fortune a few hours later when Mik suddenly froze in his tracks at the head of our caravan. He extended his hand high in the air, immediately causing us to halt and remain silent. The villagers followed our lead—this was obviously not their first time in a tense situation. Mik fixed his eyes on something ahead and signaled for us to get down by slowly lowering his hand to the ground. So, we lay on our stomachs and waited. The sound of vehicles arose faintly from the right and increased in volume as it moved past us then faded to the left. Mik waited for another minute before rising and waving us forward. We stopped at the road that the convoy had just traversed, leaving the villagers at a safe distance behind us.

"Who was that?" Nicholas asked Mik.

"I do not know."

"I guess we should get everybody across the road as quickly as possible and hurry to the rendezvous point… right?" suggested Nicholas.

"We are at the point of rendezvous," replied Mik. He moved a few paces away and began to operate his communication device, while we contemplated the possibility of additional hostile convoys rolling by. Mik returned with new orders.

"We will move backward to a new point of rendezvous," he told us. "The PRF will dispatch air transports." We reassembled the caravan facing in the opposite direction and hurried off as quickly as the Serrones could manage. After covering about a thousand yards, Mik halted us in a large clearing and instructed everyone to find cover in the nearby tree line. It felt like we had some time to kill, and I had an idea.

"Come with me," I said to Nicholas. "I want to try something." I walked over to where Mik stood. I can't say why I felt so emboldened. Perhaps I felt a hint of liberation from being in the wilderness, free of sentroids for the first time in months, watched over by a mechanic-turned-sergeant android, and surrounded by timid alien beings who feared I might savagely attack them. It's not that I was considering any kind of rash, rebellious action—not by any stretch. I had something more philosophical in mind.

"Hey Mik, can I ask you a question?"

"Yes."

"Do you like me?" Nicholas initially looked at me in disbelief. His countenance soon transformed into something akin to "let's see where this is going..."

"That is not applicable," responded Mik.

"Do you understand the question?" I asked.

"Yes."

"Do you understand what it means to *like* someone?"

"Yes." Mik seemed willing to indulge me for the moment so I pressed on.

"Are you *capable* of liking someone?"

"That is not applicable," repeated Mik. Nicholas put his hand in front of me, asking me to allow him to try a different approach.

"Mik, if Shakespeare... do you know who Shakespeare is?" he asked.

"This," Mik replied, pointing at me.

"Right," continued Nicholas, "If Shakespeare and I were in danger of being killed by rebels, would you save us?"

"Yes. It is my duty to protect soldiers and property of the People's Resistance Front."

"Good. Now, what if you only had time to save one of us?" Nicholas spoke slowly and deliberately, as if addressing a five-year-old child. "What I mean is, suppose you could only save one of us from the rebels and the other would perish. What would you do?"

Mik replied without hesitation, "In this scenario, please indicate which of you is in better physical health?" Now Mik was asking the questions and running through an endless if-then-else sequence of logic. We spent five minutes neutralizing the conditions that might otherwise influence his decision (who was closer, who was younger, who was the better soldier, etc.).

Mik finally conceded. "As you are both property of the People's Resistance Front and of equal value, my decision would be random." And with that, we were back to square one.

"Mik, would you bear false witness in order to protect a soldier?"

Nicholas asked.

"I don't think Mik has read the Bible," I said to Nicholas. "Mik, would you *lie* to protect the life of a soldier?" Mik had no reaction. "Do you understand the question?" I asked.

"Please clarify," requested the android.

I had a pretty good feel for Mik's vernacular by now, so I laid it out like this: "Consider this scenario. You have been captured by rebels. You know that Dee is in a room next to you hiding from the same rebels. Now, one of the rebels says to you, 'Mik'—let's assume he knows your name—'Mik, we will kill Dee if we find him. Is Dee in that room? If you tell us he is not, then we will not look inside the room.' Would you respond 'yes' or 'no' to the rebel?" I took a deep breath and waited for his response.

"No," said Mik.

"Do you mean that you would say 'no' in reply to the rebel?"

"Yes."

"There you have it," I said to Nicholas. "Thanks, Mik." Nicholas and I retired to the shade of a nearby tree to review the results of our experiment.

"I don't know," he said. "We might be comparing apples to oranges here. I doubt that Bar felt as though Tully's life was in danger back in the village."

"Maybe, maybe not, but he had to be aware of the tension between Jessie and Tully—Dee was aware of it. For that matter, Bar must be aware of the tension between me and Tully as well, and Charles too. He might have perceived a threat."

"But why would Bar take Tully's side?" asked Nicholas.

"Maybe it wasn't about taking sides. Ammo was already dead—he couldn't be saved. At that point, Bar had two choices. One, he can throw Tully under the bus. The result being that a fellow soldier—Tully—might be in danger of retribution at the hands of Jessie and her allies. Two, he can choose to lie and confirm Tully's story, in which case no soldier is in danger."

"And that could explain why he lied for Tully," said Nicholas, "but that means that he's only thinking one or two moves ahead. He didn't consider that we might assume he was lying and tell Jessie… Or maybe he's programmed to address the most imminent threat."

"Or maybe he's just a rotten son-of-a-bitch. Either way, Tully murdered Ammo. You saw what you saw, right?"

"I saw what I saw," conceded Nicholas. "Ammo was very much alive when I left."

"When Tully *told* you to leave."

"Correct."

Our deliberation was interrupted by a low rumbling noise. We looked up to see two aircraft hovering above the clearing. They were rectangular in shape, each about the size of a school bus and remarkably quiet. They reminded me of the spaceship that brought me to Serrone in that they shared a similar dilapidated exterior and were in desperate need of a paint job. Each descended to a position about four feet from the ground and held steady. Almost in unison, large cargo doors opened from the rear of each ship and settled into the ground, forming a ramp. I peered into the exposed holds and found them to be completely empty except for a combot standing at the top of each ramp. Mik signaled for the villagers to board the ships but they had already awakened from their naps and were heading up the ramps. We handed the backpacks up to the combots and backed off.

As we watched the ships disappear, Pablo turned to me and said, "They could have offered us a lift."

"What now?" I asked to no one in particular.

"We return to camp on foot," said Mik. If it was true that combots harbored the ability to develop personalities, Mik hadn't gotten the memo.

17

I made it back to the compound in one piece and found it to be more or less as I had left it a few days earlier. The barracks were filled with soldiers doing nothing out of the ordinary—just doing it a little quieter than usual. After checking in with my friends I headed to my bunk in the hopes of catching up on some much-needed sleep. I passed Jessie, where she lay on her bed with her fingers interlocked behind her head, staring at the bunk above her. I said nothing out of respect for her unspoken, yet unmistakable desire to be left alone.

I had not yet resolved the question of what action I should undertake, if any, with respect to Ammo. Nor would this have been the appropriate time to execute such an action. Two of the three people in whom I trusted to advise me on the matter had already weighed in. Charles was adamant in his opinion that we shouldn't stir the pot, saying that "no good can come from it." Nicholas had provided a plethora of arguments. They amounted to no practical recommendation in either direction after factoring out the pros and cons that nullified each other. And so, the matter was left up to my personal attorney, in whose counsel I placed the greatest trust anyway, and whose judgement could have trumped a unanimous opinion from the other two, if such a thing had existed.

That night, Leesheh and I absconded the barracks and snuck off to a secluded spot in a nearby thicket, as had become our routine of late. We had grown fond of a round stumpy plant with large oval leaves that were the color of eggplant. It was completely encircled by a cluster of thick, thorny bushes, as if it had its own army of sentroids protecting it. To say that we snuck is a bit hyperbolic. Our forays into the brush would have been impossible to pull off without the combots' awareness, and they paid no attention. (Nor were we the only couple rumored to engage in such trysts.) We were always mindful to stay within the close vicinity of the barracks. Sentroids rarely entered that area except for special circumstances, such as our first night in the camp. It was usually warm enough to spend the entire night outside of the hut. We had discovered a stockpile of threadbare blankets in a storage shack and hoarded a few extra.

As we lay beside each other under the canopy of the stumpy plant, I brought her up to speed on my adventures with the escort mission, recounting the experiment with Mik down to the last detail.

"Are you *sure* that's what he meant? He said he would tell a lie?" she asked dubiously. I made a wisecrack about Mik not being related to George Washington—momentarily forgetting that she was from Curacao—then assured her that there was no doubt about Mik's response. We segued into the real issue at hand: Ammo. Leesheh broke it down as if she were making opening remarks to a jury. Her accent made it sound all the more eloquent.

"It is an uncontested fact that Tully *killed* Ammo. It was *asserted*, by Tully, that Ammo was *not* going to survive his wounds, and that he killed him out of mercy. Bar *confirmed* this assertion. Nicholas *believes* that Ammo would not have died," she stated.

"Correct, he–"

"Ta-ta. You must wait sir—I am not yet finished," she added with a playful smile and a finger in my face. "We cannot prove anything. The only fact we have—by his own admission—is that Tully *killed* Ammo. The rest is speculative, although there appears to be reasonable evidence to support a case for murder."

"Exactly, and beyond a reasonable a doubt, in my opinion."

"Ah, but you see, my handsome friend, this is where you are going astray. *Your* opinion is irrelevant. What *you* must decide is whether you should present this evidence to Jessie. It is *her* opinion that matters." I found her command of the English language irresistible.

"Sure."

"And," she continued, "You must consider the consequences of presenting this evidence to Jessie."

"Right. That's where I need your help."

"Have I not been helping thus far, my handsome friend?" Her smile turned into a faux frown.

"Honestly? Not exactly. I need you to convince me whether or not I should tell Jessie.

"No problem. I will convince you to take the correct action." I looked at her eagerly. She stared back at me.

"Well?" I asked.

"Well what?"

"I thought you were you going to tell me what I should do."

"No," she clarified, "I *said* that I would convince you to take the correct action. First, you must tell me what action it is that you wish to take. Then I will convince you that it is the correct action."

"You're gonna make a good lawyer."

"Thank you." With that, I received a kiss but was no further along with respect to my dilemma.

"I'm going to tell her," I announced. "She can do whatever she wants with the information, but I'm going to tell her what Nicholas saw."

"Okay. Do I need to convince you?"

"No."

Feeling better for having made up my mind, I contemplated the best time to speak with Jessie. With respect to that, my attorney strongly advised that I wait for a while. She also added that I was still at liberty to change my mind, leading me to wonder if I had made the right decision.

Two weeks passed before a small group of PRF soldiers—not part of our company—rolled into camp crammed into a single flatbed. They numbered nine men and women, several of whom were nursing wounds. We hurried out to help them and carried the more seriously wounded into our recently christened infirmary to be examined by Charles.

Charles had gradually taken over as the company's de facto medic. The combots were capable of providing first aid, but we humans preferred Charles' bedside manner and the combots made no issue of it. We asked Cap if we could convert part of a storage building into an infirmary. Cap relayed our petition to Khan, who subsequently obtained the green light from the Chief. As you might expect, medical supplies were limited. Shipments from the city were rare, so most of our supplies were confiscated from dead rebels. Charles consolidated what we had collected into a single box that was kept inside the infirmary. We set up a couple of beds and he was in business. Charles allotted himself the perk of spending most nights in his infirmary, and as it was near the barracks, the combots had no objections, and the sentroids seemed unaware.

A few minutes after the wounded soldiers arrived, Khan and Kaiser appeared and escorted two of the healthier soldiers over to the Chief's hut. We sought our own briefing from those who remained in our care. In between mouthfuls of mushy cereal, they told us that they had been dispatched from the city to establish a new PRF camp near the village that we had recently liberated. Their group was small in number, as they were not expecting to encounter resistance. Instead, they were caught off guard by a sizeable rebel force that had moved back into the village. The rebels had nearly wiped out the entire squad of thirty soldiers, and surely would have, had it not been for the heroic actions of two combots. The combots, presumed to have been killed, held off the attackers long enough for the single vehicle to escape.

We were placed on high alert in case the retreating soldiers had been followed to our camp. Small scout teams were dispatched to patrol an extended perimeter during the night. They returned the next morning and reported having seen no evidence of rebel activity. To nobody's surprise, word soon came down from the Chief that we would be returning to the village, though not until reinforcements from another camp joined us. The unfortunate survivors of the attack were denied a return to the city and ordered to participate in the counter operation.

PRF troops began to arrive the next day and set up tents in the barracks courtyard. Most were human but there were androids and Serrones in the mix as well. I witnessed more than a few nostalgic reunions as the old-timers searched for friends among the newcomers, though nobody found much cause for celebration.

In the early afternoon, the rumor of a strange arrival proliferated through the barracks and we hurried out into the courtyard to find the source of the fuss. Strapped to the back of a flatbed truck was a large cage with vertical bars, not unlike one you might have found in a zoo a hundred years ago—before they became "zoological parks." The truck was bigger than anything we had in camp and the cage still extended a few feet beyond its sides and the rear. A large crane was attached to the top of the truck's cab. An unassuming little android, no larger than its Serrone creators, was busy attaching a hook from the crane to the top of the cage. I got close enough to see the contents of the cage as it was being hoisted from the truck bed. I cannot say that I was astonished in the least. After the events of the past few months, it would have taken much more than what I saw in that cage to shock me. Dumbfounded or bewildered might be more accurate descriptions of my reaction. Malcolm and Swag walked up and stood nearby.

"Jesus, Mister Swag," Malcolm said, "did ya ever think we'd see any of those fellas again?"

"Figured they were all dead by now," replied Swag. "Hold on—I think one of 'em's a female, Malc." He squinted for a better view. "Look—that one there."

"First of all, how can you tell, and second of all, what does it matter?" asked Malcolm.

"I dunno, mate. I just never saw a female before."

A few of us took the liberty of inserting ourselves into the old timers' conversation.

"What am I looking at, Swag?" I asked. What I was looking at were four *beasts*. That was the only word that came to mind in that moment. They had the size and musculature of large gorillas (and I'm referring to the big eastern lowland gorillas—not the mountain variety). Despite their giant size, they looked more human than ape. If someone had told me that they were representatives of a recently-discovered branch of the primate tree, it would have made perfect sense—Homo-Something-or-Other. Their large upper canine teeth indicated that meat was part of their diet and it wasn't a stretch to presume that humans might be viewed as a tasty meal. Their bodies were nearly covered with copper-colored hair and they wore loose frocks as well. It was unclear whether the clothing was their own preference or something akin to putting a sweater on a poodle. They wore boots like my own except for being thirty sizes larger, and they walked more-or-less upright within them. The most chilling aspect of this encounter was that the creatures were clearly agitated.

"Those, my friends, are what we call orcos," Swag told us, then added with a laugh, "but don't worry none, 'cause they're on our side."

"Used to be hundreds of 'em back during the big war," added Malcom. "The Serrones found 'em on some planet somewhere, and some nitwit thought it'd be a good idea to make fighters out of 'em."

"Well, they do look like they can fight," said Susan.

"Fightin's not the issue," continued Malcolm. "Gettin' them to *stop* fightin'—now that's the problem."

"And gettin' them to fight the *enemy*—that's a bit of a challenge too," added Swag. "Most of 'em ended up dead on the battlefield, but not before takin' out lots of poor ole chaps from the other side, and a few of our own. They're like tanks. They absorb a lot of damage before they eventually get taken down."

"Are they intelligent creatures?" asked Nicholas.

"Intelligence is a relative term, Nick," said Malcolm. "I'd put 'em somewhere in between a chimpanzee and the dumbest person you've ever known. They've got their own language—basic words and such, and they can be trained to a degree—but it's kinda like herding cats."

Swag pointed to the meek android who was climbing down from the top of the cage, which now rested in the courtyard. "That little robot there keeps 'em in line," he told us. "Used to be a lot more of those little guys runnin' around. I 'spose they don't have a high survival rate."

"Anyway," said Malcolm, "it looks like the General got his hands on a few and he's hopin' to turn 'em loose on that village. I'd stay clear of 'em if I were you."

"You don't have to tell me twice," I said.

"However," said Jessie, who had just joined us, "they can provide good cover. Stay right on one's heels and pray that he doesn't turn on you." I wasn't sure if she was joking.

As we watched the little android do his job, the old-timers proceeded to regale us with anecdotes of their experiences fighting alongside, and often running from, orcos in battles of long ago. The stories had obviously skewed in a humorous direction over the years. I suspect they weren't so funny at the time. The beasts were frightfully intimidating, which I suppose was the intent—the General's weapons of terror. At one point the android keeper opened the door to the cage, causing the entire crowd to gasp and take a few collective steps backward. All eyes were glued on the little robot inside the cage mingling among the beasts with the cool demeanor of a lion tamer. We were in awe of his courage, forgetting that he was merely a machine.

"The circus is in town," said Susan.

The increasing number of soldiers and other creatures in camp did little to relieve the tension spurred by the looming battle. (Perhaps the presence of the orcos helped a *little.*) We might have had superior numbers, but we certainly wouldn't have the advantage of surprise this time. Dee told us that we were going to hit the road in the morning, so I resolved to get as much sleep as possible. With all of the added commotion in camp, there was little chance of stealing away with

Leesheh for the night, and the thought hadn't even crossed my mind. I was about to climb up to my bunk when she tapped me on the shoulder.

"Can we go outside?" she asked quietly.

"I don't think we can find a good spot tonight, Lees." Absent was her usual effervescence, which I attributed to apprehension about the upcoming battle.

"No, I just want to talk to you for a few minutes."

"Sure."

We found a large tree near the infirmary and concealed ourselves from the crowd as best we could. She immediately embraced me.

"What's up?" I asked. "Is this about tomorrow?"

"Sort of. I was going to wait until I was absolutely certain, but with everything else going on now…"

"Okay, what is it?" She looked terrified.

"I'm pregnant."

There are those moments in life, perhaps not too uncommon, when your ongoing list of problems, priorities, and stresses that you mentally perpetuate and prioritize is suddenly altered for the worse. A new problem, priority, or stress that was completely unexpected and absent from your radar not five minutes earlier, has revealed itself and usurped the top position of your mental inventory. Worse still, the new issue is not so calamitous that it renders the previous holder of the top position and its subordinates trivial. No, the new problem only adds to the cumulative stress and frustration such that you think to yourself, "five minutes ago I didn't even know that this problem existed. Now it's my number one headache, and I still have to deal with all of the other crap in my life." Examples might be a homework assignment that had slipped your mind; a hard drive crash; a fender-bender; a letter from the IRS rejecting your tax return; leaving your phone in a rideshare car; or maybe you wake up in the woods one morning on an alien planet to find a poisonous, half-lizard, half-scorpion creature about to bite your nose.

Then there are those rare moments where your life is completely turned upside down, to the extent that the life you led before that moment can never return. Your future is completely redefined, and solely redefined, by this new problem. Your previous mental inventory of issues is suddenly obsolete—you cannot even recall the items that were on it. Examples might be the death of a loved one; a house fire; losing your job; losing half of your savings in a stock market crash; or learning that your girlfriend is pregnant on the eve of a battle in an alien world in which you are both enslaved soldiers, and in which children are whisked away from their parents to a remote alien city—never to be seen again.

It would be dishonest for me to write that I was not tempted to bend the truth in this narrative when describing my reaction to what Leesheh told me. It would have been easy to write that I assuaged my frightened companion with sage advice and encouragement, or that I gently wiped the tear from her cheek and told her that everything would be okay. In truth, I did nothing. I said nothing. I froze.

"What should we do?" she asked.

"You're sure?" I was probably stalling subconsciously.

"No, I told you that I was not certain."

"But probably… like ninety percent?"

"Yes."

In the span of this brief exchange I had regained my wits to the extent that I recognized that the best action—the only thing I was capable of at the time—was to make Leesheh feel confident in me. I thought it might also buy me some time to come up with a better solution. I placed my hands on her shoulders and put on my game face.

"We'll figure this out, okay? Maybe not tonight, but we *will* figure it out—together."

"Of course," she said with confidence. "Let's get through the next few days first." In that moment I realized that I probably needed her support more than she needed mine. She was mentally tougher than I was, and I wasn't ashamed to admit it.

A few hours later, I lay wide awake in my bunk pondering whether I was the only person ever in the world—any world—to be in this exact predicament (alien abduction, soldier, war, child—the whole nine yards). Of course, I wasn't. I only had to look to my right to find someone in a bigger mess. *She's* the pregnant one. *Wait—is she actually sleeping over there? Her eyes are closed...*

Then, for the first time since I heard the news, the slightest tinge of pride, the smallest hint of joy dashed through me. I permitted myself to consider the notion of being a father again. In other circumstances there would have been nothing greater than to have a child with this young woman for whom I had grown to care so deeply. In other circumstances, simply stating "in other circumstances" might have been sufficient enough to describe the predicament. But our dilemma was of other-worldly proportions. (I call your attention to the cage full of giant beasts that sat not forty yards from my hut.) I had no time to dwell on what delights "other circumstances" might have yielded. I tossed and turned, making no progress in thought, until the first glimmers of light from Wiyanga penetrated the barracks, hopefully bringing a fresh perspective with them.

18

The commotion in the courtyard just after dawn could have roused Rip Van Winkle, and being already awake, I was one of the first onlookers to the scene. It came as no wonder to find that the orco cage was at the center of the controversy. The little android and a man were fastidiously attending to another man who lay motionless near the cage. One of the orcos was monitoring the situation carefully with his head protruding from the cage as far as the thick metal bars would allow. The other three giants seemed content to eat from the trough of food at the other end of the enclosure, as if a solid wall existed between them and the disturbance.

I approached the men and the android, taking great care not to venture too close to the cage, having surmised that the large orco was likely responsible for the poor soul lying nearby, who was unmistakably dead. I didn't need Charles to tell me that his neck was broken. If the irregular angle of his spine just below his skull was not convincing, the purplish discoloring surrounding his neck cinched it. Both the victim and the man attending to him were new arrivals to the camp.

"He wanted to get a closer look at these things," his friend announced to the approaching bystanders. "I warned him not to get too close."

"It just killed him for no reason?" I asked of the android. The friend responded instead.

"Well, there was a wango on the floor of the cage. I think he intended to pick it up and feed it to the orco. The orco must have thought he was taking it from him." (A wango is an indigenous fruit named by one of the earliest slaves who felt that it tasted like a cross between a watermelon and a mango.)

"I left for only a moment," the little android interjected, as if to absolve himself. "Soldiers are not permitted to approach these beings unless instructed to do so, and only in my presence."

His advice was a little late for the guy lying in the dirt. By then a larger crowd had gathered. One of the sentroids that had recently arrived in camp pushed through the mass of soldiers and carried the body away. The crowd lingered for a short while as the conversation slowly transitioned to the subject of breakfast, at which time we set off in search of something to eat. There were no further breaches of the little android's rules.

Soon after everyone was fed, we gathered in the courtyard and proceeded to gear-up. Sentroids distributed strips of red cloth that we were to tie on our arms, to include the combots. I figured this was necessary given the number of our troops involved in the operation, which I estimated to exceed four hundred. The humans in our army represented several different races, as did the rebels. It would have been difficult to distinguish our guys from the bad guys. Swag said something about the armbands also being used to help the orcos recognize friend and foe. In light of that information, I asked Leesheh to make sure that mine was tightly secured to my arm.

While the orco cage was being hoisted back onto the large truck we piled into the flatbeds and jeeps. I climbed into the back of a truck that included my immediate friends, where we avowed to stay together, as much as possible, in the battle. Our convoy stretched for a quarter mile and included smaller, one- and two-person vehicles operated by combots in addition to the jeeps and flatbeds. I was grateful that the orcos were riding on a truck to the rear of mine, lest the slight chance of the cage door malfunctioning. We rode for hours, taking only one break for "biological needs" as the combots called them. There wasn't the slightest effort made for a stealthy approach as we neared the village. The rebel army knew we were coming and we knew exactly where they were.

I didn't know who was is in charge of the operation—the Chief or one of the Serrone officers who had recently arrived—but the strategy, which was only revealed to us as it unfolded, was simple. We slammed into the enemy almost immediately upon arriving. We had them outnumbered, probably three to one, and outgunned with superior weaponry. They had the advantage of barricades, buildings, rooftops, and other fortifications constructed from the tons of scrap material that had accumulated in the bombed-out village. Perhaps we had one element of surprise, that being the sheer stupidity or strategic genius of attacking right away, instead of spending a day or two (or even an hour) making preparations outside of the village.

The convoy came to an abrupt halt in a field where I could see the tops of buildings about a half-mile away, and the chaos ensued. We swiftly evacuated our flatbed and assembled around Dee, along with our squad mates. Dee spent a few seconds taking an inventory of his team then led us toward the village in double time, after saying nothing more than "follow me." The army split evenly in two, with a small garrison left behind to guard the Chief, the other Serrone officers, and the vehicles. We were part of a group that headed for the high ground on the eastern side of the village. About halfway across the field, the large truck carrying the orco cage overtook us at full speed. We had to scramble out of its path while maintaining our pace. I spotted the little android riding shotgun in the cab as it passed by.

We started taking fire from rooftop snipers as we reached the far edge of the field. The only option was to keep running. I was doing my best to keep one eye on Dee and the other on Leesheh, who was keeping up just fine. In fact, I was probably slowing her down a little. We circled around a wooded hill that provided natural cover from the snipers where we were able to catch our breath. I watched on one knee as the little android expeditiously opened the door to the orco cage. I readied my arc rifle in case one of the beasts had forgotten what the red armbands meant during the long ride over from camp. The orcos were in an absolute frenzy and undoubtedly under the influence of catnip or some other stimulant tailored for their physiology. They either didn't know or didn't care that they were on a suicide mission.

A small cheer arose when four of the egg-shaped drones passed overhead on their way to the village. This was twice the number that were employed in the last battle, and to our dismay, they stayed only half as long, before scooting off into safer skies beyond the horizon.

We received our first instructions during the brief respite behind the hill. Dee told us that we would follow the orcos down the east road to the village as part of an overwhelming thrust. We were to wait thirty seconds after the orcos were released before making our charge. (The combots had learned the concept of a "second" from humans. None of us wore watches—they expected us to count off in our heads.) We were told to fan out along the base of the hill, from which we would ascend in a large wave. Our commanders obviously felt that the rebels couldn't stop all of us, and Pickett's charge came to mind. All of this was being coordinated with a simultaneous, orco-less attack from the west.

The armbands seemed to do the trick, for the four beasts ignored us as they barreled over the hill, causing the ground to rumble at our feet. The next thirty seconds were filled with the sounds of gunfire whooshing, metal crashing, bones cracking, and people shouting. Then it was time for us to attack. I looked at Leesheh. She nodded back an affirmation and we ran up and over the hill with our comrades.

I had become a different person in the short time since I had last seen this village. The notion of becoming a father again had ignited a visceral spark within me. I wasn't ignorant of the challenge—the near impossibility—of keeping my family intact on this alien world. But I reckoned that I had a better chance of keeping my child safe if this so-called rebellion was quashed. At the moment, the rebels presented a major impediment to my child's future. Moreover, they would surely seize any opportunity to kill my unborn child's mother, the only person in this world whom I loved.

Some men in my situation might become more reticent and risk-averse when given these reasons to live. They might hesitate or hang back in combat, unwittingly putting their comrades at greater risk. Quite the opposite happened to me. I felt energized and empowered to create a better world for my burgeoning family. I wasn't fighting for the General, the Chief, or any other Serrone. I was fighting for my comrades and my family, which at this moment were one and the same. I doubt that this feeling was unique to me. It has probably motivated soldiers since the earliest days of war—in any civilization on any planet.

I ran to the crest of the hill and saw the plasma-riddled corpse of one orco lying in the road about a hundred feet ahead. It had apparently taken the brunt of the rebel fire while the other three advanced. They could be seen in the distance wreaking havoc amidst a cloud of dust. The surviving orcos had pushed back the first line of rebel defense such that we took little fire as we descended the west slope of the hill. As I ran forward, I fired off a few rounds from my waist aimed to suppress the soldiers on the rooftops ahead.

Within seconds we had reached the first rebel barricade at the cost of only a few casualties. One of those was the second orco, whose body was slumped over the makeshift barricade of stone, scrap wood, and vehicle parts. Rebel bodies were strewn about both sides of it. We took positions on our side of the barrier and began firing at targets deeper within the village. Leesheh was crouching beside me and discharging her weapon as if she had been born with it in her hands. I could see the remaining two orcos not far ahead tossing aside anything in their path—humans, androids, small vehicles, etc.—and absorbing heavy fire.

I was thinking that we should make our next move while the beasts were still providing a rampageous diversion. Cap must have agreed, for he soon traversed the barricade followed by the entire company. By this time, I had fully bought into the "best defense is a good offense" strategy that our leaders had implemented. I was also motivated to keep Leesheh behind me, and she appeared to be hell-bent on staying at the front of the assault. In retrospect, I might have acted a little recklessly at this stage of the battle. The constant motion probably kept me alive. In front of me stood a stone wall that was just large enough to prevent me from seeing what lay directly behind it. I had no choice but to keep moving and jump on top of it. I would have been too exposed to remain in front of it. I leaped onto the wall and fired down on two rebel soldiers that were just beginning to make a hasty retreat. Susan appeared on my right and together we took the soldiers out.

The squad continued toward the village center at a rapid pace, leaving nothing alive in our wake. I passed the bodies of the last two orcos lying beside each other, finally subdued, yet not before having fulfilled their mission of raining havoc, terror, and confusion down upon the enemy. (Did they even know they had a mission or were they just pissed off?) We came to an area where several buildings remained intact, and we began to take fire from positions within. This forced us to slow down and scatter for cover. I began to focus my fire on the second story of a stone structure to my right, from which several rebels appeared to be operating. Someone on our side flung a grenade into a window on the first level of the building. After it exploded, I watched Dee hustle into the building followed by another soldier. The grenade had surely killed anyone on the first floor but I noticed that there was still a lot of activity on the second. It occurred to me that Dee might not be aware of the threat above him.

Without further thought and without saying anything to anyone near me, I bolted for the door. I burst into the room and nearly tripped over the body of the soldier that had followed Dee. Dee lay at the foot of a small staircase about six feet in front of me. His right leg was mangled, and he was using the steps for cover while firing toward the landing above. I had a clear shot at the closest enemy soldier who was engaged with Dee. I fired my arc and he fell backward. Capitalizing on my momentum, I stepped over Dee and bounded up the steps in the hope of catching any remaining soldiers off guard. I reached the landing and came upon one soldier still alive. He was standing just a few feet in front of me and desperately shoving a fresh plasma cartridge into his arc rifle. I pointed my rifle and fired. Nothing happened. Our eyes met for an instant, both of us knowing that my arc rifle was empty. I had neglected to reload it before storming the building—a rookie mistake that could prove fatal.

Seizing his new lease on life, the rebel stepped backward and started to lift his weapon, but I didn't give him the chance to use it. I barreled into him and smashed his body against the back wall. The impact caused him to drop his weapon, so he started pounding me with his fists. I grabbed the barrel of my rifle at both ends and managed to shove it under his chin. I was much stronger than this man, and I felt his resistance weaken as the life was choked from him. Our eyes met once again, only inches apart. This time we both knew that he was about to die. He was a young man with a boyish face and could have just as easily been a student of mine many years earlier. That made no impression on me. I was gratified that he was dead.

As he slid lifelessly down the wall, I drew my first complete breath since climbing the stairs. An intense stinging pain suddenly engulfed my thigh and quickly shot up my spine. I fell to the floor in agony. Spinning onto my back, I found a rebel soldier crawling toward me. He didn't appear to have much use of his legs. *Where did this guy come from?* He must have been wounded in the initial explosion. The man ripped the knife from my leg, redoubling my pain, and raised it above my chest. I was somehow able to grab his arm and momentarily arrest his forward thrust. We remained in a stalemate for a few seconds before he was knocked backward by the impact of a plasma bullet that sheared off half of his face. At the top of the landing stood Leesheh with her rifle extended. She came into the room, followed by Susan, Jessie, and Charles.

"Thanks," I said to Leesheh as she knelt down beside me.

"Are you okay?" she asked.

"Not exactly. Doc, I'm gonna need you to look at this."

Charles did what he could to stem the bleeding from my thigh, which was essentially to apply pressure and wrap a tourniquet above the wound. He placed a stick inside the tourniquet.

"Keep pressure on the wound and turn this stick to tighten the tourniquet," he advised. "I think you were lucky today, Shakespeare. It appears to have missed your femoral. Can you walk?"

"Yeah—I think so."

Charles and Leesheh helped me to my feet while Jessie and Susan stood guard. Jessie walked over to a window and carefully peeked outside.

"This area looks clear now," she said. "Let's get outta here. We need to catch up to the squad."

"Hold on a second," I told them. I pointed down to the bloody knife that lay on the floor. "Can you grab that for me, Doc?" Charles handed me the knife. I figured that I'd earned the right to carry one. Susan removed the belt and sheath from my dead assailant's waist.

"You're gonna need these too, tough guy," she said as she held them out to me.

I came downstairs to find that Dee was no longer there, so I asked a soldier about his status. All he could tell me was that Dee had been carried out. I could have probably fought on if needed, but by the time we caught up to the squad, the rout was all but over. Just as the previous battle had ended, the village square was riddled with bodies—this time on a much larger scale.

Jessie and Leesheh walked me over to an area where the wounded were being collected and helped me to sit down with my back against a tree. This was my first experience as a wounded soldier in the People's Resistance Front and it definitely lived down to my expectations. My old combot friend Mik was performing triage and providing whatever aid he could with the help of a medical field kit that had been recycled from the Great War, though hardly replenished.

"Do you still like me, Mik?" I asked as he looked at my leg. He said nothing. "That's okay, Mik. You can get back to me on that." Charles came by and removed the tourniquet while assuring me that I didn't need it. He replaced my bandage with a clean one from Mik's medical kit, but not before dabbing my wound with a liquid from a bottle he found inside the box.

"I will be honest with you, Shakespeare," he said with a smile. "I do not know what this stuff is, but it smells like a disinfectant." When I gave him a worrisome look, he added, "I'm just yanking your chain, man. I am *almost* certain that this is a disinfectant." He seemed exceptionally proud of having incorporated American slang into his wisecrack.

Having been excused from the cleanup detail, I sat under the shade of my tree and observed the process. It amounted to little more than stacking up dead bodies and burning them. There were no villagers to liberate this time, and the village itself was in complete shambles. There was little risk of it becoming occupied again. I didn't know the exact figures of the battle. I saw very few prisoners and what must have been more than a hundred dead enemy bodies. Twenty-one of our PRF soldiers had been killed, and I watched as their bodies were laid in a row at the edge of the square. I was saddened to see that my old friend from the cargo hold, Mario the drummer, was among them. That number also included the four orcos. Their bodies were considered too heavy to move, and were thus left to the natural scavengers of the Serrone ecosystem. Two more of our soldiers would succumb to their wounds before we left the village.

The transport vehicles rolled into the village square just before dusk. The Chief delivered a short speech through the voice of Khan, telling us what a great victory this was for the PRF and that our efforts would not go unrewarded. We already knew that this reward would amount to nothing more than a few days of recuperation supplemented with extra catnip and hooch. I had no interest in a celebration, as it could do nothing to advance my cause.

As I waited to be helped aboard a flatbed, I caught sight of Tully climbing into the truck in front of mine. The hair on the back of his neck must have tingled, for he suddenly turned and looked down at me from his flatbed. We looked at each other for a moment, both of us devoid of expression, as if waiting for the other to make the first move. The moment passed as it had begun, and we carried on with our respective tasks. I had not seen as much of Sparks and Tully around the compound since they had decided to take up residence in another hut. I was sleeping a little more soundly as a result—perhaps they were too.

We reached camp late into the night and I limped to the barracks with Leesheh's help. I was a little startled to find the mangled remains of an enemy combot lying just inside the door of my hut. Cap was on his knees studying it while Dee looked on from his chair nearby. His right leg was now missing completely.

"Shakespeare," Dee said softly as Leesheh and I passed his chair, "the knife." He extended his hand. I removed the sheath containing the knife from my belt and handed it to him. He removed the knife from the sheath, inspected it for a moment then pointed it toward my leg. "Did you kill the man who did that?"

"No, she did," I responded. He replaced the knife in the sheath and handed it back to me.

"Good," he said. I figured that was his way of telling me that I would be allowed to keep the knife. Maybe there was a combot "thank you" hidden in there as well. I was curious about his leg but decided not to pursue the subject. As usual, Swag was eager to explain.

"That rebel combot's pretty beat up, but his leg'll do just fine, I reckon," he said to us when we passed his bunk. "You'll see. Cap'll have ole Dee fixed up by mornin'." Right on cue, Cap lifted up the mangled android remains and carried them out of the hut. Dee followed him out with the help of Malcolm. The soldiers in the barracks were interested in hearing my story, but I was so exhausted that even I was at a loss for words, and it would have to wait until the morning. Charles switched beds with me so that I wouldn't have to climb up to the top bunk. The raucous sounds of soldiers celebrating their survival permeated the barracks long into the night, yet I slept like a baby, knife wound and all.

19

Just as Swag predicted, I came out to the courtyard with Nicholas the next morning and found Dee standing on a new leg—new to him, at least. Its deep blue color contrasted with his reddish right arm (also a replacement) and his light gray head and torso. He looked very patriotic. My own leg would continue to be a source of pain for several days. It felt no worse when I walked, so I did my best to go about my business, of which I had plenty.

Malcolm was with Dee, and I asked if I could speak with him later. Leesheh and I planned to break the news of her pregnancy to Malcolm first, then take it from there. We had resolved to focus on the things that were within our control and not agonize over the long term. The cliché sounded reassuring when proposed, but I found it impossible to implement given my vivid and disquieted imagination. I question whether this advice has ever proved successful. Tell someone not to think of a pink elephant and what will they immediately do?

Fortunately, I had agreed to help Nicholas with a relatively minor issue. That is, it seemed minor compared to my own problems. He was actually very agitated by it. It's funny how other people's problems do not seem so terrible to us. In addition to helping a friend, his dilemma offered me a problem that I could solve, which was a satisfaction that I needed. I mentioned earlier that Nicholas wore thick glasses. He was, in fact, extremely myopic—optically. Without proper correction, anything beyond ten feet was a complete blur to him. Unfortunately, his one and only pair of glasses was destroyed in the recent battle.

It might seem morbid to someone who has not walked in our boots, but an indispensable post-battle procedure was the inspection of enemy corpses in search of vital supplies. The obvious bounties were much-needed weapons, ammunition, and medical supplies, which grew scarcer by the week. Other knickknacks proved valuable on a more personal level, such as a homemade deck of cards, cigarettes, clothing (under and outerwear), boots, or a pair of eyeglasses. None of these were of any use to their former owners and would only go to waste if left behind. As luck would have it, Nicholas had acquired a pair of glasses during the previous day's post-battle search. The prescription of the lenses was at least in the ballpark of his own, but the frames were in disrepair.

Next to the motor pool in camp was the storeroom that we satirically called the "PX," which was short for Post Exchange. The PX was nothing more than a collection of the odds and ends that had been collected here and there, and were, as of yet, unwanted. The PX was periodically subjected to sentroid inspections, during which they removed items deemed unfit for human possession. Luckily, they recognized the value in their slave soldiers being able to see, and there was a ragtag collection of lenses and frames kept on a shelf inside the shack. Nicholas was perfectly capable of piecing together a functioning pair of glasses with the materials available in the PX, to include a roll of Serrone-variety adhesive tape donated by the combots. My job was to get him there without walking into a tree.

I don't include this episode in my narrative in order to highlight my altruism or justify the importance of functional eyewear. Our visit to the PX was significant because we encountered Jessie there, and it was then that I decided to confide in her what we knew about Ammo's death. I cannot say what inspired me to tell her in that moment. In spite of my previous resolution, I had continued to oscillate between telling her and letting it go, as Charles suggested. Perhaps Nicholas' presence bolstered my confidence, or the anticipation of my own child pushed me over the edge. For whatever reason, it squealed out of me inside the shack. I told her what Nicholas saw and heard, rather than ask Nicholas to describe the events himself. I could see some trepidation in his expression and sought to relieve him of any responsibility for repercussions that might arise from the disclosure. I did my best to present the facts and only the facts, as Leesheh might have done. Jessie asked for a few clarifications but made no sort of editorial comments or declarations. She thanked me for telling her and promptly exited the shack.

That afternoon, Leesheh and I apprised Malcolm of our situation. I felt like a high school kid breaking the news to his father that he had knocked up his girlfriend. Malcolm didn't say much. He advised that we would be better off keeping the secret to ourselves for as long as possible, then referred us to Dee. The three of us found Dee near the motor pool and told him the news. Leesheh and I had decided that it was safest for her to stay with the squad for as long as possible, versus moving to the nursery. That might seem counterintuitive on the surface—choosing to fight over staying with the women and children in the nursery. However, we felt that she would be safest in the company of me and our friends. Furthermore, the rebels appeared to be all but wiped out. We pitched our idea to Dee, then he laid it out for us.

"She can stay with the squad as long as she can fight effectively," he told us. "When she can longer support the squad, she will report to the nursery and receive new assignments."

I didn't like the sound of the last part. *New assignments? Wouldn't her assignment be to give birth?* I felt like saying, *You remember that I saved your life yesterday, right?* Instead, I asked him what happens after she gives birth.

"When she is fit for combat she may return."

"Will we have access to the baby?" asked Leesheh.

"You both have unlimited access to the nursery—while you are in camp," Dee replied. We thanked him for his time and started to walk away. "You are aware," he continued, "that the child will be transferred to the city when it is old enough?"

"What age is that?" Leesheh asked.

"Three or four seasons."

There was no point in asking Dee anything else. He probably knew little more than we did about the fates of PRF children, and if he had, he wouldn't have disclosed anything that was beyond our need to know. Leesheh and I walked back to the barracks by way of a detour that took us to the stream.

"That gives us roughly two years to figure something out," I told her. "Things could be very different by then."

"Different—yes. Better? Not likely," she said. "I will not abandon my child." I admired her determination and would have expected nothing less. I doubted that she was the first human expectant mother on Serrone to make that declaration only to see her child taken away. I kept that thought to myself.

"We'll take care of these rebels first, then see about dealing with

Abasha," I asserted—and I believed it too.

Our secret didn't last long. A few days later, Swag approached me inside the barracks.

"You couldn't leave well enough alone, eh mate?" My first thought was to find out who blabbed—Malcolm or Dee? I didn't figure Malcolm for a gossipmonger, but a combot? Maybe Dee had an obligation to report it. It wasn't as if we had asked him for discretion. We just assumed that he wouldn't tell anyone. It didn't really matter at this point.

"Yeah," was all I could muster in response—not that Swag was looking for an answer.

"It's tough. I don't 'ave to tell ya that this is not a good place to have a baby," he continued in an uncharacteristically somber tone. "I had a child once—a boy."

"You did?" By now anybody within earshot was aware of Leesheh's and my predicament. I looked around to see who might be eavesdropping.

"Yeah, back during the Great War," Swag reminisced. "Didn't know his mum too well—you know, one of those kinda things. Sentroids snatched him up right after he was born—only saw the boy once."

"You don't know what happened to him?"

"No idea, mate. He'd be old enough to fight b'now. Now there's a pickle, right? That I'd end up fightin' against my boy someday. Oh well, it's a big planet. Lots of little wars goin' on. Chances are we'll never run into each other. Thing is, neither of us would know it if we did."

"I guess there's a lot of people in that situation."

"Oh, I doubt it, mate. Most people from back then died a long time ago. The boy's probably gone by now." Swag suddenly reverted to his normal jovial demeanor and patted me on the back. "Anyhow, I'll be there to help out when the day comes. In the meantime, try not to knock anybody else up, mate." I thanked him sarcastically for his sound advice.

Within a day of my conversation with Swag, the entire company knew that Leesheh was pregnant. This wasn't considered big news among most of my comrades. Pregnancies were not uncommon, nor were they limited to the women in the cathouse. Her pregnancy quickly became second hand news in camp, though our friends struggled a little when it came to addressing the subject. Congratulations were not in order. What a difference a planet makes! News that would have prompted a celebration on Earth caused foreboding on Serrone. They wanted to support us but didn't know how. Awkward attempts at conversations ensued, in which I sometimes found myself consoling *them*. I was glad when they finally adjusted to the new normal.

By all appearances, Jessie had not taken the news I gave her concerning Ammo very well. She kept mostly to herself, avoiding conversation and providing terse answers when asked a question. Most of her comrades presumed that her demeanor was simply the manifestation of prolonged grief. Someone observed that "she had been doing so much better then suddenly reverted back," to which I said nothing. It was easy for me to recognize the mounting animosity between Tully's gang and Jessie, having been so well acquainted with the feeling myself.

I told Charles about my conversation with Jessie in the PX. This made him, Leesheh, and Nicholas the only people to know what I had told her. I expected some kind of admonishment from Charles. I should have known that "I told you so" wasn't his style.

"We will need to keep an eye on her," he said to me and Nicholas. We decided not to mention anything to Malcolm or anybody else, for fear that the information might find its way to Tully. We knew what he was capable of when threatened. Charles' words from that day in the village came to mind: *no good can come from it.* I wondered what I had expected to come from telling Jessie. I thought she had a right to know, but why? Was she planning to do anything about it? The answer to the last question revealed itself on the following day.

I cannot say what triggered Jessie at that particular time on that particular day. Maybe she just passed too closely to him on a path and couldn't allow him to walk by. All I know is that someone came running into the barracks shouting something about a confrontation near the latrines. We hurried to the scene where we found a small crowd encircling Jessie and Tully. Jessie appeared to be the aggressor. For every step forward she took, Tully eased backward. He extended his arms out sideward with his palms turned upward, flaunting an expression of confusion. To me he appeared to be overacting a bit, protesting too much, but I was biased by my assumption of his guilt. Their conversation was in progress when I arrived.

"Jessie, you are a crazy woman," Tully told her, as he scanned the crowd for support. "He was dying. I did what I was told."

"*Who* told you?" she asked, inching closer to him. Tully clearly did not want a public confrontation with Jessie, she being a favorite among the majority of soldiers in camp, and he being respected only within his circle of hoodlums. He had no valid answer for her and stretched his lie further.

"Bar checked Ammo. Bar agreed with me. Go talk to Bar." Tully counted on the unlikelihood of Jessie calling his bluff. He smiled and shook his head as if he was in complete disbelief. "Jessie, we know each other a long time. You and me are friends."

I looked around for Dee or Cap. There were no androids present, nor was Malcolm. *No good can come from it.* I decided to step in. I had no qualms about being identified as Jessie's source, and I couldn't risk Nicholas being exposed. If Jessie was her normal self, there would be no danger of that, but her agitation was likely clouding her judgement. I pushed myself between them and extended my arms like a high school gym teacher breaking up a locker room scuffle.

"Take it easy," I said. "Just step back." I looked at Jessie and shook my head as if to say "not here," or "not now." She was still fixated on her opponent.

"That's right, Shake-a-spear," said Tully. "Jessie crazy. She sick in the head today." He eagerly moved back a few steps and appealed to the crowd once again. I don't know why he thought I was coming to his aid. The gall of the notion pissed me off, and I moved toward him in a threatening manner. Sparks and a few other cohorts came to Tully's defense, while Jessie and others stepped up beside me. Just like that, I had unintentionally escalated the situation into another showdown between the two emerging factions, with myself and Tully in the lead roles once again. Unlike the standoff in the barracks, which now seemed so long ago, I felt more confident and less dependent on false bravado. This time it was Sparks who took the initiative. He stepped in front of Tully.

"This not the time, huh?" he said to me calmly but firmly. "You, me, Tully, all of us—we figure things out, right? One way… or the other way… okay? Not here." He was obviously trying to defuse the altercation yet I sensed no fear behind his diplomacy.

"Okay," I responded without backing down. Although I viewed Sparks and Tully as impediments to my child's well-being, and was ready to kill them where they stood, this was much bigger than the three of us. This situation would have become nothing short of a rumble, and there were fifty-plus onlookers whose loyalties I could not predict, nor could Sparks. I understood his position. We backed off and walked away in opposite directions.

A week or so passed as if the latrine standoff had been nothing more than a dream. Other than Jessie, who continued to isolate herself and simmer, everyone around me acted as if nothing dicey had transpired. I guess our little cold war wasn't a big deal to our comrades who faced death nearly every day. To them we were just two bullies on the playground. Our Serrone masters were likely oblivious to the trials and tribulations that plagued the inferior lifeforms they enslaved. Their sentroid overseers chose not to intervene as long as none of the property was getting destroyed. The combots were more difficult to read. As I noted previously, they were aware of the conflicts among the humans, yet they seemed ill-equipped to deal with them. I was beginning to wonder if Dee sought advice from Malcolm when addressing human issues. I also sensed a growing rift between Dee and his subordinate combot, Bar.

The behavior of the combots became the topic of many discussions during idle time in the barracks. One night, our resident scientist entertained us with his opinions on combot artificial intelligence.

"The functionality of their neural networks could easily resemble that of human brains," Nicholas opined, "if you consider the similarities between life here and life on Earth." He always paused to allow for someone to question his premise. No one ever did—at least not on this planet. "If that's the case," he continued, "then you might see them as adolescents. They aren't more than twenty-five years old, right Mister Swag?"

Nicholas and Swag had become very close. The latter was very protective of the former and enjoyed his lectures nearly as much as my stories.

"That's right, Nick. These ones here in camp probably aren't more than twenty-five years old, I reckon," said Swag, visibly proud to have contributed to the discussion.

"And," continued Nicholas, "it's not as if they were sent to school. They were programmed for combat fighting but also given a basic ability to adapt."

"To learn," I added, feeling equally proud to have contributed.

"Right—to learn. Now, I doubt that anybody envisioned these

combots to last for more than a few years, and here they are, twenty years later, still learning—and doing it without any guidance. Their creators are long gone, and their A.I. has continued to grow unchecked."

"And they were designed to serve in large armies fighting conventional wars—not what we have here," Charles surmised.

"Yes, I suppose so," replied Nicholas.

It was all very interesting. It was also nothing more than hypothetical gobbledygook to alleviate the boredom. Sure, combot behavior was slightly less predictable than that of other androids, but it wasn't as if we thought of them as being anything close to human.

I was fast asleep when the lights came on in the middle of the night and Dee roused us with a voice as loud as I had ever heard from an android. It took me a few seconds to transition from deep sleep to reality, and for a brief moment the commotion in the barracks was merely a scene in my dream. We were ordered to stand in front of our bunks and remain silent. This was the closest action to being in a *real* army that we had ever experienced, though I cannot say that we were truly standing at attention.

Cap was present with Dee in the hut. He informed us that a soldier, one of our comrades, had escaped the camp. We were to be confined to our barracks until further notice. He then proceeded to the next hut and delivered the same message. Upon his exit we relaxed and soon observed that two of our fellow residents were missing. Neither Jessie nor Bar were present.

It was not unusual for Bar to be absent. Combots were not subject to the rules that limited our movements within camp. Although he typically spent his nights sitting on a chair in our hut, his absence on that particular night was nothing extraordinary. Nor, for that matter, was Jessie's. She had attained a high-level of freedom in the camp as a trusted veteran of the PRF. In fact, all of us had enjoyed a lax enforcement of rules over the past season and moved freely around the compound. We guessed that Jessie was probably visiting the latrine or pursuing a late-night snack. When she failed to return after several minutes, Malcolm confirmed with Dee that she was the fugitive.

Aroused by this remarkable development, we gathered informally in the middle of the room to mull it over. Dee took an interest in our discussion but did not actively participate. Most of us were of the same opinion. The notion of anyone escaping was preposterous, let alone

Jessie. Any of us could vacate the camp undetected without much effort. What bound us to the camp and the servitude of its masters was not perimeter security or the penalty of death, although both existed. What kept us in the camp was the bleak prospect of surviving outside of it. It was the devil we knew. As harsh as Jessie's life was in the PRF, there could be no better one awaiting her beyond it. Why would she join the rebels when they stood on the brink of defeat? Would they not kill her on sight anyway? Others called attention to Jessie's recent behavior.

"She hasn't been herself since Ammo died," someone posited.

"Where could she go?" someone else wondered.

"Maybe she reached a breaking point and just had to get out of here."

"Without her canteen?" asked Nicholas, pointing to the canteen on the floor by her bed. Her belt, sheath, and knife that usually hung on a nail above it were missing.

"Does that make sense to you, Malcolm?" I asked. I had my suspicions but I wanted to hear it from him.

"I reckon not," he answered reluctantly, hesitant to stir the pot. Armed with Malcolm's confirmation, I turned to Dee.

"Dee, let's go look for her. We can find her before anyone else does," I implored.

"Search parties have been dispatched. You are confined to quarters," he replied.

"Who—sentroids? Combots?"

"Yes," said Dee, "and scouts." The term "scouts" implied the use of the most trusted human soldiers.

"What about Malcolm… and Swag? Shouldn't they be searching? Swag's the best scout we have!" I exclaimed, while pointing to the old man. My comrades expressed their agreement vocally as our confusion ascended into discontent.

"I was not placed in charge of the search," Dee told us. "I was informed of the escape at the same time as you."

"But you understand that something doesn't add up, right?" Susan asked Dee.

"Add up?" repeated the android.

"It is doubtful that Jessie would escape without taking her canteen," clarified our resident attorney, Leesheh.

"It is dubious," admitted Dee. Under other circumstances I might have been impressed with his vocabulary. "But I am not authorized to investigate her disappearance," he added.

I sensed a hesitation in him, not in his voice—that would have been impossible. It was in the pause he took between his statements. It was as though he was computing something, or more appropriately, something *didn't* compute with him. Nothing came of it. He retreated to his chair and commenced recharging. Malcolm was the only person with any level of authority in our midst and thus became our focal point.

"I understand what you're sayin'," he told us, "but there's nothin' we can do right now. Look out that window. Adolph and Stalin are right outside. They'll zap anyone who steps out that door. You'll be lucky if they don't kill you."

He was right, not that it put us at ease. We mingled about the barracks all night contemplating various theories that might explain Jessie's suspicious disappearance.

Not long after daylight two jeeps rolled into the courtyard. We crowded the windows and porch to obtain a view. The sentroids in the courtyard prevented us from advancing closer. Bar, Sparks, and Tully occupied the first jeep; a few other native soldiers were in the second. On the back of the first jeep, where the gun mount would normally be fastened, lay a bloodied body.

The patrol was met by the Chief, Ringo, and Ratso in their chariots, escorted by their entourage of sentroids. Bar lifted the body from the vehicle and handed it to Khan. We had already guessed the identity of the body and now we could see her plainly. A few minutes later, a second patrol of Chinese soldiers and a combot pulled into camp. The sentroids then ordered all soldiers to assemble near the jeeps where they subsequently encircled us. Khan addressed us on behalf of the Chief.

"This soldier is guilty of deserting the People's Resistance Front and must therefore be considered a fugitive and an enemy of the people. Punishment for this crime is death. The fugitive attacked the soldiers of a patrol that was dispatched to capture her and was subsequently killed by them. Captain Cheefon considers this matter closed. Captain Cheefon advises the company that tomorrow we will resume our pursuit of forces rebelling against the People's Resistance Front."

"Pretty convenient," I whispered to Leesheh.

We were dispatched to the pavilion for breakfast where deliberations heightened in light of the grave development. Our suspicions and conspiracy theories fed off of each other. Few believed that Jessie left camp of her own free will. Assuming she did, nobody believed that she could have been apprehended so quickly; and if she had resisted capture, everyone agreed that she would have inflicted some level of damage upon her captors before being killed. Jessie was lethal with her knife. We saw no indication of injuries among them.

I walked over and sat down next to one of the Chinese members of the second patrol, a man whom I had come to know since my arrival in camp. He told me that they were ordered to search the area west of camp shortly after we were all awakened in the barracks. They were told that Jessie had escaped, that she was armed, and that another search party had already been dispatched. They searched throughout the night until they were recalled to camp in the morning. I asked him if the circumstances seemed strange to him.

"They did," he told me in broken English, "and we expected to find nothing out there."

We returned to find Jessie's body hanging by its feet from a rope tied to a branch high up in a tree near the courtyard. Her arms dangled toward the ground, as though reaching out for someone to grab them and help her down. I guess the Chief wanted to drive his point home.

We were confined to the barracks for the rest of the morning, where we continued to seethe. We couldn't determine the details of the incident but we were convinced of foul play. The specifics of how Jessie could have left the barracks without anyone noticing were difficult to reconcile. Nobody could recall if Jessie was inside the hut when the lights were turned out. If she was, it's entirely possible that she left for the latrine, where she could have been snatched.

"But her knife," said Charles. "She would not take her knife to the latrine, would she?"

"No," replied Susan, "which means that someone retrieved it later."

"And forgot the canteen," added Leesheh.

It was conceivable that someone like Sparks could have snuck in and fetched the knife while we slept, yet that would have been risky given that he no longer resided in our hut. But there was someone—*something*—who had easier access: Bar. We turned to our scientist for confirmation.

"Who knows? I'm beginning to think that anything's possible with them. Why don't you ask *him*?" Nicholas said, nodding toward Dee.

"What do you think, Dee?" I asked. I didn't expect an illuminating response, nor did I receive one.

"I can only draw a conclusion based on the facts. Jessie left the camp without permission and was apprehended," he said.

"Then you believe it to be a fact that she left the camp of her own volition?" asked Leesheh. Dee paused for a few seconds before responding.

"I cannot say."

"What about you, Malcolm?" I asked. "What are we gonna do about this?"

"I dunno. I don't see that there's much we *can* do."

"Come on, mate," Swag said softly to Malcolm, "It's Jessie."

"I bloody well know who it is, Swag," replied Malcolm defensively. "It's not like we 'aven't been down this road before, mate. It's no good—you know that as well as anyone."

"Well I'm gonna do something about it," I said.

"The only thing you're gonna do is get yourself killed, Shakespeare. You need to cool down and collect your wits," chided the Aussie.

I wasn't mad at Malcolm, only disappointed. I had once looked up to him as a role model but that image had been swiftly eroding in recent weeks. I felt like the son who grows up to learn that the father he had worshipped like a superhero had the same faults and weaknesses of most men.

"So that's how it is?" I said soberly. "That's how you survived for so many years on Serrone? By keeping your head buried in the sand? Kissing android asses?"

"I'm still here."

"Yeah, you're still here. And you can have *all of this*. I'd rather die trying to make this a better place. If that means killing some asshole soldiers or Serrones, then I'm ready to do it."

"Shakespeare," whispered Leesheh. She then mouthed "Dee."

"I don't care if Dee hears me," I said in full voice. "You understand, right Dee? Are you *loyal* to Jessie, Dee? She was a good soldier, wasn't she? I'm a good soldier too, right?"

Dee said nothing, for which I was a little relieved. Having made my point, I took my foot off the accelerator and walked to the back of the hut. In retrospect it was a harsh judgement of Malcolm, a man who clearly cared about our well-being. Still, I felt no regret for having made it. His goal was survival; mine was victory. I was still unsure of how that victory would be defined other than including the freedom and well-being of my family.

Another concern occurred to me shortly after my diatribe. If Sparks and Tully (with a complicit Bar) premediated Jessie's murder, might they not seek to eliminate the only witness to Tully's murder of Ammo? Would they not assume that Nicholas was the source of Jessie's suspicions that prompted her to confront Tully near the latrine? The repercussions snowballed in my mind. I suddenly felt the weight upon my shoulders and sunk down to the floor. I was responsible for Jessie's death. I was responsible for any danger that Nicholas now faced. I was responsible for any retaliation against my friends. I concluded that my only recourse was to squarely shoulder that responsibility and to do it publicly.

We were released from the confines of the barracks shortly before dusk. I found Sparks and Tully loitering near one of

the Chinese huts sharing a bottle.

"Can I talk to you for a minute?" I asked of them. I put up my hands up as they walked cautiously toward me. "I'm not looking for trouble."

"Okay, Shake-a-spear," said Tully, "you talk." As I hoped would happen, a small crowd gathered to watch the adversaries square off once again.

"What Jessie said yesterday—about Ammo. That came from me. I saw Ammo get shot in the village. I didn't think he was hurt badly, and I told Jessie what I thought."

The two men thought about my words before responding. "I don't know what you talk about," said Sparks, "Bar saw Ammo. Bar made the choice. Tully follow orders. We told you that."

"As for Jessie," I continued, completely ignoring his response, "I know what happened last night."

"Yeah, Jessie escaped. We ordered to find her," said Tully as if I must have been the most gullible person on the planet.

"*As for Jessie,*" I repeated, "I *know* what happened last night. You and you, stay away from me and my friends." The two miscreants responded with their typical sham claims of confusion and denial, but I had already turned and walked away.

20

Time began to pass more quickly for me. My life became a series of routines comprising smaller routines, layered upon monotonous tasks consisting of repetitive steps. The days dragged on but the weeks flew by. I only looked forward, yet I had little to look forward *to*, beyond the birth of our child. I woke up on a particular day and realized that I had survived my second season on Serrone and was well into my third. I was alive. Leesheh was alive. I had lost no friends since Jessie's problematic death. This period in my story is characterized by considerable personal changes to me, some gradual and others nearly instantaneous, which I will summarize in this chapter.

Droplets of information managed to trickle from General Abasha himself down to his slave soldiers in the most remote camps of the People's Resistance Front. But we didn't need to be told that we had the rebels, those sworn enemies of the Serrone people, on the ropes. We were often gone for weeks at a time as our patrols pushed farther into the outskirts of Region Seventeen in search of combatants. Encounters with rebels occurred less frequently, and the size of their factions dwindled. We liberated scores of villages and killed anyone and anything that tried to stop us. It was only natural that we would begin to feel invincible.

We camped in conditions that made the barracks back in the compound seem like the Ritz Carlton, yet there was something rustic about sleeping under the stars and pondering what other strange worlds might be out there. Leesheh was with me on every patrol. In spite of an ever-expanding midsection, she continued to hold her own in combat. We used to joke that she was fighting for two. Never on patrol with us was Sparks, Tully, or anyone else from their gang. I suspect that our segregation was no coincidence and had been orchestrated by the combots—Dee in particular.

In contrast to the relentless mental anguish and anxiety, my physical body was thriving on the new planet. Whether on the road or in camp, I found time to work out with Susan nearly every day. I became obsessed with physical conditioning and enjoyed the mental and physical edges that it provided. I added muscle to my frame while losing fat and increasing flexibility and endurance. We had no scales; Charles estimated my weight to be in the neighborhood of two hundred and twenty-five pounds—not much heavier than when I left Earth but of a much stronger and leaner constitution. I loved to eat and was ribbed for having a ceaseless appetite. There was one thing about this planet that I preferred over Earth: the food. I attributed some of my physical enhancement to the mysterious vitamin pills that were rationed by the sentroids. I had voluntarily increased my daily dosage to two a while back and seemed no worse for the wear.

Susan devised a variety of creative exercises incorporating whatever was on hand—logs, branches, rocks, etc. We used the weight of our own bodies more than anything else, which meant a lot of pushups and pullups. The daily workouts caught the attention of a few others and before long we had five or six regulars in Susan's "boot camp." Even Pablo showed up every now and then, though I think that had more to do with his growing interest in Susan.

One morning, Ying, the gritty little Chinese woman, and pound-for-pound the toughest warrior in the company, showed up to boot camp and jumped in without saying a word. She soon became a regular participant and expanded on Susan's knowledge of Tai Chi by showing us some new moves (and somehow did it *still* without saying a word). In part because I had a bet with Susan that I could make Ying laugh, and in part because I wanted her to teach me, I approached Ying one day after boot camp and asked her to show me a few tactics. I was particularly interested in some of the moves I had witnessed her perform in combat. I tried to describe what it was that I wanted to learn.

"Ah, you want to be Bruce Lee," said Ying—the first words she ever spoke to me. I would come to learn that she was a student of Wing Chun, a style that was widely practiced in China and popularized by Bruce Lee.

"I guess so," I responded hesitantly, unsure if she was making fun of me.

To my delight, she readily accepted the challenge of adding some finesse and technique to my brute force aggression. We trained regularly and became friendly. ("Friendly" was a relative term with respect to Ying. As far as I could tell we were friends.) As the days piled on, I was able to coax more and more words out of her until we finally established something resembling a conversation. Ying had arrived approximately two years before I did, part of the consignment of slaves that preceded mine. She opened up about her life in camp but was reluctant to discuss her life before abduction.

"That life someone else," she said in fragmented English. "Not mine."

I understood the feeling and didn't press her—however curious I was about her civilian life. Ying must have grown to like Susan, myself, and the others in our squad. I could never have surmised this but for the fact that she showed up on patrol with us one day and never left. Like Swag, Ying was one of those veterans who seemed to have earned a degree of latitude with the combots. She was a welcome addition to Dee's squad and her presence provided me with ample opportunity to win the bet with Susan. I eventually made Ying laugh, not once, but twice. The first time came a few days later when I slipped onto my butt during training.

As was the case with many of the soldiers in camp, Ying took a particular liking to Monte, perhaps because he was also undersized. She seemed to take a special interest in his safety and well-being. Watching them fumble through a conversation soon became one of our simple pleasures.

With each enemy altercation my aggression and tenacity increased, not by design, yet also without repentance. The number of foes I killed increased beyond which I cared to count, and with it grew my reputation as a warrior. My objectives churned within my mind like a mantra: defeat the enemy, defeat my captors, return to Earth with my family—one obstacle at a time. I had long since abandoned my arc rifle for a smaller weapon that I confiscated from a dead rebel soldier. I called it my "Uzi," despite having no idea if it resembled an actual Uzi submachine gun. It had a shorter range of accuracy but was better suited for close-quarter combat, which I had come to favor. I took advantage of my size and quickness to overpower opponents; as such, many of my kills came from the blade of my knife. Twice during this period my resolve was truly tested.

We surprised a small band of rebels bivouacked in a meadow during a heavy downpour. There were only twenty of us on the patrol but we still had them outnumbered and outgunned. We fired a few shots into the camp then pounced on their tents before they had a chance to react. I dove into a small tent with my knife drawn and my Uzi ready to fire, only to find two young faces staring back at me in sheer terror. The sight of these children—not yet teenagers—paralyzed me and halted my knife within inches of one's throat. One of them, a girl, shifted her eyes toward an arc rifle lying nearby. I shook my head, extended my hand toward the rifle and slowly pulled it away from her. I raised my finger to my lips to keep them quiet and slowly backed up to the front of the tent so that I could be seen by my comrades while keeping the children under guard. The slaughter was over in less than a minute, after which I removed the boy and girl from the tent and called out to Dee. This was my first encounter with adolescent soldiers, but it wasn't his. Dee spelled out their fate—well within earshot of them.

"Captain Cheefon would order us to kill them." Was it possible that Dee was leaving the door open for another option?

"But Captain Cheefon is not here," I pointed out, then asked Nicholas to take the children away from us.

"If the captured soldiers were to provide valuable information leading to the location of the larger rebel faction from whence they came, then they are worth more to us alive than dead," Dee suggested. We already had a pretty good idea where that faction was, and I could not help but detect a touch of shrewdness in his words.

We took the rebel children back to the compound, conveniently arriving in the dead of night, and smuggled them into our hut. Dee exited to brief Cap and Ringo, and returned later with good news. He had informed his superiors that the children had provided valuable intelligence about the location of a rebel faction. This was a fact; they *had* provided us with some information. In turn the children were to be sent to the city for what Dee referred to as "re-indoctrination." We knew that this wouldn't be a pleasant experience for the children. Nevertheless, it was the best possible outcome given the circumstances.

In light of the narrative above, and specifically with respect to my seemingly bold interaction with Dee, I should recount other developments that came to pass during this prolonged period. From the time of Jessie's death, I no longer viewed Malcolm as a leader and gradually forged my own relationship with Dee. This coincided with my ascension into the unofficial position as the highest-ranking human soldier in the camp, which was known colloquially as the Human in Charge (HiC). This was not a role to which I had laid claim; it was gradually bestowed upon me by my comrades, and I eased into it with some humility. It came with no speech or ceremony. We meant no disrespect to Malcolm and continued to rely on his wisdom and experience for our safety and survival. Dee recognized that I had gained the confidence—and loyalty—of my comrades and treated me accordingly.

This brings me to the final incident that I wish to highlight within this period of my story, as it likely influenced my newly-formed perspective of the combots as peers rather than overseers. I'll skip the details of how I found myself alone with a rebel combot in a foxhole. Suffice to say that the circumstances leading to that precarious position were the result of a fluke rather than an intent. I zigged where I should have zagged, lost sight of my comrades, and jumped into the nearest hole for cover. Why the rebel combot was alone in that hole is moot. The supposition that one or both of his legs were incapacitated I will neither confirm nor deny. I will readily admit that he was very much alive and intent on taking my life.

It would have been fortuitous for me to have jumped directly on top of him rather than land squarely in front of him, but I should be thankful that I landed too close for him to extend his weapon and blast me into pieces. In the nanosecond I was airborne, in between discovering the combot and landing in the hole, I considered the likelihood of my knife penetrating his android armor. I quickly dismissed the idea, in spite of my confidence with that weapon. I also took note of the knife in my opponent's belt and his assured confidence in its ability to penetrate my human flesh.

I seized the initiative by putting one arm around his neck and grabbing his wrist with the other hand in the hopes of preventing him from grabbing his knife (or mine). I fully expected to be tossed away like a rag doll. I was pleasantly astounded to find that I was somehow a match for his strength, though I knew that I could never match his endurance. Noticing that a large rock protruded from the dirt wall behind his head, I took a calculated risk. I released his wrist and used my free hand to thrust his head into the rock. It seemed to have little effect other than afford me an opportunity to repeat the move, which I did, three or four times.

I could feel him weakening. I grabbed his head with both hands and smashed harder and faster against the rock. His body went limp and I relinquished him to gravity. He fell forward, exposing a gaping hole in the back of his head. Bits and pieces of mangled alien machinery were visible inside the opening, swimming in a thick yellow liquid that was leaking into the foxhole.

Exhausted, I sat and studied the mangled robot. I had always pictured the inner workings of the Serrone androids to resemble the circuit boards, wires, and solenoids of the old pinball machine that my father tinkered with in our basement. The inner workings of the combot's head looked nothing like that. It appeared far less complex and mechanical than I had imagined. None of it made much sense to me, but then again, neither had the pinball machine.

I was proud of my conquest and a little confused as to how I was able to pull it off. Was his battery low? Does he even have a battery? Were combots less durable than we had assumed? Were some of them constructed better than others?

A few of my comrades soon discovered me in the hole with the combot, at which time I decided to ignore my skepticism and focus on what I *did* know: I had killed a combot. As we dragged the remains of the android to where the squad had assembled, I described the events that led to me defeating it. (The details of how his legs had become damaged were purposely left vague and open to interpretation.)

21

The time came when Leesheh was no longer able to participate in combat activities and was confined to the nursery. For a while she was permitted to spend the day with her squad in the barracks, if we were in camp. For reasons undisclosed to us humans, she was not allowed to spend her nights in her own bunk, nor was I permitted to sleep in the nursery. Eventually, Charles recommended that she remain in her bed at the nursery as much as possible. He was the closest thing we had to an obstetrician, save for the older woman who had delivered a handful of babies since arriving on the planet. The doc and the midwife agreed that the time was near.

I could be found in the nursery for most of the day sitting at Leesheh's side and doing my best to distract her with stories. The few toddlers who were there at that time usually gathered around and listened with such awe that one might have thought I was delivering the Gettysburg Address. Even when telling children's stories, they were hopelessly puzzled by my words and nonetheless thoroughly entertained. They burst into laughter at the most inexplicable moments, which caused us to laugh along with them. Swag became a regular visitor as well. He told me that he wanted to "make sure the girl is alright," though I suspected that he was equally interested in hearing the stories.

I made it part of my daily routine to visit the ladies in the cathouse and bring them whatever food and sundries I could scrounge. There were only six women left there including, to my anguish, the addition of the young prisoner, Saba. A few women had perished over the past season, undoubtedly due to some combination of sickness, abuse, and melancholia. With no new arrivals since my own group of abductees, the ranks in the cathouse had not been replenished. This might have been considered a good eventuation, if not for the fact that the remaining women had become increasingly abused. On a particular day, just a few prior to Leesheh going into labor, the controversy surrounding the cathouse that had simmered within me for so long finally reached its boiling point.

Charles and I entered the cathouse and found Tina lying in her bed and Saba sitting beside her in a chair. Saba was dabbing a cloth on various areas of Tina's face, which we found to be covered with cuts and bruises upon drawing closer to her. Tina was unconscious, but Saba apprised us of the circumstances that led to the beating just a few hours earlier.

"She don't want to be with him," Saba told us. "She told him 'no more.' She hit him."

From Saba's account and those of the other women present, it was apparent that Tina had reached the end of her rope and refused the advances of a soldier. The coward reciprocated her defiance by beating her to within the last thread of her life. I asked the women to identify the man responsible. I knew who he was and where I could probably find him. He had arrived on Serrone the same day that I did, a prisoner in the other cargo hold. It was this man with whom I had been ordered to fight on that first day in camp, after my bogus sparring session with Leesheh had failed to convince the combots. He had soundly whipped me that day, using more force than I felt was necessary to appease our evaluators.

Since that day our paths had diverged. I had grown stronger, quicker, and resolute. He had grown fond of catnip, moonshine, and gambling—popular camp vices that I cannot begrudge anyone in our plight, but the extreme to which he indulged I found irksome. As members of the same squad, I had many opportunities to witness his timidity in battle, despite being one of the more physically capable soldiers in camp. This, too, is a behavior that I cannot hold against a conscript such as we were, though I was vexed by his disinclination to defend the comrades who were defending him. It was the depravity of his frequent visits to the cathouse for which I held him in flat-out contempt.

I found myself in a fevered state that until this point had been reserved for the battlefield. Charles told me afterward that my eyes turned from blue to bright green. He said that he had tried to calm me down, though I have no recollection of the conversation. I do remember instructing him to care for Tina and setting out for the barracks. I found the man where I expected him to be, inside the first hut in the barracks row. He was enjoying a leisurely day—free from patrol, and bantering with his buddies. I didn't take the time to hear the actual subject of their conversation. In my unbridled imagination he was recapping his recent trip to the cathouse, which only increased my rage.

I grabbed him by the collar and yanked him out into the courtyard, followed by the befuddled soldiers who had been laughing with him only seconds earlier. Had I cared for dramatic effect I might have informed the man of the crime for which I had passed judgement and sentence, but my vehemence would not allow for it. Nor did any of the bystanders demand an explanation for my assault, indicating afterwards that I appeared far too enraged for them to attempt an intervention. (I had no awareness of anyone watching until after I had finished with the man.) For his part, the convict protested vociferously from the time of his apprehension until my first blow landed squarely into his midsection and knocked the wind out of him.

Had you asked me to hypothesize earlier that morning whether I was inclined to physically punish a fellow soldier who had harmed a friend, I would have earnestly affirmed, for violence had taken residence in my character and was as natural to me as my sense of humor. Whether I thought myself capable of killing a man for this offense was questionable. Was this a case of temporary insanity? A crime of passion? Or perhaps the man who was beating this degenerate to death was who I truly had become: an amalgam of the good, the bad, and the ugly—a product of my environment. None of that crossed my mind as I pulverized the man's face. Nothing whatsoever crossed my mind, as if I was an android executing the instructions programed within me.

He had likely been dead for a minute or so before I finally stopped the onslaught. As I stood over him and caught my breath, a strange calm came over me, accompanied not by remorse or satisfaction, only consolation. It was then that Nicholas and Susan stepped in and gently pulled me away from the grisly corpse. My wits soon returned and displaced the savagery that had temporarily commandeered my faculties. That's when the idea to further advance my convictions dawned on me.

"The cathouse is closed indefinitely," I announced to the flabbergasted soldiers encircling me. "Anybody who touches one of those women without their consent will answer to me. Understood?"

Nobody said anything, which I accepted as affirmation. I was ready to exit the stage when I noticed Tully in the crowd. I used the advantage of my momentum to call him out specifically and show the others the coward that he was.

"Tully," I asked, "Do you understand what *indefinitely* means?" He huffed and shook his head slightly, as if to say "whatever," though I don't think that word was in his vocabulary.

I went back to the newly defunct cathouse to check on Tina then walked next door to be with Leesheh. I wanted to explain my behavior to her before anyone else did. It wasn't that I felt a need to justify it. I simply wanted her to know the correct version of the events, and perhaps preemptively downplay witness accounts of my fury. Leesheh knew as well as I that death was a part of our life on Serrone. As anticipated, she took no umbrage with my actions, though I cannot say that she was ecstatic. I quickly pivoted to the subject of her status and the imminent birth of our child. Nicholas and the others joined us shortly thereafter and redirected the conversation back to what had transpired in the courtyard.

"Did you see Cap and Dee?" Nicholas asked. "Nearly all of the combots were there." I told him that I hadn't noticed. "Isn't that weird?" he continued excitedly. "I don't know how long they were there but they made no attempt to stop you." I saw where he was headed and was equally curious of the combots' puzzling behavior, but I was a little embarrassed to belabor the topic in front of Leesheh, or anybody else for that matter.

"Yeah, I don't know," I said dismissively. He started to respond and I cut him off with a quick glare and slight shake of the head. He got the message. I intended to resume the conversation with him and Charles in the barracks later, then something happened that caused me to wonder if I would ever have the opportunity.

Dee stepped into the nursery and told me to join him outside. A sudden chill shot up my spine, and I did my best to suppress it in front of Leesheh and the others. In response to her look of concern I mouthed "It's okay" and followed Dee outside, where I found Cap and the sentroid we called Stalin waiting. Stalin ordered me to come with him. I looked behind to see the somber expressions on my friends, then followed the sentroid, flanked by Cap and Dee.

The chill within me heightened into a fear that I had not experienced in a long time. I'd had plenty of occasions to fear death since arriving on Serrone, but none that afforded this much time for internal deliberation—not since waking up on the transport ship. I couldn't help but imagine that this tranquil walk was like the final steps of a condemned man heading for the gallows. There was no point in asking my sentroid executioner or the combot sergeants escorting me about my fate. I knew they would not speak.

I wallowed in my self-pity for a moment longer before my brain kicked back into survival mode, and I began to reassess my situation. Why would I be taken away for execution? The Serrones had no qualms with public executions. Would they not want to make an example of me in front of the company? Why are these two combots, my chain of command, here with me? Something felt different about the situation. If I was marked for certain death I would have probably been disposed of already. I might be in peril, yet there must be some uncertainty regarding my circumstance—some unresolved question.

Our destination soon became clear. We entered the section of the camp that was strictly off limits to the human soldiers and headed toward the Chief's quarters. *So, this is the deal? I'm being taken to see the Chief?* Kaiser, one of the Chief's two sentroid bodyguards, stood in front of the building. I expected our party to stop there and await the Chief's arrival, but we skirted to the side of the building and walked behind it. Well-hidden behind the hut, whether by design or coincidence I couldn't say, was a small ship. It was a smaller version of the airships that evacuated the refugees after the first battle in the village. Waiting for us in front of it was the Chief's other personal guard, Khan. Stalin halted us there where we stood quietly for a minute or so.

I had never witnessed or heard any account of a human soldier ever being brought before a Serrone officer. My mind raced. Was I being called to explain my actions—to plead for my life, perhaps? That didn't make any sense—I was nothing more than livestock to the Chief. Sentroids and combots dealt with these "human resource" issues, not Serrones. There was something more to this—perhaps an opportunity? A door opened on the ship. Was a door opening for me? I was running out of time and I had to think fast.

The Chief emerged from the darkness behind the door, dressed in his colorful frock, with his shaded visor nearly covering his face completely. My brain went into overdrive. *Does this guy want a conversation with me? How should I deal with this arrogant alien? Wait—maybe his air of superiority is the key. I'm just an animal to him—a lower life form. He would never give me credit for being clever or cunning.* I decided to call upon my acting skills to defend my barbarism. *If he wants a conversation, then I'll give him one—and I'll lay it on thick.*

"Captain Cheefon wants to know why you killed a soldier of the People's Resistance Front," said Khan. (The combots sometimes used the "PRF" acronym but the sentroids never did.)

"I killed a traitor, not a soldier of the People's Resistance Front," I replied confidently. There was a moment of silence as the Chief pondered this declaration. The little lights on the side of his visor twinkled.

"Explain," said his interpreter.

I had already decided the direction in which to take this. There was no use in mentioning the incident with Tina at the cathouse, as the Chief was incapable of empathy for humans. However, he was surely sensitive to the destruction of his property, or why else was I there?

"The soldier betrayed the People's Resistance Front. He harmed other soldiers in the company, rendering them unable to function properly," I opined. I didn't know how long I would have the floor and was determined to hold it until told otherwise.

"The soldier was ineffective in combat," I continued steadfastly. "He refused to engage the enemy and placed other soldiers at risk." I was actually starting to enjoy it a little—the crazier the better. "I eradicated the soldier in order to improve the combat efficiency of the unit." (Combat efficiency seemed like a nice touch.) "The man was not a worthy soldier of the People's Resistance Front," I proclaimed. "The People's Resistance Front is better–"

"Quiet," interrupted Khan.

"Okay." I glanced around while the Chief digested my bullshit. There was nothing to read on the android faces.

"You have killed many rebels," Khan said.

"Yes…?" I didn't know if it was a question or a statement.

"You killed a rebel android."

"Yes." I saw no need to go into the extenuating circumstances of that particular event, but I did see another opportunity. "My success in battle is due to the great leadership of these combots here beside me," I said while gesturing to Dee and Cap. I didn't expect that remark to register with the Chief, but I hoped that it might trigger something within Dee and Cap—the loyalty bias, as Nicholas called it.

"Remove your clothing," ordered Khan. This demand was a bit of a surprise. I readily complied, as any loyal soldier of the PRF would.

The Chief began to walk forward. Khan extended an arm toward me and firmly collared my neck with his claw. At the same time, I felt something jab into my ribs. I glanced downward to see his other arm with the dreaded taser appendage protruding from it. I should have been frightened by this turn of events, yet I wasn't. If the Chief wanted me dead it would have already transpired. The Chief circled me at a safe distance. I had never been so close to a Serrone—not even the village refugees. He seemed so diminutive. I could have easily crushed him with a single blow, if not for the robotic claw choking my neck. What was he doing? I supposed that my balderdash must have been convincing, and that he was now taking a closer inspection of his prized bull. After a couple of revolutions, he returned to his perch and Khan withdrew his restraints.

"Captain Cheefon wants to know if you are happy fighting for the People's Resistance Front," said Khan. I dared to believe that I had the alien eating out of my hand.

"It is what I live for. The rebels must be killed, and I live to kill," I blurted in a stream of consciousness, while feigning a wild expression that bordered on insanity. I was a tamed beast, fully indoctrinated and ready to unleash my frenzy upon any threat to the PRF. At least, that's the impression I was aiming for.

Then it was over. The Chief retired to the confines of his house-ship and I was dismissed without commendation or punishment. Dee waited as I put on my clothes, then we walked back to the barracks together.

"Why was I brought to see the Chief?" I asked.

"I do not know why."

"I think the Chief likes me," I joked.

"You are the property of the PRF and nothing more," warned Dee. "Do not forget that." His admonishment seemed a bit ominous and would have killed my buzz, had we not soon reached the barracks, where I was warmly greeted by a throng of human soldiers. Many of them seemed surprised to see me alive.

My impulsive, violent behavior had paid unforeseen dividends beyond my imagination, and my head swelled accordingly. I had, for the time being, put an end to the abuses against the women in the cathouse. They would remain there of course, lest the Serrones suspect that the reproduction machine had been impeded. Secondly, I had captured the attention, if not the favor, of my master. I might one day utilize this connection to find a way back to Earth. Finally, I had furthered my reputation among my comrades and heartily welcomed their admiration. The cost for these prizes?—nothing more than the life of a despicable man. It seemed perfectly justified as I reveled in glory, Dee's warning having been already forgotten.

22

The birth of my son came to pass as smoothly as I could have hoped. Charles and the conscripted midwife performed admirably within the miserable conditions of the nursery, as did Leesheh and, of course, the baby. The color of his hair, skin, and eyes mirrored his beautiful mother, yet there was something in his appearance that brought back memories I had buried long ago. On the first night of his life, I held the child in my arms as Leesheh slept. In his eyes I could see his sister looking back at me. I choked back the tears knowing that the two would never meet. I couldn't help but wonder if she was better off than he was—better off than this poor child whom I had carelessly brought into this alien world in bondage. He would likely never read a book, ride a bicycle, or use a smartphone. He *would* likely take the life of another human being before he reached the age of sixteen.

"I'm sorry, little man," I said to him. "You're not supposed to be in this world. We're going to take you to a better one—our world. But until that happens, we're going keep you safe and teach you how to survive in this one. And I'm not just talking about your mother and me. There's Uncle Charles, Uncle Nick, Aunt Susan, Uncle Swag… oh, and Aunt Ying too. Aunt Ying is a badass. She'll teach you how to defend yourself."

"Shakespeare–" Leesheh said softly. I hadn't noticed that she was awake.

"Here's the thing, little man," I continued, "As long as your mother and I are here, you're safe. And guess what—we're not going anywhere without you—I can promise you that. As long as–"

"Shakespeare." She sat up in her bed and gently touched my arm.

"You cannot promise him that. He does not belong to us," she said softly.

I handed the baby to her and wiped my eyes on my shirt sleeve. I stood silently for a moment then sat down on the bed facing away from Leesheh.

"I'm his father."

"You are. And I know that you will do everything in your power to keep him safe. As will I."

"Everything in my power."

"But we have to prepare ourselves—and prepare him—for the possibility that he will be taken from us. Some things we cannot control."

I was upset that she said it but I knew she was right. There wasn't much within my power other than fighting and trying to find a way home. The door opened and a soldier peered inside. He called to me in a loud whisper.

"Shakespeare, Dee sent me. You have to return to the barracks."

In consonance with their reactions upon learning of Leesheh's pregnancy, our friends were reluctant to congratulate us. I fully understood their reticence, just as I had nine months earlier. In spite of the awkwardness surrounding the uncertainty of the child's fate, they were eager to help in any way they could. Charles, of course, was a constant presence in the early days of the baby's life. Nicholas and Susan doted over him as well. I recall entering the nursery a few days after my son's birth and finding him in Monte's arms as Ying patted his head. Monte appeared a bit flustered later when Leesheh and Ying simultaneously attempted to teach him the Dutch and Mandarin words for baby.

Unfortunately, happier moments like that were the exception. The clock was now ticking loudly. Our best guestimate was that we had two seasons—maybe a little longer—before the child would be taken away. The gloom and uneasiness even caused us to briefly consider not giving him a name, as if that could somehow make it easier to detach ourselves from his destiny. Having dismissed that preposterous notion, with each of us blaming the other for having conceived of it, we decided to call him Jasper, after Leesheh's father.

Complicating matters was the rumor of evacuating the camp. The remnants of the rebel army had been pushed to the outer boundaries of

General Abasha's region and it was becoming logistically inefficient to launch patrols from our position. We had heard that other PRF camps had already been relocated. Leesheh and I knew that a decision to move our base of operations might hasten the transfer of the camp's children to the city. I asked Dee if he could confirm the possibility of evacuating the camp. Not only did he confirm it, his affirmation was delivered with additional compelling news.

"I have been told to expect the arrival of more soldiers from Earth," he told me. "The relocation of this camp will be delayed until the new soldiers have been oriented." He didn't know the estimated timeframe for their arrival, and I gleaned that communication between Abasha and his interstellar spaceship was sporadic and unpredictable. I shared the information with the squad and we began to deliberate the ramifications of new troops in our ranks. The spirited discussion reminded me of our days back in the cargo hold when we spent hours knocking around the possible explanations for our abductions.

"Well," said Susan, "I'm sorry that another bunch of Earthlings had to get abducted, but I'd rather get *them* than a ship full of orcos." Nobody could disagree with that.

"I wonder what they're thinking at this very moment," said Nicholas.

I was distracted from the conversation by a flurry of ideas swimming around my head. Could the arrival of the ship present an opportunity for escape? I couldn't see how to make it work. We would have to take out the sentroids… and what about the pilots? Could we hold them at gunpoint? I shared my audacious thoughts with the group. Most of them dismissed the notion. To my surprise, it was Malcolm who took the idea seriously, though he also noted its futility.

"It's tempting, mate," he said. "I know it is. I can't tell ya how many times we thought about it. Not recently, but back in the day—right, Swag?"

"Right," answered Mr. Swag. "We're not talkin' about an airplane. It's a bloody spaceship."

"I don't think I've told you people about the uprising, have I?" asked Malcolm. When we replied that he had not, he recounted the story of a revolt that occurred many years ago, near the end of the Great War. There were more than a thousand slaves—mostly human—in their army. The number of Serrones and androids had severely declined, and there was still an abundance of interstellar ships coming and going at their base. Human leaders planned the operation for weeks then gave the signal when an opportunity presented itself. Both Malcolm and Swag participated.

"We actually took control of one of those big freighters for a little while," Malcolm told us.

"Didn't know what to do with the bloody thing," added Swag. "We just sat there on the ground in a standoff until… until they brought those spiders in. Damned spiders." It was a visibly painful memory for the old man.

"Wiped out two hundred of us, even after we tried to surrender," said Malcolm. "The plan worked beautifully—up to that point. We even thought we had a pilot—a little Serrone we captured inside the ship. He just sat there and refused to do anything. I doubt he understood a word we said. And what could we do with him—kill him?"

"We were like a dog chasin' the neighbor's car every day," said Swag, "Wouldn't know what to do with it if he ever caught it. Well, we caught it. We bloody well caught it that day."

"See? I know it's tempting, Shakespeare," Malcolm said. "But it's a just a dream. I told you when you got here you were never goin' back home. This is your home now. Keep making a difference here, and one day there might be more of us than there are of them."

This was the first time I had known Malcolm to even slightly endorse the concept of defeating Abasha and whoever else that ruled the planet. Even if hijacking a spaceship wasn't a possibility, I wasn't ready to abandon all hope of returning to Earth; however, I did view it as a long-term objective. For the time being I had to concentrate on protecting my child.

A few days after giving birth, Cap ordered Leesheh to return to the barracks and resume combat duties. Tina and Saba pledged that little Jasper would never leave their sight, and his parents resolved to visit him every hour of every day. I don't know if we were being tested, or if it was the Chief's way of telling us that the child was his property, or if it was merely a coincidence, but one day after Leesheh was reassigned to the squad, she and I were dispatched on a long patrol.

It was a difficult separation for me and even worse for the new mother. She fretted about Jasper even as plasma bullets flew overhead during a brief firefight. She emptied her weapon then crouched down next to me behind a rock.

"You think he's okay, right?" she asked me as she jammed a new cartridge into her arc rifle.

"He's fine," I assured her. I don't think she heard me, for she had already reengaged the enemy. We pulled into the courtyard after two weeks on the road to find everything more or less in the state we had left it, including our son. That night, we smuggled him out of the nursery and slept as a family under the stars in our favorite spot near the barracks.

Several more weeks passed without the arrival of the starship. Patrols had ceased—we were simply too far away from the action. We were one of the PRF's largest companies and we had a fully-replenished supply of weapons and ammunition that we had captured over the past two seasons. We were far too valuable to be left on the sidelines. Soldiers from other units stopped in camp on their way to and from Abasha City. They told us that victory was imminent. I know that I shouldn't have cared, yet I found myself yearning to be part of the action. It was as if I had earned the right to see it through. I wanted to fight alongside my comrades. If I had only known how soon that opportunity would present itself.

I was down by the stream when word came that the ship was only minutes away. I hurried to the courtyard where I saw a small group of combots and sentroids huddling. It appeared as a bunch of androids engaged in a staring contest but I knew that they were communicating in their robotic way. Dee broke off from the group when he saw me approaching.

"Shakespeare, Captain Cheefon wants you to greet the new soldiers," he said. I couldn't help but chuckle at his use of the word "soldiers." Those poor abducted souls had no idea what lay in store for them. I didn't want to be the person to have to break the news, and I figured that Malcolm could do a better job anyway. I thought it might be a nice gesture to send him up to the landing site, given how much his leadership role had diminished since my arrival. I suggested the substitution to Dee and he concurred immediately, which meant that he didn't seek approval up the chain. It would have certainly been denied. Dee had ostensibly made a field-level decision, which I found intriguing. I located Malcolm in the barracks.

"Cap wants your expertise up at the landing site. Take two soldiers with you." I spuriously elevated the order up a level to Cap for effect.

Charles was nearby and had just heard the news.

"I'll go," he said eagerly.

"That's fine, Doc," I said, "You can make sure nobody needs immediate medical attention, but we're gonna need a couple of… well, *enforcers* to help the sentroids keep everything in order. No offense." I called to mind my first impressions of Sparks and Tully at the landing site.

"None taken," responded Charles. "I'll fetch my kit."

"I'll grab a couple of lads from the Chinese huts," Malcolm offered.

"Let's not have any natives, okay?"

"Right." He understood whom I meant.

As much as I wanted to avoid dealing with the newbies during their first minutes on the planet, I still wanted to see the big ship land. Several of us walked to the camp entrance with the intention of continuing up the path to the edge of the clearing that would serve as the landing site. Chairman Mao was waiting at the entrance and stopped us there. Not far behind him and safely in his chariot stood Ringo.

"You are not authorized to leave the camp," Mao told the group. I decided to test my recently-acquired status.

"I need to be at the landing site when the ship arrives. I need to make sure there are no problems," I asserted. Mao stood motionless and I could sense that something was churning along the network.

"You only, may proceed," he told me. I had passed the test, so I decided to push for extra credit.

"No. I need assistance from her, her, and him," I said, indicating Leesheh, Susan, and Nicholas. I waited while Mao silently tapped into the network again.

"Proceed."

I felt bad that the others couldn't come with us but I didn't want to press my luck—not yet. We walked up the path a short way before I muttered, "suckers." Nicholas speculated that I had attained a rank equal to the combots. I told him that I intended to continue to gain favor with the Serrones by kissing their asses and doing their bidding.

"The more they trust me, the more damage I can do when the time is right," I boasted.

We waited at the edge of the site about a hundred yards from the actual landing spot. Dee, Malcom, Charles, and two other soldiers waited with a couple of sentroids that I believed to be Adolph and Stalin. Mik the combot was there too—probably for medical support. It wasn't long before Susan pointed out a dot in the sky that was growing larger. We soon recognized the old ship that had brought us to Serrone. It looked even shoddier than I remembered, but it somehow managed to maneuver silently and smoothly onto the landing spot. Malcolm and Charles positioned themselves in front of the large side door and waited for it to open.

"What's that?" asked Leesheh. She was pointing to a figure moving far away on the other side of the clearing. We suddenly descried a few others—then more. They were forming a perimeter on the far side and slowly encircling the ship.

"We're under attack," I said in disbelief. "Malcolm—take cover! We're under attack!"

There was not much we could do from our position. We had no weapons other than my knife.

"Nick, Susan—go get help," I ordered, then grabbed Leesheh by the shoulders. "Get to the nursery."

"What about you?" she asked anxiously.

"I'll wait here. They can't see us. Nick—grab my Uzi. Go. Leesheh, *go!*"

They scrambled down the path as I retreated a few feet into deeper cover. The welcoming party looked confused as they tried to make sense of the situation. I don't think they had completely understood me. If Adolph and Stalin knew what was happening, then they would have surely contacted the camp. As of yet, nobody was coming up the path.

Then the door to the ship opened. The best course of action would have been for everyone to take cover inside but it wasn't happening. Instead, a sentroid came out of the ship. I wanted to shout to them again, but the enemies were closer now and I would have been easily discovered. I watched helplessly as one of the soldiers fell to the ground. A shell exploded near the ship—not close enough to injure anyone. The soldiers and androids regrouped near the door and began to return fire, with little success.

"Get inside," I said quietly to myself, attempting to will them into action. "Get inside, get inside." A single shell could have taken them all out in their huddled position.

The enemy soldiers cautiously drew closer, enabling me to get a better look at them. These were not rebels—not the rebels I knew. There were some human soldiers and combots scattered among their ranks, but the vast majority—a hundred or more—were a kind of creature I had never seen. They were humanoid in shape and much shorter than humans. They had two arms, two legs and no discernible head—just a bulge extending from the shoulders, resembling a large neck. (I later compared it to the old television cartoons when one character pounded another's head down into his body using a giant hammer.) They wore no clothing and were covered with a brown scaly skin that was reptilian in appearance. The creatures carried lightweight rifles, and I confirmed later that they possessed no natural weapons, such as a venomous bite, which had come to mind upon first sight. Their most impressive attribute I observed that day was their quickness. They darted to and fro with amazing dexterity and the ability to switch directions or stop on a dime, all while staying close to the ground.

It looked as if Malcolm and the others had finally decided to take refuge inside the ship. One by one they climbed inside as those that remained outside provided covering fire. To their credit, or perhaps due to their programming, the three sentroids were the last to move inside. It looked as if the third and final sentroid would get inside the ship just before the attackers reached them. Then something went awry. The sentroid (later identified as Stalin) took heavy fire and fell dead inside the doorway, making it impossible to close the door. The soldiers struggled frantically to pull the weighty, disabled hulk inside while taking heavy fire. Several enemy creatures—maybe fifteen—gained entry into the ship before the door finally closed behind them. The fate of those inside was now, quite literally, sealed.

It was as that time that the cavalry arrived from camp, albeit in a very chaotic fashion. Soldiers scampered up the path haphazardly with vehicles not far behind. If I had not signaled for them to stop and take cover, we would have surely lost several on the spot. Cap found me and knelt down.

"What is the situation?" he asked. I quickly filled him in, then suggested that we bring the jeeps forward and unleash the heavy mounted weapons. They could provide covering fire while the soldiers fanned out into positions along our side of the perimeter. The attackers had since noticed us and began to take up defensive positions in and around the ship. Nicholas crawled forward and handed me my Uzi.

"Malcolm and Charles are stuck inside the ship with some of those animals," I told him.

"Geez. What are those things?" he asked. A shell suddenly exploded nearby causing us to crouch down even more.

"They could have easily taken out the entire ship and welcoming party with that artillery," I said. "But they didn't use it."

"Maybe that's why they're here," he said. "They came for the ship." That made perfect sense. They wanted the ship and they needed it intact—passengers and all. He who controls the slave trade controls the planet. For the moment they had turned their focus away from securing the ship and onto us. We couldn't allow them to break through and overrun the camp, yet we were losing ground and taking casualties. We were too spread out and disorganized, having overreacted and overextended upon arriving to the confusion.

"Fall back!" came the order from Cap.

We slowly gathered our wits and organized a defense while keeping the ship in sight. The combots divided us into makeshift squads and commenced to execute a concerted strategy. We could ill afford to allow the enemy access to the ship and needed to keep them occupied with our plasma fire. It was possible that the enemy had already gained control of the ship, though I highly doubted that the peculiar creatures inside were capable of operating it.

The battle melted into a standstill. Targets became difficult to hit and both sides reduced firing in order to conserve ammunition. The enemy shelling had ceased as well, and we took the calculated risk of assuming that their artillery stocks were depleted. They had superior numbers but we had a key advantage: we knew the surrounding terrain. There was a patch of high ground near the right flank of the enemy line. It appeared to be unoccupied and undiscovered by them. I proposed to Cap that I take a small team and attempt to gain the position. We could then rain down on them from above. When they're forced to shift resources to counter us, we would smash them on their left flank and pinch in toward the ship.

Cap okayed the plan and put Dee in charge of the team instead of me. Dee quickly pulled me aside.

"Pick the soldiers you want," he said. "You will lead." I had no time to ponder the profound implications of his decision. I quickly assembled a team of fifteen soldiers whom I could trust with my life, including two combots from the Chinese squad. A larger contingent would follow if we were successful. We retreated into the woods and started on a slow, circular trek toward the hill. We had plenty of cover and reached a position within fifty feet of the base of the hill without issue. Dee and I decided that I would take half of the team to the base of the hill while he and the other half provided cover, if needed.

We slowly crept out from the wooded canopy and reached the exposed area at the bottom of the hill. After checking our weapons, we began to ascend the hill on our stomachs. We heard them before we saw them, as they alerted each other of our presence using high-pitched shrills. Several of the brown creatures came barreling over the crest of the hill. My guess is that they had spotted Dee's group farther away and were surprised to find us looking up at them from the hillside. Our advantage was slight and short-lived. We rose to our knees and opened fire, while Dee's group rushed forward to assist. We were able to dispatch the first wave with our weapons. When the second wave made contact shortly thereafter, we found ourselves in close-quarter combat.

I threw my Uzi over my shoulder and drew my knife. Suddenly my entire world consisted of the two feet of cylindrical space that surrounded me. I slowly inched my way up the hill by slashing and smashing everything in front of me. The creatures were weaker than us, yet they were tenacious and hungry for a fight. They came at us relentlessly. As I made my third kill with a direct knife thrust into the midsection of one, I felt a sting in my lower left leg. I glanced down to see blood but had no time to deal with it. Just to my left I saw a creature hanging around Susan's neck. They fell to the ground in a tangled heap. I leaped over to them, pulled the animal off of her and slammed it into the hard ground.

Within two minutes we had reached the summit of the small hill. We dropped onto our bellies and began firing down on the onrushing enemies, forcing them to retreat and take cover. I took advantage of a brief respite to survey the damage behind me. One of our combots and five human soldiers lay dead or wounded. At least fifteen enemy reptilians were killed on the hill, plus one human soldier. I saw a commotion erupt on the opposite side of the landing site as our comrades pounded the enemy's left flank. Shortly afterward, Cap led the remaining forces on a charge from the middle of the line. My team held its position and cut off any chance of an enemy escape to their right.

I had completely forgotten about my leg when the pain suddenly returned with a vengeance. Ying noticed me wincing.

"You hurt?" she asked. I flipped onto my back and nodded toward my leg. Ying briefly inspected the plasma wound on my calf. "Nah, not bad," she said with a smirk, as if accusing me of faking it. "You a big boy. Suck it up."

I directed an expletive at her, which only made her laugh—the second time I ever made her laugh. She was right, though. The plasma round had only nicked me and I had narrowly averted disaster.

"I have to go now. *Somebody* have to fight," she said and took off down the hill with the others toward the action. I managed to regain my feet and limped behind them.

Despite having gained the upper hand, the battle persisted for a while longer and not without significant losses to our side. The enemy continued to hold a position at the rear of the ship and repel our attacks. The fire coming from their location finally ceased, at which time five of our soldiers slowly approached. As soon as they came within a few feet of the position, a huge explosion detonated, taking their lives and completely ripping apart the aft section of the ship. The concussion knocked most of the soldiers within a hundred-foot radius off their feet. Unable to gain their prize ship, the enemy had rigged a boobytrap to render it useless for anyone else.

We eventually linked up with Cap's team and the group from the right side of our line, just behind the ship. Still alive and in our custody were three of the odd brown creatures, two human soldiers, two Serrones, and one small android that reminded me of the little guy who minded the orcos. Many other enemy combatants had likely escaped into the woods.

As I limped to the side of the ship with Cap and Dee, the Chief and his two lieutenants approached cautiously in their chariots. Word of my flanking maneuver had already spread throughout the camp's Serrone-android network.

"Captain Cheefon congratulates you on your accomplishments in this battle," Khan said to me. "This combat robot," he continued while gesturing toward Cap, "informed Captain Cheefon that you devised a plan to counter the enemy offensive." I had to give it to the combots—they never stole credit for anything. Their penchant for honesty was just as strong as their loyalty.

"I did what was necessary for the defense of the People's Resistance Front," I replied with a straight face.

"You are injured," said Khan. "You must be attended to." On cue, Cap and Dee began to look around. Then it occurred to me. They were looking for Mik, and Mik was inside the ship! I had completely forgotten about Malcolm and Charles. I had also neglected to brief Dee and Cap on the situation inside the ship when they first arrived on the scene.

"The ship!" I cried. I quickly apprised everyone within earshot of what I had witnessed at the start of the attack. The three Serrones quickly retreated to a safe position as we approached the door.

"We are unable to establish contact with anyone inside," Cap said. "We must open the door ourselves."

We regrouped and formulated a plan to enter the ship simultaneously from two doors and the hole that was blown open at the aft section by the boobytrap. Kaiser exposed a panel next to the side door where the welcoming party and attackers had entered. Chairman Mao did the same next to a door on the opposite side of the ship. Dee was to lead a team through the first door, Cap through the second, and I would take a team into the aft section of the ship via the blast hole. Cap suggested that my injury might hamper my abilities but there was no way I was sitting this one out. Malcolm and Charles were in there somewhere.

The signal was given and the sentroids opened the doors. I turned on the flashlight that I had taped to my Uzi and limped into the darkness. At my feet were the remains of the enemy creatures that had been annihilated by their own boobytrap or killed in the firefight that preceded it. A putrid stench filled the air just inside the ship, an amalgam of melting metal and burning flesh—human and otherwise.

We passed cautiously through the rear of the ship, pushing back loose wires with our rifles and avoiding the sharp edges of the wreckage that jutted into our path. Then we heard the sounds—a chorus of moaning, sobbing, and screaming. I stopped and slowly directed my flashlight all around, as did the others in my party. The horror engulfed us from all directions. We were already standing in the rear cargo hold—the same cargo hold that was once my home. Whatever wall existed between it and the aft section of the ship had been obliterated. Mangled bodies were pressed against the sides of the hold in various contortions; many remained strapped to the wreckage by one wrist and one ankle, having not yet been released before the surprise attack commenced. I surmised that I was probably standing near the location of my own berth.

We made our way a few more feet and shone light onto the first survivors we encountered. Some were injured; all were terrified. It was extremely frustrating that we could do little for them until we secured the ship. I tried to assuage their fears with words of encouragement, but what does one say in such an inconceivable predicament? I recalled Malcolm's first words on my first day as I stood bewildered outside the ship: "You are now soldiers of the People's Resistance Front." I decided it would be best to hold off on that one.

What could I tell these forsaken people? Don't worry? You're safe now? We'll have you on your feet and fighting lizard creatures before you know it? I just implored them to calm down, and pledged that things would soon become clearer. Some of them cowered in fear as we passed and recoiled to the back wall of their cubicles. I tried to reassure one frightened young woman that I was one of them by holding my flashlight under my chin in order to illuminate my face in the darkness. Far from being placated, she shrieked like a child listening to a ghost story around a campfire. It probably didn't help that the flashlight was taped to the barrel of my Uzi.

We finally came to the hatch at the front end of the hold. It was tightly sealed, so I dispatched a soldier to go back and find out what was happening on the other side of the door. I assumed that any potential danger on that side had already been eliminated by Dee or Cap.

"Tell them that we're clear on this end. They can open the door from that side," I said.

The hatch slid open a few minutes later and I stepped into the small room that we once called the yard. It was empty except for Chairman Mao, who had opened the door. I waited for the sentroid to say something—maybe give me an order. He just stood quietly. I took the initiative, even though I was still very apprehensive around those powerful androids.

"Can you release the people in the hold back there?" I asked. I pointed to my wrist. "The straps?" Mao waited a moment then walked past me into the hold. I asked the soldiers with me to remain behind and assist the newcomers. "Keep them in there until you hear back from me," I instructed. I crossed the small room and entered the next one where I encountered Cap.

"How many soldiers are alive in that section?" Cap asked.

"I didn't count."

I left him there and entered the front cargo hold. Coming from the rear, this was the room before the one into which Malcolm, Charles, and the others had retreated. The lights above the corridor were turned on. The abductees in the back of the front cargo hold remained strapped into their berths and appeared to be unharmed. It was eerily silent—a familiar sensation to me. The newcomers' curious expressions indicated that they had likely been ordered to stay quiet. I walked toward the front of the hold and spotted Dee ahead in the next room with a couple of soldiers. I moved toward them but didn't get far before encountering an obstacle in the corridor, the body of a brown scaly creature. I took a heavy sigh and surveyed the carnage that lay before, beside, and above me.

The dead creatures were scattered everywhere. I imagined that they had darted into every nook and cranny upon entering the ship. Most of the newcomers I encountered in that section of the hold were dead or near death. The hatch leading from this hold to the small room where Malcolm and the others had entered the ship must have been opened before the attack. I stepped over the twisted remains of an android that I recognized as Thing Two, then made my way into the small forward room into which the welcoming party had retreated at the start of the attack.

This was clearly where most of melee had occurred. Bodies were scattered about, overlapping each other as if they had been killed somewhere else then tossed inside here. The walls and floors were splattered with a mix of human blood, yellow android fluid, and whatever it was that coursed through the veins of the scaly creatures. It was difficult to find patches of bare floor on which to step. I could see what looked like a sentroid underneath a pile of five or six enemy corpses. I pulled one off the pile to reveal what was left of Thing One. It was obvious that he hadn't gone down without a fight, nor did any of the other soldiers who were trapped there. It must have been a gruesome and tumultuous brawl, transpiring in such a tiny space that it was probably over in seconds.

I eventually reached Dee, who was standing over Malcolm's lifeless body. Malcolm was sitting with his back against the wall and his legs outstretched. His body was riddled with wounds. A strange little rifle lay across his stomach, with one of his hands draped over it. I recalled that neither Malcolm nor Charles were armed when they set out to meet the incoming ship. Malcolm had likely wrestled this from one of the enemy creatures.

Slumped across Malcolm's legs was Mik's torso; his severed robotic head lay a few feet away. The sentroids Adolph and Stalin had already been removed from the ship and laid on the ground nearby. They appeared to be less damaged but were also lifeless. I counted the remains of sixteen enemy creatures strewn about the forward room and the front cargo hold. One was found inside a lower berth alongside the body of a newcomer. It had probably sought cover there. I peered inside and imagined the terror that poor abductee must have felt when that thing climbed into his compartment. Then it occurred to me that I hadn't seen Charles. I nudged a few enemy bodies here and there using my feet to see if he might be lying underneath. He wasn't.

"Where's Charles?" I asked Dee. He looked confused. "Doc," I clarified.

"Outside," said Dee.

"Alive?"

"Yes."

I hurried to the door but was halted by Dee's outstretched arm.

"Shakespeare—he will not live."

I found Charles lying barely conscious in the grass near the door of the ship. A few of our comrades were doing what they could to halt the blood that was escaping from multiple wounds. A jeep pulled up from which two soldiers carried over a stretcher. I helped load him onto the stretcher and tried speaking to him as the soldiers carried him back to the jeep.

"Hey Charles," I said. I couldn't find the right words to continue.

"Ah, Mister Shakespeare," he mumbled. "Good to see you, man."

"We're taking you to the infirmary. You might have to tell us what to do."

"Not much you can do, my friend. Maybe fetch me some of that moonshine."

"Sure thing."

I rode with him to the infirmary where we laid him down onto a bed. Susan came in with a bottle but he was too weak to drink. Nicholas entered with Leesheh, whom he had fetched from the nursery.

"I am lucky," Charles said softly. "Now they will have to discharge me and send me home." He laughed weakly at his joke then quietly died.

Leesheh and I walked back to the landing site where I reconstructed the events of the battle. The bodies from both sides were being collected into piles for incineration. The remains of Mik and the sentroids that had been destroyed were loaded onto a flatbed. I doubted that the PRF had the expertise to repair them, but they held residual value for spare parts. The Chief had returned to the battlefield and was overseeing the cleanup process, flanked by Khan and Kaiser—two of the three sentroids that still functioned. Cap and Dee were busy assembling the newly arrived soldiers. As much as I dreaded it, I figured I could be of use there. I told Leesheh that she might as well go and spend time with Jasper while the Serrones and sentroids were too preoccupied to notice.

Thirty-seven of the newcomers walked off of the ship under their own power. Sixteen wounded newbies were carried off and every one of them died before the end of the following day. Thirty-five more had been killed during the battle and subsequent explosion. They were carried from the ship and heaped onto the mounds of dead soldiers. I was one of the few wounded soldiers to survive the battle. Even if our medics, Charles and Mik, had not both been killed, we still lacked medicine and supplies. Fortunately for myself, my leg had been superficially grazed; a week later it was nearly healed and permanently scarred.

We lost fifty-one human soldiers in the battle, plus three combots. The number of soldiers in camp had dipped below 100, down from nearly 150 when I first arrived. We now had 84 humans including the new conscripts.

Perhaps the most consequential loss was the rickety old spaceship that lay in ruins outside of camp. Rumor quickly spread that it was the last of its kind. I held out hope that there might be another functioning starship somewhere on the planet. Deep down I knew that the idea of returning to Earth was quickly deteriorating into nothing more than a fantasy.

23

As the enslaved property and non-ranking members of the PRF, we were never briefed on the reasons for attacks such as the raid on the ship. Yet fragments of information, as I mentioned before, somehow made their way from General Abasha's circle of trusted advisors down through the android hierarchy to the combots, where they were eventually shared with the de facto leaders of the human slave population.

As you are aware, I had risen to such a level within my own camp. In addition to winning the confidence of my human comrades, I had apparently gained the loyalty of several combots. I also claimed, at that time, to have earned the admiration of the Serrone officer presiding over the company to which I belonged, at least in the way that a prince might value his prized stallion. Make no mistake—my future was bleak. But in the context of my surroundings, and relative to the other humans on this planet, my bleakness seemed brighter than most—one of the brightest in the entire world.

And so, I learned that the People's Resistance Front was now at war with King Tosso, venerated leader of the Kingdom of Toghan, our neighbor to the north. It was the king's army that attacked us. The surprise attack occurred only days after King Tosso withdrew from a non-aggression pact with General Abasha. The agreement had been in place since Abasha seized power following the assassination of the President (for life) of The Republic of Whatchamacallit, a.k.a, Region Seventeen. The reasons for King Tosso's revocation of the peace treaty with the PRF did not find their way down to me. It's possible that the king had decided that General Abasha was getting too big for his britches, or maybe the king had his heart set on possessing the last starship.

We felt immediate repercussions of this new war and the sneak attack on our camp. Malcolm's loss greatly impacted morale. We would all sorely miss his wisdom and experience, and none would miss his friendship more than his old buddy Swag. They had spent more than twenty years together on the planet, first as slaves schlepping ammunition for massive android armies, and ultimately as warriors in the PRF. Swag kept mostly to himself for a few days following the attack before his affable front returned, though I suspect that his grief lingered for some time after.

The company suffered immeasurably from the loss of Charles' medical expertise. His death affected me more deeply than I had thought it could. I didn't realize how much he had meant to me until after he was gone. He was like the older brother I never had. Death was now a regular part of my life and I had grown a thick skin to insulate myself from its influence. I had been troubled by the losses of Ammo, Jessie, Malcolm, and others, but not shaken. The loss of Charles took longer to process and might have crippled my resolve if not for the presence of Leesheh and little Jasper. All of us who benefited from Charles' leadership and equanimity in those early days on the cargo ship were impacted, including Susan, Nicholas, Pablo, and several others from the hold who had outlived him.

Other repercussions of the war were soon revealed, all of which would have a negative impact on me and my family. I had feared that we would abandon the camp after the arrival of the new soldiers. One day after the attack, Cap informed us that the order for relocation had been issued by General Abasha, and for much different reasons than before.

Firstly, the Toghans were feared to have a larger army than the PRF. We had witnessed firsthand their use of other alien races, specifically the "lizzies," as they were known by the old-timers. Cap intimated that the PRF had little intelligence regarding the capabilities of their forces—aircraft, androids, weaponry, troops, etc. As a result, we had been ordered to consolidate with another PRF camp to the south, and closer to Abasha City. Nor could we have remained in the camp anyway, as we were all at once too small in number to defend it. We were ordered to evacuate the camp within five days.

Secondly, a small scout team was to break off from our company and move north in search of Toghan forces. It would be a very risky mission, to say the least. The team was to be led by Bar, who would undoubtedly take with him the likes of Sparks and Tully, and I would be more than happy to see all of them go. I would not expect to see them again.

The most troublesome development, albeit the least surprising, was that the children and non-combative women in camp were to be evacuated to Abasha City. I suppose the General wished to consolidate his slave reproduction in one place and out of harm's way. Leesheh and I tried to mentally prepare ourselves and each other for this day. We began to make whatever preparations we could to ensure the survival of our eight-week-old son. The most immediate and obvious concern was perhaps the easiest to solve. There was a wet nurse in camp who was ready and willing to take over for Leesheh. She would be traveling with Jasper to Abasha City where, we were told, several women divided the nursing duties for the community of slave children there. Although Leesheh was uncomfortable with the idea of relinquishing her rite of motherhood, she was relieved that her son would not go hungry.

As more information describing the conditions for slave children in Abasha City trickled down to me from various sources, I became less apprehensive about parting with my son. There could be no substitute for having him with us, but having reconciled that luxury to be unattainable, there was something to be said for the safety in numbers offered by Abasha City. I expected that we would soon see our son again, and repeatedly, if only sporadically. I didn't know how close our new camp would be to the city other than that it had to be closer than our present location. Surely there would be some reason for us to visit the city.

Late in the afternoon of the day following the attack, Leesheh and I called upon Tina and Saba in the cathouse. They were as jittery as anyone concerning the recent developments and peppered me with questions about the upcoming changes. After telling them everything I knew, Leesheh disclosed the reason for our visit.

"Shakespeare and I have a favor to ask of you," she said eloquently. "We know that you have your own lives to worry about, and we know that it will be difficult to survive in Abasha City. You will be faced with… new challenges…" She seemed to regret having started down a particular path. The challenges facing these young women were obvious to everyone and did not need mentioning.

"Would you consider watching out for Jasper—if you can?" I asked.

"Well, I don't consider that a favor," Tina said without hesitation. "I would have looked out for Jasper even if you'd never asked. I just assumed it was my job now."

"Me too," said Saba.

"Hell, Shakespeare, you saved our lives," Tina continued. "Of course, I'll take care of the boy—who I happen to adore, by the way."

We thanked the women profusely and remained with them for a while doing our best to talk about more lighthearted subjects, of which there were so few. On the way back to the barracks, Leesheh and I discussed how much Tina had changed since we arrived on Serrone. Most of us had changed physically—arguably nobody more than myself. In Tina we both noticed something beyond the toll of the physical abuse she had sustained. It was in the way she looked at us and the way she spoke. She had been one of the more optimistic captives in the cargo hold, and now there was little sign of any spirit within her. It was like talking to an old woman who had lived her life and was waiting for it to end. She could not have been older than twenty-five.

"That could have been me," said Leesheh.

"Yeah." The image it conjured gave me a chill.

"But if I lived there, in the cathouse, I could still be with Jasper."

"There probably wouldn't be a Jasper, and you'd probably be dead. I think we made the right decision."

"You're right," she said. "I think Jasper will be good for Tina—and Saba."

"I agree. Saba's a good kid."

I think that Leesheh and I were feeding each other contrived positive expectations in the hopes of receiving genuine positive expectations in return. The result of this feedback loop was that we both started to believe that everything might be okay. I even imagined a nursery school in the city with a bunch of kids singing songs led by a group of exuberant young women smiling and clapping their hands. I returned to the barracks feeling cautiously optimistic—*very* cautiously—about the future of our child. My optimism was rooted in little more than a fabricated hope. Nothing I had experienced on this planet warranted such expectations, except for one thing: I believed that I was different. I believed that I had cracked the code to the Serrone masters.

The sentroids undoubtedly milked the Toghan Serrone prisoners for intelligence then duly executed any that survived the interrogation process. I presume that the two humans died from torture as well. I cannot say whether the lizzies possessed a level of intelligence worthy of extraction or if they were simply disposed of. I saw nothing of the prisoners after they were taken from the landing site following the battle, including the little android. I doubt that he would have been destroyed, as androids were becoming a rare and valuable commodity on Serrone. If it were true that there were no more starships, then humans, lizzies, orcos, and all other alien slaves would also increase in value as we decimated each other at the whims of our masters. The longer I could survive, the more valuable I would become.

I wasn't sure what to make of the new war with the Toghans. That we would transition from one conflict to another without a peaceful hiatus was not unprecedented. Based on my knowledge of Serrone history following their Great War, it should have been expected. King Tosso had likely been biding his time while the PRF and the rebel factions slugged it out, severely weakening each other. I had no knowledge of Toghan strengths and capabilities other than the lizzies, which I felt confident in defeating based on my limited experience fighting them. They seemed blindly-aggressive and prone to overextending their lines. That is, I thought they were in too much of a hurry. That might not be so bad if the king had multitudes of lizzies to spare, which I questioned.

The relocation of the children and evacuation of the camp were inevitable. I couldn't attribute those to the new war. Nor did the new war cause me to reconsider my personal objectives. The new enemy would provide opportunities to increase my skills and gain the trust and confidence of the Chief, which I could exploit to reunite with my son and find a way back to Earth. And if along the way I reduced the population of Serrones, androids, otherworldly aliens, and humans wishing to harm me and my family, then all the better. The more I thought about it, the more I liked what this new war could do for my vengeful quest. I resolved to become stronger, tougher, and nastier.

From a military standpoint, I was much more concerned about the setback within my own company. Our depreciated numbers left us vulnerable. Although the starship was beyond repair and no longer a prize, a second attack by the Toghans was not out of the question. In addition to making preparations for the relocation, it was imperative that we provide whatever training and orientation we could for the thirty-seven new conscripts. That task fell upon Cap, Dee, and myself. The duties of the three surviving sentroids were limited to the personal security of the Chief and his two lieutenants. The sneak attack on the camp seemed to have rattled our Serrone masters. They had become even more scarce, and seeing less of them was okay by me. Not surprisingly, the Chief retained the services of Khan and Kaiser for himself, while Ringo and Ratso were forced to share the protection of Chairman Mao.

Following the battle, the newbies had been marched down to the courtyard where they sat for hours in a state of mental anguish and confusion underneath the vigilant eyes of Bar, Sparks, and Tully. The Chief and his entourage finally showed up, and I listened to Khan deliver a condensed version of the lecture that we had received on our first day. Not only was the speech shortened, it had also been updated to note that the PRF was at war with the "nefarious" Kingdom of Toghan, and that the "vicious war crimes" of King Tosso would not go unpunished. Absent was any mention of women being assigned to reproductive duties. I guess it was an all-hands-on-deck situation for the Chief. No soldiers could be spared for any job other than defending him.

I had no intention of addressing the group in spite of an overwhelming sense of empathy that rushed over me while watching them listen to Khan. Once the Chief had departed, Cap and Dee both looked to me, as did Leesheh. The combots were disinclined to speak to the newcomers and wanted me to fill Malcolm's shoes as the person responsible for their well-being. I doubt it was intentional, but they successfully exploited my increasing self-conceit as the alpha male in the company. On top of that, Leesheh whispered something about everyone counting on me. She accompanied her message with a disarming gaze that melted my defenses—as always. And so compelled, I addressed the neophytes.

"My name is Shakespeare. Now, I know you're confused…" It was as if I had channeled Malcolm's ghost and it was speaking through me. I wondered how many of the newbies would refuse to accept my advice, as I had once renounced his. I told them to forget about ever seeing Earth again, even though I still held on to the dream. I told them that I would do my best to keep them alive, even though my only concern was to protect my family and friends. I told them that I would teach them how to survive, even though I cared more about killing enemies and winning the war. I told them that they should respect the power and authority of the sentroids, even though I pondered ways to take them down. I employed my acting skills to mask my insincerity and even fooled Leesheh.

"That was a good thing you did," she told me. "They will look up to you now, and you should protect them."

"I will."

There was no point in trying to consolidate the new conscripts into a single hut, as they would only be residing there for a few days. We fed them then dispersed them among the five huts so that they might mix in with the veterans and learn via osmosis. Although the group of newbies comprised citizens of the Northeastern United States and Canada, we insisted that some bunk with the Chinese and Africans. A few ended up in my hut. They proceeded to barrage me with questions as I had done to Malcolm on my first night. I did what I could to mollify them, though I mostly just pawned them off to Nicholas, who was eager to pontificate on the astronomical ramifications of their long voyage. I finally ordered them to their bunks and climbed into my own, hampered by the sting of my injured leg. A young African-American man wearing stylish eyeglasses approached the side of my bed.

"Can I sleep here?" he asked while pointing down to Charles' bed. I sat up on my elbows and studied the young man. Maybe it was a trick of the brain, or because he had just brought Charles to mind, but his resemblance to my old friend was uncanny. I reminded myself that Charles only had daughters and told the man that he could have the bunk.

"My name's Mike," he said while offering his hand. I hadn't heard that name in a long time.

"Shakespeare."

"Are you in charge here?"

"Nah… I don't know. I'm just a slave like you." For some reason his question made me uneasy. I enjoyed my elevated reputation but I didn't want to shoulder the responsibility when these newbies started dying. I changed the subject to his eyeglasses. "Remind me tomorrow about your glasses. We can strengthen them up with some tape. Nick over there can help you. Now, you should try to get some sleep, even though we both know that you won't."

"Thanks."

We led the conscripts on a brief tour of the camp following breakfast the next day, which simply means that we took them to the stream. They already knew where the latrines and the food pavilion were, and there was no point in taking them anywhere else. Cap informed them that the rest of the camp was off limits and that anyone caught in an unauthorized area would be shot or tasered. The veterans found his bluff comical; the newbies were still naïve enough to believe it.

All available security resources, i.e., those not assigned to protecting the Serrones, had been deployed along the camp perimeter. It was now a much more lenient camp than it had been when I arrived. This was the result of deficiency, and not by choice. I felt very insecure in the camp and actually would have appreciated a few more sentroids looking out for us. I kept my Uzi strapped to my shoulder and Leesheh near my side at all times, except for when she was with Jasper at the nursery and I was unable to join them. In those instances, I asked Susan or Ying to keep an eye on them. Jasper was still under my care and I redoubled my efforts to protect him.

I suggested to my combot comrades that we dispense with the one-on-one grappling matches for the newcomers, to which they agreed. We concurred that the most valuable lesson we could impart was how to operate the arc rifles. (We now had more rifles than soldiers and plenty of plasma cartridges to load into them.) As we marched to the makeshift firing range, I wrestled with the notion of a covert task that had occurred to me while listening to Khan's speech on the previous day. I considered it a necessary undertaking but doubted that I could pull it off without the consent, or at least the acquiescence, of the combots.

I decided to confide in Dee and nudged him away from the group as we walked. Dee had continued to be such an enigma to me. Just when he seemed almost human, he would revert back to the company line, as if he had been reprogrammed overnight. Nicholas was more optimistic about the changes he had perceived in Dee and some of the other combots. I hadn't fully grasped the science of artificial intelligence and was reticent to acknowledge it. Still, I had little choice but to trust the android.

"There are two women here among the newcomers who would not make good soldiers," I suggested to Dee. "I think it would be in our best interest, and theirs, if we send them to the cathouse."

"There are no reproductive activities allowed in camp," he noted. I'd like to think he was referring my recent ultimatum, though it was more likely the result of Khan's speech to the newbies.

"I know, but if they're in the cathouse, then they'll be sent to Abasha–" I quickly stopped myself. I was never sure which slang terms the combots understood. "To the *capital city* in a few days where they can be used for reproduction and other duties." Dee silently processed my proposal. It occurred to me that he might be running it by his superiors. "Maybe we should keep this to ourselves," I added. "The Chief… um, Captain Cheefon might not understand why this is necessary."

"Yes," replied Dee, "the Chief would not understand that this is the best course of action." I could have sworn that he had emphasized the word "chief." Maybe this was his way of telling me that we were of a like mind.

"Thanks, Dee. I'll take care of it." It was the first time I had ever thanked an android, and it was heartfelt.

I made my way discreetly to the first of the two women whom I had designated for the cathouse. Unlike Leesheh, there was no time to allow for them to decide their own fate. I truly believed that they had a better chance for survival in Abasha City. I had convinced myself that they might escape the habitual misogynistic practices of the PRF there. I further surmised that if they remained with us, they might find themselves assigned to a cathouse in the new camp, which could be a far worse fate. I might not have the clout to protect them there. I pulled the petite woman aside and told her to wait while I quickly fetched the other. The second woman was even frailer than the first. My hand wrapped around her upper arm with plenty of room remaining for my fingers to touch.

We started walking together, purposely falling back from the group. I tried to explain my plan for them as pragmatically as possible, without too much emphasis on the positives or the negatives.

"I'm taking you two to meet some friends of mine," I said nebulously. "I have an idea to help you get by."

"Can you take us home?" asked one. I realized that she needed a large-scale reset of expectations.

"I'm sorry, no. That's not possible." I stopped them and addressed them earnestly. "You need to understand that you're a long, long way from home. This planet... this world, is a very dangerous place. There's nothing good here. There are no… positive alternatives." They looked at me with such trust and innocence that I unexpectantly found myself fighting back tears. "I can send you away from here—away from the fighting. But you have to understand that where you're going is also not a pleasant place." Tears now quietly rolled down their cheeks and I quickly wiped my own eyes. "You have to trust me. When things are really bad *there*, you have to trust me that it would have been a lot worse *here*. Okay?" What choice did they have? They nodded in affirmation and we continued to the building that had formerly served as the cathouse.

"I have another favor to ask of you," I said to Tina upon arrival. I started to introduce the young women then realized that I didn't know their names. Once they introduced themselves, I explained my plan to Tina and Saba, somewhat cryptically, to avoid painting a bleak picture in front of the neophytes. I also didn't want to imply to Tina and Saba that I expected them to be forced back into unthinkable atrocities in Abasha City. It was a subject best left untouched. As I expected, Tina and Saba were eager to help.

"You'll need to act like they've been here all along and didn't just arrive on the ship," I advised. "I think that the Serrones are too distracted these days to care."

"Got it," said Tina.

"If there's a problem," I continued proudly, "I'll do what I can to intervene. I have some leverage with the Chief."

The two newbies thanked me. They seemed a little perplexed about exactly what it was they were thanking me for, yet they were gracious nonetheless. Their gratitude made me feel a little better about my decision and about myself. When I joined the others at the range, Cap had finished instructing the new soldiers on how to load and fire an arc rifle. I recalled the incident in which one of my fellow newcomers had willfully blown off his own head. In a peculiar attempt to prevent a similar action, I picked up a loaded rifle and delivered a short speech. It was undoubtedly fueled by the vanity and pride stemming from my actions regarding the two women.

"Before we start practicing, is there anyone here who would like to take this arc rifle and blow off his or her head? No? You can end it all now—just stick this end in your mouth and push these two buttons." I paused for a few seconds and scowled at the crowd. "Okay then, let's begin."

I handed the rifle to Dee who commenced with the individual firings.

As I write this, I can see how absurd my behavior seems. It was a misguided intent to avert potential acts of what I considered to be cowardice. It occurred to me later that I hadn't judged the man who killed himself to be a coward at the time. I remembered how much his courage had impressed me that day.

The session transpired without incident and we returned to the courtyard where Cap briefly discussed tactical maneuvers and non-verbal signals to be employed during combat. That concluded their training and we shifted our focus on the impending evacuation.

Despite slight misgivings about abandoning Mike and the other neophytes in my hut, I spent the night with Leesheh and Jasper in our usual spot under the stumpy plant with the eggplant-colored leaves, encircled by our personal guard of thorny bushes. We awoke before daylight and stealthily replaced Jasper into his wooden basket inside the nursery. We returned to the barracks in time to accompany the troops to breakfast.

Upon returning to the barracks, Leesheh and I were happy to find the small scout team busy assembling in the road near the courtyard. As I had hoped and expected, Bar had recruited Sparks, Tully, and a few other natives to join the team for the perilous northern expedition. Rounding out the group of ten were a second combot and some soldiers selected from the Chinese contingent. A few us stood nearby and deliberated the bleak prospects of the reconnaissance mission. Before long, most of the company had gathered in the courtyard, as if to pay their final respects. Nobody expected to see anyone return from what seemed to us as a suicide mission deep into enemy territory. I sympathized with the few acquaintances I had on the patrol and silently bid the others good riddance. As they loaded supplies onto a jeep and single flatbed, I wondered how far they would be able to drive them without being spotted.

The Chief, his lieutenants, and the three sentroids appeared when the convoy was loaded and ready to depart. I was astonished to watch Ratso take a seat in the rear of the jeep. I wasn't surprised to see that he had been assigned to the team, but this was the first time I had witnessed a Serrone PRF officer go anywhere without a sentroid escort. The Chief was evidently unwilling to part with one of his two bodyguards for the welfare of his underling.

We waited several minutes longer for the patrol to get underway.

There appeared to be some issue delaying their departure. Bar and Cap were engaged in a conference with Khan and presumably, the Chief. We thought little of it until Bar and Cap began looking in my direction periodically. It was very difficult to discern when androids were in disagreement, but this particular conference was clearly displaying some of the subtle indications. They looked my way again. A dreadful thought occurred to me.

"I think Bar is trying to recruit me for the mission," I said to Leesheh and the others nearby.

"Do you think so?" Leesheh asked doubtfully.

"They keep looking over here. I can see why he would want me. I'll just tell the Chief to keep me here." Bar broke from the conversation and walked toward me. "Geez, here he comes," I groaned.

My mind started racing again. I had to think of a good reason for staying with the company, and I couldn't stop wondering why they would want me on the mission. Did the Chief not realize it was a suicide mission? Bar stopped in front of us and pointed to Leesheh.

"She is to go with us," he said.

"Wait… *what?*" I couldn't find any other words. This bombshell was completely out of left field.

"She is to go with us," Bar repeated. "Come now, into the truck."

"This makes no sense!" I yelled. "Why would… Hold on… Cap! Dee!" They did nothing. Leesheh's legs wobbled and she grabbed my arm.

"I… I need to get some things," she stammered.

"We have supplies in the truck. Come now," said Bar, as he reached out his hand and grasped Leesheh's arm. She let go of me as Bar began walking her to the truck. I froze in place and looked around—everywhere—anywhere—for support. My friends returned sympathetic looks of consternation, but what could they do? Leesheh turned back to me, her face overcome with dread. I regained some of my equilibrium and darted toward the truck.

"You can't take her!" I shouted. "She needs to–"

Before I could say another word, my entire body turned to jelly as fifty thousand volts coursed through it. I fell to the ground face first, paralyzed and convulsing, and barely conscious. I don't know how much time elapsed before I regained enough awareness and ability to roll onto my back. Khan stood over me with his taser appendage extended, fully prepared to repeat the process.

"Stay here," he commanded.

As I struggled to compose a plea to the Chief, Swag approached.

"I'll go along too. You can use someone like me," he said directly to the Chief. Then I heard Ying's voice, followed by Susan's, also volunteering for the mission. After a moment, Khan spoke.

"He goes," the sentroid said, pointing to Swag. The magnitude of Swag's gesture—his sacrifice—combined with the sight of Leesheh in the back of the flatbed, reduced me to tears.

"Swag… thank you," I said. He bent down on one knee and put his hand on my chest.

"No sweat, mate. I'll keep her outta trouble," he said softly, then headed for the truck. I knew that his pledge would be impossible to uphold. I tried to regain my feet and appeal to the Chief. Khan placed his arm on my shoulder and nudged me back down.

"Silence," Khan said. As the convoy slowly pulled away, Leesheh called to me from the back of the truck.

"Shakespeare—Jasper!"

"I will!" I shouted back. We both knew that there was little I could do for my son, yet I needed to assure her that I would do whatever I could for him.

Tully's diabolical voice was the last thing I heard from the convoy. "Don't worry—we take good care of her, Shake-a-spear!"

When the vehicles were out of sight. Khan ordered the crowd to disperse. I tried to rise but he pushed me down once again. The Chief stared at me through his tinted goggles.

"Captain Cheefon has a message for you," Khan began. "You are a soldier in the People's Resistance Front. You do not fight for a woman and child."

Now it became clearer to me. This was not Bar's design—this order came directly from the Chief. Did he see through my schemes? Why did he question my loyalties? Where had I messed up? I must have underestimated his awareness of what transpired within the camp. I wanted to ask him but held my tongue. A discussion between the master and his slave would not be allowed. My time would have to wait, but it would come. I swore it to myself.

"There are other women with whom you can breed," continued Khan. I considered lunging for the Chief but knew that I wouldn't get anywhere near him. Khan was practically on top of me, and beyond him stood Kaiser. I decided to double down and let the master think that he had broken me.

"I fight only for the People's Resistance Front," I announced. "King Tosso must be brought to justice."

The Chief and his sentroids left the courtyard without further comment. I remained on the ground sobbing until my friends came to collect me. My life was shattered. Leesheh was gone and my son would soon be taken from me as well. Perhaps the Chief had broken me after all.

24

The Chief's "message" for me persisted into the following day. I awoke early following a restless night and headed for the door with the intention of visiting Jasper in the nursery. Dee stood inside the doorway blocking my exit. He extended his hand out as I approached.

"Wait," he said. "The women and children are evacuating to the city today."

"I know. I'm going to see my son."

"No, Shakespeare. You are confined to quarters today."

"Dee, he's my *son*," I entreated. Dee said nothing and turned his head toward the courtyard behind him. I peered over his shoulder and saw Kaiser. I knew then that I would have no chance of saying goodbye to my son. All I could do was ask Nicholas to check on him and wish Tina and Saba good luck from me. A few hours later, a small aircraft landed in a remote part of camp, remained there for a short while, then returned to the air. My confinement to barracks ended shortly thereafter.

I walked down to the nursery and sat quietly for several hours on Leesheh's empty bed. My mind raced back and forth, mulling over ways to bring her back, and plotting the demise of my Serrone masters. I came up empty on both fronts and resorted to pitying myself. I would almost have rather seen her die than have to imagine the different ways she might be tortured and abused. I remained in the nursery long after nightfall. The Serrones didn't seem to care so much about my whereabouts any longer. Eventually I wandered off to the old spot encircled by the thorny bushes and fell asleep, only to be awakened by a torrential rainfall a few hours later. Another season on Serrone was coming to an end.

Although it provided little consolation to me at the time, I discovered that the two women I had placed in the cathouse had successfully departed for Abasha City with the others. Maybe the Chief was throwing me a bone? *Not likely,* I figured. He probably agreed that the women were of better use in the city or simply hadn't noticed them. As I pondered the horrors to which I might have condemned them, I seemed to feel sorrier for myself than for them.

We spent two more days preparing to leave the camp, sludging through mud and muck during the day while trying to sleep under leaking roofs at night. I was in no mood for conversation and my friends gave me a wide berth. Nobody was more gratified than I when the jeeps and trucks were finally lined up and loaded for departure. As soon as I could get out there—anywhere—the better chance I would have of finding her. I knew we'd be heading in the opposite direction of her reconnaissance party, but staying put wasn't a viable option. I wanted to get far away from the camp that I had recently come to loathe more than ever.

Like my comrades, my personal belongings were few and fit easily into a rucksack that I had fabricated by sewing together some well-worn shirts. Inside were my secondary knife and sheath. This was a smaller, serrated blade. I had become fond of wearing both knives in battle and employed a two-handed martial arts technique that Ying had taught me. The sack also contained some spare boots, socks, shorts, shirts, and underwear that I had recently washed in the stream using my trusted cereal mush detergent. Finally, I stuffed in a box of plasma cartridges and a few grenades that I had illegally cached.

There were very few personal items to be found on Serrone. We probably missed photographs as much as anything else. I made it a daily habit to picture Leesheh and Jasper in my mind so as not to forget their likenesses. I sometimes asked my friends to describe their own recollection of Leesheh's face, in the unlikely event that there were details I had forgotten. There were rumors of old books, wristwatches, pens, and other Earthly knickknacks to be found in Abasha city. I had yet to see any trace of those items other than some pencils and a few scraps of paper, and I dismissed the rumors as fantasy.

My only other possession, and perhaps my most prized, I wore on my head as we pulled out of camp for the last time. It was a tan beret, very similar to the black headgear worn by the Chief and other Serrone officers in the PRF. I had snatched mine from a dead rebel Serrone a few seasons back. I usually only wore it in combat. I feared the Chief might not appreciate one of his slaves donning Serrone attire, and I could count on him to be absent during combat situations. But it was raining pretty hard that day and I didn't care too much for what the Chief thought at that point. If he wanted the stupid beret, he could have it. I guess he didn't mind or didn't notice, for the beret rarely left my head from that day until the day it finally disintegrated.

We headed south beneath the unwelcome escort of storm clouds that continued to pour down incessantly for the first two days of our expedition. We huddled in the back of the flatbeds underneath flat sheets constructed of a plastic-like material salvaged from old buildings. They rested on top of our heads like tiny shanty roofs. When positioned correctly, which was about half the time, the water would flow down the sheets and over the side of the vehicle. The occasional odd flying creature flew into our laps, either by accident or in an attempt to escape the interminable rain. This never failed to panic the newbies and supply the rest of us with a good laugh. Even I managed to crack a smile before returning to my state of perpetual misery.

At least seven times we had to vacate the relative dryness of our truck in order to help free a vehicle stuck in the bottomless mud. There happened to be a few rain ponchos in the company's inventory, but they were designed to fit an average Serrone and useless to someone of my size. There was also an unofficial rule that the ponchos were reserved for the unlucky soldiers assigned to man the large guns mounted on the backs of the jeeps. Those poor souls were fully-exposed to the rain all day.

We spent the first night huddled in leaky, soggy tents by the side of the road. Somebody might have drowned in his sleep if not for the fact that nobody slept. On the second night we happened upon an uncharted, abandoned village and slept on cold wet floors, for which we were eternally grateful—not that it was in the least bit comfortable, but the elbow room was appreciated. After a few hours of fitful sleep, we were back on the road as Wiyanga climbed into the early morning sky.

The gray clouds finally parted, and we lowered our rain shanties to find ourselves on a much different terrain. It was at nearly the same time that we turned onto a road with a paved surface, which caused more than one person to note the obvious: that we could have used the pavement *before* we left the wet climate. The forests of green and purple flora that we knew in the North were soon replaced by a sparse rocky and arid environment. The rocky hills must have been rich in oxidized iron, for they presented a reddish color that was similar to what I had seen in the deserts of Utah.

The only trees in this region were gigantic timbers with vast yellow canopies. They were spaced hundreds of yards apart, as if they were hoarding all of the ground water in the vicinity, and thus denying the chance of life to anything else except the smallest of plants. As such, they stood out on the horizon like giant lampposts. Animals were scarce too, as would be expected in such a dry region. The giant yellow trees were home to a variety of winged creatures, some of which reminded me of large bats. The skittish critters wanted no part of our convoy and scattered in every direction if we drove anywhere near one of the trees.

Following a brief chow break under the pale blue light of the setting Wiyanga, we climbed back into flatbeds. It promised to be the most disagreeable night of the trip thus far, for we had been informed that the convoy wouldn't be stopping to bivouac. The new kid, Mike, sought me out and wrangled a seat next to me, where he subsequently riddled me with questions about everything under the Serrone sun. He was either very innocent, very brave, or had not received the memo that I was to be left alone. I caught Susan wincing out of the corner of my eye, probably hoping that I wouldn't slice off the young man's head. I indulged a few of the kid's questions and soon found myself quite disarmed by his enthusiasm and charisma. He seemed to be absorbing the shock of his first week on the planet in a pretty good stride. We conversed through most of the night while our comrades lay scattered around us attempting to steal moments of sleep.

Mike hailed from Upstate New York and was a journalism student at Boston University at the time of his abduction. That explained his eagerness to interview me. He was very interested in my history—specifically in my life after abduction. I provided a detailed account of my experiences on Serrone and found the disclosure to be somewhat therapeutic. I appreciated Mike's optimistic expectation of my reunification with Leesheh, though I knew that he had no clue of its futility.

"I think I'll call you Scoop," I told him. "And now, Scoop, I'm gonna to try to get some sleep. You should do the same." I managed an hour or two of light sleep before it was interrupted by an excited commotion among my companions in the truck.

"Something just flew over us—heading north," Nicholas informed me. I asked him the nature of the aircraft. He described a small winged drone that was unlike the jittery eggs we had seen in support of the PRF. We concluded that it probably wasn't one of ours.

"Well, they know where we are," I said. "If the king has any makings of an air force, then we might get a taste of it soon." The Chief must have agreed with my assessment because the convoy soon accelerated, pushing the shaky old flatbeds to their limits. After about thirty minutes we came to the crest of a hill and caught sight of our likely destination—a good place to take cover from a possible airstrike. We were awestruck by the enormity of the old city rising out of the desert, surrounded by vast expanses of nothing in all directions. Soaring skyscrapers were bunched together in the center of the black silhouetted skyline, encircled by smaller edifices. From our distance, still many miles away, the city appeared to be alive and vibrant in the midday light.

This was surely one of the grand Serrone metropolises that the old-timers had described with so much reverence. The cities were the culmination of the once great, now former Serrone civilization. But Jessie, Malcolm, and Swag were not there to enlighten us further on the majesty and efficacy that these cities once boasted. Scoop and the other neophytes in our truck turned to me for an explanation of what lay before them. I admitted that none of us had ever been to one of these cities. As the skyline grew closer, Nicholas and I did our best to reconstruct the depictions that the old-timers had provided to us. No one was more interested in our descriptions than Monte, though I questioned how much of it he understood. It occurred to me later that this was probably the first city he had ever seen, on Earth or anywhere else.

Before long we had reached the outskirts. There were no suburbs; the demarcation between desert and urbanity was unmistakable. Equally undeniable was the evidence of devastation and annihilation. Most of the towering superstructures were now bombed-out husks. Many others had toppled down to cover the streets and smaller buildings—casualties of what must have been massive explosions. Those skyscrapers left standing were gradually progressing toward the same demise as a result of abandonment and deterioration.

We were forced to slow down upon entry and even required to stop periodically to avoid obstacles that littered the main thoroughfare. The city was enveloped in a spooky silence that promoted the appearance of an artificial façade, not unlike an abandoned movie set. Sporadic gusts of wind whistled through the corridors, constantly repositioning loose debris and dust. We gawked and rubbernecked while pointing out peculiar attractions to each other like tourists on an open-top bus.

In many ways the alien metropolis resembled a large Earth city, though not without several odd variances. There were no signs—no street signs, billboards, storefronts, or otherwise that were recognizable to us. Some of the buildings displayed intricate symbols and others were constructed in strange shapes resembling the same symbols, as if the building itself was conveying a message. Everywhere were exotic contraptions and structures in such a state of ruin that we could not determine their purpose, not that we would have been able to do so if they were brand new. Some appeared to have once facilitated mass transportation, others might have been used for lighting or mass media.

We eventually arrived at what appeared to be a large city square. A tremendous metallic structure planted on a large granite base occupied the center. It sprawled asymmetrically from the base in all directions, increasing in breadth as it soared to the violet blue sky—at least five hundred feet above the ground. Our vehicles passed by quietly enough that we could hear a chorus of arcane tones emanating from the structure's thin metal leaves as they swayed ever so slightly in the breeze. Strange looking characters were inscribed on the granite base, and the consensus in my truck was that the structure served as some kind of monument. We were sharply divided on the question of whether the structure had been damaged, as it was difficult to establish if its current shape was the intent of its creator. Nevertheless, I felt strangely moved in the presence of this mystical object, and impressed by the society that warranted such a wonderful monument to their achievements. I wondered in disbelief how so much could have been squandered and left in the hands of the reprobates that now governed the planet, and my contempt for them increased.

We saw no Serrones in this part of the city, yet it was far from uninhabited. The once-grand metropolis had been inherited by curious creatures of all shapes, sizes, and colors. None were more prevalent than the giant rodents we called cappies. The ubiquitous varmints ruled the city with an intrepid boldness, suggesting that any predators they once had were long extinct. They seemed unfazed by our sudden presence and became agitated when forced to make way for our oncoming vehicles, as if annoyed by our rudeness.

At one point the convoy halted for reasons unknown to us subservient soldiers. Susan joked that the Chief was lost and needed a moment to study his Michelin Guide. After a brief hiatus, we turned east onto a shadowy side street and proceeded at a reduced speed. The slow pace troubled me. Some of the towering ruins seemed on the verge of crumpling on top of us, and I would have preferred to slip under them as quickly as possible. We eventually made our way to the eastern edge of the city which appeared to have been less impacted by the ravages of the war. There we discovered the probable cause of our diversion into this sector.

What first seemed like tricks of our imaginations were soon visually confirmed as the presence of Serrone civilians. Their faces appeared in windows and a few came out to the street and stood motionless as we crept by. We had come to learn that the color of Serrone clothing indicated status. Based on their apparel, these Serrones must have occupied the lowest rung of the social ladder. They wore gray, threadbare frocks, and none donned the ornamental hats or shaded visors that we typically saw on their well-to-do cousins. In short, these Serrones were surely the destitute survivors of a merciless war. The conspicuous squalor of the city's inhabitants made the villagers that we "liberated" a while back look like aristocrats.

Nevertheless, these were citizens of the PRF, and the Chief evidently required an audience with their leaders, for we came to a halt amidst the gathering crowd. Cap ordered us down from the trucks for a quick stretch and a chance to refill our canteens from a large water tank nearby. This sent the local denizens scrambling into their dilapidated buildings, desperate to put a safe distance between themselves and the savage beasts that we were. I no longer felt the slightest desire to dissuade the meager Serrones from seeing me as such a danger, and even delighted in my intimidation. I did nothing to taunt them other than act as if they didn't exist. I purposely walked over to the wall of a building, sat down, and started eating my fruit while ignoring the dozens of alien eyes that studied me through the safety of nearby windows.

An opportunity to further bewitch them soon presented itself when I noticed an unusually large cappie sauntering toward my vicinity. The portly rat seemed unaware of me, or more likely unimpressed, as it searched for its next meal among the piles of debris heaped against the building. I reached for the smaller of my two knives and held it up by the blade using my thumb and forefinger. I performed this move slowly and smoothly solely for the benefit of my audience; the cappie was too disinterested to be spooked by any sudden moves on my part. As soon as the oblivious rodent ventured within ten feet of me, I flung the knife end-over-end towards it. I fully expected the knife to strike the cappie somewhere on its bloated body. I was pleasantly surprised to see it penetrate the animal just behind its head and kill it instantly, presenting me as a more skillful marksman than I actually was. I casually walked over to the corpse, removed my knife and wiped it clean on the cappie's fur. I then returned to my previous position and sat down as if nothing had happened. I doubt that cappies were part of the local Serrone cuisine, but I left it there for them to admire.

Being wholly satisfied with my performance, I closed my eyes in the hopes of stealing a few minutes of sleep before resuming the journey. I don't know how long I was in this state of semi-snooze before being suddenly roused by the sense of something in my immediate presence. I opened my eyes to find a very small Serrone standing not three feet in front of me. I froze and quickly glanced from side to side to see if anyone in authority, particularly a sentroid, had noticed my proximity to this Serrone—ostensibly a mere child. It seemed that nobody was aware of our close encounter, at least not anybody who would take a corrective action at my expense.

I turned my head back to the child and locked eyes with it. Its face was porcelain smooth and the color of an eggshell. Perhaps it was my imagination, but I perceived it to display an expression of fearless, innocent curiosity. It wore only a tattered shawl that resembled a potato sack. I instantly found myself equally drawn to this little being, wishing to placate it and somehow convey that I was harmless, in spite of my beastly appearance and recent theatrics. I wanted it to know my entire history, to know that I had a small child, and to understand what brought me to its home that day.

I could do none of that. Instead, I slowly extended my hand with the palm facing up. The little guy studied my hand for a while then carefully brought its own hand near it. It quickly touched my hand then pulled away as if testing the temperature of a hot stove. Realizing that its hand had not been destroyed, it slowly replaced it in my palm and left it there. It felt more like plastic than flesh. I would have liked to examine it further but I dared not move my hand in fear of spooking the courageous child.

"Shakespeare!" Nicholas called out to me, having just caught sight of my situation. His voice quickly jolted me back to reality, and I feared for my safety. I carefully withdrew my hand from the Serrone's and motioned it away.

"Go," I whispered loudly while waving my hand to the side. The child took a moment to realize what I was demanding then scurried off. I scanned the perimeter once again and concluded that my extraordinary encounter had gone undetected by the sentroids. I sat quietly reflecting on my experience before noticing another strange development.

The Chief stood in the street near the lead vehicle, engaged in conversation with a couple of the residents. Given that the locals were not equipped with the visors that seemed to facilitate a non-verbal form of communication, I listened closely, attempting to hear the odd squeaks and squeals of a natural Serrone conversation. I was too far away to hear them but I noticed the Chief pointing toward me a few times. Knowing that it was seldom a good omen to be singled out by the Chief, I walked over to Dee, who was much nearer to the conversation, and asked him what was being said. I specifically wanted to know what it might have to do with me.

"Toghan soldiers have been seen in this area. Captain Cheefon is questioning the loyalty of these people," he said.

"What does that have to do with me?"

"Captain Cheefon told them that he would unleash you upon them if they betrayed General Abasha. He told them that he would leave you here until you had captured and devoured every one of them."

I wasn't quite sure how to feel about that notion. It felt a little bit like a compliment. After all, he did choose *me* as his weapon of intimidation. On the other hand, it made me feel a little like a demonic monster—at least the part about eating them did. I was somewhat mollified knowing that, unbeknownst to the Chief, the local Serrones had just witnessed my interaction with the small child and had surely noted that I had not devoured it.

"Do they know that he's exaggerating about me eating them?" I asked.

"That is doubtful. Citizens are taught to believe that alien soldiers, such as yourself, are eager to devour them. It helps to maintain control." I could see that the propaganda might not have been too far from reality in the case of orcos, and perhaps lizzies, yet in light of my recent encounter, I didn't care to be thought of as such a barbarian. Killing and maiming for my own survival were acceptable traits. I drew the line at eating.

"You know that I would never do that, right?" I asked Dee. For some reason I needed to know his opinion on the subject, as he was my comrade.

"I have no reason to believe that you would," Dee replied. I would have preferred a simple "yes," though his answer was somewhat reassuring. We regrouped on the flatbed where I shared my experience with the others.

"The poor little guys have it nearly as bad as we do," remarked Pablo. "They just want to be left alone."

"Yeah," Susan added. "Their children are probably sick of hearing their parents talk about how great everything was before the war."

We left the city, turned south once again, and continued for a few hours before reaching the new camp. It was a village not unlike the ones we encountered in the North, although in better condition, having escaped the collateral damage of clashes between the PRF and rebels. The company we joined there was equally decimated and not much larger than ours. The resident soldiers came out to watch our vehicles pull into a paved square on the eastern end of the village. As we looked each other over, a few soldiers exchanged friendly waves. They appeared to be an ethnically-diverse group. I soon learned that their veteran members hailed from all four corners of the Earth. They were the amalgam of former companies that were combined and recombined over the years. I recognized a few soldiers who had passed through my former camp at one time or another.

The first thing I did upon jumping down from the rear of the flatbed was to inquire about Leesheh to every stranger I encountered. I doubted that anybody would have seen or heard of her, as Bar's scout team had set off in the opposite direction from us. My intent was to call attention to the matter and alert them to keep an eye out for her in the future. I received a few polite commitments to help, though I was certainly not the first person to be searching for a missing friend or loved one on the planet. They were surely aware of the fruitlessness of my quest and were kind enough not to mention it.

Later, when the opportunity presented itself, I interrogated human enemies that I encountered in close-quarter clashes and threatened to brutally punish those who could not provide intel about Leesheh's whereabouts. Of course, none of them had useful information and subsequently felt the wrath of my frustration and anger. I now regret that they were forced to pay for the Chief's decision in the form of a tortuous death. But those encounters were still several weeks away.

We spent the next few days acclimating to the camp, which was known among the local soldiers as Little Vegas. Whereas there was plenty of poker to be found in the village, the name derived from its proximity to the large abandoned city in the desert, which had been dubbed Vegas by human slaves several years earlier. The village we now occupied was likely constructed when the city first came under attack.

Little Vegas, or "LV," couldn't have been more different than my former camp. Instead of living in hastily constructed shacks and huts, we utilized the existing Serrone buildings, some of which still had fully-operational automatic doors and windows. Naturally, the nicest dwellings were occupied by the Serrone officers and guarded by their sentroids. The slave soldiers and combots were assigned to a cluster of two-story buildings on the eastern edge of the village. This served to insulate the Serrone officers from an outside attack. More significantly, it further isolated the humans from the western half of the village, in which a colony of Serrone civilians resided.

I could not determine if the buildings that served as our barracks had been built specifically for this purpose or if they had previously provided some other function. The former seemed more plausible, for they resembled military barracks on Earth. The second floor consisted of one long room full of nothing but single bunks—fifty or so in all. The first floor comprised two rooms: one large dining hall and a multipurpose area that we utilized for a lounge, meeting room, and gym. A small outhouse had been constructed near the barracks, as the latrines were too far away for a midnight stroll.

There was very little shade in Little Vegas. A few of the large yellow trees could be found in the village, but none were near our barracks. The seasons in that region of the planet were slightly more pronounced than those to which I had become accustomed—the cool season was cooler, and the warm season produced a few very hot days. We found ourselves spending more time inside the barracks there than in the previous camp.

As you might expect, the humans were forbidden from entering the western sector of Little Vegas. A makeshift wooden fence spanned the entire north-south axis of the village to remind us. Nobody living on either side of the fence was inclined to venture anywhere near it, and we humorously referred to the area as no-man's land. The only time we caught a glimpse of the civilians was when we were assigned to patrol the western portion of the village perimeter. Every soldier in the camp participated in sentry duties.

To my dismay, Little Vegas was not without its version of a cathouse. I never strayed close to it and avoided eye contact with any of its residents loitering outside. There was nothing I could do at that time to help those unfortunate women, and I had no desire to meet any of them. Knowing them personally would only hamper my efforts to achieve indifference. There was also a handful of toddlers scampering about.

At the LV camp we ate our meals inside the large dining room, aptly named the chow hall. There was no stream to provide water and sewage disposal. Truckloads of mostly-potable water arrived weekly. We emptied our latrine buckets into a nearby landfill that had subsequently become the preferred habitat for millions of unearthly insects. I dreaded latrine duty and unashamedly exploited my revered status among the soldiers to avoid it.

LV had a large motor pool and even a few transport aircraft parked in the middle of town, though one of them did not appear to be airworthy and was likely a parts donor for the other two. We brought with us most of the inventory from our infirmary and PX, which we merged in with the local counterparts. There was an abundance of weaponry and ammunition in the village, including both large and small ordinances. Although I would have preferred to have a larger complement of troops, I felt much more protected there than the previous camp.

We numbered approximately two hundred human soldiers. Humans were the slave of choice among the leaders in General Abasha's PRF. As such, there were no orcos or other alien warriors in the camp. I'm fairly certain that the Chief was the highest-ranking Serrone upon his arrival to Little Vegas. I base that assumption as much on the variety of color in his clothing as anything else. He and Ringo added to the three Serrone officers already in the company. They were closely guarded by a total of nine sentroids, including the three from our contingent: Khan, Kaiser, and Chairman Mao. Fifteen combots now served alongside us as our sergeants. I wondered if the respect I had earned from Cap and Dee would translate to the others. It appeared that Cap was at the top of the combot hierarchy in the company, so my prospects of continuing as the human-in-charge (HiC) were favorable.

In Little Vegas I found a level of carousal and debauchery that wouldn't have been tolerated in my former camp. The General's grip on his army appeared to be loosening in the wake of recent defeats. The village was rampant with catnip and rotgut. My Chinese comrades exchanged notes with the local distillers and soon there were multiple varieties of moonshine from which to choose. Availability was determined by the particular fruits and vegetables that were shipped in. The camp boasted a small brewery as well, and I grew partial to the concoction, despite bearing no resemblance to any beer I had ever tasted.

This brings me to another development of my life about which I am reluctant to share. Nevertheless, I feel it necessary in order to help frame subsequent events into a proper context. It was not only the beer in which I began to indulge. My consumption of moonshine increased well beyond the occasional snip I used to take in the former camp. Worse still, I found myself chewing the catnip leaves in defiance of the oath I once swore to myself. It would be disingenuous to blame my irresponsible behavior entirely on the recent separation from my family. It was merely the spark that ignited the powder keg. I didn't realize how much Leesheh had kept me grounded until she was gone. Fortunately, catnip was scarce unless a battle was forthcoming. On the idle days I softened my cravings with moonshine.

Gambling was the most popular pastime in the village. Homemade chess sets, playing cards, and dice were ubiquitous in the barracks. They weren't the only sources of wagering. The soldiers found a way to bet on any mental or physical challenge that one could imagine, ranging from the benign to the bizarre, and eventually to outright lunacy. Predictably, many wagers were based upon eating and drinking, in both quantity and quality. Several native species of animal and insect were devoured until the ingestion of a particular green worm led to the violent death of an unfortunate gambler. Challenges involving feats of physical endurance were popular as well. Contestants competed to see who could stand on his or her head the longest, or who could stay awake the longest (without the aid of catnip). I believe the winner lasted five days before collapsing. The combots mostly turned a blind eye to our shenanigans. They finally intervened when a few sadists decided to stage the first annual "Knife Olympics," which included contests involving juggling and catching very sharp objects.

What did we wager? The most common currency in camp was the canine teeth of lizzies. They had replaced cigarettes, which had all but disappeared due to a scarcity of anything in the desert that could be smoked. I found it interesting to see how much value soldiers placed upon these teeth given how little there was that could be purchased with them. There were very few personal possessions among the soldiers. The most valuable items were weapons—superior rifles or blades won from enemies in battle—and only a fool would part with those at any price. I guess it was our proclivity for competition, domination, and good old bragging rights that bestowed so much value on those teeth. Soldiers wore them with pride in the form of necklaces, and fistfights over their possession were common. I found little value in them myself, though I enjoyed watching the peculiar contests that were waged.

My new vices did nothing to hamper my primary addiction: increasing my strength, conditioning, and fighting ability. Susan, Ying, and I combined forces and knowhow with a few of the local workout junkies and convened on a daily basis. Pablo and Monte occasionally joined in. The former joined for aforementioned reasons; the latter joined at the incontestable request of his mentor, Ying. Monte's English had improved to where I could understand and converse with him without much more difficulty than I had with Ying. His inexplicable charisma carried over into Little Vegas where the local soldiers came to love and protect him as much as we did. There was no shortage of amusing moments at the expense of Monte and his self-appointed mentor Ying. I suspect that her knowledge of colloquial English was only slightly better than her protégé's. I recall them both cringing in disbelief when someone remarked that he would give his left arm for a stack of blueberry pancakes.

I cannot pinpoint the precise moment, but it was around the time of my first bizarre audience with the Chief back in the old camp that the "spear" in "Shakespeare" began to wither away. The connotation of the moniker disappeared along with it. In its place rose the legend of the Shaker, seeded in fact and nurtured in fiction. Its origins might be traced way back to that second battle in the village; perhaps it was fueled by the legend of a man who took down a combot with his bare hands—or was it two combots? Maybe it was fostered by the threat of a chivalrous warrior who wouldn't hesitate to crush a man's skull if he so much as looked at a woman the wrong way. Was this not the same warrior who dared to address his Serrone master as if he was an equal, and live to tell about it? I cannot attest to any of that hype. I never claimed to be half the warrior they believed me to be, but I will confess to one incident in which I might have passively endorsed my new epithet.

Several weeks after I arrived in Little Vegas, another company of approximately one hundred men, women, and combots joined our camp, increasing our ranks to more than three hundred. One morning, I happened to walk in the vicinity of a conversation between a few of the newly arrived soldiers and a member of my own company. The latter called me over.

"This is him," my comrade told the new arrivals.

"You're the *Shaker*?" asked one of the soldiers, a young, wide-eyed native. I was a little taken aback to find that my reputation had spread beyond the old camp.

"Yeah," the comrade answered eagerly in my stead. "He shakes the life out of his enemies." I didn't correct him and went about my way.

My closest remaining friends, with the possible exception of Nicholas, heartily embraced my new identity and readily adopted the recently-evolved nickname. It seems that their own reputations were enhanced as a result of their associations with me. I have no doubt that my good friend Charles and my own Leesheh would have continued to call me Shakespeare. They were two of the final tethers that held me to the person I was in the cargo hold and during those early days on Serrone. I fought to retain the memories of them in the forefront of my mind. The relocation had the effect of rendering events that occurred at the old camp to seem longer ago than they actually were. The combots also began to address me as Shaker, though this was not so surprising, as they seemed inclined to imitate us.

I look back on this period of my life as a series of dichotomies. Even with the lens of time through which I view it today, I am still unable to properly analyze or explain them:

I grew my hair and beard longer. Maybe I no longer cared about my appearance, or maybe I cared immensely about my appearance, only now I was trying to impress an entire camp instead of one woman.

My reckless behavior on and off the battlefield could have indicated that I considered myself to be already dead—I do recall that sentiment crossing my mind; or was my ultra-aggressive behavior a byproduct of my resolve to reunite with my son and his mother?

As I implied in the anecdote about my encounter with the Serrone child, I began to humanize the alien victims of the endless fighting and empathize with them. Simultaneously, my hatred of the world's greedy, cowardly alien leaders increased daily. My eagerness to eradicate them would eventually rival my desire to find my family members.

I was still called upon to entertain the barracks with stories and I willingly complied. But my narratives were less often based on movies and classic literature in favor of honoring fallen comrades and sharing memories of our exploits in battles. I enjoyed playing the role of the Shaker and found it increasingly difficult to suppress his flamboyant personality, though I still inwardly thought of myself as Leesheh's Shakespeare.

I remember being reasonably aware of my destructive tendencies and choosing to engender them. To this day I cannot say whether my stubbornness was borne of self-pity, despondency, or grief.

25

We were fortunate in that we spent the better part of that first warm season in the new camp—more than fifteen weeks—without any combat-related activities. As usual, the rank and file were uninformed, and we had no idea where we stood in relation to the front lines of the war with the Toghans, or "Tongs" as they had become known. I recall two noteworthy events that occurred during those early weeks in the new camp. Both were derivatives of the complacency in which the camp was immersed, yet they could not possibly have been more contrasting in nature.

I'll begin with the more lighthearted incident. For whatever reason, the soldiers in this camp were more sociable (and I daresay festive) than those in my previous community. The native-born young soldiers in Little Vegas seemed more amicable than the menacing ruffians with whom I had parted ways at the old camp. The young men and women in LV reminded me of Ammo in that they were eager to learn from the earthly veterans, and there was no shortage of the latter possessing the same amiable intentions as Jessie. Although LV comprised soldiers abducted from all seven continents, it lacked ethnic divisions. We lived in our own little melting pot, united against our enemies. A few of the Chinese and Africans from the old camp bunked in my barracks, and some of my companions from the cargo hold now resided with the soldiers that preceded us there in Little Vegas.

Rather than enforcing the old squad assignments, the combots adapted to the organization of our new barracks and reconstituted the squads accordingly. We had a much larger ratio of humans to combots in LV. The Serrones had long since squandered the capacity to produce new combots, yet the ability to reinforce the human population was only recently lost with the destruction of the last remaining starship. Thus, only one combot resided in our barracks and supervised more than fifty of us. I was happy that our sergeant was Dee. I maintained a certain rapport with the enigmatic android despite my inability to predict his behavior.

I cannot recall exactly how the idea originated, but it came to pass one day that the camp should hold a talent show. It likely evolved from the increasing popularity of a cappella karaoke in one of the barracks. The entire camp was soon abuzz with chatter about the event and a committee was formed to determine the proper time and place for it. The safest location would have been inside one of the barracks halls. The problem was that none was large enough to accommodate the attendees, which was anticipated to be the entire human population of Little Vegas.

It was decided to stage the show in the yard between the two most remote barracks halls. The Serrone officers rarely ventured into the barracks area—especially those so close to the city perimeter. (It would have been interesting to see their reaction to such a spectacle.) As the HiC, I was cajoled into running the idea by Cap, in spite of having advised the committee to proceed without conferring with the combots. I pulled Cap and Dee aside after morning chow and initiated a bizarre conversation, the recollection of which still brings a smile to my face.

"Cap, I need to ask you something."

"What is your question?"

"Um, the soldiers… well, you understand the importance of a soldier's morale—a human soldier, right?" I probably should have rehearsed my pitch.

"Yes," said Cap.

"Good. I mean, I should tell you that the current morale in the camp is very low." Nothing could have been further from the truth. The camp had become a rival to Sodom and Gomorrah in response to the relative peace we had experienced in recent weeks. I continued my spiel. "And I'm concerned that the low morale might impact the soldiers' ability to fight when the time comes."

"The soldiers' morale does not appear to be low," replied Cap. He wasn't buying it.

"Nevertheless," I added undauntedly, "the soldiers have requested to… stage… an event that will improve—increase—their capacity and willingness to fight for each other. That is, it will increase their loyalty." I finally remembered to play the loyalty card.

"What is this event?" asked Cap.

"Well, it's not a big deal—it's nothing serious—just a chance for the soldiers to entertain each other."

"They entertain each other already," he pointed out. I decided then that their permission probably wasn't necessary and tried to downplay it further.

"You're right. This is nothing more than that. I just wanted to be sure that the Chief… um, Captain Cheefon, is okay with it." A quiet pause ensued during which Cap and Dee stared at each other. Dee then turned and stupefied me.

"Shaker, it seems that Captain Cheefon could not disapprove of something about which he had no knowledge."

"Right… Um, we plan to hold the event in the barracks yard near the city perimeter," I told them.

Dee continued his thought as if I hadn't spoken at all. "As such, I recommend that this event be conducted early in the morning, when Captain Cheefon and the sentroids are less likely to be in the vicinity."

It certainly wasn't our first choice for a start time but I wasn't about to look a gift horse in the mouth. I reported back to the committee, and the newly titled "Breakfast Talent Show" was scheduled for the following week.

The show went off without a hitch and was thoroughly enjoyed by all. We unanimously resolved to make it a recurring event. Most of the combots—all except for the four assigned to guard duty—attended and stood like statues in the back of the audience. They must have been absorbing the unique display of human loyalty, as it had been sold to Cap. Even the four combots on guard duty managed to walk by several times more than their normal route would have required.

As predicted, most of the acts were singers, including a well-rehearsed barbershop quartet and several would-be divas representing whatever popstar was in the limelight at the time of their abductions. The virtual curtain was brought down at the end of the show with a tear-jerking rendition of *Time to Say Goodbye* by a man and woman who could have easily been opera stars in their lives before. I had been on the fence during the days leading up to the show as to whether I would perform. Nicholas' and Susan's incessant pestering finally pushed me over. I decided to recite one of the few poems I could still recall:

"Behold this ruin! 'Twas a skull
Once of ethereal spirit full,
This narrow cell was life's retreat:
This space was thought's mysterious seat.
What beauteous visions filled this spot!
What dreams of pleasure, long forgot!
Nor hope, nor joy, nor love, nor fear
Has left one trace of record here.
Beneath this mouldering canopy
Once shone the bright and busy eye:
But start not at the dismal void—
If social love that eye employed,
If with no lawless fire it gleamed,
But through the dews of kindness beamed
That eye shall be forever bright
When stars and sun are sunk in night.
Within this hollow cavern hung,
The ready, swift and tuneful tongue:
If falsehood's honey is disdained,
And when it could not praise, was chained;
If bold in virtue's cause it spoke,
Yet gentle concord never broke,
This silent tongue may plead for thee,
When death unveils Eternity!"

The audience was stunned—not captivated by my performance so much as they were surprised to see the ferocious Shaker in such an uncharacteristic light. An awkward moment of dead silence followed the last line of my delivery, then a spontaneous cheer erupted. I couldn't hold back my smile at the risk of tarnishing my reputation. In retrospect, my thespian talents probably served to enhance my mysterious persona rather than diminish it.

If my renewed affinity for poetry had weakened my warrior reputation to any extent, it was undoubtedly restored by the second noteworthy event that occurred during this period. It had been made known to us peons via the trickle-down pipeline that the Chief was the senior PRF officer within Little Vegas. What also seemed apparent soon after the arrival of the third company was that his leadership was not without opposition. I do not believe this rivalry endangered the Chief's position, yet there must have been some sort of gauntlet thrown down, or at least a friendly challenge brought forth which the Chief felt obligated to accept. The resolution of this challenge required my direct participation, as it was conveyed to me with little advanced notice one morning in the dining hall, when Khan approached me.

"Come with me," ordered the sentroid in his stoic monotone. I complied without question, though not without a little apprehension. I followed him for about a hundred yards to a smooth patch of the sandy desert where the Chief and the other Serrones waited in their chariots, flanked by a full complement of sentroids. Standing in front of them was one of the soldiers from the recently arrived third company, a man of similar size and build to my own. The only visible difference between us was his closely cropped black hair and beard that clashed with my wild, barbaric appearance.

I glanced at him with the hope of learning the purpose of our meeting. He returned a similar look of puzzlement. Some of the soldiers had noticed that something might be going down, and they approached slowly and quietly to witness it. The sentroids permitted them to remain, and held them back at a safe distance from the Serrones. Within a few seconds, most of the camp had gathered and formed a semi-circle around us. Khan stripped me of my belt which housed my knives. The other man wore no weapons.

"Fight," said Khan, never one to mince words. My opponent said something in a language that sounded like Russian to me. I found out later that he hailed from Bulgaria.

"Him?" I asked. I already knew the answer. I was merely stalling in order to ascertain the circumstances surrounding this duel. It wasn't difficult to see that this amounted to little more than a Serrone cock fight, and I was the Chief's prize fighter. I was not the least intimidated by my opponent and I quickly saw an opportunity to increase my standing with the Chief, though I was no longer under any illusion that he would ever see me as anything more than a beast of burden. I should note that my opponent likewise did not appear to be intimidated in the least, and was further bolstered by words of encouragement offered by his supporters in their native tongue. I decided to make this a wrestling match instead of a boxing match and thus save us both some unwelcome lacerations. I quickly settled on a plan to utilize some of the moves that Ying had taught me. I hoped to subdue the big man and choke him out.

"Fight him," replied Khan. "Now."

I moseyed over to the man and attempted to grab him around the neck. He quickly countered with a sharp blow to my ribs. *Okay, that was my mistake.* I needed to take this a little more seriously. I came at him a little more forcefully and failed to defend my head. He promptly struck me squarely in the jaw, nearly knocking me to the ground. For reasons I cannot explain, I lacked conviction and was a little put off by his aggression, which seemed a little excessive to me. Perhaps I had gone too long without a brawl.

"Dude, this isn't a fight to the death," I muttered as my tongue combed through my mouth in search of missing teeth. He responded by saying something in Bulgarian and delivering another strong shot to my gut. That did it. The switch flipped, and I'm not referring to the standard light switch metaphor. A more appropriate image is the large lever that Dr. Frankenstein yanked down to infuse life into his monster. My own monster within, which I had managed to suppress for so many weeks, was suddenly unleashed and in control of my body.

Call it what you will: waking the sleeping giant, poking the bear, triggering a survival instinct—any and all applied. My motor revved up and accelerated from zero to sixty in about two seconds as I bull-rushed the large Bulgarian and slammed him into the ground with my 250-pound body landing squarely on top of him. Before he could catch his wind, I landed a flurry of body punches into his ribs then moved up to his face where I eagerly repaid him ten times over for his blow to my jaw. He was probably out cold after the third blow, yet I couldn't stop. It was as if I was just another spectator watching this hellion deliver his terror along with everybody else.

The Chief must have recognized that his prized beast was on the verge of snuffing out another one of his valuable soldiers, for I suddenly felt a firm hand on my upper arm start to pull me away. Still under the influence of my frenzied trance, I instinctively spun around and wailed on the combot that had been charged to break up the fight. My fist caught him squarely in the head and he fell to the ground. I stood over him fully prepared to continue the scuffle when my body was once again completely overwhelmed by a familiar surge of electricity, and I collapsed to the ground. Somehow it didn't hurt as much this time. Maybe Khan lowered the voltage for this one, or maybe I was developing a tolerance for it. It still rendered the desired effect and jolted me back to reality.

As I lay on the ground, the Chief and his cronies departed with no further comment. Nicholas and Susan helped me to my feet as the Bulgarian was aided by his friends. I walked over to him and extended my hand as he sat up.

"Sorry," I muttered half-heartedly, though I felt little remorse and no regret at that time. As far as I was concerned, he was lucky to be alive and should have been thanking me. This incident had no storybook ending. The Bulgarian and I did not become fast friends, with one of us saving the other's life in battle, or anything sappy like that. As far as I can remember, he was dead within a month. However, I did feel bad for striking the combot, and not only because I had severely bruised my hand. I walked over to him and apologized, which might seem odd to someone reading this narrative. To me (and most of my comrades), the combots were living beings. This particular android, whom I did not know, accepted my apology. We even shook hands. Dee then walked over and kindly advised against striking a combot in the future, as it was more likely to damage my hand than the android. *Yeah, thanks for the advice.* I nursed my hand for a few days and listened to the yarns about me knocking down a combot grow by the minute.

This outlandish incident marked the end of our extended noncombative period in Little Vegas. Just when a sense of complacency and relative security had taken hold of the entire camp, we became painfully aware that we were on the verge of clashing with the Toghan army, and they were bringing the fight to our doorstep. A routine patrol rushed into camp one evening and reported that a large enemy force was approaching from the north. Orders came down to set up a defensive position on the northern perimeter of the village, just a short walk from our barracks. We kicked into gear and dug in at the top of a sandy hill on the edge of town. It sloped down to a flat ravine where huge boulders protruded from the desert floor. The ground sloped up from the other side of the narrow ravine where it met a line of small dunes, not a hundred yards away from us. It was behind these dunes where we first caught sight of the enemy force a day later. They seemed to be content to remain where they were, so we proceeded to stare each other down for the time being.

Our position was fortified by various objects we hauled over from the village, such as old vehicles, chunks of stone walls, wooden poles, and other debris. In front of the makeshift barricade lay our entire stock of barbed wire that had been shipped in from Abasha City—one of just a few items they had spared for our cause. Behind the barricade we dug a series of foxholes and trenches, which were manned by our entire complement of soldiers, minus the patrols that were dispatched to watch for flanking maneuvers. The enemy strength appeared to number in the hundreds, with the majority of their force consisting of the crazed lizzies, which we occasionally saw darting back and forth on the dunes, just beyond the practical range of our arc rifles.

It was torturous to see the relative comfort of the barracks only a short distance away and yet so far from reach. We passed away the hours swapping the same old stories and jokes as we did in the barracks, minus the singing. I decided that I should trim my hair and beard in anticipation of the forthcoming battle. We had Jessie's old supplies, but there was nobody in the vicinity of my trench with the skills and experience for the job. There were a few volunteers willing to learn, but I had no intention of being their first customer. Ying was particularly eager to try. The idea of her holding a sharp knife anywhere near my neck was very unsettling, and I politely declined. I finally consented to Nicholas giving it a go. After waiting for a half hour while he second-guessed his approach, I told him to forget it. In the end it was Monte who stepped up. He proved to be quite the artisan and went on to become the most sought-after barber in the camp.

We were able to rest at night with relative ease, knowing that the lizzies had poor night vision. In fact, it was midday when the Tongs launched a small attack to probe our defenses. A wave of thirty to forty lizzies sprung over the dunes on a suicide mission without artillery support—only covering fire from small arms. We figured that the Tongs were not yet ready to reveal the magnitude of their armaments. We took down the feisty little creatures with relative ease. Only a few made it as far as the ravine.

The second wave, twice as large, attacked not an hour later. We showered them with plasma once again. This time they reached the ravine in greater numbers, though none made it more than a few feet up the sandy hill in front of us. Their numbers were clearly larger than we had estimated and it was blatantly obvious that they were trying to draw us out into the open by sacrificing scores of their monkey-lizards. That is, it was obvious to everyone but the Chief or whichever incompetent Serrone imbecile was in charge of the battlefield that day. A few minutes after we defeated a third, larger wave, Dee came over to my position in the trench and delivered the news.

"Prepare the squad for an offensive," he told me. Susan and Nicholas were within earshot, and we exchanged winces of disbelief before I responded to Dee.

"You know that's exactly what they want us to do, right?"

"Possibly, but if they attack again, we will counter." He believed this was wrong. I don't know how I knew that—I could just feel it.

"I guess the Chief thinks they've been weakened by these failed attacks?" Dee didn't respond to my rhetorical supposition. "We have no idea what kind of army they have hiding behind those dunes," I continued. "King Tosso has won a lot of battles. He didn't do it by making foolish decisions."

"We have our orders," said Dee. "Prepare the squad."

"Okay," I relented. I knew that there was no point in trying to convince a computer to defy its programming. "But they clearly have superior numbers," I added.

"That is probable," said Dee. It was the best he could offer in acknowledgement of my protest.

I had no fear or concern for my own safety. I was long since engrossed by a lethal combination of sentiments: invincibility and resignation. But I did care about my comrades, and I despised the Chief even more for his ineptitude and indifference that would surely result in senseless deaths. Dee, Nicholas, and I made our away through the trench preparing the soldiers for the counter attack. Although my experience fighting lizzies was somewhat limited, I knew that hand-to-hand combat was inevitable. I advised the men and women to affix bayonets to their arc rifles using the trusty Serrone adhesive tape that had worked so well for us in the past. I preferred to keep my own knives in their sheaths, and my Uzi was too small for a bayonet anyway. I disallowed grenades; they would be useless in the close-quarter fighting and an easy target for enemies firing down upon us from their hill position.

I came across Scoop, the young journalist from New York, who was crouched on the other side of Nicholas. He seemed a little unnerved yet surprisingly calm. I had taken a liking to the kid and was troubled by the notion that he was unlikely to survive his first taste of combat.

"Scoop, stay close to me," I advised. As he nodded in affirmation, Nicholas gently poked me and pulled me aside.

"Shaker..." He was struggling to find the words. "I don't think that's a good idea."

"What?"

"You're not the best... I mean, it's not safe for him to be with you."

My friend's words cut deeply but he was right. How could I be trusted to protect anyone at this point? I felt sad that it had become so obvious to others, and sadder yet to know that I wouldn't change in the wake of this revelation. I just didn't care enough.

"Scoop, stay with Nicholas," I muttered, then moved along.

It wasn't long before the Chief got his wish. Again, I can only assume that it was the Chief who was making these tactical decisions, for there were no Serrone officers anywhere near the front line. The fourth wave of lizzies emerged from the dunes and bounded down the hill. The size of this attack was notably smaller than the previous wave, as if to feign the action of a desperate and depleted force. The Chief took the bait. Dee's squad and another, totaling approximately one hundred soldiers, were ordered over the wall.

Several wooden platforms about the size of doors were pitched over the barbed wire so that we could safely bridge the razor-sharp barrier. We scampered over the platforms and fanned into a line spanning about a hundred yards. We moved slowly down the hill while firing upon the lizzies as they came into the ravine below us. To the surprise of no one—no human—the Tongs responded to our attack with an immediate artillery barrage, targeting us on the hill as well as our remaining forces behind the wall. Simultaneously, a second wave of lizzies and human soldiers emerged from the dunes and descended down the hill to meet us. The remainder of their force unloaded continuous suppression fire over our barricade, rendering it nearly impossible for our forces to do the same in support of us. In short, we were in some serious shit.

We successfully eliminated most of their initial attack force before reaching the ravine. Once there, we found cover behind the large boulders and braced for the second wave to reach us. We were only able to discharge a few rounds each before they were upon us. The Tongs seemed bound and determined to turn this battle into a confused brawl, which played to the strengths of their numbers and the fighting penchant of their lizzies. Huge clouds of dust kicked up in the ensuing melee, and my entire world was suddenly reduced to a five-foot radius.

Susan, Ying, and I typically preferred to fight together, and we soon found ourselves standing back-to-back-to-back in a triangular formation. The two women were also aggressive fighters, though they exerted more structure, control, and precision than I. Their prudent styles complemented my unfettered approach, and we likely saved each other's lives many more times than we noticed that day. Susan preferred her bayonet while firing the occasional shot at close range. Ying and her student had flung our small rifles behind our backs and drawn our knives immediately upon entering the ravine. I had recently replaced my primary blade with something akin to a small machete, and it served me well that day. The lizzies seemed drawn to it like a magnet, or maybe it possessed a mind of its own, for it seemed to have slashed several of them without my knowledge.

For all the success of our little triumvirate, the company was sustaining a large number of casualties overall. Despite killing far more of them than they were of us, they seemed able to afford the losses and more than willing to pay the price. My attention was suddenly drawn to a comrade nearby. He had just been wounded, and not as the result of a stab wound or plasma round. The sight and sound of his death knell was unmistakable—something I had long thought to be extinct. I looked up the hill beyond the ravine and spied the dreaded bursts of light and the treacherous spider responsible for them. It was slowly descending toward us while spraying the ravine with its voltaic projections, indiscriminately eradicating both friend and foe. I pointed it out to Susan and Ying, then quickly fought my way over to Dee, who was just a few yards away.

"Look. We need to get out of here!" I implored, while calling his attention to the metallic, multi-legged threat coming toward us.

"Agreed," he replied. "Pull back the left flank. I will handle the right."

I darted back to the left and began shouting the command to retreat. My comrades behaved as well as the finest-trained armies on Earth, continuing to fire on the enemy as they traversed the hill behind them in an orderly fashion. As I reached the edge of the ravine, an idea came upon me for which I had no time to contemplate. If I had, I probably wouldn't have gone through with it, even in my foolhardy state. Rather than retreating with the rest of the squad, I remained hidden behind a large boulder.

"What are you doing?!" Susan shouted to me above the battlefield racket.

"Go!" I waved her back while trying to convey that I hadn't lost my sanity. My hope was that it would appear from the Toghan vantage point that all of the surviving members of our team had retreated. I couldn't see what was happening on the opposite side of the ravine, but it sounded as if the spider android was continuing to advance. Its heavy weight, though dispersed among six legs, resulted in loud footsteps that reverberated on the compacted desert surface. It was closer than I had estimated. I had hoped to be several yards away when it emerged onto our side of the ravine. Now it sounded like it was just behind the very same boulder that sheltered me. I stood nervously with my back to the rock, trying to recall the maneuver executed by Dee and Bar on the day of my very first battle, when they exploited the spider's vulnerability to close-range fire. I nervously checked that my Uzi was loaded. I checked it again. The spider was only a few feet away. If it detected me first, I would stand no chance.

The first hint of a golden leg appeared beside a rock not three feet from where I stood. Without hesitation I jumped out from my position and volleyed several rounds into its midsection. It managed to fire off a few bursts in my general direction but I was too close for it to zero in. It first fell forward, as if kneeling on its front legs and paying homage to its assassin. I reacted with shots into its rear legs, bringing it fully to the ground. My final round was placed into its head at pointblank range. The entire act probably lasted no longer than five seconds. I can remember it only in slow motion, where it felt like five minutes.

I looked up toward my comrades on the hill to find that they had reversed and were coming back into the ravine to ensure my safe recovery. What they had noticed, and I had not, was that several lizzies were still active in my vicinity. I became painfully aware of this when one jumped onto my back and clasped its hands around my neck. I rocked my torso forward and downward, causing the animal to flip over my head and onto the ground, where it met a swift death, courtesy of Ying's knife. We rushed up the hill, scampered over the wooden bridges, and dove into the trench. I caught my breath amidst a chorus of cheers from my comrades. I had never seen an army so delighted in the wake of what could only be described as a decisive loss.

The Tongs must have been content to call it a day and take stock of their losses, for we faced no additional attacks that day. The loss of their spider android undoubtedly stung deeply. It was surely a miscalculation to place it at such risk, and the leaders on the other side of the ravine were likely recalculating their opponent's fighting capacity, if not their tenacity.

Our ability to withstand four attack waves, capped by the moral victory of taking down the arachnid prize, came at a great cost to us—one that we could ill afford to pay again. Nearly ten percent of our company's fighting force lay dead or dying in the ravine, which soon became known as the Devil's Den. A few of us recognized the allusion to the American Civil War; *all* of us came to recognize it as a place of savage and inhuman violence, for it would surpass its namesake in brutality many times over.

We spent the next few hours resting in the trenches and doing whatever menial tasks we could conceive to distract us from the sounds of our wounded lying in the Devil's Den. We could do nothing for them. Many of the Toghan lizzies also clung to their last threads of life and wailed out in high-pitched squeals that sounded like fingernails scraping down a blackboard. I am not ashamed to admit that it was a relief to wake the next morning following a brief and fitful sleep, and see that the last of our comrades and enemies had succumbed to their wounds. The natural undertakers of the alien planet, so much more numerous and expeditious than their Earthbound counterparts, had already taken custody of the ravine. I only wish that the wormlike creatures and their unseen microscopic cohorts could have worked even faster. I will never be able to cleanse my mind of the awful images and stench brought from the partially decomposed bodies that lay before us for several days.

26

We could only conclude that the lizzies reproduced like jack rabbits, or that their home planet had been cleaned out of every last one of them. Wave after wave was thrown at us for the better part of two weeks until the Tongs finally relented—for a while. On two occasions the lizzies breached our wall only to be beaten back. Otherwise, we were able to repel their challenges without a single Tong—lizzie or otherwise—making it out of the Devil's Den alive. We were ordered into the Den ourselves one other time during the early days of the battle. It was only a week after the first clash I described in the previous chapter, which was apparently enough time for our Serrone masters to forget the calamity that it was. My squad was spared the misfortune this time. We did our best to protect our comrades from above, yet the company once again sustained reprehensible casualties.

And still we had no idea of the big picture—no sense of the magnitude of this conflict with the far-flung king and his lizard army. Were we winning? We certainly weren't winning in our little speck of the war. We had lost nearly twenty percent of our soldiers and had little to show for it. Was there a strategic value in holding this town, or was the goal to win by attrition? The latter seemed to be the preferred tactic of our enemy, and it was not without success, from what we could tell. We were fortunate to receive reinforcements in the form of fifty soldiers dispatched from Abasha City, but Dee informed me that there would be no more coming. The endless supply of lizzies would surely wear us down. How many battlefronts were there like ours? The soldiers dispatched from the city knew little more than we did. They spoke of companies being sent to other fronts and had no knowledge of any soldiers returning. I was particularly disappointed to hear that.

Following this initial phase of the battle, both sides dug in and waited. The women of the cathouse and the handful of children they minded were evacuated to Abasha City. The civilians living in the western section of town started leaving in droves. Some might say they were like sheep or frogs sensing an oncoming storm before we humans could see the signs. I think that the writing on the wall was fairly obvious to everyone. Most of the civilians headed north into the captured Toghan territory. Clearly, they were betting on the other team.

We assumed that the Tongs were awaiting reinforcements. Nobody could quite figure out what our own leaders might be waiting for. One optimist submitted that our job was simply to keep this Toghan army at bay while we crushed them on other fronts. After we had a good laugh, he too admitted that he didn't actually believe his theory. Even without their presumed reinforcements, we were probably outnumbered and outgunned. This realization added a measure of mental torture to the impasse as the days piled on. Most of us had long since surrendered to our probable demise, and the stress brought forth by the belief that we lived solely at the pleasure of our enemy made it more unbearable. We could neither see nor hear them but we knew they were there, just beyond the dunes. *Why were we still there?*

We continued in this holding pattern for the entire cool season. Things became calm enough that we were able to rotate back into the barracks for a night or two, in small groups. The respite and inactivity only dampened my spirits and pushed my disposition into dangerous depths. I raised my moonshine consumption up a notch in a counterproductive effort to compensate for the dreariness. Even Susan made a comment about my drinking, but I was too pigheaded and withdrawn to notice.

Time was as much an enemy to me as were the Tongs and the Chief. There was nothing I could do to reunite my family while I was bogged down in the trenches around Little Vegas. I secretly hoped that the battle would resume in earnest so that progress could be made in one direction or the other. Something—anything—needed to happen. The chances of finding Leesheh alive diminished with each passing day. I felt isolated in my quest to find her. My friends had stopped mentioning her name soon after we left the old camp. I know they did that out of respect for my feelings, wishing to spare me their opinions of her certain demise. I found it odd that we often spoke of our fallen comrades—Jessie, Malcolm, Charles, and the others—yet Leesheh and Swag were rarely mentioned, at least not in my presence. I suppose they were consigned to a limbo status until I gave the "okay" for them to be honored along with the other deceased.

I struggle to recall any significant moments during this monotonous period of waiting for the inevitable bloodshed. In hindsight, it seems to have lasted no more than a few weeks, though I know it spanned the majority of two seasons. In light of reflecting on my thoughts toward Leesheh during this time, and how the subject was so delicately avoided by my friends, a particular conversation comes to mind. It confounded me then but not so much today, and I cannot help but smile as I begin to transcribe it.

It happened one evening on which a small group of us had been discharged from the front line to spend a night in the barracks. It must have been during the seasonal transition, for I distinctly recall rain, and rainstorms were so infrequent in that region. I lay in my bunk staring at the ceiling and thinking of little more than the hypnotic patter of the rain on the roof. My serenity that evening was interrupted by Susan, who sat down on the edge of my bed and proceeded to make small talk. Absent was her characteristic dry sense of humor, and I sensed that she had an ulterior motive for this conversation.

"Hey, can I ask you something?" she said after a brief moment of silence. After I assented, she proceeded to ask my opinion on a series of vague questions about relationships. She seemed to be zeroing in on a very specific one.

"What do you think my husband is doing now?" she asked. "Do you think he's moved on?" I had never known her to be sentimental in the least. I had an idea of the answer she was seeking and it happened to be aligned with my own feelings on the matter.

"It's been years," I said. "We have to assume that our families have moved on. Not that they've forgotten about us—only that they've accepted that we aren't coming back."

"Don't get me wrong," she said, preparing me for what was about to follow. "I really miss my children—and my husband—but it feels like that was somebody else's life—not mine."

"I know what you mean."

"You were married before, right?"

"Divorced," I said. Susan already knew that, but I indulged her. By the time we left the cargo hold, all of us knew each other's histories as if we had grown up together.

"She's probably remarried by now, right?"

"I would hope so."

"My kids—I'm never going to see them again, am I?" She was jumping all over the map.

"I don't think so."

"So… you think my husband has moved on?" she repeated.

"I really can't say, Susan, but I can tell you this: he would understand if *you* needed to move on."

"Sure, I guess… I mean—why do you say that?" she asked, feigning surprise.

"Is that not why we're having this conversation?"

She bit her bottom lip and looked at me guiltily.

"Susan, it's okay," I continued. "You're literally on a different planet now. Nobody here will condemn you and nobody on Earth will ever know."

"Yeah, but my kids…"

"What does this have to do with your children? If you got a divorce on Earth, you would still have your children in your life, right?"

"Yeah... My husband has probably moved on, right? Do you think he's moved on?"

It was time to call in reinforcements, and I beckoned for Nicholas to join us. It was a risky move because I had to keep him focused.

"Nick, answer a question for us. Let's say, hypothetically, that Susan was able to travel back to Earth, leaving tomorrow."

"I don't see how that's possible," said Nick. "As far as we know there are no ships–"

"*Hypothetically*, Nick. Let's assume that she travels back on a ship identical to the one that brought us here."

"Okay."

"Good. Now, how many years will have elapsed on Earth from the time she was abducted?"

"How long does it take the ship to travel back to Earth?"

"That's what I'm asking you."

"Does the ship travel at the speed of light?"

"How should I know? Let's assume that it does."

"But according to Einstein, traveling at the speed of light is impossible."

"Damn it, Nick! A ship brought us here, didn't it?"

"I'm just saying that we were probably in a state of suspended animation for quite some time."

"Okay, fine. Assume that."

Nick stroked his chin and looked up to the ceiling as if the answer might be scribbled on the rafters. "Well," he started, "if she traveled at a speed *approaching* the speed of light…" Not finding the answer on the ceiling, he looked to the floor. "I suppose that upwards of fifty years could have elapsed on Earth during which Susan only experienced a few years."

Bingo. It was like pulling teeth, but I got him there. "You see Susan? Even as we speak, life on Earth has already advanced fifty years."

"Not exactly," added Nicholas. "This is just a theory. It's possible that–"

"Nick, that's good enough. You told us what we needed to know."

"I'm just saying that it's apples and oranges to compare where we are right now to what is currently transpiring on Earth. If I had more time I could–"

"Nick! We're good, man." I had released the bird from its cage and it was flapping all over the room.

"I get it," said Susan. "Thanks, Nick."

"So, the real question, Susan, is who are we talking about?" I asked. This was the only time I had ever seen her blush.

"You know who," she replied. I assured her that I had absolutely no idea of whom she was speaking. "You really don't know?" She seemed genuinely surprised. I shook my head.

"Don't know what?" asked Nicholas. We ignored him. Susan looked at me and mouthed the answer.

"Pablo."

The only answer that might have shocked me more was Monte. I knew that Pablo had a thing for Susan, but I had never witnessed the slightest inkling of reciprocation. On the contrary, she often ridiculed his affections. I could see now that it had all been a pretense to disguise her true feelings. Over the ensuing days, as word of this union spread throughout the trenches, Susan grew increasingly dumbfounded when discovering that not a single person had any idea. I began to wonder if

Pablo had known anything about it before I did. He definitely seemed happier from that day forward, though I noticed little change in Susan. She periodically slipped into her old habit of ridiculing his advances, prompting us to remind her that we already knew all about their relationship.

That anecdote stands out in my memory because such moments were rare during our standoff in Little Vegas. The tension grew thicker as the influx of supplies began to wane. We were not under siege, at least not at the hands of the Tongs. King Tosso was undoubtedly aware that our supplies were dwindling without him having to spare the resources to physically encircle us. Water continued to be flown in on dilapidated airships. We wondered why the king didn't employ his superior air force to deny us such a precious resource. It finally became a forgone conclusion that he no longer had a superior air force. We couldn't recall the last time we had seen a drone from either side of the war. Airships in Serrone had a funny habit of dropping out of the sky, and none were being manufactured to replace them. The war had thus digressed to one of land (and possibly sea, though we had no knowledge of any naval battles).

Late into the second season we began to receive trickles of soldiers arriving from the east and west, sneaking past the Toghan patrols at night. They spoke of defeats on all fronts that were driving the PRF back toward Abasha City. The arrival of these refugees bolstered our ranks slightly, but that was overshadowed by the degradation of our morale caused by the dismal news they brought. We couldn't help but wonder why we were being spared. Our spirits sunk into the depths of the trenches, where the last morsels of frivolity, hope, and optimism disappeared into the sand.

Before long, we were ordered to make preparations for a retreat. Instead of lifting our moods, the action felt more like a stay in execution. We discreetly loaded up the vehicles with our diminished supplies of food and water, then returned to the trenches to wait for the evacuation order. Rumors spread that the Chief was already long gone, having hopped on the last transport aircraft out of the village. We stayed on the front line, mired in a state of puzzlement and agitation for two more days, wondering why we were still there.

The attack finally came nearly a year after the first wave of lizzies had emerged from the dunes. In the first light of the morning, a short barrage of artillery was followed by the emergence of a large band of lizzies methodically approaching from the dunes. This army was larger than I had ever imagined, and I was amazed at the discipline of the lizzies as they held formation. We waited until they reached the Devil's Den before firing down upon them. They absorbed our fire without hesitation, seemingly resigned to sustain a calculated number of casualties in exchange for winning our position. Their slow, businesslike approach was terrifying. They stepped over their fallen comrades without taking their eyes off of us and started up the hill. All of this was done without firing a shot, which rendered them all the more intimidating.

When a second wave of lizzies, humans, and combots appeared on the dunes, the order to pull back and abandon Little Vegas was finally issued. Strangely, the Tongs did not increase their pace in response to our haphazard retreat. It was as if they merely wanted to chase us away and rid the village of our pestilence. We fled to the awaiting vehicles in a near panic. The first wave of lizzies soon reached our front line, where they halted and proceeded to unleash a volley of plasma fire into the backs of our ranks. They killed tens of retreating soldiers and would have surely killed dozens more if they had pursued us in their typical rabid fashion.

I stayed toward the rear and provided covering fire until my ammunition was depleted, then jumped onto the last vehicle just before it sped away. A few lizzies betrayed their masters by breaking ranks and chasing after us like unleased dogs. We easily picked-off the pursuers while the majority remained at the edge of town and watched us drive away to the south. My comrades that were crammed into the flatbed with me began to relax as we put some distance between us and the Tongs. I was not so naïve to think that we had escaped them just yet. I couldn't help but feel as if we had been herded rather than attacked.

27

We continued on a southernly route for a week without stopping for anything longer than a chance to relieve ourselves and distribute what remained of the rations. The gargantuan yellow trees of the desert gradually gave way to clusters of green and purple leafy trees, and the sand was soon replaced by rolling hills covered in lush vegetation. I was content to put the desert behind me, having spent nearly two years there in a disquieted haze. If the scuttlebutt among the flatbeds was true, we were headed to Abasha City. I slowly began to allow myself to believe the prospect of seeing my son once again.

There was no sign of the Chief in our convoy. Leadership of the company seemed to have been handed down to Ringo or one of the other Serrone officers that had stayed behind with us. Whoever was in charge must have believed that we were out of immediate danger after a week on the road, for we bivouacked near a stream on the seventh night. It was a welcome change to eat fruit fresh from the nearby groves and sleep under the stars. In the morning I asked Cap if we were heading to Abasha City. He could not say for certain—even the combots were in the dark at this point. We jammed into the flatbeds once again. It was even more crowded than before following the breakdown of one of the decrepit trucks.

We followed the small brook through a beautiful countryside and a couple of abandoned villages until it fed into a wide river that crossed our path. Spanning the river was a long bridge constructed of exotic stone and metal alloys that I couldn't identify. The stones formed elegant roman arches beneath the roadway. Tall towers adorned with grand metal sculptures rose from each end of the bridge. Smaller sculptures lined the rails on each side of the span, watching over all who crossed the architectural wonder. How the elegant bridge had managed to survive the endless wars while the towns on either side had been reduced to rubble, was a complete mystery.

On the other side of the river was a tent encampment on the edge of a decimated village. I saw several PRF soldiers emerge from tents and stand on the opposite embankment as we approached. After crossing the bridge, the convoy came to a halt near the center of the camp. As we disembarked and assembled, the camp residents—maybe a hundred soldiers in total—walked over to meet us. I looked in all directions for a glimpse of the Abasha City skyline and saw nothing but rolling hills beyond the village ruins.

"Are we staying here?" I asked Dee.

"Yes."

"For how long?"

"Unknown," he said. I cursed myself for allowing the faint prospect of seeing my son to germinate into full-blown anticipation during the previous week.

Our arrival was expected. The small group of soldiers that greeted us was relieved to have their numbers fortified. They had already erected tents for us, though there was only enough tent space for about half of our company, so the junior soldiers were relegated to sleep outside. I sought out a veteran of the company and was directed to a tall, wiry woman from London who had been on the planet for more than ten seasons. We swapped stories of our recent histories and found them to be very similar. Her outfit had been driven back from a position to the west of Little Vegas following heavy fighting against infinite waves of lizzies. It was her impression that we were now under orders to hold the current position, as it was one of the main roads leading to Abasha City.

My ears perked up when she mentioned the city, and I inquired about its proximity. She told me that she had been there several times over the years and that it was no more than a day's ride south. My hopes began to rise again, and I fought earnestly to suppress them. The British woman was in the middle of a sentence when a tremendous explosion erupted behind me. The sound of the blast and shock of the concussion startled me, causing me to stumble to the ground.

"I should have warned you that we were blowing the bridge," the woman said with a laugh. "You might want to cover your ears. I don't think they've finished the demolition quite yet."

I regained my feet and turned just in time to see a second explosion bring down the grand tower on the near side of the bridge.

"We can't have those Tongs crossing over now, can we?" she added. I made a remark about it never being a good sign when your own army is destroying bridges in its wake.

"Well, they've got us on the run—that's for sure," she said.

I managed to secure a tent for myself, Nicholas, Susan, Pablo, Ying, Monte, and Scoop. I filled them in on what I had learned and how close we were to the city. We stayed up most of the first night discussing our prospects.

"We'll get there soon enough," said Susan. "I can't imagine us lasting very long out here in the open, with only the river to protect us."

"They could have wiped us out back in Little Vegas," suggested Scoop. "Why didn't they?"

"I've been thinking about that," Nicholas said. Rather than simply telling us his theory, he proceeded to lead us there as if he was teaching a class. It was no wonder that more and more soldiers were calling him "Professor."

"What is the most important commodity on the planet right now?" The Professor asked us.

"Water?" suggested Scoop.

"Water is a valuable *resource.* I'm talking about a valuable commodity. Think about it. What does every leader need to stay in power?" I could see where he was going.

"Us," I said.

"Right—an army. More specifically, an army of human slaves. You, you, and you." He pointed to each of us for effect.

"And we're in short supply," said Susan.

"No more human come here," added Ying.

"Correct," said Nicholas. "No more humans, lizzies, orcos, or any other aliens are getting added to this game. And no more androids are being constructed either. All of the pieces are on the board and in play. He who controls them controls the world."

"It doesn't take a rocket scientist to see that the Tongs are on the verge of taking out Abasha," said Susan.

"Sure, but the PRF might be small potatoes to the Tongs. Who knows what else is out there? How much of the planet does the king control? One third? One tenth? He needs us alive to conquer and hold it," lectured The Professor.

"Maybe the Tongs are driving us back to the city in order to get the entire PRF in one place, where they'll exact a surrender," I suggested.

"Makes sense to me," said Pablo. To nobody's surprise, Nicholas proceeded to question his own premise.

"That may be true," he told us, "but they risk provoking an epic battle in which thousands could die."

I proposed the idea of surrendering to the Toghans. I conjectured that we could delay the inevitable and save human lives. I cannot say how serious I was at the time, but the notion of a rebellion took root that night. Could the king be any worse than Abasha? There were humans in his army, and as far as we could tell, they took a backseat to the lizzies when it came to serious combat. Nobody else would admit to taking the conversation seriously either, yet we indulged ourselves by trying to conceive of a plan. We concluded that the androids would be too large of an obstacle to overcome. The combots could not be relied upon in a rebellion, and the sentroids were far too powerful. Still, the numbers of both were being reduced by attrition, and we agreed that the day might come when we could gain the upper hand. I slept better that night than any night since we dug the trenches outside of Little Vegas.

This camp had no name. It did not host talent shows. There was no gambling, no contests, no catnip, no cathouse, and limited quantities of alcohol. Nevertheless, it promoted a level of camaraderie that I had not experienced since arriving on Serrone. Many seasons had passed since anyone had tasted victory in battle. The triumphs once so common to the People's Resistance Front had been replaced with a pervasive feeling of gloom and loss.

It was this shared misery that brought the soldiers closer together. Many seemed disappointed in the inevitable defeat, paying no regard to the circumstances which brought them to the planet in bondage to fight someone else's war. I wouldn't go so far as to say they were victims of Stockholm syndrome. It's just that nobody likes to lose. I could relate to this sentiment but I didn't feel it. I harbored no illusions of defeating the Toghans. I was tired of the war and was willing to fight for whichever side could end it faster. Whereas the others dreaded the arrival of the Toghans, I couldn't wait for them to show up and slaughter us or drive us back to the city where I could find my son. The way I saw it, the evil

Tongs were much less of a hindrance to me than the PRF.

It was not long before my wish came true. Early one morning, a few weeks after arriving at the camp, Scoop rushed into the tent to rouse me from a deep sleep.

"Shaker, get up! You have to see this!"

I couldn't tell if he was in a state of panic or elation. He just seemed bewildered. I heard nothing but silence from beyond the tent so I grabbed my gear and headed outside. Wiyanga was still below the horizon, but the parent star had risen high enough in the sky to provide a dim light, similar to a very cloudy day. The entire camp, more than three hundred soldiers and androids, stood on the bank of the wide river with their backs to me. I made my way to them and took my own place in the line. Facing us on the opposite bank was the Toghan army, or a large portion of it at the very least. It could have been described as our mirror image had their numbers not been ten times ours. We stood one deep, shoulder to shoulder. They were amassed three or four deep in a line that extended hundreds of feet beyond our flanks.

The scene felt far more surreal than ominous. No weapons were drawn. No artillery was aimed in our direction. Both armies stood motionless while gazing at each other across the river in silence. Ours comprised humans and androids. Theirs was a mix of lizzies, humans, androids, and a few other species that I couldn't identify from such a distance. I wondered what the chances were that any of us knew any of the people that stood across from us—not from Serrone, but from Earth. Maybe somebody over there was from Virginia, I thought. It wouldn't have made any difference. I just remember having that specific thought at that moment.

"What happens now?" Scoop asked me.

"We go to the city, I suppose." It dawned on me that Nicholas' theory was probably a reality. They wanted us—at least most of us—alive.

"Load the trucks!" ordered Cap from some distance away. His voice snapped me into soldiering mode.

"You heard him. Let's move it!" I shouted.

Most of the Toghan force remained on the opposite bank of the river and watched us prepare for our withdrawal to Abasha City. One might have never guessed they were there, given the sober, businesslike manner in which we proceeded to break camp and load the trucks. There was no way for them to traverse the river in time to catch us, even if they had so desired, which we doubted. They knew where to find us.

I decided to ride in the cab of a flatbed and continue my conversation with Evelyn, the British veteran whom I met upon crossing the river. My earlier interaction with her made me realize how much I missed the company of Jessie, Swag, and Malcolm, and how much I could still learn from an old-timer. I couldn't tell how much older Evelyn was than I. Serrone had a polarizing way of accelerating the aging process in some people while enabling others to thrive in the hostile environment. Evelyn's reddish-brown hair included gray streaks that looked as if they had been dyed rather than the result of natural aging. I attributed her rugged appearance to her years as a soldier and tried to picture her before her abduction. I imagined that she was once quite attractive, and asked her about her life before.

"God Shaker, it's been a long time since I thought about her," she replied as we climbed into the cab. Evelyn drove the rig while I sat in the middle and Dee rode shotgun.

"Her?"

"The woman I was before coming here. You wouldn't have recognized me. I was a chubby girl." She seemed a little embarrassed of who she was before.

"I can't imagine that," I replied. I wasn't just being polite—it was difficult to imagine that the slender woman sitting next to me was ever an ounce overweight.

"It's true. I was nearly two hundred pounds. And here's the funny part: I was attending a weight-loss camp out in the countryside when they snatched me up."

"Are you kidding?"

"It's true. I was a city girl—born and bred in London. It was my first time north of Yorkshire and look what happened. They pulled me and another girl right out of our beds."

"That's crazy."

"But you must look on the bright side, Shaker."

"What's that?"

"Well, I lost the weight, didn't I? You have to admit that the Serrone weight-loss program is damned effective. You don't see too many chubby people running around on this planet, now do you?"

I admired her sense of humor. It seemed to be one of the common denominators among the old-timers, and a key to long-term survival.

"Is the other girl still around?" I asked.

She replied without skipping a beat. "Oh no, no. She didn't survive the trip here. Some sort of sickness, I suppose." Any grief for her friend had long since dissipated. She could have just as easily been talking about a pet that died thirty years ago.

We drove on and I asked her and Dee to tell me as much as they could about Abasha City. I was mildly surprised to learn that Dee had never been to the city, though he seemed to know nearly as much about its history as my new friend. Evelyn told us how she had been brought to the city as a slave of the Southern State more than twenty seasons ago, when the humans referred to it as "Konkoro"—a bastardized version of the Serrone pronunciation. Dee attempted to teach us the correct pronunciation. Neither Evelyn nor I could master it.

"It's just Abasha City to me," I told them.

"You are incorrect, Shaker," Dee responded. "Abasha City and Konkoro are not the same place."

"Okay, now I'm confused. Are we not going to Abasha City?" I asked.

Evelyn proceeded to clear up my confusion, while occasionally deferring to Dee for confirmation of a specific detail. Abasha City sat just to the north of Konkoro. It was originally built to house the thousands of slaves brought from multiple planets in support of the Southern State army. She provided comical accounts of the numerous quirky and freakish aliens that were brought to Serrone on an experimental basis. She was more somber when describing the countless human slaves that were sacrificed in gruesome combat trials. She said that orcos were once the preferred combat weapon of the Southern State but the supply was nearly depleted after only a few years, a result of the orcos' aversion to defensive tactics. I asked her about lizzies. Her knowledge and experience were nearly as limited as my own.

"Lizzies were a northern thing," she said. "They were terribly ineffective against orcos and not used much in the Great War until humans were placed into combat. They fare a lot better against us."

I speculated that there must be thousands of lizzies on Serrone and whimsically suggested that trillions more must live on their home planet. My comments struck a chord with Dee, who had been mostly silent during the trip thus far (in concert with his normal disposition).

"Thousands were brought from their planet," he chimed in. "Many more were born here."

"You seem to know a lot about it," I said, not expecting a response.

"I made several trips to that planet. I was part of a team that was sent to retrieve them."

"You flew on a starship?" I asked. Once again Dee had surprised me with an odd factoid about himself.

"Yes, shortly after I was created."

"How could you abduct so many without being detected?" asked Evelyn. Dee paused before replying.

"Detection was not a concern. We took them by force. Thousands perished—many more than we captured," he said. Evelyn and I exchanged anxious glances.

Dee must have sensed our uneasiness and felt compelled to elaborate. "It was not my choice. We were ordered to do so." It was probably my imagination, but I sensed a hint of remorse in the seasoned android's voice. We sat quietly for a few moments before Dee broke the awkward silence.

"Shaker, you know that I would never do that, right?" he asked. I instantly recognized my own words from that day in the old city, when the Chief warned the inhabitants that I would eagerly devour them. Was he just mimicking me? Was he telling me what he thought I wanted to hear? Did he actually *feel* remorse? Do combots harbor their own war demons? I couldn't wait to share this turn of events with Nicholas.

"I have no reason to believe that you would," I said, purposely repeating his response to me from that day. I wasn't being facetious. I was trying to communicate with him in a way that he might understand.

To my relief (and perhaps Dee's as well), the discussion returned to the history of the city and the differences between Dee's Great Northern Army and the Army of the Southern State, in which Evelyn was enslaved. The two former adversaries deduced that they had once fought against each other in a particular battle. They agreed that the battle ended inconclusively after thousands of lives were lost. (I would have been shocked to hear that it had ended in anything other than a stalemate.) I suppose that in the era of warlords, where factions were continuously intermixing, reunions such as this were common. As expected, Dee was able to recount every detail of the battle, yet so was Evelyn. To my amazement, they traded accounts of every move they made during that fateful day. I thought about it and realized that I was also able to recall every second of every battle in which I had participated—and in vivid detail, as if it had transpired in slow motion.

I first caught sight of the lifeless Konkoro skyline after riding for a half-day in the truck. It stood less prominently on the horizon than the first Serrone city I encountered back in the desert. Nothing could ever match the experience of seeing that magnificent oasis rise out of the infinite, flat sand. Konkoro was as large or larger than that desert metropolis, but at this distance it was intermittently blocked by the hills and forests that stood between us.

However pleased with myself I might have been for having chosen to ride inside the cab, my jubilation doubled when a steady rain began to fall upon my soggy comrades in the flatbeds. It was about this time that our road merged onto a wider highway that made a straight line for the city. We soon passed a small group of Serrones walking on the side of the road. There were about fifteen in all, young and old, walking alongside a large cart that hovered a few feet above the ground. Packed within the cart were crates, pieces of furniture, and other miscellaneous items that I assumed constituted everything they owned in the world.

Before long we passed another group of refugees heading for the city, then another, until they formed a near-continuous line on the side of the road. We saw a few more of the hovering carts, though most of the refugees' belongings were piled into more traditional carts—the kind with wheels. These carts were pulled by hairy oxen-like creatures that were larger than a compact car. Only a few of the Serrone youngsters turned to look at us as we drove by. Their elders trudged along the muddy shoulder looking no farther than their own feet. I'm sure we weren't the first convoy to pass by, and there was obviously no expectation of assistance.

The rain subsided a little, paving the way for a misty fog to descend upon the city. Visibility was reduced to a few hundred feet, so I didn't recognize the large stone wall for what it was until the convoy stopped at the gate.

"What is that?" I asked.

"The wall," said Evelyn. "You didn't know that Abasha City was surrounded by a wall?"

"I guess I had pictured something resembling chain-link and barbed wire. This looks like something out of the Medieval Period."

It really did. The massive beige and gray wall stood more than thirty feet high and extended in both directions for as far as I could see. It was constructed of large carved stones and mortar. When we drove through the iron gate I could see that the wall was several yards thick. I surmised that it must have been constructed fairly recently, for in the inverted world of Serrone, the more primeval a structure appeared, the newer it probably was. High-tech, large-caliber plasma cannons were mounted on turrets and evenly spaced along the wall. I knew there was an anachronism there somewhere, but I couldn't decide if it was the wall or the guns. Once inside, Evelyn called my attention to the ruins of a smaller, more contemporary-looking fence.

"That's what kept us inside the slave camp back in the day," she said. "Abasha built the stone wall a few years ago when he made it his capital." Beyond Abasha City to the south stood the towering, dilapidated skyscrapers of Konkoro looking down upon us, as if searching for the best spot to fall and maximize damage. If you stared up at them long enough, you'd swear that they were falling at that very moment. I learned later that there was no direct access to Konkoro, as Abasha City was completely walled in. Rumors of who and/or what resided in the ruins were plentiful. The only things I ever saw in Konkoro from the vantage point of the wall were cappies—thousands of them. There might have been Serrones living in there somewhere, because none of the refugees were being allowed into Abasha City. Most of them just kept walking farther south, well past Konkoro. The walled stronghold seemed to be reserved for General Abasha, his officers, a handful of Serrone aristocrats, and the slave army that protected them. Anybody else was on their own.

28

Abasha City was far from the Emerald City that I had once envisioned, yet it was still the largest and most advanced settlement I had seen since arriving on the planet. The soldiers in my company were eager to explore the offerings of their new home but I had only one purpose since our arrival: to find my son. I hadn't taken catnip since leaving Little Vegas yet my heart still pounded as if it might crack a few ribs. Cap assembled us just inside the main gate where we stood silently waiting for something to happen. Ringo idled by in his chariot alongside Chairman Mao, who had made the trip to Abasha City with him. We stood and grumbled for what seemed like an hour before the Chief finally appeared with my old buddies, Khan and the Kaiser.

Khan briefed us on our new assignment. He stated that our only official duty was to protect General Abasha. When he elaborated further, it sounded a lot more like the emphasis was on protecting the Chief. The Chief's role in the PRF at this point was vague. We were told that Ringo had taken charge of our company, and that he was assigned to manage and protect a pie-slice sector that amounted to about one eighth of the total city. This area was called sector seven by the androids. It was a substantial area given that the city was nearly two miles in diameter. The soldiers we had joined with at the river were split between our company and the one that occupied the adjacent sector to the south. That slice of the pie was called sector eight, and it stood between ours and the ruined city of Konkoro. I was disappointed to find that Evelyn was among those to be transferred, though it made sense. Our neighboring sector lacked veteran leadership, and she was well-suited to fill the void.

Following Khan's remarks, we were ordered to proceed to our sector and take up our barracks. I was now a bona fide nervous wreck, having come so close to my son without being able to see him. I thought about begging leave from Cap but decided it wouldn't be a good idea for the HiC to steal away on a personal mission. Cap wouldn't have allowed it anyway, and I had yet to figure out how to navigate my way around the camp. The notion that my son might not even be in the city threatened to cross my mind and I quickly shoved it aside.

The barracks were nicer, if only because they were newer, and it was great to have a roof and a bed once again. The buildings were of a similar design to those in Little Vegas—long, two-story structures with single bunks upstairs and multipurpose rooms downstairs. The outlandish rumors of indoor plumbing in Abasha City turned out to be just that, though we did have a water pump outside the main entrance. I would be remiss not to mention that the latrines were cleaner than any others I had encountered, once again due to their recent construction. I was far above latrine duty at this point. It would have otherwise been significantly less repulsive than previous camps, which I duly noted to Scoop and the other junior soldiers when I assigned the duty to them.

After settling into the barracks, I tried once again to break away and search for little Jasper. I took a chance and told Dee about my plight. He didn't grant me permission to leave but he provided a little hope that I might get away later, in his customary cryptic fashion.

"You cannot leave the sector. We have to take the company to chow," he told me, then added as he walked away, "It is much easier to move around the city at night."

The sector dining hall was close to the barracks and the short walk over to it afforded me no opportunity to see more of the city. Had I not been so preoccupied, I would have been overjoyed to find my favorite cereal mush laid out for us. Instead of savoring the dish that I hadn't tasted in several seasons, I wolfed it down in the hopes of hurrying everybody else along so that I could plan my evening escapade.

"Why you eat so fast?" asked Ying.

"He wants to find Jasper," said Susan. "You must be about to crap your pants, Shaker."

"Yeah, you could say I'm a little anxious. I'm gonna try to find him tonight."

"Good plan. We go too," said Ying. By the time we finished dinner the entire table had volunteered to help find Jasper, and I was worried about causing a spectacle. We finally agreed that Nicholas, Susan, and Ying would accompany me. We came out of the dining hall into the darkness and made our way across the small courtyard to the barracks. The lights went out about an hour later. I climbed out of bed and walked over to Dee, who was recharging in a chair by the door. The others followed my lead.

"I'm heading out," I said softly to Dee. When I saw no reaction, I repeated myself. After this Dee turned slowly and looked at me.

"Why are you telling me this?" he asked. Message received. We entered the courtyard stealthily and made our way to the edge of the sector as if we were sneaking behind enemy lines. There were plenty of lights on around the camp and we were more than a little embarrassed to notice a few soldiers casting strange looks in our direction. It turned out that there was a lot of activity in the city. It was business as usual, and nobody seemed to mind that we were out and about. It felt as if we were the only company that had been sent to bed, while our older siblings got to stay up late. That was the first and only night that our company was subjected to a curfew.

We were technically confined to our sector, yet there were no hard boundaries between the sectors, and it was easy to move freely around the entire city. There were ostensibly too many soldiers for the sentroids to track, not that they appeared interested in doing so. I approached a couple of my new comrades lounging on the steps of a building and sharing a bottle.

"Where are the children kept?"

"The kids? They're in the middle of town—green building."

"Thanks."

"You got a kid there?"

"I hope so."

"Good luck. Are you guys new?"

"Yeah. Got in today."

"What's going on out there? We don't hear shit in this prison."

I didn't want to be rude and would have enjoyed trading information with these guys under difference circumstances, but I just couldn't be delayed any longer. I told them as much, thanked them again, and we made our way toward the center of the city. After asking for directions twice more, we found ourselves in front of a stone building that was painted lime-green. It stood out from all other buildings in the area—not so unique for its pastel color as for being the only one with a sentroid standing in front of the door.

This development threw me a little in light of the relaxed atmosphere I had seen on the walk over. The others halted while I proceeded without breaking stride and attempted to walk right past it, as if I had the authority to enter. Acting the part might have worked on a combot, but sentroids possessed no capacity to perceive or interpret something like self-confidence. By design, everything to them was black or white. As expected, the sentroid stepped into my path.

"No access."

"I have business in there," I told him.

"What business?" the sentroid asked. I was pleasantly surprised that he was at least sniffing the bait.

"I'm a doctor." The sentroid paused for a second, probably accessing some sort of database.

"You have no business here," he said. For a fleeting moment I considered rushing past him, then thought the better of it. I was in no mood for a taser and would have only found myself in hot water with the Chief—or worse, the General. We huddled a few feet away from the stringent android and contemplated our next move. The sentroid paid no further attention to us whatsoever. We might as well have been a mile away.

"We can try again tomorrow," suggested Nicholas. "We need to figure out how things work around here."

"I just want to see him. I need to know that he's alright."

"Come on, Shaker. We'll try again tomorrow," said Susan as she gently tugged my arm. We began to walk away and passed a woman heading in the opposite direction. After a few more steps I heard a voice.

"Excuse me," said the woman. We turned and looked at each other in the dim light. Her face looked familiar but I was unable to place it. She walked over to us, keeping her eyes studiously on mine, as if surprised to see me.

"Do you remember me?" she asked. In that instant—maybe it was her voice—I did remember her, and a warm feeling rushed over me. She looked healthy and assured. Frankly, I was astonished that she was still alive. Of the two women I snuck into the cathouse that day, she was the more fragile, and I had little confidence that either would survive.

"I *do* remember you. How are you?" My face lit up. I felt like a proud doctor meeting a young woman he hadn't seen since delivering her in childbirth.

"Okay," she answered. I told the others about my brief encounter with this woman and the other that occurred a few days before we abandoned the old camp. I could sense that the young woman was not convinced I had made the best decision on her behalf. Seeing her now, in direct contrast to my tough-as-nails comrades, Susan and Ying, I was certain that she wouldn't have survived the past few years with us. I didn't feel that it was my place to point this out to her, though Ying had no problem in doing so.

"Good thing you come here, or you be long gone dead," she said bluntly.

"I guess so…" said the woman.

"Shaker save your life!" continued Ying. I was grateful that she had no filter, and also a little embarrassed, so I changed the subject.

"How is the other woman?"

"She's here in the city." I felt still more relief to hear that they were both alive—then my thoughts returned to my son.

"Do you—I'm sorry, I don't remember your name."

"Janet."

"Janet, do you live in there? My son… Jasper—is there a boy called Jasper in there? I can't get inside."

"Wait here," she said. She walked past the sentroid and climbed the three steps into the green building. About thirty seconds later the doors burst open and the woman reappeared with two others, whom we all recognized immediately.

"Shakespeare!" shouted Tina as she bounced down the steps. She skirted around the sentroid with her arms outstretched and leapt onto me. Behind her came Saba, the young rebel prisoner whom Charles had saved. Tina looked a little older in the face, yet the maturity somehow enhanced her beauty by making her appear more confident. Saba appeared as young and vibrant as ever. Nobody else could have looked so out of place on a military installation. We all exchanged greetings in front of the sentroid, who couldn't have cared less for our reunion. Although both women seemed as content as could be expected, I was haunted by the idea of what they had been subjected to since leaving my protection.

It was Susan who first asked about Jasper.

"He's fine," said Tina with a smile. "He's getting big."

"Can you bring him out here?" I asked.

Her smile faded as she turned to look at the sentroid. "I don't think so. Not now." Then she lit up again. "Saba, can you bring Jasper over there?" She pointed toward a window several feet away from the door, then turned back to me. "We can do the next best thing. Come over here."

Saba went back inside as Tina led the rest of us over to the open window. It was a few feet above my head and I stood just below the narrow sill.

"Not too close," said Tina, gesturing back toward the sentroid. "He probably wouldn't like it if you came into contact with the children. We shouldn't push it—not today."

I reluctantly agreed and stepped a few feet backward. Saba soon appeared in the window holding my son. I don't know why I was so taken aback to see that he was no longer an infant. He had grown so large that Saba struggled to hold him. Instead, she stood him on the sill and placed her arm around his waist. It was clear that he had been roused from a deep sleep and was not too happy about it.

Even in the dim light of the evening I could see that the boy had inherited his mother's caramel skin and brown eyes. I saw little resemblance to myself, which was also noted by Susan in the form of a quip about the boy being so lucky. Tina politely disagreed and attributed Jasper's nose and sheer size to my genetic contributions. The mention of his size segued to the calculation of his age, which on Earth would have been definitive, but on Serrone was much more imprecise. We knew how many seasons had transpired since his birth and we knew that a Serrone year comprised two seasons (warm and cool). We deferred to our resident physicist for a conversion rate between our home planet and our current planet. I allowed for Nicholas to debate with his self for a few minutes then cut him off and settled on an estimated age of two and half Earth years.

"That's your father, Jasper," said Saba. Jasper didn't seem too interested in me, and that was okay. He was alive and would eventually come to know me better. We spent a few minutes talking to the toddler. It was generally a one-way conversation, though Jasper tossed in a few words here and there to our delight. When Saba took him back to his bed, I attempted to wipe away the tear on my cheek before anybody noticed it. If they did, they were kind enough not to say anything—even Susan.

Tina next filled us in on the status of the children in Abasha City. There were nearly one hundred living in two buildings side-by-side, with a fenced-in play area in between. Tina, Saba, and Janet were among those assigned to look after them. There was no charter for educating the children beyond basic communication skills, but the ladies of the nursery had taken it upon themselves to teach the children whatever they could.

"We have lots of pencils and paper here in the city," Tina told us. "The sentroids make sure that the nursery has plenty to go around."

"How is that possible?" asked Nicholas.

"I guess someone convinced the General that literate soldiers make better fighters," she said.

Though we were all in such high spirits, I couldn't shake the question of whether Tina and Saba had been forced to endure unspeakable atrocities.

"So, that's all you that you ladies do here—watch the children?" I asked delicately.

"Like I said, we try to educate them as best we can," Tina replied, apparently missing the gist of my question.

"Yes, but that's *all* you have to do, right? No other… duties?"

"Oh—we're okay, Shakespeare. We're lucky, but there's still a lot of that stuff going on here." She pointed over to a cluster of buildings nearby. "The General always needs more soldiers."

"Sandra wasn't so lucky," said Janet. I had all but forgotten that she was still standing with us.

"Sandra?" asked Susan.

"The other woman that he sent here with me," Janet added, while pointing at me. My heart sank and I looked to the ground.

"Shaker, you did what you thought was best," said Susan calmly.

I had no doubt that my motives were well placed, but Janet didn't seem to agree, and it really bothered me. I don't know if Tina was just trying to change the subject when she suddenly burst out with an epiphany of sorts.

"Shaker? You're *the* Shaker?" she exclaimed.

"Yeah, that's what they call me now."

"Wow. You're big news around here—a real legend, dude."

"They've heard of me here?" I asked. This was not false humility. I was genuinely surprised that my reputation had reached Abasha City. I figured I was just a big fish in a small pond out in the fringes of the PRF territory.

"*Heard of you?* I'm telling you, man. You're a big deal here. Did you really kill one of those spider things?"

"I had some help."

"Are you actually embarrassed, Shaker?" said Susan with a laugh. "I'm a little surprised. What happened to your giant ego?"

"Yeah, you my hero," said Ying. Sarcasm was apparently uninhibited by her steep language barrier. I was grateful for the ribbing. It was true that I generally enjoyed the adulation of my comrades, though it seemed a little misplaced in that moment, in the presence of Janet.

"We should get back to the barracks," I said. I looked over to the lime-green building once more and added, "I'm gonna figure out a way to get in there."

29

It might have been the very next day when I first heard the rumors of a human settlement somewhere on the planet far away from Abasha City. Nobody seemed to know anything firsthand. All I heard were stories of someone who knew someone who heard something from someone else. I dismissed the gossip as nothing more than wishful thinking and put the idea out of my head. My immediate priorities were to acclimate myself to the city and find a way to spend time with Jasper.

Following breakfast, during which I was more appreciative of the cereal mush I had missed so much, a combot from another sector led the company on a tour of the city. The city was shaped like a pie with the bottom third missing. Into the missing wedge jutted the northern portion of the old city, Konkoro. The stone wall ran along the entire border of Abasha City, meaning that the only access to Konkoro was via a large, heavy gate at the apex of the missing pie wedge, and it was rarely opened.

Many of our soldiers had been to Abasha City before but were not permitted to opt out of the tour, as did our new Serrone leader, Ringo, whom we would seldom see from that day forward. The first stop was the portion of the great stone wall within our own sector. We were shown the various ladders and staircases leading to the elevated landing on our side of the wall, on which we could stand and see out beyond the city. There we received a short briefing on the operation of the two large-caliber plasma cannons that were mounted within our sector. It was our responsibility to monitor our portion of the wall and man the guns at all hours. Cap ordered the combot squad leaders to devise a schedule. Dee passed the duty for his squad down to me.

The immediate view from our section of the wall faced to the east and was nothing spectacular. All forestation within a half mile of the wall had been cleared, leaving nothing but grasses and weeds in front of us. Somebody questioned why there was no moat and drawbridge, a question which our combot tour guide took seriously, rendering it impossible for us to suppress our snickering. Beyond the cleared area surrounding the wall were endless hills and forests. The forests contained a large variety of tree species, sprouting a vast array of colored leaves, as if stuck in a perpetual autumn. Over our right shoulder was a view of the northeastern edge of the old city, where our attention was immediately drawn to a particular skyscraper that appeared to be leaning in our direction. The decaying structure was easily two thousand feet high and probably just out of reach of our sector. Looking down the wall, I could see a few of the unfortunate soldiers in Evelyn's company patrolling the adjacent sector under the shadow of the colossal structure and the foreboding threat of its collapse.

On the grounds just within the wall was a battery of anti-aircraft artillery that looked as ancient and ineffective as the aircraft it was intended to destroy. My suspicions of its inoperability were all but confirmed when our tour guide breezed past it without any elaboration. The interesting part of the tour commenced when we departed our sector and headed for the center district of Abasha City. The cathouse, infirmary, and PX were situated there, as was the nursery complex that I had visited on the previous night.

We entered the PX and discovered a narrow warehouse containing two long rows of wooden shelves in three tiers that were somewhat reminiscent of the cargo hold I once lived in. Sitting at a small desk just inside the entrance was a grumpy old veteran with a bushy gray beard who went by the name of Luther. We surmised that the old man must have been one of the first humans abducted, and that he must have been in his sixties when it happened. The scuttlebutt around camp was that he had never seen a minute of combat duty, which I believed wholeheartedly after getting to know him and his crafty ways. He had a knack for acquiring items and knowledge, none of which he be provided without a price. Very little transpired in the city without Luther knowing about it.

I don't believe that Luther took a liking to me initially, but he must have seen some value in forming an alliance with me. I guess my reputation and imposing appearance surpassed those of the two thugs he had currently in his employ. From the moment we met he schmoozed me with phony praise and false humility. I too saw a value in the alliance and pretended not to detect the spurious nature of his affections. Although we never verbalized our agreement, it was obvious that Luther was interested in physical protection, and that I desired access to information and the vast assortment of knickknacks in his store. And so it was that the old codger invited me to return that evening for a private, more comprehensive tour of the PX.

I returned later with my small entourage, on which he frowned, then agreed to permit upon my insistence. We found the collection of wares in the PX to be widely disparate and peculiar. We were even more curious to know how certain items could have possibly found their way to the planet. This category included toenail clippers, dried out felt-tip pens, worn toothbrushes, old magazines, a deck of forty-nine playing cards from the Trump Taj Mahal casino, a broken Casio LED wristwatch, a barbecue cookbook, a DVD of the movie *Spartacus*, and a coffee mug inscribed with "The World's Greatest Dad," all of which had obviously been smuggled from Earth. We concluded that some humans must have been brought there in a much more liberal manner than we were, as it would have been impossible for us to have smuggled any such articles with us. Nicholas opined that some of the items might have once been souvenirs brought back by Serrone astronauts in the early days of the slave trade. How they ended up in Luther's hands I never knew.

The majority of the PX inventory comprised native items which were far more interesting to me—especially the blank sheets of paper. The recent decline in Serrone civilization had spurred a comeback of the written word in hardcopy format, following an absence that had probably lasted for centuries. Supplies of a thick and resilient papyrus resembling an ancient Hebrew scroll began trickling down to the human soldier population, along with an alien cousin to the ballpoint pen. Luther maintained both in stock. It was around this time that I began to keep a diary of sorts that would become the foundation of this narrative.

The PX also boasted a hidden cache of weapons that could be purchased at exorbitant prices—usually in the currency of lizzie canine teeth or cigarettes. Knives, grenades, and plasma weapons in all shapes and sizes were available to any soldier willing to pay the price, and daring enough to brandish them in front of the androids. Some of the combots were known to tolerate the appearance of exotic weapons while others were likely to confiscate them (after which some of them mysteriously found their way back to the PX). Cap and Dee fell into the former category, and I soon replaced my Uzi with a faster, more accurate and more powerful plasma rifle with a higher capacity (which I also referred to as my Uzi). As Luther's new partner, I had the pick of the litter. I was always wary of the sentroids and I retained a complement of conventional weapons to display in their presence. Fortunately, sentroids were rarely close at hand on the battlefield, as it was their commission to protect the fainthearted Serrone officers. I also added a small handgun to my combat ensemble. It fit nicely inside my new black boots that laced halfway up to my knees.

My new accessories did not come without a price. I found myself performing various chores for Luther that more often than not involved physical force or intimidation. My reputation usually sufficed in accomplishing the task, though fisticuffs were required on a few occasions. Susan and Ying took advantage of my PX connections to bolster their own weaponry—new serrated knives for Ying and a powerful rifle for Susan. Nicholas passed on the opportunity. Even then I could see that he frowned upon my degenerate behaviors. I pretended not to care, or perhaps I really didn't care, and he continued to benefit from my protection.

I have digressed from describing the city tour in favor of introducing my collusion with Luther. I should return to the original task, because the bountiful PX was by far not the highlight of the field trip. Nor was the infirmary, which we visited next. I was impressed with the relative cleanliness of the facility and the thirty-plus wooden beds that looked far more comfortable than anything I had slept on since arriving on the planet. The beds were mostly empty except for a few patients suffering from non-combat ailments and one or two others brought in from distant battlefields. There were three resident "doctors"—two human and one little android. I use the term loosely for I am highly doubtful that either of the humans had been licensed to practice medicine on Earth. One them lectured us briefly on the best method for providing first-aid to a plasma wound. We found the information to be moderately useful, if not a few years overdue. We stocked up on fresh bandages on our way out.

Our guide led us in a southernly direction for a few minutes before coming to a barbed wire fence that enclosed a small compound within the city. Behind the compound was the southernmost portion of the stone wall, and behind that was the entrance to the old city. Inside the barbed wire fence stood several modern structures that resembled larger versions of the Chief's residence in the old camp. Patrolling the compound inside and out were numerous sentroids. We knew that this was the General's headquarters before our guide told us as much. I figured out later that our own Chief and other Serrone officers had taken up residence within this secondary fortification as well. I hoped to catch a glimpse of the mighty General but we were not so lucky. As predicted, our combot guide advised us that the compound was strictly off-limits to us, and quickly ushered us away.

We visited a few other facilities, including a motor pool and an airfield, before turning back in the direction of our own sector. We happened to proceed on a different path from whence we came. Whether by intention or happenstance, our route took us near a large metal pen situated in a southwestern sector of the city, where we came to an impromptu halt to view the curiosity. The rectangular enclosure occupied a footprint of about two hundred by one hundred feet and reminded me of a supermax prison. Two fences surrounded the pen. The inner fence was constructed of horizontal metal bars and included several outward facing signs with lightning bolts on them. The outer fence was not electrified and consisted of vertical steel bars. In spite of the two fences with crisscrossing bars, it was fairly easy to see inside the enclosure. A tall wooden shack rose up from the middle of it. The enclosure itself made for quite a spectacle, yet it was the inhabitants that stupefied us.

Within the pen were eleven orcos in various states of temperament, ranging from deep sleep to moderate agitation. Inside the cage, mingling freely with the menacing giants was what appeared to be the same little android who had accompanied the orcos that fought to their death in the village with us so long ago. He was being assisted inside the enclosure by a couple of brave soldiers wearing red armbands. The wide-eyed soldiers were doing their best to keep their distance from the orcos *and* the electrified fence, challenges that undoubtedly conflicted from time to time.

"I didn't think there were any of these things left," I commented to Dee. When I realized that he wasn't going to respond to an implied question, I rephrased my thought in the form an actual one. "How many of these orcos are left?"

"These are all that remain in the PRF," he answered.

"What will happen to them?"

"I do not know. They are marginally effective in battle. They are nearly as dangerous to our own troops as to the enemy."

"I guess they still make an effective deterrent," I said.

"I think these creatures are fascinating," said Nicholas. "I wonder what it takes to get assigned to this duty."

"I doubt there's a waiting list," said Susan. It then occurred to me that it might be worthwhile to have a trusted friend involved with the orcos, though I couldn't think of a reason at the time. I later spoke to Cap about volunteering Nicholas to assist the little android in his care and feeding of the beasts. He approved, then asked me if Nicholas was taking the assignment willingly or if I was punishing him. I told him that it was Nicholas' desire to take the position. On the following morning I accompanied Nicholas to the cage, where he eagerly replaced one of the assistants. The man seemed equally shocked and ecstatic upon hearing the news that he was to be permanently relieved.

During the tour I had noticed that numerous small vehicles were available to soldiers for transportation within the city. This ridesharing pool consisted mostly of two-person scooters and a few jeeps. I had never operated a Serrone vehicle in all my time on the planet. I had generally preferred to ride in the back of the flatbeds with my comrades and saw no reason to learn how to operate the alien vehicles. (Not to mention that drivers were often the first targets in an ambush.) Now it was imperative to learn. The city was just too big to traverse on foot. Pablo had a lot of experience driving and I asked him to show me. It took all of about five minutes to master, as these particular little vehicles were essentially self-driving. I still preferred walking, but it could take forty-five minutes to walk from one end of the city to another.

Having settled into the new environment and having seen my son for a second time through the window, I set out to mingle with soldiers in the other companies and gather whatever intelligence I could about the city and the war. The comrades with whom I met seemed generally comfortable and secure within the formidable stone wall. They had heard talk about the Toghans pushing PRF forces to the south but felt that the front was still miles away. Although I disagreed with their optimistic assessments, I kept my doubts to myself for the time being.

The fact that more and more soldiers and refugees had been retreating to the city should have been a red flag to them. The General's propaganda machine within the walls was obviously very effective. In fact, there had been no enemy sightings from the wall, and most of the soldiers were under the impression that we were winning the war. Nevertheless, I was certain that the Tongs were lurking in the forest just beyond the perimeter. The river where we had encountered the large army was only a day's ride away. For now, at least, it was business as usual in Abasha City.

A week or so later, I learned that business as usual included one-on-one fighting matches for the amusement of the Serrone officers. Several of us were lounging on the first floor of the barracks one morning debating whether it would be better to be a sixteenth century European monarch or someone living just above the poverty line in the modern-day United States. (As I recall, compelling arguments were made for both sides.) Dee interrupted the lively discussion to tell me that my presence was required outside. I came out of the barracks to find Khan waiting for me in the small courtyard.

"Follow me," he said. We proceeded to an area near the General's compound where a sizeable crowd of spirited human soldiers had gathered. I quickly deduced that they were there to witness some sort of corporeal event in which I was destined to play an integral role. A small ring in the grass had been roped-off just outside the barbed wire fence that surrounded the General's compound. A group of Serrone officers stood nearby the ring and behind the fence, within the protection of the compound. The three sides of the ring outside of the compound were surrounded by enthusiastic soldiers who seemed to know a lot more about what was transpiring than I did. A cheer arose when Khan ordered me into the ring after removing my knives. (My contraband pistol remained hidden in my boot.) A second cheer followed when a shirtless young male soldier, likely native born, climbed over the rope and started bobbing back and forth like a boxer warming up for a prize fight.

I looked into the compound in the hopes of catching my first glimpse of the General. I recognized the Chief sitting among several other Serrone officers donned in frocks of various color combinations. None seemed to exhibit the adornment, or command the deference that I had envisioned for the General. Then I saw him—it had to be him. He was sitting on a balcony on the third story of a metallic building, several yards back from the fighting ring, and well within the safety of the compound. From where I stood, he looked less like a general than he did a 1970s stereotypical street pimp. His swanky frock can best be described as a zoot suit of yellow, green, and red neon colors. Instead of the traditional PRF beret, he wore a wide-brimmed hat that clashed with his multi-colored suit. It was difficult to identify from such a distance, yet something resembling a large plume extended into the air from the brim of his hat. His eye visor seemed darker and larger than those worn by his subordinate officers, and it nearly covered his entire face. Two sentroids sat closely on either side of him, practically blocking his field of vision, which seemed a little superfluous given his safe distance from the action.

"Fight. No death," said Khan, calling my attention back to the ring in which I stood. My opponent instantly started toward me with his fists cocked and ready.

I extended out my hand toward him at arm's length. "Hold on a second—just hold on, okay?" Then I turned to Khan. "What are the rules here?"

"Fight. No death," he repeated.

"I know *that*, but how do we determine the winner?"

"One soldier is unconscious, one soldier cannot get up, one soldier surrenders; no faking," rattled off the sentroid, as if reading from a manual.

I supposed that there must have been suspicions of fighters taking dives in past fights. That wouldn't be a problem with me. I turned and faced my opponent, who immediately charged at me with reckless abandon. I dispatched him quickly without inflicting too much damage upon his body or face. He was no match for me, so rather than knock him into oblivion, I held him down on the ground in a headlock and choked him out. No death.

The discordant roars from the human spectators indicated that lots of lizzie teeth and cigarettes were about to change hands as a result of bets won and lost. I received several pats on the back from complete strangers as I climbed under the ropes and entered the crowd. The Serrones remained stoic, though I'm certain that some kind of alien currency was wagered among them as well. After all, we fought at their desire.

This event marked the beginning of a pattern that lasted for several weeks. Each morning following breakfast I distributed the days assignments among the soldiers—always dispatching Nicholas to the orco pen. I then made my way in a roundabout fashion to the PX, stopping to consort with soldiers and combots from other sectors along the way. Our interchanges were often accompanied by catnip and moonshine, which were quite abundant in the city and mostly tolerated. Despite halfhearted attempts to resist, I had resumed my vices shortly after arrival.

I sometimes hung around the front gate in the hopes of gathering intel about the war from newly arrived comrades, as small bands of retreating soldiers were arriving at an increasing rate. I would eventually find my way to the PX and sit with Luther for the afternoon to cultivate our burgeoning friendship, i.e., alliance. I visited the nursery every day before dinner and talked to Jasper as Tina or Saba held him on the window sill. He was beginning to warm up to me, but progress was slowed by my inability to gain access to the lime-green building. I had made no progress on that front.

Every three or four days I would be summoned to the ring just outside of the officers' compound for a match. Nicholas placed bets with the local bookmakers on our behalf and we prospered in the initial fights as I soundly defeated my opponents. Unfortunately, the odds were soon reduced to the point where there was very little wagering on my contests. I might have made a fortune by taking a dive if my ego would have allowed it. The betting action among the Serrones had probably dried up as well. Nicholas and I speculated that I would no longer be called upon to fight, in favor of holding a contest between two more evenly-matched opponents. That would have been fine with me, but we were mistaken.

One evening, several weeks after my arrival in Abasha City, Khan brought me into the ring in front of a crowd that seemed more raucous than usual. There was a flurry of activity as the soldiers engaged in a high volume of wagering transactions. Across from me stood two medium-sized soldiers, a man and a woman, both of whom appeared capable of handling themselves.

"Which one am I fighting?" I asked Khan.

"Both."

"At the same time?"

"Yes."

I looked at the General up on his balcony, then over to the Chief in his chariot. I wasn't sure about the General, but I was certain that I had won the Chief a lot of Serrone currency—whatever that was. Now I stood to make him a lot more if—*when*—I defeated these two opponents. I quickly weighed my options: The Chief held all the cards; he had burned me before; I was his slave. All of that occurred to me, yet something was different. The General was there, and my guess was that he had wagered on me. Maybe I could put the Chief in a tight spot. It all sounds a bit ill-conceived as I write this. My brash behavior was undoubtedly fueled by catnip.

I walked closer to Khan and spoke to him quietly.

"Ask Captain Cheefon what I get if I win."

"You get nothing. You must fight or you will be killed," replied Khan without hesitation.

"Yeah, I get *that*, but tell the Captain that I'm not feeling well tonight. I don't feel confident that I can win."

"What is wrong?"

"Tell him that I lack… *motivation.* A good soldier needs incentive in order to fight effectively. I'm sure that General Abasha would like to see me at my best." I looked directly at the Chief and waited nervously for an answer.

"What is it you need?" asked Khan.

I wasn't exactly prepared for this response. If I asked for access to the nursery specifically, it might put Jasper in danger. The Chief knew that I had fathered a child. "Unlimited access to all facilities in the city—except the officers' compound, of course."

"It will be granted if you win," said Khan following a brief pause. Wow—I hadn't expected that. It then occurred to me that my victory was in no way guaranteed. I needed a strategy for fighting two soldiers simultaneously. I had fought multiple opponents in combat on several occasions, but this was different—there were no weapons involved. Luckily, Nicholas had used the delay to mingle in the crowd and garner some intel about my opponents. He came up to the rope and called me over.

"The woman is the better fighter," he said quietly. "The guy is fairly new and hasn't seen much combat."

Armed with that limited information, I formulated a basic strategy. The way I saw it, two against one was not a fair contest. So, before Khan could give a signal to commence fighting, I ran over to the man and belted him squarely in the jaw. By the time he landed on the ground I had already turned and engaged the woman. She put up an admirable fight, employing karate-style kicks and quick jabs while trying to avoid my advances. Eventually my size was too much for her to repel, and I put her on the ground and into a chokehold. Before she lost consciousness, her partner collected himself and attempted to pull me off of her. I was forced to postpone my chokehold and address the man again, this time in the ribs, before returning to the woman. Just as she went out cold, the man took a wild swing in my direction, to which I responded with the deciding blow.

I brushed myself off and headed straight for the nursery, ignoring the cheers and pats on the back from those who had invested in me. As soon as I put my foot on the first step of the lime-green building, the sentroid in front snatched my arm into his grasp and yanked me firmly to the ground, where I found its taser appendage at eye level, about six inches away.

"No access."

I climbed to my feet carefully and moved a few steps backward.

"I do have access," I claimed. The sentroid remained silent. "Check again. I was just granted access."

"No access," he repeated. There wasn't much left to do there that didn't include me absorbing fifty thousand volts of electricity, so I returned to the barracks. I hoped that my recently-granted access just needed some time to make its way through the PRF bureaucracy. I fared no better on the next morning. I stood and stared at the nursery for several minutes, listening to the sounds of children playing in the yard behind it. I had gained nothing. For all I knew, I already had access to every facility except the nursery prior to the fight. Even in my furious state I knew there was nothing I could do that would not endanger my son.

So, I headed to a nearby sector known for its intemperance and drank myself into a stupor. I cannot account for much of the afternoon, though I distinctly recall standing in the darkness outside of the nursery window and yelling for my son. Suddenly, Tina had magically appeared at my side and was pulling me away from the building. Next, I lay on the ground laughing as she was reaming somebody out, then realized that I was the subject of her tirade.

"You need to pull yourself together, Shakespeare… or Shaker—

whatever the hell your name is." Her sharp reprobation had a temporary sobering effect. "Do you think you're the only person who's gotten screwed here? Look around."

I muttered incoherently before she cut me off.

"You used to be a guy who could get things done. Now you're just a big baby. Grow up."

She said a lot more before I finally formulated what I thought was a cogent response, yet by then she had magically disappeared, and I wondered if I had dreamt the whole conversation. I got to my feet with aid of a lamppost but I have no recollection of anything else until early the next morning, when a strange grunting sound brought me back to reality. I saw nothing but grass when I first opened my eyes. I lifted my throbbing head to find that I lay at the outer fence of the orco pen, where several of its inhabitants were sizing me up.

"Hi guys," I mumbled. "I'll just be getting out of your way." I dragged myself to my bunk and collapsed.

30

I am ashamed to admit that Tina's verbal rebuke didn't spur me into immediate rehabilitation. I even sunk a little lower before the lights within came back on for good. I fought in the ring several more times against various pairs of soldiers until the wagering dried up once again. Finally, the Chief decided to put me up against a trio of young soldiers. I was unprepared, overconfident, overmatched, and slightly inebriated. I managed to inflict a little damage before they overpowered me and took me to the proverbial woodshed. I woke up in the infirmary feeling the symptoms of a severe concussion, and remained there for a few days.

I was visited off and on by my friends while confined to the infirmary, but I mostly passed the time alone, mired in my own thoughts. I'd like to think that I had become more or less resolved to clean up and refocus my priorities. The thrashing I had received certainly felt like rock bottom, and Tina's words had never left the forefront of my conscience. Having said that, I'm not sure that I would have followed through if not for a final nudge from an unlikely source.

Ying and Monte paid me a visit on the morning of my third day in the infirmary. We struggled to carry on a superficial conversation. The two of them were never much for words, so we mostly sat in an awkward silence. Monte then spoke out of the blue.

"You need get better," he said.

"Yeah, I feel better. I should be back in the barracks tomorrow."

"No. You need get *better*," he repeated. "Here and here." He pointed to his head, then his chest. "War come soon. Shaker in charge—all of us." He waved his arm in grand sweeping gesture as he spoke the last phrase. Something about his innocence cut me deeply. It was as though my own son was entreating me.

I spent the next few weeks cleaning up my act and preparing myself and my company for the imminent arrival of the Tongs. I even gave Ying permission to cut off my testicles if she saw me partake in a drink or a wad of catnip. I'm not sure if she fully understood that I was exaggerating, which added more incentive to steer clear of the vices. I found that my son's future and the safety of my comrades was incentive enough, and I was never again tempted to dilute my problems with those toxins.

With Cap's permission, I ordered mandatory morning workouts for the entire company. We drilled for urban warfare and made preparations to defend our sector in the event of a full-scale invasion. Before long we were the model company of the city, and similar practices were ordered in the other sectors. As a result, Cap was assigned to oversee conditioning and drilling for the entire human army. He subsequently called upon me to implement the procedures across the city and I found myself outside of my own sector more often than not.

I had less free time now, and I used it wisely. I spent an hour a day outside the nursery window with Jasper. He was a bright child and eager to learn. My goal was to teach him one new word per day. To my delight, he had finally started calling me "dad." I made it a point to check in with Luther at least once per day to exchange the latest city gossip. I spent most of my remaining leisure time at the cathouse.

Perhaps that previous statement warrants further explanation. Prior to my sobriety, I found it easy and convenient to ignore the moral aberrations that were tolerated under the pretext of proliferating the species. Now I was determined to put my citywide authority and notoriety into action against them. In short, why not put the overblown Shaker myth to good use? Inspired by my actions in the old camp, I concocted a scheme and briefed my friends, who eagerly agreed to help. I was even able to convince old Luther to play along with the ruse and cultivate a few rumors.

On the next day, Nicholas and I planted ourselves in chairs on the porch of the large cathouse. Before long, a couple of veteran soldiers sauntered up the steps and made their way toward the door, greeting me cordially along the way.

"Hold on a minute guys," I said politely. "We need your names and the name of your company sergeant." On cue, Nicholas took out a sheet of paper and prepared to write.

"What the hell for?" asked one.

"It's kind of a long story," I told them. "Here's the thing…" I proceeded to explain how the General had recently concluded that too many "soft" babies were coming out of the nursery, and that selective breeding was needed in order to ensure a powerful fighting force in the future.

"So what?" he asked.

"So, do you want to put your name on the list?"

"What list?"

"The list of applicants," said Nicholas. "You'll need to pass a test in order to prove that you have what it takes to father the next generation of soldiers. If you pass, you'll be granted unlimited access to the cathouse." One of the two men appeared to see where I was heading with the yarn. The other was a little dim.

"What kind of test?" asked the slower man.

"It's simple," explained Nicholas. "All you have to do is fight. If you *win*, you're *in*. The General himself came up with the slogan."

"Yeah, you have to show us that you have the balls," I added with a smile.

"I have to fight him?" the dimwitted man asked, pointing to his buddy.

"Oh, no," I said. "We would never ask you to fight your friend. You'll be fighting me, or maybe Ying. Do you know Ying?"

"Not to the death," added Nicholas. "At least, not intentionally."

"Maybe I'll just come back when you're not here," proposed the dimwit.

"I guess you could," I said, "but the ladies will let us know. Then your name will go on the *other* list—the one that goes directly to the General."

"This is ridiculous."

"You are entitled to your opinion, sir," I said. "In fact, you should report your grievance to the sentroid stationed in front of the officers' compound. I'm sure that the General would love to hear from you."

"But you would probably take personal offense to that, right Shaker?" suggested Nicholas. I followed his lead.

"That's true… I probably wouldn't be too happy about it—especially since the General chose me, *personally*, to lead this initiative. I would probably feel obligated to bust your head open. You know that I meet with the General on a weekly basis, right?"

"Yeah, I heard that," said the buddy. *Did he really just say that?* So far, our scheme was working out better than we had imagined. *Were they stupid enough to believe that I actually met with the General?*

The two men ultimately declined to toss their hat into the ring. Remarkably, a few soldiers did accept the challenge and signed up over the next few days. I didn't mind climbing back into the ring for a good cause. It might have been a little suspicious to some that the ring was relocated to a secluded spot near the front gate; or that the fights were held late at night; or that the Serrones were never present for the matches. Thankfully, nobody ever questioned the validity of the new ordinance. More importantly, nobody earned the right to enter the cathouse. I handled most of the contests, though Ying dispatched her share of applicants with an impressive display of quickness and power. I was glad to have her on my side.

In order to protect our grand hoax, we even allowed the ladies of the cathouse to believe that the General's decree was a real thing. This meant that there would be little gratitude for us. That was okay—we didn't do it for the gratitude. I rarely ventured inside the cathouse. I found that the women were afraid that I might be there to cash in on my rights of conquest, and I didn't want to cause them any additional discomfort.

Our plan was more successful than we had imagined, and after a few weeks we feared that the Serrones might notice the conspicuous lack of activity in the cathouse. Nicholas came up with the idea of sending in a regular rotation of trusted men to hang out there. Some were designated as "overnighters" who slept alongside the women under a shared blanket. We had no idea how closely the cathouse activities were monitored, so we needed it to look real.

Of course, in order to implement Nicholas' plan, we had to brief the women on the entire operation. We swore them to absolute secrecy, to which they eagerly and gratefully complied. I daresay that Nicholas' plan spawned a few romances among the women and our male volunteers—something we hadn't considered but welcomed nonetheless. Over the course of a few more weeks, several soldiers caught on to our sham, yet we never faced a challenge. Luther described it to me this way:

"Only the complete idiots haven't figured it out, but it doesn't matter whether they know or not. What they *do* know is that one way or another, you or that Chinese stick of dynamite are gonna end up kicking their ass, and it's not worth it. The smarter guys know it's a scam, but they have too much respect for you to defy the order."

We realized that the General might eventually detect a pronounced decline in new pregnancies, but that was months away. As it happened, other events would soon render that concern a much lower priority.

The influx of soldiers took a dramatic increase around the time that I completed my first full season in the city. The battered warriors brought with them stories of harrowing defeats that were occurring closer and closer to us. Nobody was surprised to hear it. That the Toghans were taking so long to close in on us was bewildering and terrorizing. Nicholas continued to postulate his theory that King Tosso's slow advancement was all about limiting human casualties and should not be interpreted as a weakness. He made sense, *but where were they?*

I happened to be on the landing above the front gate one morning when a single flatbed truck limped up the road. After a brief inspection, the combot stationed outside the wall signaled for the gate to open, and the vehicle proceeded into the courtyard where it promptly died. I watched the small group of ruffled soldiers help each other climb down from the flatbed. They had clearly been through the ringer, and I wondered how many of their fallen comrades were left behind. A lone combot climbed out of the passenger side of the cab. He looked familiar—but it wasn't possible, *was it?* I took a closer look and there was no mistaking it. The combot was Bar.

My adrenaline spiked as I visually swept the group frantically. My heart sank. There were no women among them. Surely there must be others whom I would recognize. I looked them over again from above. Nothing. *Wait—one of them does look familiar.* He had changed quite a bit—older perhaps—but I recognized him. *If that combot is Bar, then it has to be him. It has to be Sparks.* I checked for a third time and determined that the remaining soldiers were strangers to me. I turned away to avoid detection. Next, I considered running down the steps and confronting them, then decided to wait until I could get Sparks away from Bar. Bar would only impede my efforts to obtain information. Sparks belonged to me, and I would face him when the time was right.

After the new arrivals departed, I conferred with the combot in charge at the gate. He told me that he had ordered the new soldiers to report to his own company, which happened to be stationed in a sector on the opposite side of the city from my own. I hurried back to my barracks, and with every step a new butterfly took flight within my stomach. Hopes and dreams I had suppressed long ago suddenly began to wake from a deep slumber. I tried to minimize them. I repeated to myself that it just wasn't possible. I came upon Dee and Cap standing together near the barracks and told them what I had seen as I tried to catch my breath.

"Can you debrief Bar?" I asked. "Can you find out what happened to the patrol?"

"If ordered, I will do so," replied Cap. In retrospect, I should have realized that they would neither comprehend nor share my excitement. I left them and bounded into the barracks where I found Susan and Pablo. Within minutes, all of my friends had been apprised of the startling development, and we assembled at a table in the dining hall to weigh our options.

"You need to speak with him as soon as possible," said Nicholas. "Time is of the essence, if… well, if she…"

"It's okay, Nick," I said to him calmly. "You can say it: 'If Leesheh is still alive'."

We decided that Susan and Nicholas should accompany me over to the other sector—for my own protection, as they put it. Each had the intent of preventing me from killing Sparks on sight, albeit with different motivations. Susan merely wanted to ensure that I had obtained all actionable intelligence before dispatching the miscreant. Nicholas was concerned about protecting me from my own erratic behavior and keeping me out of the Chief's doghouse. Ying wanted to come along as well but we concluded that she was a greater risk than I was to start a riot. As we headed out, Nicholas pulled me aside.

"Shakespeare, the fact that there are two survivors of the patrol and no sign of the others is not necessarily a positive development."

"I get it. I just want answers. Any information is better than not knowing, even if it isn't what I want to hear."

We found Luther snoozing in his homemade Adirondack chair just inside the PX door. Luther rarely spent nights in his assigned barracks, feeling that the inventory was far too valuable to leave unguarded. I refer not to the general items that were freely available to all soldiers—spectacles, utensils, paper, etc.—but rather to the private cache of exotic weapons, books, magazines, and other items that could fetch a lofty price on the city's black market. Luther enlisted a small gang of henchman to assist with the guardianship of his treasures; however, his general distrust of all human beings resulted in his seldom vacating the premises. On this night the old man was forced to make an exception. I called in a favor that required him to venture over to the sector in which we expected to find Sparks.

We decided that it would be too difficult to deal with Sparks in his own sector. Curious soldiers might poke their nose into our business, or worse, Bar might intervene. Instead, we waited in the shadows outside the infirmary while Luther fetched Sparks under the pretense that he was needed there for a physical examination. We stood against the back wall of the infirmary for about ten minutes before seeing two figures approach on the adjacent path. As they passed by, I grabbed the taller, slender figure by the arm and yanked him toward me into the darkness, while the older, slouchy man continued walking on the path as if he was alone in the world. I thrust the younger man into the back of the wall and held him there with my hand clasped firmly around his neck.

"Welcome home, buddy," I said through gritted teeth. "Remember me?" His expression morphed from startled to terrified when my maniacal smile came into his focus.

"Shake-a-spear… It's you… yes! I was planning to see you tomorrow," he proclaimed disingenuously.

"Well then, I'm glad I ran into you. Where is she?"

"She? I don't know who…" I loosened my grip momentarily then slammed him back against the wall, allowing just enough air in his windpipe for him to whisper. He put his hand on my wrist but lacked the strength to do anything more.

"Where is she?"

"I... I don't know," he gasped. I released my hold on his throat, grabbed him by the collar with both hands and pulled him in closer.

"Tell me what happened."

"Tongs attack at night—sneak up in the bush."

"When?"

"Long time ago. Few days after we leave camp."

"What happened to her? Was she killed?"

"I don't know… no—not yet. We get away. Me, Bar, Swag Man—and lady soldier too."

"She got away? Then what?"

"I don't know... we... Bar..." He seemed to be choosing his words carefully.

"Then what!?" I tried to shake the words out of him.

"I don't know... the lady... she hurt bad."

"How bad? What happened!?" He shook his head at me. His eyes appeared on the verge of jumping out of his head. I calmed down a little and spoke slowly, emphasizing every word. "Tell me exactly what happened."

"Bar... he..."

"Did Bar kill her?"

"No. Bar want to leave her in the bush."

"So, you left her there?"

"She hurt bad—real bad, Shake-a-spear. Bar left her."

"And you?"

"Bar made me leave too... I like the lady." I shook him again.

"Bar? You're gonna blame this on a robot?"

"It's true. Bar... and Tully. Tully's idea. Tully want to take the pretty lady from camp—away from you. Bar said okay. Chief said okay." I took a deep breath. I was ready to end the man's life then and there. If not for my sobriety, I surely would have.

"But Swag Man stay, Shake-a-spear," he added, as if Swag's gallantry might somehow bolster his own case. "Swag Man stay with her in the bush."

"She was still alive when you and Bar left them?"

"Yes—still alive, still alive," he said while nodding vigorously.

"What happened to Tully?"

"Don't know. I don't see him after that night."

"Did the Tongs kill him?"

"Don't know. Maybe. Probably. I don't see him after that night." He proceeded to tell us how he and Bar hid in the bush for several days while moving south under the cover of night. They eventually stumbled into a PRF squad and had remained with them ever since.

There was nothing more to learn from Sparks, and my thoughts quickly shifted to his fate. Over my left shoulder was the devilish Susan, nodding her approval to finish the asphyxiation. Over my right shoulder was the angelic Nicholas. He could see that I was about to carry out the death sentence.

"Hold on—just wait a second," Nicholas said gingerly. "Let's think this through."

"What's there to think about?" I said. "He's responsible and he has to pay." I returned my hand to Sparks' neck and started to squeeze. He began to convulse and choke.

"He's just a dumb kid—a follower," Nicholas implored. "Let him go." I don't know if it was Nicholas' words as much as the horror I saw in Sparks' eyes that caused me to loosen my grip. I wasn't ready to let him off the hook but I was willing to appease Nicholas for the time being. I released Sparks, who immediately collapsed to the ground and rolled onto his back. I placed my boot upon his neck.

"I'm not finished with you. You'd better watch your step," I told him, then walked away.

Not long afterward I lay in my bunk replaying my conversation with Sparks over and over. Hearing that Leesheh was alive but badly wounded provided no closure and left me feeling more anxious and tormented than before. It was as if an old wound that had nearly healed was violently ripped open once again. The fact that Swag was with her provided a faint glimmer of hope, but the old man wasn't a magician. The chances of a wounded soldier surviving in the bush were negligible. I concluded once again, as I had so many times since she left me, that it would be better to know for certain that she was dead than to be haunted by an infinitesimal chance that she was alive. What I had learned from Sparks gave me no reason to think that she was still alive.

The others left me alone in my thoughts and remained downstairs. My solitude was eventually interrupted by the sound of footsteps ascending the wooden steps. I turned my head to see Dee approaching.

"Shaker, did you meet with Sparks tonight?" he asked from the foot of my bunk.

"I did."

"He and Bar are the only survivors of the patrol?"

"Probably. They were attacked a few nights after leaving camp. A few got away."

"Leesheh?"

"She was wounded. Bar and Sparks left her in the woods. Swag stayed with her." I was curt. It was painful to recount Sparks' testimony aloud and I couldn't understand why the combot was interrogating me about it.

He stood and looked at me for a moment before responding. "Bar left them there?" Another pause. "Swag is a good soldier. I am sure that he did what he could to help her."

It then occurred to me that Swag was probably dead as well. I recalled in detail the manner in which he had volunteered for the mission—solely to protect her.

Dee broke the silence once again. "And the Serrone officer you call Ratso? Do you know his fate?"

"I didn't ask."

Dee stood for another second or two then headed for the stairs. I called out to him before he reached the landing.

"Hey, did you ask me because you're my friend, or because you have an obligation to report this up the chain?" Dee stopped and waited for a few seconds before turning toward me.

"I asked because you are a loyal soldier."

"What does that even mean?"

He started walking back to my bunk. "Shaker, is it your belief that I approved of Bar taking Leesheh on the patrol?"

"You did nothing to stop it."

"You overestimate the power and authority granted to combat androids. You fail to realize that we were created to be soldiers on the battlefield and nothing more. We are not much different than yourself."

"You're saying that you're like *us*?"

"Perhaps some of us more than others." He turned and walked down the stairs.

I slept very little that night. I couldn't help but contemplate how the fateful attack on the patrol might have gone down. I conjured up various scenarios and replayed them in my mind like video loops. I imagined the moment when Bar and Sparks abandoned Leesheh. I pictured her dying underneath stumpy bushes with eggplant-colored leaves—like the ones we used to lie beneath in the old camp. I could see Swag trying to save her, then being riddled with bullets as the Tongs closed in on him. I couldn't have been more agitated if their ghosts had stood before me in the barracks. I must have dozed off at some point early in the morning hours, for I was roused just after dawn.

"Shaker, wake up." Still half asleep, I stretched my mouth wide open in the hopes that my eyes would follow suit. Luther nudged me again. "Get up."

"What's going on?" I asked. Luther looked around and noticed that my friends were watching us. I assured him that it was safe to speak in their presence. He then used his eyes and a quick tilt of his head to direct my attention to Dee, who was sitting in a chair near the stairs.

"Outside," Luther said. I wasn't concerned about Dee, but it was just easier to follow Luther outside to the grassy area near our barracks.

"What is it?"

"The boy you met with last night."

"Yeah?"

"He went over the wall."

"He's missing? How do you know he went over the wall?"

"No, you don't understand. He went over the wall. They found him lying there with a broken neck."

"He's dead?"

Luther responded with a certain shrug—the non-verbal equivalent of saying "duh." We headed over to Sparks' sector where I met with the soldiers who had discovered his body. I asked them if they thought it was suicide.

"Nah, he probably misjudged the height in the darkness, or maybe he slipped before he was ready to jump," one of them told me.

"Maybe the fall itself wasn't suicide," added the other. "But goin' out there all alone sure would have been. He wouldn't have lasted a day."

"What do you mean? Why wouldn't he have lasted a day?"

"Because they're here."

31

I saw no evidence of the soldier's ominous declaration at that time, yet no more than an hour passed before the city was placed on alert and we were ordered into our defensive positions. I was outside of the green nursery building visiting Jasper and Saba through the window when the alarm sounded. I hurried anxiously back to the wall within my sector and climbed up to the landing, where I found my comrades in various states of consternation. At the edge of the tree line far beyond I descried the busy movements of the Toghan soldiers, like a large colony of ants. Only the leading edge of the force protruded from the trees, but it was sizeable enough, and ten times that amount was surely lurking in the dense forest behind. From a distance they appeared preoccupied and oblivious to our presence, though we knew that we were the sole reason for theirs.

Their apathy only made them more intimidating. They were well out of range of our small arms. We could have showered them with artillery or fired our wall-mounted plasma cannons randomly into the forest, but this would have only played into their hands. They evidently knew that our stock of plasma shells was limited. And so, we faced off against each other once again, only this time the stakes were considerably higher and there was no river between us.

Following a day in which our entire force stood at the wall in anticipation of an invasion, we receded to a high-alert status. We carefully watched the Tongs for several days. The situation outside of the walls changed little as life inside became much more rigid and solemn. Soldiers were generally confined to their sectors so that they could assume their defensive positions on a moment's notice if word of an attack came down from the rotating watch. I retained my freedom to move about the entire city. This was due to my role as the HiC for soldier readiness, and not a result of the agreement on which the Chief had reneged. I still lacked permission to enter the nursery, so I continued to meet with Jasper through the window.

Soldiers spent their time moving between the barracks, latrines, and dining halls in their sector. In my company we passed the hours by playing cards, spinning yarns, and discussing the prospects and aspects of a potential Toghan attack. I was once again called upon to ease the tension with the levity of my narratives from classic literature; however, I found it increasingly difficult to recall the details of those stories and often resorted to fabricating plot elements. The years that had transpired since leaving my home world now seemed like decades. My preoccupation with the hardships on Serrone had robbed the brain of cycles that might have otherwise been allocated to retaining memories of my life before.

At first, there was an abundance of theories and opinions of how the Toghans might proceed against us.

"They could never get inside the city without taking a lot of casualties," claimed a young soldier in the barracks one evening.

"You don't think the lizzies could get in here? They've got plenty to spare," said another.

"They *can* get in, but they won't," offered Nicholas. "Too many lives—human lives—would be lost. No, they're gonna be out there for a while. We're under siege."

Nicholas proceeded to expound on his recurring theory once again, and it was difficult to poke many holes into it. Yet if this was a siege, then the vice was being tightened very slowly. Water still flowed freely from underground springs and wells into the vast storage tanks. It would be difficult for the Tongs to disrupt the supply of fresh water. The influx of food from the roadways was halted, but cargo aircraft still flew in and out of the city on a regular basis. For the time being we were allocated full rations. Nicholas had an explanation for this as well.

"The king wants to weaken us before we realize we've been weakened. He doesn't want an epic battle. He prefers a surrender, but if we don't, we'll be too weak—mentally and physically—to put up much of a resistance to his overwhelming numbers. We're the frog in a saucepan, and we'll start to feel the heat soon enough." Everybody waited for Nicholas to second guess himself. For once he seemed resolved.

"Maybe General Abasha has a trick up his sleeve," suggested Scoop.

"Yeah, maybe," I responded. "I guess we'll find out soon enough."

The "heat" to which Nicholas referred slowly started to manifest itself over the next several weeks. Fewer flights were seen in the skies above the city and fewer aircraft were seen parked on the grounds. The aircraft were disappearing somewhere, either breaking down or shot down—it just wasn't happening near the city. We weren't privy to the source of our food supply. It obviously didn't come from the fields surrounding the city. Perhaps it was being shipped in from a neighboring region whose ruler was allied with the General. If so, then it would only be a matter of time before King Tosso's expanding influence and the General's dwindling prestige would dissolve any such alliance. Sure enough, we noticed one day that our rations were slightly reduced, though no official notice was given. Two weeks later they were lessened again. The water in the saucepan was starting to simmer.

I cannot say if the Tongs had spies inside the wall, but they certainly had eyes above it. Ying was the first person to notice the sporadic movements high up in the deserted skyscrapers to our south. I had always likened the old towers to a mob of giant gawkers waiting to see what happened between the PRF and the Toghans. Now we were literally being watched from them. It became a sort of game to spot one of their soldiers lurking around fifty stories above us. I don't know why they attempted to hide from us. It wasn't as if we could do anything to stop them.

I should note that during the siege I happened to find myself in Bar's sector on occasion. Following my intimidatory encounter with Sparks and his subsequent demise, I had decided to avoid any interaction with Bar. Although the combot was still somewhat junior in rank, he did have access to the android network—i.e., the sentroids. I couldn't trust him, and the less he knew about me, the better it was. In those instances where our paths crossed, I simply acted as if I didn't know him. Whether or not he bought into my deceptive performance I cannot say. In either case, he seemed content to leave me alone.

As much as I enjoyed the company of my friends in the barracks, the monotony was sometimes too much to bear. On occasion I took advantage of my unrestrained access to the city and wandered along the deserted streets and paths during the night. Sometimes I ended up in the PX and passed the time listening to the old man's stories of his exploits on Serrone. If only half of Luther's tales were true it still amounted to a fascinating life. One thing was certain—he had been among the very first human slaves brought to the planet. I learned a lot from him once I determined how to filter out his hogwash.

On a particular evening well into the siege, we sat sharing a cigar. Luther proclaimed that it contained actual tobacco, and that it originated under a shroud of mystery from the far reaches of the planet. He told me that it had traveled there at the hands of various slaves, soldiers, Serrone generals, and monarchs until he alone was able to procure it using his vast influence and connections. He failed to recall, nor did I remind him, that I was present not two weeks earlier, when he rolled the stogie himself using the dried, bitter leaves of an indigenous plant which grew in large quantities within the city. It was subsequent to this fabrication that the following conversation ensued. Having been predisposed to his hyperbole pertaining to the miraculous cigar, I was more skeptical than usual, and my bullshit radar was on full-alert.

"What do you know about Plymouth, Shaker?" he asked.

"As in Plymouth Rock?"

"No. The human settlement here on Serrone." He took a puff on the cigar and passed it back to me.

"Is that what they're calling it now? I know nothing about it, because there's nothing *to* know."

"Don't be so sure, my friend. I know some things." He extended his hand toward me and beckoned with his fingers. I handed the cigar back to him.

"I suppose you're going to tell me that you know where this magic kingdom is—or perhaps that you've been there?"

"I don't know exactly where it is, but I know someone who does. Someone here in the city." He took a final drag on the cigar and smooshed it into the table. I was at the very least, entertained, and decided to further indulge him.

"Oh, really? And you're telling me this… why?"

"We're going there. We could use a man with your talents."

"Okay, I'm interested. I'd like to meet your friend." I was interested only in seeing how far he would take this. I was also enjoying my role—it was very cloak and dagger.

"Meet me back here tomorrow night," the old man instructed.

"Fine, but I'm a package deal. My friends come too."

"Ah, your Chinese sidekick? Her skills will prove very useful indeed. The other woman is welcome too. She's a tough cookie."

"And Nicholas."

"No way. We're too many already."

"*And* Nicholas."

"I suppose his intellect might come in handy," conceded Luther.

"Then I'll see you tomorrow."

At breakfast I told my friends about my clandestine interchange with Luther, and added that if they were interested, I'd figure out a way to sneak them over to the PX with me later that night. They readily consented. Susan was looking for a laugh, and Nicholas seemed genuinely intrigued. As for Ying, who knows? I rarely knew what she was thinking.

"There could be something to this," said Nicholas.

"Yeah, we're off to see the wizard," added Susan. "I get to be Dorothy."

I decided that the best tactic was to be blunt. After dinner I told Dee that I was taking the others over to the PX to look for weapon upgrades.

"Be careful not to be detected," he advised. "Those other soldiers are not permitted outside of the sector."

As long as we avoided the sentroids we would be fine, and the worst thing a sentroid would do is order the others back to the barracks. Plus, sentroids were rarely seen in the middle of the city. Anybody else (i.e., combots) would assume that I had the proper authority. We made it to the PX without a hitch. I wasn't surprised to see that Luther was alone.

"What happened? Your friend couldn't make it?" I asked sneeringly. The old man looked us over, looked the room over, looked out the window, then looked us over again.

"It's clear," he said over his shoulder. The door to the back room opened.

"It's you?" I asked in disbelief. An air of credibility swept over the room as she entered.

"Hello Shaker," said my British friend, Evelyn.

"You're behind all this?"

"There are several of us involved. I trust that we can count on your silence, whether or not you agree to help us." Her serious tone and posh accent made me feel like I was in a James Bond film.

"Of course."

"And your friends?"

"Absolutely," I vouched. They nodded in concurrence.

Evelyn told us everything she knew about Plymouth. I wasn't yet convinced of its existence but I had no doubt that she was. She had spent most of her years in the PRF assigned to a camp located near the southeastern border of the region. It was much farther from Abasha city than my original camp had been, and in the opposite direction. In that part of the planet, rumors of a free human settlement were common. It was said that a sympathetic Serrone ruler had recently set aside land under his protection. The land was supposedly more than two thousand miles away by land—shorter by sea—and that a sizable mountain range lay in between.

Evelyn told us a captivating story about a small group of soldiers, her comrades, that escaped from the camp one day, long ago, to find the free territory. She was a member of the search parties that were ordered to locate the AWOL soldiers. They found nothing. A year passed, during which the rumors persisted, fueled by the fact that the missing soldiers had never been found.

One night, one of the escaped soldiers snuck back into the camp and into the hut in which Evelyn lived. He quietly roused a girl whom he loved, a young native soldier who occupied the bunk next to Evelyn. There in the darkness, he told the girl that he had been to Plymouth and had returned now to bring her back with him. He described the route to get there. He described the land, the people, and the free society they were building. He declared to the girl that he wanted none of that without her by his side. She was frightened and would not commit to leave with him. The brave soldier spent two days hiding in camp while trying to convince her to escape with him. Unfortunately, his luck ran out and he was discovered hiding under the mess hall by a combot. He was branded a rebel spy, tortured, and killed as an example to the others.

"Why didn't you try to go there?" asked Susan.

"I wanted to," replied Evelyn. "Security became much tighter in camp. I couldn't find anybody willing to risk it, and I lacked the confidence and ability to make it on my own."

"And now that camp is long gone," I said.

"It is. You met the other survivors with me at the river."

"What about the girl?" asked Nicholas.

"Sadly, she's no longer with us. But there's more. The area southeast of here is loosely controlled by the Tongs now. I've heard of mules that operate out of an abandoned village near my old camp."

"Mules?" asked Susan.

"People that might be willing to take us to Plymouth. It's worth a chance. We just need to get out of the city and into the forest."

"And therein lies the problem," said Luther, who had remained unusually quiet up to this point.

"Even if we got over the wall, we'd never get past the multitudes of Toghan soldiers that surround the city," I said.

"The wall isn't a problem," replied Evelyn, "but yes, the Tongs are a major impediment at the moment."

"What do you mean 'the wall isn't a problem'?" I asked.

"Perhaps this is a good stopping point for now," Evelyn told us. "Shaker, if you could come back to my sector with me, I'd like to show you something."

I agreed to meet her outside of her barracks after escorting the others back to our own. After they were safely inside, I made my way over to sector eight, which was our neighboring sector to the south. Evelyn greeted me on the path well before I reached her barracks.

"Are you alone?" she asked.

"Yeah. What is it?"

"Not here."

She led me over to a small storage shack. The nearby lamppost was inoperative, which was likely not a coincidence. A soldier leaned against the wall of the shack with his arms folded over his chest. Evelyn gave him a slight nod, which he likewise returned, then softly rapped on the door twice. I could hear a noise from inside that I likened to the sound of a wooden latch being lifted from it. Evelyn and I stepped into a small room where she lit a flashlight after quietly closing the door behind us. Waiting for us inside were two soldiers whom I recognized but did not know. Evelyn introduced them to me as Rajev and Petey. Rajev was a stiff, thirty-something man from Mumbai. Petey was only slightly more relaxed and appeared far too old to retain such a youthful moniker. He hailed from the hills of Northern California. Evelyn interrupted our brief introductions by shining her flashlight in Rajev's face.

"Show him," she said. Rajev looked at her dubiously, to which she responded, "Go on now."

The two men pulled up several loose floorboards and laid them aside. Evelyn shined the light into the newly-revealed space where I saw a large hole, about four feet in diameter, dug into the ground.

"A tunnel?" I asked.

"Yes," replied Evelyn.

"Where does it go?"

"Under the wall and into the old city about a hundred meters away," said Petey. "We're pretty sure it opens up into an alleyway."

"Pretty sure?"

"We don't want to pop out until just before we're ready to go," explained Evelyn.

"What's the plan?"

"We're not certain," she said, "It's obvious that we cannot go anywhere as long as those lizzies are out there."

"That's definitely a problem."

"Yes, Mr. Shaker," said Rajev, "but you see, at some point the Tongs will have to come into the city and–"

"And vacate their positions near the forest," added Petey. He seemed overly eager to be the person revealing the information, lest someone else might receive credit for formulating the plan.

"So, they come in with the tide, and we go out with it," I said. "It sounds tricky."

"We were hoping you could help us with that," said Evelyn.

I professed my doubts, though truth be told, I was all in. Seeing the tunnel cinched the deal. I wasn't buying into the notions of a sympathetic Serrone ruler, the so-called mules, or a promised land. I just liked the idea of getting out of Dodge. Now that I was seriously considering this, there were other conditions that needed to be discussed.

"I can help," I proffered, "but my son comes with me."

"Shaker," started Petey, "I wish we could bring everybody in camp with us, but there's a limit to–"

I cut him off and appealed to my friend. "Evelyn, he's my *son*."

"We'll work it out somehow," she said.

"There's more. I owe my son's life to two women in the nursery. They aren't fighters but they're young and capable. They won't hold us back."

"Shaker–"

"I'm not finished. Susan and Ying—you agree that they're indispensable?"

"Of course."

"Well they both come with baggage. Susan has a man, Pablo. He won't set the world on fire but he can handle a weapon. He's managed to survive this long—and he's a good driver."

"I'm familiar with the man."

"And then there's Ying. I can't imagine she would leave without Monte."

"Who's Monte?"

I couldn't help but chuckle. The subject of Monte always brought a smile to my face, even in the context of this weighty discussion.

"Shaker, who's Monte?" she repeated.

"I think you know him. He's the Indian—Native South American. Kind of a little guy."

"Can he fight?"

"He can. Two years ago, I would have said no. Now I'd trust him with my life." I thought about what I had just said. I really had come to feel that confident in Monte.

Evelyn sighed and said, "My god, Shaker. You've just doubled the number of people on our team."

"I'll get the job done," I said assuredly.

"And you will be responsible for bringing all of them here when the time comes," she countered. "We won't be available to help you with that."

I felt a little as though I was being scolded. "Of course."

We discussed a few options and parameters before I retired to my own barracks. The gears in my head were grinding away. A new flame had sparked in my gut. I felt rejuvenated. It was a crazy, farfetched scheme that might get us all killed. And I was one hundred percent onboard.

I brought the others up to speed the next morning at the breakfast table and advised them—ordered them—not to tell Pablo or Monte yet. I could see that Nicholas' imagination was already tugging him in multiple directions. It was my job to keep him focused. He touched on a critical point before we left the dining hall.

"If the General surrenders before the Tongs attack, we'll have no chance of escaping." We agreed that this could soon become our biggest problem.

"However," Nicholas continued, "our job now is to protect General Abasha. The king wants Abasha dead but he needs *us* alive. Don't you see how that puts us in a unique position?"

Two more weeks passed, during which the camp ran dry of cigarettes, moonshine, and catnip. The infirmary quickly filled to capacity with soldiers complaining of withdrawal symptoms. There wasn't much that the phony doctors there could do to alleviate them, and many others toughed it out on their own. Only a small percentage of the nearly fifteen hundred soldiers in the city would have been characterized as full-on addicts, yet that still amounted to a lot of sick people. Some speculated that this was the impediment that the Tongs had been waiting for, but another week passed with no break in the siege. It was nice to have complete sobriety in the camp; however, any advantage it afforded us would soon be offset by a nutritional decline. The end of the warm season was marked by another reduction in rations.

I became increasingly concerned about Jasper and the other children in the city. I worried that the General might deem them an unaffordable drain on the food supply. I began to sneak extra rations into the nursery with the help of Tina and Saba. My apprehension heightened when Nicholas brought related news. He informed me that the little android had hinted about the orcos being euthanized soon. The Serrone officers apparently felt that the beasts were consuming too much of the precious food supply.

The Serrone officers themselves had been scarce since the Toghans arrived. There was talk that some had evacuated, but I knew they were still in the city. The officers' compound remained under a constant, heavy guard. Cap and combots from other sectors reported to the sentroids on a daily basis. The Serrone cowards might have been hiding, but they were still in the compound. Where could they go? This was the General's home. It was too late for him to secure sanctuary in some other region. He had lost too much political capital. The Serrones in the PRF were running out of time, and so were we.

32

"Here they are," said Luther, pointing to a shelf containing several large wooden boxes.

"How many of them are there?" asked Nicholas.

"Maybe two thousand or so."

"That's more than enough," I said. "Let's get these onto the truck."

The old man watched Nicholas, Pablo, and me carry the boxes out of the supply building and load them into a flatbed that I had secured for "official business." Nobody was around to notice, not that anybody would have raised an eyebrow. The Serrones remained sequestered in their cozy compound, and had drawn most of the sentroids into a tight formation around it. Implementation of the defensive strategy for the greater part of the city was left in the hands of the combots, who had no choice but to rely on the support of veteran human soldiers. Of the latter group, I was fortunate to be considered in the highest regard. I found that my reign and latitude increased each day that the siege progressed. Furthermore, the sentroid who had steadfastly regulated traffic in and out of the nursery had recently been reassigned elsewhere. I was now able to hold Jasper in my arms, though my sessions with him were often shorter than I would have liked.

Pablo climbed into the driver's seat while Nicholas and I entered the cab from the other side. We needed Pablo to operate the flatbed and had recently brought him up to speed on the plan. The plan, which we sometimes referred to as "Operation Tide," was coming into focus, and not a minute too soon. The city and its soldiers were starting to show signs of fatigue brought on by the siege. Some of the smaller, weaker soldiers were becoming noticeably sluggish.

We stopped at each of the sectors, starting from sector one in the southwest and circling clockwise to Evelyn's sector in the southeast. At each location I relayed the following order from Cap to the combot in charge:

"Each soldier is to store an armband on his or her person at all times. The armbands are absolutely not to be worn until combat begins. Take only as many as you need—no extras. Any soldier who loses his armband may see me for a replacement."

The first part of the order was, indeed, from Cap. I had suggested to him that it would be a good idea to colorfully distinguish ourselves from the humans serving in the Toghan army, should they invade the city. The remaining stipulations were of my own device. I didn't want any surplus armbands circulating around the camp.

The first two deliveries went off without a hitch. We entered the third sector where I asked a passing soldier to fetch the combot sergeant in charge. I knew that Bar was a member of this company and that he wasn't the ranking combot. Bar and I had successfully ignored each other since his arrival, and I didn't expect to see him now. When the sergeant approached, Bar was at his side. I relayed "Cap's" order as Pablo unloaded a box of the red armbands and placed it at their feet. The combot sergeant acknowledged the order and carried the box away. Bar remained behind and eyed me for a moment. My paranoia got the best of me. I imagined that he had figured out the entire plan in that very moment.

"Tell me again, soldier, what is the purpose of these armbands?" he asked.

"Exactly what I just said to your commander. They are to be worn in the event of an attack." I did my best to disguise my nervousness.

He questioned the logic of the order. "Is the General concerned that we might confuse the Toghan lizzie soldiers with our own humans?"

"I don't know what the General is concerned with," I replied. "I have never met him. My orders come from Cap." Bar stood quietly. I relaxed a little, knowing that he was not within range to communicate with Cap at that time. Even if Bar could speak to him, Cap was sure to confirm the order.

"Is there anything else?" I asked. He turned to Nicholas.

"You are assigned to the orcos?"

"I am," answered Nicholas.

"How are they faring? Are they strong?"

"They've lost some weight, but they're strong."

"I suppose they are very hungry," Bar continued. "Too difficult to control. They would be useless in battle. Do you agree?"

Nicholas answered cautiously. "It's not my place to decide that."

"We need to go," I interjected. Bar stood motionless as we boarded the truck and drove off.

"What was that all about?" asked Pablo.

"I wish I knew. Hopefully nothing," I replied.

After distributing armbands to the remaining sectors, we drove to the PX, where the old man stashed the remaining supply in a hidden compartment. We returned to our barracks in plenty of time for lights-out.

On the following afternoon, Nicholas and I headed over to sector eight and met Evelyn outside the small shack that covered the tunnel. Nicholas carried a large empty box which served no purpose beyond establishing a reason for us to be entering a storage shack. We figured that meeting in plain sight would attract less suspicion from combots, or in the unlikely event that a wandering sentroid might happen by. Waiting for us inside were Petey and Rajev. I briefed them on my progress since our last meeting, two days prior.

"And how are things going on your end, Nicholas?" asked Evelyn.

"Pretty good. I think we're ready," he answered.

"Not *too* ready, I hope?"

"Ha. Yeah, let's hope not."

"Let's get to the good stuff," I said. "Did you get through?"

"We did—the night before last," Rajev announced.

"How did it go?"

"Well, I'm still here," he cracked. "We had to shift a few meters, but we were able to pop through in a dark alleyway."

"That'll work," I said.

Rajev described the area of the old city that surrounded the tunnel exit. He had spent hours hiding in the alley on the first night and saw no sign of any Toghan or civilian activity.

"What time should I be here tonight?" I asked.

"Midnight will be good," Rajev replied.

I returned to the shack that night at the agreed upon time, where Rajev and Petey were again waiting. I latched the door behind me and helped them remove the floorboards. Rajev climbed down a rickety wooden ladder into the tunnel where he stood looking up at us from about ten feet below. I started to follow him, when Petey grabbed my arm then pointed to my flashlight.

"Hold on. Is your battery fresh?" he asked. I looked at him curiously and he busted out laughing.

"I'm just kidding, man. Good luck." The Serrone flashlights did not require batteries. Their source of power was as much a mystery to us as the hovering chariots. I descended to the small landing area where Rajev waited. Petey began to replace the floorboards above, causing a modicum of loose dirt to fall down upon my head. Rajev had conveniently moved out of the way, this not being his first experience in the tunnel. He grinned as I brushed the dirt out of my hair.

I had envisioned crawling on all fours through a narrow, claustrophobic hell. I was pleased to find that the tunnel was tall enough that I could traverse it on two feet, though I was forced to slump forward to a significant degree. I still experienced an element of claustrophobia as we slowly made our away along the muddy floor. I could hear the sound of water trickling in from multiple sources along the walls.

"How safe is it down here?" I asked.

"Well, I wouldn't want to live down here," replied the tunnel rat. I guess a silly question deserved a silly answer.

I was happy to discover that we had reached the other end sooner than I had expected. Rajev threw me the shush sign then extinguished his flashlight. He climbed the ladder and carefully pushed aside a piece of wood that covered the hatch. I replicated his moves and soon found myself crouching down beside him in a dark alley. We were somewhere in the northern district of the old city, Konkoro. We found cover in the ground floor of an abandoned building nearby where we could take safe refuge. There was a fair amount of ambient light emanating from various celestial bodies. This provided some visibility of our surroundings and it also made us susceptible to detection.

"The eastern edge of the city is in that direction," Rajev pointed out. "From there, it is probably seven or eight hundred meters to the tree line." We decided to proceed in that direction for a short distance to establish a potential escape route. It would have been nice to plot the entire route through the old city, but we couldn't risk being sighted. That night was the last opportunity to be out there before the actual escape. The rustling sounds of cappies and/or other scavengers froze us in our tracks on several occasions. We saw nothing of them, and my nerves were starting to get the best of me. I began to think that the risk of being discovered far outweighed the reward of finding a direct escape route. We knew that the Tongs utilized the skyscrapers in this area to watch Abasha City from high above. Their spies might be close by. I tapped Rajev on the shoulder.

"Let's get back," I whispered.

We scampered back through the tunnel and knocked softly on the loose floorboards that blocked our return. Petey soon lifted them away and we climbed back into the relative safety of the storage shack. Evelyn was there to greet us. We reported what we had seen in Konkoro, which wasn't much. Everyone agreed that the tunnel was ready.

The delicate Operation Tide was as ready as it could be, and we couldn't hold out much longer. The timing depended somewhat on the Toghans and the General, and it could be any day now. It was time to bring Tina and Saba into the fold.

"You're here early," noted Tina when I showed up inside the lime-green building on the following morning.

"Is there someplace we can talk in private?" I asked quietly.

"Sure, out here." She gestured toward the enclosed grassy lot that separated the two nursery buildings. I saw Saba fetching Jasper at the other end of the long room and walked over to her.

"Say hi to daddy, Jasper," she said as I approached.

"Hi daddy!"

"Hello Jasper. Saba, let's leave him here for now. Can you come with me?"

Jasper was a little confused and not too happy with such a brief visit. I assured him that I would be right back. Once outside, I told the women as much as they needed to know about Plymouth and Operation Tide.

"Of course, it's entirely up to you, but I assure you, things are gonna get pretty messy around here by the time we leave," I warned. "Either way, Jasper is coming with me."

Saba looked at Tina, as though granting her the proxy to decide for both of them. Tina looked over in the direction of one building, then the other. She next exchanged a glance with Saba, who responded with a slight nod.

"You know I'd follow you anywhere, Shaker. It's just that… all these kids. What happens to them?"

I knew it was coming. I knew how Tina cared for every child as if it was her own. Their well-being and education gave her a reason to live. I had wrestled with the same thoughts—and not just about the children. What would become of my comrades left behind to deal with the Tongs?

I did my best to convince Tina and Saba that the children would likely end up as slaves in the Kingdom of Toghan, and that their lives in that capacity could not possibly be worse than being a slave in the ill-fated PRF. I told them how Nicholas was convinced that King Tosso wanted to bolster his army with human soldiers, and that it was in his best interest to minimize human deaths. Then I foolishly promised to do whatever I could to bring more children with us.

"Thank you, Shaker. I trust you with my life. Just tell us what to do," Tina said. She hugged me then went inside to fetch Jasper.

I met up with my friends near the old anti-aircraft battery in our compound. They were glad to hear that Tina and Saba were finally in the loop and onboard. I didn't mention my promise to Tina regarding the children. That left Monte as the sole unenlightened conspirator, and we agreed that it would be best not bring him in until the operation was underway. I turned my attention to the anti-aircraft weaponry.

"Have you figured it out?" I asked Pablo.

"I think so," he said. "We can lower the angle and reduce the charge… here." He pointed to various controls on the apparatus. It all looked alien to me. "We probably won't hit anything but it should get the job done," he added.

"These guns seem to have been designed to target low-flying drones," said Nicholas. "We can make it work."

I slept soundly that night for the first time in weeks.

33

Another day passed. Then another. Then we caught a break. Some speculated that a deadline had come and gone with no response from the General. We had no way of knowing if any diplomacy had been exchanged between the two warlords. Others opined that the king must be a devotee to Serrone astrology, for it was a rare day on which Wiyanga and its parent star aligned together in the morning sky. The most agreed upon explanation was that the king had finally decided that we had reached our breaking point. For whatever reason, he brought his army out from the sanctuary of the forest and tightened his circle around our city.

The alarm sounded a few hours after breakfast. I was with Cap near the camp's front gate at the time. We ascended to the landing above the gate and watched the force advance toward us. They moved slowly and did not appear to be on the verge of attacking. Sure enough, they halted a few hundred yards short of the wall. In the front of their line stood the lizzies, three to four bodies thick. Behind them was a thin band of humans and androids. Just beyond that, we could see soldiers assembling field artillery weapons—the ones we liked to call giant mortars. Lavish vehicles trailed behind the soldiers and fanned out across the entire line, with a higher concentration near the front gate. Most were fully-enclosed, but we didn't need to see inside to know that they contained the Serrone leaders of the Toghan army. The king himself was likely in one of them.

Cap remained at the front gate while I hopped on a scooter and rushed over to sector eight to view the battlefield from that perspective. The Toghan line thinned to the south, yet it extended in that direction as far as I could see. I had no doubt that all exits from the old city were covered. I returned to my own sector to assist Dee with the defensive preparations, though there wasn't much to do other than wait. The rifles were already clean. The ammunition was already stockpiled in strategic locations. My comrades were battle-ready and manning their positions. The two armies stood staring each other down, like two prizefighters receiving their final instructions from the referee. Neither side blinked, and the rest of the day passed stressfully and uneventfully.

Before darkness fell, I met separately with each of my co-conspirators in the sector. I dispatched Nicholas over to the orcos pen after telling Dee that the little android had requested his presence to help monitor the situation there. I climbed to the landing and met with Susan, who was manning one of the large plasma cannons on the wall. I checked in with Ying, who was positioned on the landing at the other end of the sector. Monte was by her side. I descended the wall and met with Pablo near the anti-aircraft guns. I instructed all of them to standby for the signal. Maybe it would happen later in the night and maybe it wouldn't. I scooted back over to sector eight and found Evelyn at her post on the wall, where we quietly conferred.

"It's probably too late for a surrender today," I said.

"Yes, but for all we know, a surrender might have already been arranged for the morning," she posited.

"So, we go tonight?"

"What choice do we have, Shaker? A surrender would finish us—absolutely finish us."

"Are your guys ready?"

"Of course."

"Then wait for the signal," I instructed. "You should hear it when that star reaches… right about—there."

I stood behind Evelyn's shoulder and directed her line of sight to a bright star that was rising in the dusk. It had become common practice to use the relative positions of planets, moons, and stars when relating the passage of time. We would have preferred clocks, but there was only one in the entire city—the broken Casio LED wristwatch which Luther wore proudly. The estimate I provided to Evelyn represented about three hours, which would put us in the dead of night. And a dark night it would be. Wiyanga and the parent star had both disappeared until morning.

I stopped by the PX and grabbed Luther on my way to the nursery. He would be needed there when the signal was given. Luther had armed himself with a beautiful handheld plasma weapon that looked like an antique.

"Does that thing even work?" I asked, as he climbed on the scooter behind me.

"Yup."

He also carried a heavy knapsack, of which I relieved him. I looked inside to verify that it was full of hand grenades, then strapped it over my shoulder. We pulled in front of the lime-green building only to find that the sentroid had returned to his post. Tina was sitting on the steps behind him. As soon as we pulled up, she approached us anxiously. We maintained a safe distance from the android as we spoke.

"How long has he been there?" I asked.

"Since the alarm sounded." She seemed frantic. I calmed her down and assured her that nothing had changed, except that Luther would have to return to the PX until the operation commenced. I glanced over to the sentroid.

"This guy's not gonna know what hit him. He might even be gone by the time this goes down," I said. "Now, have you picked them out?"

"Yes. It was tough, Shaker—really hard."

"I know." I placed my hands on her shoulders to keep her focused. "How many?"

"Eight," she said. I unleashed a considerable sigh in reaction to the number.

"I thought we agreed on six."

"I know, but they can do it, Shaker. I promise."

"Okay. Eight it is." I owed her that much.

I had decided not to tell Evelyn in advance that my entourage would be showing up at the tunnel with six—now eight—children in addition to Jasper. I considered it a price for my services, and there was nothing she could do about it. I had hoped to review Tina's eight selections at this time, ensuring that they were old enough to follow directions and nimble enough to move on their own two feet. The unanticipated return of the sentroid had rendered that impossible.

"Tell Jasper that I'll see him soon." I looked over toward the sentroid and an idea occurred to me. "Tina—hold on a second." She came back over to us. "Quietly move everybody to the other building and have them put their armbands on now. And don't let that chucklehead sentroid see you do it." I dropped the old man off at the PX and returned to my sector. I found Dee near the base of the wall and probed him for information.

"What are you hearing?"

"I have been told that King Tosso has demanded the General's unconditional surrender," said Dee.

"What's the General planning to do?"

"I do not know. He is meeting with his advisors presently."

"In the compound, right?"

"Correct."

"I don't see the king allowing him to live."

"It is unlikely."

"I know what happens to me if we surrender. What happens to you?" I asked.

"I do not understand."

"Have you thought about what would happen to you if the General surrendered?"

"No."

"But can you? Are you able to consider your options?"

"Are there options?" asked Dee.

"Maybe." The old combot looked at me and said nothing. I walked over to the wall, climbed up to the landing, and waited quietly with Susan. It was one of the darkest nights possible on the planet. We could discern very little of our enemies beyond the occasional flicker of light. I finally patted her on the shoulder.

"It's time." She nodded, then I walked over to Ying and Monte.

"Go ahead and tell him," I whispered to Ying, then made my way back down and crossed the open ground toward the barracks. I stopped at Pablo's position near the old anti-aircraft guns.

"I guess the Tongs aren't coming tonight, eh Shaker?" he said as I approached.

"I don't know about that. Let's give them a reason to pay us a visit." I glanced furtively toward Dee, then walked casually into the barracks where I waited for a few minutes before slipping out a back door and hopping onto a scooter I had stashed there. I rode over to the PX and found Luther waiting inside.

"There's a slight change in plans," I told him. The cue to initiate

Operation Tide was supposed to be the detonation of a few grenades, by me, near the PX. The idea was that the explosions would be heard across the entire city without anyone knowing exactly where they had occurred. My revised plan took us over to the cathouse, where I parked the scooter then went inside and quietly told the women to put on their armbands and stay put. Luther and I then moved stealthily over to the side wall of the nursery, where we affixed red armbands just below our shoulders. Luther lifted up the bag of grenades.

"Two should do it. Take the rest to the tunnel," I instructed.

He handed me two grenades. I inspected them to ensure that there were no visible defects. I would need to hold them for a few seconds after pulling the pins, and a short fuse would be deadly. In the darkness these two grenades looked as good as any, so I told Luther to get ready. He turned his back to the wall, crouched down and covered his ears. I poked my head around the corner. The sentroid stood about thirty feet way and just in front of the steps—exactly where I needed him to be. I pulled the pins, waited for what seemed like the longest four seconds in my entire life, then rolled them to the sentroid's feet. One detonated early and only brought the stunned sentroid to the ground. A moment later the second detonated just inches from his head. I could not have planned it better. There was no way that he could still be functional. Still, I ran over and poured a few rounds into his fractured head just to make certain. I called out to Luther. He peeked around the corner then shuffled into the nursery.

I hustled back to the cathouse with my eyes fixated on the sky in the direction of sector seven—my sector.

"Come on, Pablo... that was the signal, let's go," I said to myself. I reached the scooter and stood watching the sky. Nothing happened. "Do it, Pablo." I couldn't wait any longer. Then, just as I mounted the scooter, my eyes caught the streaking tracer low on the horizon. A quick flash came and went like a distant lightning strike. The echo of an explosion followed a second later.

"Way to go, Pablo."

At this point, many things started happening simultaneously in locations throughout the city. I can tell you precisely what I saw, and what I did; I can also tell you what the others were *supposed* to be doing, and what I *believe* transpired.

I heard the sound of a plasma cannon coming from the direction of my sector. This was likely at the hands of Susan, in response to Pablo's firing of the anti-aircraft shell. The anti-craft shell likely made contact far behind the enemy line, but it was intended for effect only—to spur the Tongs into action. The sounds of plasma cannons slowly multiplied, spreading in a counter clockwise direction along the wall relative to my position, as if a spark was traversing a fuse. Within seconds, the sounds of battle emanated from all sectors. The battle for Abasha City was underway, and so was Operation Tide.

Having commenced firing from the wall, Susan, Ying, and Monte were to remain there for a few minutes then gradually make their way to Pablo under the cover of the battle chaos. From there, the four conspirators would sneak out of the sector and rendezvous with me at the nursery. I had another task to perform before meeting them there. I instructed the women in the cathouse to take cover and remain in the building, then headed out to my scooter.

It was the riskiest, shakiest, and probably the stupidest phase of Operation Tide. I rode southwest from the cathouse and arrived at the orcos pen, where I found Nicholas waiting anxiously outside. I dropped the scooter and hurried over to him.

"The little android might be a problem," he said fretfully.

"We figured as much. Where is he?"

Nicholas pointed to a small building next to the pen. "In there."

"Get started. I'll take care of him." Nicholas took a single step before I grabbed his arm. "Hey—how sure are you that this isn't going to backfire in our faces?" I asked.

"As sure as I can be under the circumstances."

"Like... ninety percent?"

"More like seventy-five."

"I'll take it. Go!"

He ran over to the large gate that separated the eleven orcos from the rest of the city. I burst into the small building and discharged the little android with a single shot to the head. If I wasn't so consumed by what was about to ensue, I might have had time to feel some remorse for the little guy. Instead, I darted outside and lifted up the scooter. The sight behind me was almost comical. Nicholas was walking quickly toward me while trying his best not to run and not to appear so nervous. The hungry orcos followed behind him, gawking in all directions and salivating at their new freedom. Nicholas turned back, waved them forward, and shouted a strange command (which he later told me meant "food").

"This is crazy," he said as he jumped on to the back of the scooter. He was understandably apprehensive, yet I felt a surge of confidence. I knew him well enough to know that he wouldn't have released the animals if he didn't think our plan could work. We headed south as the battle raged on behind us.

We reached the officers' compound and found it buzzing with activity. Agitated sentroids and Serrones were moving in all directions with no sense of purpose. As expected, none of them wore red armbands. We skidded to a stop and darted out of the orcos' path. Nicholas shouted more commands, although I'm not sure they were necessary. The orcos slammed through the fence and started tangling with the unexpectant sentroids. I would have loved to stay and witness the melee, but we couldn't trust the effectiveness of the armbands we were wearing, and we weren't about to stick around to find out. Plus, we had places to be.

Within minutes we were inside the nursery, where Susan, Ying, Pablo, and Monte were waiting for us along with the others.

"Are they coming?" I asked Susan. She knew that I was asking if the Tongs were advancing on the city.

"Yes."

"How are we holding up?"

"Okay for now, but there's a lot of them—and I mean, *a lot* of them," she said. "They just keep coming."

The news was both good and bad. It was good in that it was exactly what we had hoped for—the chance for a clear path to the forest. It was bad because now our time was running out. The Toghan army would likely breach the wall before long. Evelyn and her team should have been making their way to the tunnel and securing it by this time. I knew that they wouldn't wait there very long.

I took a moment to review the present state of affairs in the nursery. Tina stood nearby holding Jasper. She was attentively hanging onto every word we said—a trooper awaiting orders. Next to her was Saba. She was holding the hand of a young girl who represented the first of eight, hand-in-hand chain links that decreased in height down to a spritely boy who couldn't have been older than four. The looks on their faces varied from oblivious curiosity to sheer terror.

"Are you ready?" I asked Tina.

"Let's get out of here," she replied ardently. As she spoke, the door leading to the enclosed yard opened. Janet entered the room holding an infant child in one arm. Her other hand stretched down past her waist where it clasped the hand of a disheveled young girl, who in turn, clutched an equally tattered doll. The sight of them standing in the doorway rivaled any scene ever portrayed in a Dickens novel.

"What's going on? Are we under attack?" asked a disquieted Janet. My first instinct was to order her back to the other building. I opened my mouth but nothing came out.

"Aaahhh!" I grumbled loudly. "Come on—we're getting out of here." I ran over and scooped up the little girl, grabbed the doll which had fallen to the floor, crossed the room and rushed out the front door. One-by-one, the entire party followed me down the steps and skirted around the scattered remains of the sentroid. Our daring escape must have resembled *The Sound of Music* more than *The Dirty Dozen.*

The wall appeared to be holding, for the path between us and the little shack in sector eight was deserted, and the sounds of battle seemed distant. Closer, more ominous noises emanated from the direction of the officers' compound. I was as much afraid of a stray orco coming our way as I was the Toghan army. I jogged toward the tunnel entrance with my Uzi extended out in one hand, and the little girl in the other, with her tiny hands locked around my neck. Remarkably, Operation Tide seemed to be working.

We came upon Evelyn and Petey waiting outside the shack. They were facing away from us, ready to fire upon anyone or anything that appeared from the direction of the wall. I called out Evelyn's name as we approached so as to avoid startling them into a friendly fire incident. Needless to say, her astonishment at the size and composition of my party was quite evident.

"Not a word," I demanded.

"Hurry!" she implored. "It sounds like the fighting is getting closer!"

With the girl still in hand, I peeked inside to find the shack empty except for Rajev kneeling next to the hole, waiting to assist us. The rest of Evelyn's team was already under ground. There wasn't nearly enough room to fit everyone in the shack. We had to send people inside in small groups while the others waited outside, fully exposed. I handed the girl to Evelyn and told her and Petey to go ahead into the tunnel. After they disappeared, we started sending the children in, interspersed with adults to shepherd them. Susan, Ying, and I stood guard outside. I peeked inside periodically to monitor the progress. Some of the children resisted the descent into darkness but there was no time to soothe them. Down they went, tears, dolls, and all.

One by one, my friends disappeared into the tunnel. Luther went first. Tina carried Jasper down. Saba, Janet, and Nicholas followed amidst a flock of children. Monte followed without hesitation and was likely as clueless as the child he carried. Pablo went next. Rajev waved me in as he descended down the ladder. I pulled Susan into the shack and ordered her down the tunnel. Then I spoke to Ying. I don't know exactly when the notion had first entered my mind—it was somewhere between the nursery and the shack. In the short time it took to get everyone into the tunnel, the idea had morphed from a frivolous whim into a firm resolution.

"You go ahead," I told Ying. "I need to take care of something. I'll catch up." I hadn't intended for Susan to hear, but she did. I hoped that Ying would understand, and I feared that Susan wouldn't allow it. I was right.

"What are you doing?" Susan yelled. Only her head was visible above the hole.

"Just go!" I shouted. "I need to make sure... Just go ahead—I'll catch up—don't worry!"

Susan started to climb back up while chastising me with her fiery eyes. "Dammit, Shaker. You don't think I know what this is about?" She looked down into the tunnel and said, presumably to Rajev, "Get going. We'll meet you in the forest." Then she walloped me in the stomach. "You know the Chief won't survive this. Just let it go."

"The king will kill him," added Ying. "He a dead man."

"That's not good enough," I replied. "I have to know for sure. You two go ahead. I'll catch up. I promise."

"Like we're just gonna let you go out there by yourself, you big oaf," Susan said, then punched me again, though not as firmly this time. "Come on, let's go before I change my mind."

I turned to Ying with the intent of insisting that she go down the tunnel. The look she returned told me that it would have been futile. I sincerely wanted them to go with the others. There was no time to argue.

"Load up," I told them.

I suddenly felt selfishly reassured to have them at my side. I shut the door to the shack and we made our way southwest on foot toward the officers' compound. The sounds of random skirmishes came from nearby, lending a chaotic feel to the surroundings. There was no action in the immediate area, but it was closing in.

"They're inside the wall," Susan said. "We need to step it up."

We rounded a dark corner near an empty building and simultaneously came to a halt in the face of an arc rifle pointed in our direction. We believed that we were heading away from the bloodshed and hadn't expected to encounter hostiles in front us, at least not until we reached the compound. Thus, we were caught by surprise and had no chance to take out the operative, though we outnumbered him three to one. The point of his rifle was just visible under the beam of a floodlight above. The soldier holding it was veiled in the shadow. It appeared to be a combot. I assumed he was an ally; a Tong would have dropped us as soon as we came into sight. The combot stepped forward and revealed himself. He was neither friend nor foe, exactly.

"What are you doing here?" Bar asked, looking squarely at me. I felt like asking him the same question, but I was the one with the rifle pointed three feet away from my gut.

"We're going to check on the south gate," I proffered.

"There are soldiers already positioned at the south gate. You should be defending your sector."

Well, we're not, I thought to myself, and remained silent. He held the cards at the moment, and I had no idea how he intended to play them.

"You are deserters," he said. "You are to be executed in accordance with the laws of the People's Resistance Front." A sinking feeling swept over me. I glanced over at my comrades.

"I'm the one you want," I told him. "These two will return to the sector."

"You are all guilty of desertion."

My options cascaded down my mind in the space of a microsecond. I could reach for my knife faster than my Uzi; my knife would have little effect on a combot; the Uzi was my best choice; Bar was obviously going to shoot me first; maybe Ying and Susan could get a shot off if I distracted him. I reached for my weapon…

Boom! Bar was knocked backward and onto his back. I drew my Uzi and fired two more shots into him. Who fired the first shot? Ying?

Susan? They were casting bewildered looks in my direction. Then—the sound of footsteps behind us. We turned to find Dee with his arc rifle extended. He walked past us and stood over the lifeless Bar.

"I could not allow him to execute you," he told us calmly.

"How did you… why are you here?" I asked.

"I followed these two soldiers when they departed the sector. I had not seen you, Shaker, since the battle started."

"So, you saw… in sector eight… what's inside the shack?"

"I already knew about the tunnel. I have been watching you."

"What happens now?" I asked.

"I believe I know where you are headed," Dee said as he walked toward me, then looked in the direction of the officers' compound.

"And?"

"We should hurry if we hope to have any chance."

There was no time for analysis. Dee killed Bar. Dee was with us. That was sufficient for now. We had to get moving. I thought it might already be too late when we surprised a small group of lizzies wandering on an otherwise deserted path. A couple were already severely wounded and we quickly dispatched the rest. Nothing was said between the four of us. Whether the lizzies had come from the north or the south made little difference at this point. We were too close to the compound to turn back.

We found the officers' compound still mired in conflict and disarray, though most of the hostility was confined to a few isolated pockets. The rest of the grounds were littered with the remains of sentroids, Serrones, and orcos. At least two orcos were still breathing and engaged with what remained of the sentroid force. Nobody seemed to notice or mind our presence. Perhaps each thought we were there to reinforce their side.

I quickly scanned the bodies in the yard and found no sign of the Chief. I knew his ostentatious attire well, and it was not present in the muck. The sounds of encroaching warfare grew closer. We stood facing the collection of alien abodes. I had no idea which one might be harboring the Chief.

"That one," Dee said, as if he had read my mind. He pointed to a structure straight ahead. I had no doubt that he was correct, for we came upon the remains of Kaiser lying outside the door. I fired into the door's locking mechanism, kicked it open, then burst inside with reckless abandon. Fortunately, there was nothing there. I could have easily been killed as a result of my carelessness. Susan closed the door behind us then extended her hand to me, imploring me to regain my composure.

I scanned the room. Another closed door faced me from the opposite wall. Susan and Dee stood guard while Ying and I approached the second door. Using signals and whispers, we decided that she would fire on the locking mechanism and I would kick open the door. We executed the maneuver then quickly moved away from the open door. There was no sound from within. I pivoted into the room with my Uzi aimed forward. There I found the Chief cowering in a corner, holding some sort of small weapon. I kicked the weapon out of his hand and pushed the point of my Uzi into his porcelain face.

"Do it, Shaker. We gotta go," Ying said. She was right but I wasn't about to let him off so easily. I pulled off his beret, then his visor, and squatted down to meet his dark beady eyes a few inches from my face.

"Can you understand me?" I said softly but sternly. The only other time I had been this close to a Serrone it was a juvenile eyeing me with innocent curiosity. The Chief's expression was nothing like that. It had to be sheer terror. Here was his prize beast, sprung from its cage—tortured, beaten, persecuted—but not broken—and ready to collect its due. I saw what the Serrone civilization had once been. I saw how far it had fallen at the hands of blood-thirsty, power-hungry warlords. I had no doubt that the Serrones understood hatred and revenge. The Chief knew why I was there, even if he couldn't understand my primitive language. I slowly removed my large, serrated knife from its sheath and raised it to his scrawny neck.

"Shaker—now," implored Ying.

"This is for Leesheh," I proclaimed, then thrust the knife into his midsection. He opened his mouth wide and emitted a shrill squeal. Pain. "And this is from me." I stuck the knife into the side of his neck and his lifeless body slumped forward.

"Let's go!" shouted Susan from outside the door. Her voice thrust me back into reality. I rose to my feet and followed Ying into the other room. Susan stepped cautiously up the to the door leading back out to the compound as the rest of us stood close behind with our weapons at the ready. She carefully cracked the door open and leaned into the opening to see outside.

The next moment is so etched into my memory that it feels as though I'm recounting something that happened only yesterday, and not so long ago. My hand trembles a little and I am forced to lay down my pencil for a moment. I have no choice but to relive the anguish and culpability that I had managed to repress in recent years, though I have never tried to evade the responsibility for what happened.

The long steely blade penetrated the front of Susan's neck and propelled through the other side so quickly that the motion was nearly imperceptible. It appeared to materialize within her in an instant. In a reflex action, she placed her hands on the blade, causing deep cuts in her palms. Blood gurgled from her throat and dripped from her hands in such volume that she quickly lost consciousness and died without having to endure the pain for more than a few seconds. She remained upright in death, held in place by the silver blade that protruded at least a foot beyond her neck.

We were stunned only for a brief moment before taking action. We couldn't see the agent of her demise but his location was obvious. We fired in the direction of the blade's origin. The culprit bullied his way into the room, and finally retracted his arm to release Susan's body. He stepped over it and continued toward us, absorbing round after round of plasma while we slowly retreated toward the opposite wall. He would have easily overpowered one of us, and possibly two, but three of us were too much for him to handle. Khan fell at my feet with a heavy a crash. I had to jump backwards to avoid the long blade from slicing my boot. I had never seen such an appendage on a sentroid before.

As I surveyed the mesh of metal and wires beneath me, Ying had already moved to the doorway leading outside. She froze and turned back to us with a look of consternation.

"Shaker," was all she said. I knew that it was over.

We laid our weapons on the floor of the Chief's quarters and slowly walked out into the compound, one by one, with our hands raised in front of us. Hundreds of Toghan soldiers were approaching from all sides. Some had their weapons pointed at us while most just watched curiously. The majority of them were lizzies, panting and growling—fresh from battle. There were several human soldiers among them, and it appeared that they were holding the lizzies at bay.

34

I was able to fulfill the fantasy of my personal vendetta at the cost of Susan's life, Ying's freedom, and a renewed separation from my son. As our captors escorted us north through the city, I couldn't help but entertain delusional thoughts that the Chief had somehow planned his death to transpire on his own terms—that he exploited my resentment and stubbornness to torment me one last time. He was probably looking up at me from Serrone hell at this very moment and laughing.

"I'm so sorry," I said to Ying as we knelt on the ground outside of the compound.

"Was my choice," she responded, without looking at me.

I wanted to apologize to Dee as well—and also thank him—but he had been taken away separately, presumably with the other combots that had been captured. I never saw him again.

Four human soldiers escorted us northward, though not before they engaged in a spirited game of rock, paper, scissors to determine how our weapons would be divided among them. The winner chose my Uzi for his grand prize, and my large serrated knife was selected by the runner up. When it was over, I directed their attention to the pistol hidden in my boot, which a soldier then sheepishly removed. I had no intention of using it.

There wasn't much to see in the middle of the city. We passed the nursery, cathouse, and PX. All were empty and relatively unscathed. As we approached the front gate, bodies began to accumulate. Toghan soldiers, human and android, were busy cleaning up the carnage. They barely looked up as we walked by—just two more prisoners to process.

Other than corpses, there was no sign of the thousands of lizzies that spearheaded the attack. I guess their job was done, and they would be of little service in the aftermath.

Morning had broken by the time we reached the north end of the city. The gates were wide open and our escorts led us through them, where we came upon seemingly endless rows of prisoners sitting cross-legged. There were easily a thousand or more, with most still wearing a red armband. I breathed a small sigh of relief to see that so many of my comrades had survived. Nicholas was probably correct about the king's intentions. How many more might have lived if I hadn't detonated those two grenades just a few hours ago?

We were led toward the back of the assemblage and ordered to sit down. There would be no special treatment for the mighty Shaker here. The Toghans didn't know me from a hole blown into the city wall, and that was fine with me. I was happy to become lost among the multitudes.

"I don't see nobody," said Ying once the guards had left us. She continued to pivot her head in all directions. "Nobody here."

It took me a second to comprehend what she was telling me. There was no sign of the tunnel escapees. The children captured from the nursery were being held nearby—close enough that I could clearly see their faces. I didn't see any of the children that we put into the tunnel a few hours earlier. They would likely be sitting right over there with the others if they had been caught. This by no means guaranteed that my friends and my son were safe, but it was a positive sign.

We sat under the light of Wiyanga for what seemed like hours. A few scattered plumes of smoke rose from inside the wall. We were lucky enough to be upwind and were spared the pungent, morbid odor. The Toghan guards walked languidly up and down the rows to keep tabs on us. A few sought to break up the monotony by chatting with prisoners. A middle-aged Asian guard eventually made his way to me. I kept my eyes fixed on the ground in front of me, hoping that he would pass by.

"Where's your home?" he asked with a slight accent.

"It used to be right there," I said, pointing toward the city. I knew what he meant but I wasn't in a very sociable mood.

"No. I mean *before*."

"America. Virginia." I tried to exhibit several non-verbal signs of someone who didn't want to be bothered. I guess he was too bored to care.

"I'm from Manilla," he volunteered. I managed a nod and hoped that he would move on to a more gregarious prisoner. He did not.

"A guy back there told me that you're one of the PRF's meanest badasses," he said. I followed his eyes back in the direction of where he was looking, then returned my gaze to the ground and put a blade of grass in my mouth.

"Nah, he's mistaken me for somebody else."

"Well, either way, you're one of us now."

"Great."

"The king treats us well."

"I can hardly wait."

"No, seriously. I think you'll like it better." Why was he trying to sell me on Toghan?

"He'll grant us our freedom if we ask him nicely?" I asked.

"Well, no, not that. I just mean that he takes good care of us."

"So, as far as brutal dictators go, other than expecting you to die for him, he's pretty good to his slaves. That is, those of you that are still alive. I wonder what your buddies who died last night would have to say about it."

He finally moved along, undoubtedly having grown weary of my sarcasm. My thoughts returned to Susan's death, then on to Pablo. I dreaded having to face him with the news. I suppose the miniscule odds of ever seeing him again offered me a bitter solace. My self-loathing soon transitioned to the subject of my son. How does the expression go? Abandon you once, shame on me; abandon you twice, and I'm the world's worst father. *Maybe it's for the best*, I thought. Tina would raise him like her own, and Nicholas would be there too. *Yeah, he's better off without me—I hope they aren't still waiting for us in the forest…*

A few times during the course of the day I took a merciful break from my introspective brooding to glance at Ying. That she was speechless was not unusual, yet I sensed that she was mentally drained, and felt it would be best to leave her alone for the time being. I was probably her closest friend on the planet, if she allowed herself friends, which was difficult to say. I hoped that she would soon forgive me for selfishly exploiting our relationship.

The tedium was eventually relieved by the arrival of a legion of trucks. Our conquerors loaded them in an orderly fashion, leading us over to the convoy in groups of ten while the other prisoners remained seated in the grass. When my time arrived, I lumbered along with my group in a semi-catatonic state. A familiar voice interrupted my trance.

"Shaker."

I turned to see Scoop, the young soldier from New York, sitting amongst the remaining POWs.

"Where were you?" he asked quietly—practically mouthing the words. I could only shrug my shoulders and shake my head in a vague sort of way that evaded his question. I had no way to explain my actions.

We rode north, stopping only for hurried meals of stale cereal during the day and open-air bivouacs during the night. We were subject to the constant and close supervision of armed humans and combots, which I found puzzling. We had nowhere to run. I perceived that many of my fellow POWs were somewhat relieved and looking forward to a change of pace under a new master. The years of captivity had rid most of them of aspirations to anything greater, and I too, felt apathetic, if not a bit broken.

For the first handful of days, our route was nearly identical to the one which I had taken in the opposite direction a few years earlier. We crossed the wide river on a hastily constructed pontoon bridge that seemed on the verge of sinking under the weight of our convoy. It spanned the river only a short distance away from the ruins of the majestic old bridge, which appeared to have been looted of its sculptured ornaments. The lone surviving tower was inclining dangerously to one side, and the gap between the stone decks reaching out from each shore had further deteriorated and grown much wider.

We found ourselves in the company of the giant yellow trees in the vast desert once again, where our speed quickened and our rest stops decreased. The Toghan Serrones in charge of our caravan didn't seem fond of the dry climate. We didn't travel within eyesight of Little Vegas, nor did we pass through the city from which its named derived, though we did catch a glimpse of the colossal skyline off in the distance. Before long I began to notice the familiar topography of the subtropical region that was my home upon arriving on the planet.

We continued due north for three more days before stopping for good at a large encampment that rivaled Little Vegas in size and structure, though without the sand. In the distance not more than ten miles away was a moderately-sized Serrone city on a hill. I was told that it was a vibrant, functioning Toghan metropolis despite being considerably underpopulated. I cannot validate these claims, for I was never permitted to venture anywhere near it.

The camp was surrounded by a short, unintimidating wire-mesh fence that served as a reminder more than an enforcer of our captivity. We were loosely marched through a similarly unimposing gate and taken to a collection of two-story buildings set in perfectly parallel rows. The buildings were constructed of a plaster that had the appearance of stucco. I would guess that they had been newly-constructed for us—the deluge of new slaves acquired from the recently defunct People's Resistance Front.

We assembled in front of the quarters and quietly awaited our barracks assignments. I stuck close to Ying in order to increase the chances of us being housed together. There were very few faces from my old company among us, not that I would have felt inclined to reside with any. I might have sought the companionship of Scoop, if not for the awkwardness of our brief exchange on the day after the battle. I was staring blankly at the heels of the person in front of me when a fusion of distant, familiar sounds caught my ears. They had been present all along—I simply hadn't taken notice. There was a low, gentle rumbling accompanied by an incremental whoosh, as if a giant was repeatedly sighing. I had not heard these harmonies in so long—not since my life *before*—that I was momentarily dumbfounded, or merely in a state of disbelief. But there was no mistaking the source—waves breaking on a beach. When I reached my assigned bunk on the second floor, I hurried to a window that faced in the direction of the sounds but could not visually confirm them.

Our long narrow room was furnished with two rows of double bunkbeds and little else except for the small wooden lockers that separated them. Ying and I laid claim to a set of beds near the middle of the room, not for any reason other than it being the next available when we entered. We sat quietly on my lower bunk for a few minutes before a combot entered the room. He introduced himself as our supervisor and told us to address him as Viz. The sixty or so slaves assigned to our room formed his "workgroup," as he referred to it. Viz did not entertain questions and promptly ordered us to assemble in front of the building.

He led us around the entire camp. It comprised nothing but sleeping quarters, latrines, and a large mess hall. The latter building was the final stop on our tour. It stood on the threshold of a beach that led into a vast sea. I doubt that our conquerors intended to reward us with such a picturesque dining experience, yet I had never seen such an impressive vista. The water reflected the pale blue hue of the parent planet. The beach was blanketed with black sand and littered with large charcoal-colored boulders. It was a particularly windy afternoon; six-foot breakers routinely crashed into the sand and rocks, adding a bright white foam to the sooty palette.

The semi-circle fence surrounding the camp extended into the ocean for about fifty yards, approximately two hundred yards down the beach on either side of the mess hall. Viz walked us up the beach to the northern edge of the fence where he pointed out an endless array of rolling green hills in the distance. He told us that the hills were a source of food for the Toghan army, and that our workgroup was now part of the larger group of farmers assigned to cultivate them.

The next morning, we assembled in front of the barracks with a few other newly-formed workgroups and waited for more than an hour before a small procession of vehicles pulled into the yard. Two small hovering cars flanked a larger, wheeled truck that was about the size of a delivery van. The vehicles were spotless and in remarkable condition compared to the jalopies that transported us during the waning years of the PRF. All were fully-enclosed with darkly-tinted, bubble-shaped covers. I have to admit that I was a little disappointed to see only a single entity emerge from the middle vehicle—an android, no less. I hadn't expected an audience with the king, but an appearance by some representative of the "royal family" might have been intriguing.

The android was, as far as I could tell, a sentroid, yet something was different about him. Perhaps he was a later model, or maybe it was just that he had been spared the ravages of combat. He was well-polished in appearance, if not demeanor, which was as robotic and emotionless as any other I had encountered. He lectured us for several minutes. The gist of the speech was the same as the one I endured on my first day on the planet—substituting "Toghan" for "People's Resistance Front," and "King Tosso" for "General Abasha" here and there. (It turns out that King Tosso was the rightful ruler of the hemisphere all along. Who knew?) The android made vague references to ongoing conflicts between the Kingdom of Tosso and "unlawful" or "rebellious" regions and factions, and I inferred that none of the action was transpiring near us.

Following his speech, the sentroid disappeared into his vehicle, which subsequently sped out of camp along with its escorts. The excitement of the day now over, we climbed into flatbeds and drove out to an orchard full of wango trees where we received instructions for harvesting the ubiquitous fruit.

35

My first year in the Toghan army passed slowly, followed by a handful that passed quickly, followed by a few that, in retrospect, seem to have been compressed into a single month. It was not until later that I was able to more precisely estimate the number of years that transpired during this chapter of my life. A detailed chronology of this period would consist mostly of immaterial nothingness. I would be unable to distinguish one season from another if I tried. I will instead describe the milestones and events that shaped my disposition and state of mind, and eventually led me to where I am today.

The camp was known among the slaves as Ocean City. Our duties were confined to the army's agricultural needs, which varied along with the seasons. In the warm season we tended to the wango orchards; in the cool season, which was much wetter in this part of the planet, we harvested a grain that grew in pools of water and tasted like chalk (or so I was told). Some of the wangos made their way to our own dining hall, while most were loaded onto trucks and shipped out to the troops. We suspected that the chalky grain was earmarked for the hordes of lizzies in the Toghan army.

Viz was a constant presence in our lives during that first year. He spent his nights in our barracks and escorted us to our worksite each and every day, where he remained to ensure that each of us was pulling his weight. Of all the combots I had encountered, Viz exhibited the least inclination toward subjective reasoning. His personality, or lack thereof, was much closer to a sentroid than his combot brethren. He rarely spoke more than one word at a time, such as "work," "eat," "stop," "yes," and "no." I wondered if the repurposed android, who was presumably once a sprightly warrior, resented his new status as an overseer. Or maybe he was the recipient of a combot lobotomy.

When not toiling in the orchards or the fields, the workgroup was confined to quarters or the courtyard just outside. My fellow slaves in the workgroup entertained themselves with songs, stories, and games similar to those that had helped us pass the time in the PRF. Vices common in the PRF were mostly held in check in Ocean City. I saw no alcohol or stimulants of any kind during my stint there. There was also no systematic program for involuntary reproduction; however, activities leading to the voluntary variety were tolerated, and rather prevalent. Its participants were conspicuously undeterred by the dearth of privacy, too. One woman in our group became pregnant early on. She was whisked away during her final trimester and returned several weeks later, childless. There weren't any prize fighting or other abusive activities in the peaceful camp for the amusement of our masters. In fact, I never laid eyes upon anyone ranking higher than a sentroid within Ocean City, though the lavish vehicles that came and went from time-to-time were surely occupied by well-connected Toghan Serrones.

We were sometimes permitted to swim in the ocean following a warm day in the fields. Most of the beach was rocky, but there was one area that was naturally devoid of any dangerous obstacles. I took advantage of every opportunity to immerse myself in the salty water. I could close my eyes and imagine that I was back in the cool Atlantic Ocean, if only for a short while. Otherwise, I mostly kept to myself. My days of storytelling were long behind me. I couldn't recall the details of the classics and lacked the inclination to fabricate new ones. I was generally regarded as a loner and left to my own designs. I periodically wrote in my journal and kept it on me at all times, safely folded inside a pouch. Entries during this period were few and far between.

The slow passage of time during that first year can probably be attributed to my general feelings of disconsolation and hollowness. It's true what they say about warriors returning from combat to find that they miss the war. I had come to despise the bloodshed as much as the next soldier, yet suddenly I felt a loss of purpose, mission, and brotherhood. As a fighter in the PRF, I had sensed that I was advancing my own cause—making something happen. I didn't want to be a fighter, but I sure as hell wasn't cut out to be a farmer. Compounding my gloom was the loss of my son and my friends, for which I had only myself to blame.

The exception to my self-imposed detachment was Ying. Any resentment she might have harbored toward me following the battle of Abasha City had faded during the first weeks in the new camp. Our bond solidified in the years that followed, and she became like a sister to me. Our relationship was not nurtured by our shared history, in that we never rehashed or commiserated about the past. In fact, we hardly spoke yet rarely ventured out of each other's sight.

There were inklings that I (and Ying) had remained an intimidating figure in the early years and perhaps beyond. Although it had waned, the legend of the Shaker had not fizzled out entirely. This was not an image that I propagated or validated through any actions or words. I shrugged off any admiration that was bestowed upon me, as if it was my penance to disclaim it. Looking back, I might have squandered opportunities to hearten my comrades who were likely feeling as distraught as I was.

It was toward the end of the cool season, a couple of years or so after beginning our agricultural pursuits, that the winds of change began to blow once again. We gathered in the courtyard following our breakfast ("cereal by the sea" I called it), where Viz informed us that we would not be working in the fields that day. The trucks brought us, along with several other workgroups, to a large pavilion where we stood en masse—maybe five hundred in all—facing a raised platform. A few minutes later, a colorfully-adorned Serrone and his android entourage entered from the back and stepped up to the platform. The Serrone wore a tinted visor not unlike the Chief's, and a red wide-brimmed hat with a short crown and several feathers stuck into the band. His traditional Serrone frock clashed with his hat, and even more so with itself. The top half resembled a tie-dyed shirt of rainbow colors while the bottom comprised red and white vertical bars, resembling a candy striper volunteer. His wardrobe display was impressive, though I'm pretty sure that he wasn't the king.

One of his sentroids informed us that we were being asked to swear an oath of loyalty to King Tosso. Specifically, he asked if anyone present was unwilling to swear the oath. Needless to say, nobody declined the opportunity. On the ride back to camp, Ying and I discussed the implications of the bizarre ceremony.

"My guess is that things are about to change for us," I said.

"Now we Tong soldiers. Soon we fight again somewhere," she responded.

"Yeah, I think so."

Although it wasn't obvious at the time, I can see now that we became soldiers on the very next day. We were ordered to pack up whatever personal items we could carry and climb into the trucks waiting for us outside. (Unlike the PRF, the Toghans permitted us to retain certain personal belongings. If we could carry it, we could keep it.) Before long, hundreds of newly-sworn defenders of the king shipped out and headed north. Viz was left behind, undoubtedly to foster the next group of incoming agronomists. I wonder if he envied us.

We continued north for at least a week before arriving at a small camp that was bustling with military activity. We were shepherded into a facility where we exchanged our farming shorts and tee shirts for warmer apparel. The new garb consisted of fresh undergarments, full-length cargo pants, a long-sleeve shirt and a knit cap—all in the color of forest green, otherwise known as Tong green.

Following a quick meal, we were told to return to the trucks. Each of us was handed a heavy parka and a pair of waterproof white pants that were designed to fit over our new cargo pants. Both items were arctic-white in color. The outside of the parka was constructed of a synthetic fiber and the inside was lined with fur donated by some unfortunate hairy creature. These two final pieces of the ensemble were somewhat foreboding. The temperature was cool but pleasant—there was no need for such a heavy coat where we were. We guessed that we wouldn't be staying in this area for long.

We continued northward for days, and still farther northward for several more days, until the heavy parkas and white pants had become permanently attached to our bodies. The gradual ascent of our trucks into the mountains became far less gradual, and our pace slowed as they struggled upward. These were the first mountains I had seen up close since arriving on Serrone. What struck me was the intense shade of red within the rocks that pervaded throughout. I didn't need Nicholas to tell me that they were rich in iron oxide. Contrasting with the red rocks were the dark green coniferous trees and the snow, which was a brilliant white with a hint of blue-violet reflecting from Wiyanga. The snow eventually blanketed everything in sight. Just when it seemed that the trucks could go no farther on the ice-packed roads, we reached another camp.

The human soldiers there called their frigid village Ice Station Zebra. The day after we arrived, an equal number of soldiers gleefully shipped out in the same trucks that had delivered us, noting that any destination would be better than where they were. A couple of unclad combots (apparently impervious to the cold) briefed us on our new assignment. We stood at the northeastern border of the Kingdom of Tosso, where various rebel factions lingered, allegedly for the purpose of gaining entry into the kingdom and wreaking havoc upon its loyal subjects. As the newest and least trustworthy soldiers of the Toghan army (or so it was implied), it was our responsibility to rid the mountains of this pestilence. It was widely-known that lizzies performed the lion's share of combat duty for the Tongs, but the reptilian creatures couldn't survive in these temperatures. That explained why we were there, and probably explained why the rebel factions were there as well.

We were issued ancient arc rifles that might have met a minimum quality standard during the Great War or the decade that followed, though even that assumption was debatable. We found them to be dangerously unreliable in the frigid climate. Each of us was also provided with a basic field knife that came in handy for gutting local critters, and we soon discovered that our food intake depended heavily upon our hunting skills.

Each of the wooden barracks was heated by a single wood stove that was located in the center of the room. Thus, it became a nightly contest of first-come, first-served to determine who slept in the choice bunks closest to the furnace. All of the beds were shoved so closely together at night that there was no room to walk between them. Those who tended to need the latrine in the middle of the cold night were usually banished to the outer reaches of the barracks (or they kept a convenient bottle handy). Any bed inside the barracks was considered a luxury. We spent most nights bivouacked higher up in the mountains, huddled in white canvas tents that were sparsely heated by small oil burners.

As I wrote earlier, this was the beginning of a period that swiftly glossed over me. We fell into a repetitive pattern that boiled down to the following: climb up, camp out, hunt, wait, hunt, wait, hunt, break camp, climb down. This was carried out in combot-led teams of seven or eight soldiers, several of which were deployed throughout the area at any given time. We encountered unfriendlies on a regular basis, but our skirmishes rarely resulted in casualties, which seemed more than agreeable to both sides. Eventually, the mutual lack of aggression morphed into an unspoken truce. By the time I left Ice Station Zebra, opposing soldiers regularly swapped cigarettes, supplies, and stories high up in the mountains. We found that many of the enemy soldiers were simply runaways in hiding—avoiding the servitude and bloodshed at the hands of Serrone warlords. I respected them, though I never felt compelled to join their ranks. I saw no way for them to ever escape the mountains.

There was no change in seasons, so it is difficult to estimate how much time I spent at Ice Station Zebra. It was easily three years if it was a day. During this time, I emerged from my funk and entered into a state of indifferent complacency. In a way, it was the best of both worlds: I was a soldier once again, enduring shared hardships with my comrades, yet with little chance of being injured or killed. Even the so-called hardships were not so difficult. I acclimated to the beauty and serenity of the red, white, and blue-violet mountains with ease.

Then one day out of the blue, the order came to leave the mountains behind. Rumors soon abounded. Perhaps we had proven our worth and loyalty to the king and had earned a more hospitable post, or maybe we were desperately needed somewhere else.

The answer lay to the southeast, not far from my original camp. The king had held the territory since pushing us out after the attack on the starship years earlier. And now some upstart hoodlum was trying to muscle in. That's what we theorized—nobody told us anything. What else could it be?

We arrived at a temporary encampment on a hill in the middle of the afternoon. It seemed strange to walk among the familiar plants and wildlife again. In a way, it felt like home, albeit a home that evoked vastly mixed emotions. The makeshift camp was crawling with lizzies, which I found a little unnerving. They clumped together in a huge horde and weren't constrained by an enclosure of any kind. I had killed a lot of their cousins in my day, and I hoped they'd received the memo stating that I was now fighting on their side. Making matters worse, the hill seemed awfully exposed, which I pointed out to one of the soldiers who had greeted us upon arrival. He was a stocky Asian-American who seemed pretty laid back. Maybe it was just his San Fernando Valley accent.

"It's not a problem," he told me. "They're out numbered and pinned down in a village a few miles up that road. We've got 'em by the balls."

"Then why am I here?" I asked.

"Look around. We don't have enough minders."

"Minders?"

"Humans. Don't worry—the lizzies'll take care of the heavy lifting. We just gotta keep 'em organized and pick off the bad guys who get away from 'em."

"I don't know the first thing about being a minder," I said.

"Don't sweat it, bro. Mainly you just follow behind them. We'll tell you what to do."

As he was talking, one of his colleagues approached to ask him something. I didn't take much notice of the man other than his long, dark, neglected hair and beard. He had clearly seen better days. I saw him shudder slightly when he caught sight of me. He proceeded to take a half step backward and look in the opposite direction with an unnatural twist of the neck. I didn't make anything of it and started to walk away.

"What's up with you, Tully?" the Asian-American man asked of his colleague. "You look like you just saw a ghost, man."

I stopped in my tracks and slowly pivoted. Now I could see him plainly—just as he looked on the last day I saw him, all those years ago.

"He did," I said. Tully grew more jittery by the second and remained silent. I walked closer and glued my eyes onto his. "Tully and I go way back."

I thought about everything bad that had happened since that day. I could blame him for all of it. I could kill him—maybe not in that moment—but soon. It would be easy, and I could see by the trepidation in his eyes that he agreed.

I could also blame myself for everything bad that had happened since that day. Killing him would only end *his* misery. It would likely do little to assuage my own. Then and there I decided to let it all go. I wasn't forgiving him, nor was he asking for forgiveness. I just didn't want anything to do with the miserable wretch. I didn't want him to have the satisfaction of getting under my skin any longer—alive or dead.

"This thing with us is over, Tully. Just stay out of my way. Don't stir it up."

He answered with a brief nod and we parted ways. I turned around to find Ying standing there. She had been watching my back the entire time. She nodded her consent, and I patted her on the shoulder.

"Let's find something to eat," I said.

It turned out that the lizzies were just intelligent enough to distinguish friend from foe. On the day after we arrived, we watched from a relatively safe distance as the horde of monkey-lizards plowed through the small village and shredded the wannabe warlord and his thugs. I learned that only the female lizzies fought. It occurred to me that I had never seen a male lizzie until that time. They existed in smaller numbers and were used for mating purposes only. They were slighter in stature than their female counterparts and had a vertical crown of hair that resembled a mohawk. All things considered, they had it pretty good.

Our small, agile corps of humans, combots, and lizzies patrolled the greater area for the better part of two seasons. We uprooted and dispatched several crews that allegedly posed a threat to the kingdom. Some of our targets seemed like political threats to the king, rather than violent threats to his kingdom, but who was I to say anything? Tully was with us for the entire period. He managed to stay clear of me, and we never exchanged another word.

On a particularly warm morning we were told to load the trucks as usual, which meant that we herded the lizzies into a few of the flatbeds before climbing into our own. We drove due west for three days—uncharted territory for me—and reached the outskirts of a large Serrone village. There we joined up with a large force of soldiers—a thousand or more—complete with an artillery unit. *Now this was the real Toghan army*, I thought—the same kind that kicked us out of Abasha City.

We had no idea where we were or whom we were to be fighting. The combot in charge of our company told us that we would be sweeping through the village with the objective of eradicating a large rebel army that had taken hold there. A soldier who had been stationed there for a while told me that the so-called rebels had inhabited the small city for years. It seems the king was looking to expand his empire. It made little difference to us.

Our large army lobbed a few shells into the village then we invaded it in the usual order, with the lizzies leading the charge. Ying and I blended in with the mass of soldiers. We weren't looking to be heroes. I cannot recall if I killed any rebels that day—I doubt it. My arc rifle misfired nearly as often as it fired, so I tried to maintain a safe distance between myself and the melee. We captured the village without much difficulty, and the king had another feather for his pimp hat.

Following the battle, my comrades were divided and reassigned to various companies in the large army. I suspect that the idea was to dilute the former PRF members among the Toghan "regulars." Ying and I were lucky enough to remain in the same company. We stayed with this army for a year or more, patrolling the area from our newly-established base in the village. The village was nondescript, as was the time I spent there. There was a lot of talk about Plymouth amongst the human soldiers. I hadn't heard much about it during my time up north, which was fine with me. The notion of a human settlement perturbed me more than ever, for I had grown to impugn its existence in recent years. While the fantastical idea of Plymouth provided hope to some, for me it was a hurtful reminder that my son and my friends probably died trying to find the imaginary city. Or worse, they were enslaved by another savage warlord who snatched them up. Whenever I heard soldiers talking about Plymouth, I walked away. I made it very clear that I wanted no part of it.

In the early days that followed the attack on Abasha City, I regretted not leaving through the tunnel with my son and the others. Now I regretted letting them go. Here in the Toghan army we were still slaves but we were relatively safe. It was certainly better than life in the PRF. In the years since Abasha City, I had convinced myself that finding happiness on Serrone was a pipedream. Why chase a rainbow when complacency suited me just fine? I still had my sister Ying; I'd made a few acquaintances in the company; I had my journal; and I had my beloved cereal mush. When looking back on my life in the PRF, it seemed as detached from me as my life on Earth. Now it was all about to change once again.

36

Ying and I were caught completely by surprise that night. I can remember the cool, breezy evening like it was yesterday. We were members of a small squad assigned to patrol the dense forest, just as we had done countless times before. There were ten of us: nine human soldiers and our combot sergeant. We had been assigned to this particular squad for several weeks. Although they were decent soldiers, Ying and I preferred to keep to ourselves—friendly, but not friends. We were the only former members of the PRF in our unit.

We piled into two vehicles. One was a jeep with a heavy weapon mounted in the rear; the other was a traditional flatbed truck. I quickly fell asleep in the back of the flatbed, a useful skill I had honed from spending thousands of hours riding in them. Ying nudged me awake when we arrived at the starting point for the patrol. I stood up and walked toward the rear of the bed, allowing the soldiers in front of me to hop down first. Ying was ahead of me. When it was her turn to climb down, a soldier on the ground raised his hand to stop her.

"Hold on a second," he said quietly, while looking attentively toward the jeep.

"What's going on?" I asked. The soldier raised his hand again.

"Wait," he mouthed to us. Something was going down. Had they heard a suspicious sound in the woods? None of the soldiers had his weapon drawn and none were seeking cover. The combot started walking up the road, then turned back toward the vehicles.

"It is time to go," he said to the squad. "What are you waiting for?"

The crackling whoosh of the heavy machinegun spooked me and I instinctively ducked down in the truck. Through the gap between the wooden slats I saw the plasma rounds hit their intended target, one after the other. The combot wriggled and shook in response to the first few hits, like a dancing string puppet. The fourth put him down for good. The woman behind the gun ceased firing and stood up to survey the damage. The other soldiers walked over to the combot as Ying and I remained in the truck, completely dumbfounded. I raised my rifle, not knowing what to expect, or whom to trust.

"Lower your weapon, Shaker," said one of the soldiers. He walked toward us with his rifle slung over his shoulder. "You too, Ying. Nobody is going to hurt you." We jumped down and walked over to the group. The man who spoke to us was an older German gentleman called Bird Man. I never asked about the origin of his nickname, though I suspect that it had something to do with his curved nose that resembled a beak. The Bird Man (or "Bird" for short) appeared to be the leader of this little mutiny.

"Sorry if we scared you. We didn't know if we could trust you enough to tell you ahead of time."

"I take it you couldn't trust the sarge," I said.

"He's an android," said Bird.

I might have disagreed with his assumption but it was water under the bridge. "What's going on?" I asked.

"We're getting out of here. We can leave you two here or you can come with us. It's your choice, but if you choose to stay, we need you to give us the entire night before you report back."

"It would take us all night to walk back anyway. I assume you're taking the vehicles."

"We are."

"Where you go?" asked Ying.

"Plymouth," said the woman who fired the heavy gun—a Kenyan woman named Huso.

"Geez," I said with a sigh. "That's what this is all about?"

"You know how to go?" asked Ying.

"We have an idea," said Bird.

I was not impressed. "An *idea*?"

"We hear that it is safe travelling once we reach the Kinshan Territory," said Huso.

"And where exactly is that?" I asked. It didn't ring a bell with me. Bird was about to reply when Huso interrupted.

"Bird, we have no time for this. We *have* to go now."

"In or out, guys. Make up your minds," Bird said in a very business-like tone.

I didn't have a good feeling about it. Even if Plymouth existed, which I doubted, this team seemed to lack the knowhow and supplies to make it there safely. And once we committed, there could be no turning back. I turned to Ying to ask her what she thought. I could already read the answer in her face.

"You wanna do this, huh?"

"You decide, Shaker," she said.

I owed her so much. There was no way I was going to let her down again. I would have rather died.

"Let's go," I said to the Bird Man.

We quickly dug a shallow hole for the combot near the side of the road and covered him with dirt, leaves, and twigs. Then we scurried into the vehicles and continued moving away from the village. We made it a hundred miles or more before daybreak, at which time we drove the vehicles into the woods and covered them with loose branches. It would have been too dangerous to continue traveling on the road. We spent the daylight hours hiding in the brush, where I took the opportunity to ask Bird about his plan for finding Plymouth. He pulled out a crumpled sheet of parchment that showed what appeared to be a hand-drawn map.

Where did you get that?" I asked.

"I found it on a dead soldier," said Bird. I took a look at the map and found that there wasn't much to it, just a few crudely drawn pictures, words, lines, arrows, and the letter "P" with a circle around it. It did little to bolster my confidence in our journey.

"This is all you've got?"

"I am sorry that we do not have a yellow brick road for you," replied Bird.

"This is supposed to be Plymouth—here?" I asked, pointing to the "P."

"What else could it be? Look, this arrow points south. We will need to find this river down there then turn east. We should come to this place—see where it says 'yellow arch'? It should be close to where the river meets the ocean."

"That's supposed to be an ocean? What does the yellow arch mean?"

"That's where we find help. You have heard of the man at the yellow arch, right?"

"No."

"That is how the story goes. We get there and we are home free."

The entire plan seemed like one assumption layered upon another, sitting on a shaky foundation of wishful thinking. All we needed was a little fairy dust to sprinkle on top. At that point I figured that my role would be to keep this crew of pilgrims safe. Fortunately, I had swapped my rifle with the dead combot's. His was in much better condition. (Ying had the wherewithal to grab his knife.) Bird was about to fold up the map when something on it caught my eye.

"Hold on. What's that?"

"That is a bridge. We head south to the river, then east from there," he said.

"I know that bridge, and I know where that river is." The picture was rudimentary, yet there was no mistaking the majestic towers. "It's just north of Abasha City."

"You know the area?"

"Ying and I lived there. We saw that bridge get blown up years ago."

"We don't need to cross it."

"Have any of you ever been that far south?"

"No."

"Here's the problem. You see this?" I circled my finger around a sizeable blank portion of the map above the bridge. "This entire area is a desert—a *serious* desert. There's a big city in the middle of it, too, and it's populated with Serrones."

"A desert?" lamented a crestfallen Huso.

"I guess we cannot walk through it," said Bird.

"Even with vehicles we wouldn't make it through there without being spotted. There's only one road," I told them. Then I pointed out that it wasn't too late to concoct a cock-and-bull story about an ambush or something, and make our way back to the village. The look of disappointment proliferated across their faces—including Ying's. I felt bad for raining on their parade—our parade. I guess I didn't want to see the pilgrimage end either.

"There might be another way," I said as I moved my index finger along the map. "We could head east from where we are, and a little south, and try to reach the coast just below Ocean City. It seems to me that *this* river empties into *that* ocean. From there we could move back westward to find the yellow thing."

"Yellow arch," added Bird assuredly, as if lending his stamp of approval to the new plan. The others readily agreed in light of the bleak alternative. Having set us on a dubious course to the wondrous destination, I crawled under a shady bush and tried to catch a little sleep.

We made our way east for days, encountering no signs of current civilization, and only a few signs of bygone civilization, in the form of abandoned villages and vehicles. We were careful not to enter any of the villages, in the remote chance that nomadic Serrones might have taken refuge there. Food and water were plentiful in this region of the planet. We stayed in the forest and replenished our canteens with water from the copious streams that flowed in our direction and pointed our way to the sea. It was there that I tasted my first roller, courtesy of Huso's adept hunting skills. The roasted version of the venomous creature was far less intimidating than the one that had nearly bitten off my nose.

The forest eventually gave way to an open field at the crest of a hill. We stood at the edge of the tree line and marveled at the great sea below us, less than two hundred yards away. The easy part of our journey was now over. After reconnoitering the area for a few hours and waiting for nightfall, we turned south and carefully paralleled the coast while staying just inside the tree line. By the third dawn after reaching the ocean, the forest had deserted us. Looking down into a southward valley, a single road snaked through rolling fields that extended in every direction except where they were halted by the sea on our left. The road led to a small village in the distance. Small clumps of trees, insufficient to conceal us, dotted the open landscape.

We remained on the hill for two days, watching the occasional vehicle wind its way up or down the little road. None appeared to be the property of the Toghan army. We reckoned that we were in the middle of King Tosso's southern empire, formerly the eastern border of the PRF. There was no need for the king to maintain a large military presence there. Still, sneaking our way past the village on foot seemed far too precarious.

"We're soldiers, aren't we?" I posited. "It can't be unusual for these Serrones to see soldiers passing through their village. We look the part, we act the part, we hide in plain sight."

"Just march through town?" asked Huso.

"With no vehicles, and no combots or sentroids escorting us?" added another concerned pilgrim.

"If we act the part—I mean, act like we're supposed to be there—those little guys will run and hide in their little huts until we're gone," I told the group. "Trust me, they're more afraid of you than you are of them." Everyone was tired of lying on the hill and nobody had a better idea, so my plan was accepted by default.

"We'll go as soon as it gets dark," said Bird.

"We should go right now," I said. "First, Serrones are less active at this time of day. Second, we'll look less suspicious walking through town in broad daylight. That's what 'plain sight' means." This part of my plan was met with less enthusiasm; however, Ying and Huso were onboard and helped me to convince the others.

We headed down the hill and made a straight path for the village, avoiding the road as much as possible. When we came to within a quarter-mile of the village, we stepped onto the road and marched single-file with our rifles over our shoulders and our faces brimming with confidence. The villagers were not as sedate or reticent as I had hoped. They had probably grown accustomed to soldiers passing through. A few younger Serrones ventured near us for an up-close view. This spooked some of my fellow pilgrims, whom I had to remind to stay in character.

We reached the opposite edge of the town without consequence, as far as we could tell. We had no idea if a suspicious villager had contacted any local authorities. We continued to walk in formation until we came to a large truck parked on the side of the road. A small building sat at the top of a rise a few hundred yards away. Seeing that the vehicle was unoccupied, Bird assembled us behind it so that we could regroup under its cover. The truck was some kind of civilian transport vehicle, with an enclosed cargo space that cast a large shadow. The building on the hill appeared to be vacant as well.

"What now?" someone asked. "Do we keep walking?"

"We have to," replied Bird. "We can't stay here." There was nothing ahead but the small road and endless fields that melted into the horizon. The beach was too rocky and also too exposed. It seemed that we had avoided one obstacle only to find a larger one ahead of us. Ying broke the silence.

"Why we don't drive?" she asked, while patting her hand on the side of the truck. Everyone exchanged glances. It seemed too obvious to be feasible.

"Does anyone know how to operate this thing?" I asked.

"Jonesy can drive it. He grew up in a motor pool," said Huso, referring to the lanky, native-born soldier in our group. He looked all of eighteen years old.

"Are you up for it, Jonesy?" asked Bird.

"Sure," he replied nonchalantly, as if Bird was asking to fetch him a beer. Natives tended to be either cocky bastards or just plain imbeciles. I hadn't known Jonesy long enough to determine which he was, but I was leaning heavily toward the latter. Despite his confidence, the notion of driving out of there felt a little risky. Nobody appeared willing to make the call.

"It does seem pretty serendipitous," I added. "It's like this thing is begging us to drive it." For the first time we took a group vote and the vehicle idea prevailed seven to three. I volunteered to ride in the hot, stifling cargo area, but Bird insisted that I ride shotgun with him and Jonesy. I was relieved to oblige.

It turned out that Jonesy was a savant when it came to alien vehicles. Through my novice eyes, he looked as if he was casting a spell on the arcane controls. He waved his hands around some buttons, pushed another, touched a few more, and we were on our way. I asked him where he had learned so much about operating the machines. He told me that a combot started teaching him when he was just five or six seasons old. The conversation reminded me of Mik, the old motor pool combot in my first camp.

We stayed on the road all day and half the night, tensely passing through two more villages along the way, until it began to veer away from the shore. Bird directed Jonesy to pull the vehicle into a small patch of woods near the road. We did the best we could to camouflage it, but it was simply too big to hide. The only course of action was to put as much distance between us and the truck before dawn.

Wiyanga rose a few hours later to find us walking along the dark sandy beach. The area seemed desolate, so we agreed to push ahead in the daylight. Huso noticed it first. It was a narrow line of trees far off in the distance, running perpendicular to our direction. It appeared to be the kind of tree line that followed the bank of a river. We hurried our pace and came upon the massive estuary, just as I had guesstimated. Assuming this was the same river as the one on the map, our yellow beacon was somewhere along the bank, to the west of where we stood.

There was a lot of natural cover around the estuary, so we camped there for the night and the entire following day before resuming our journey under the stars. I remained a Plymouth skeptic, though I was enjoying the thrill of the quest. I could not allow myself the hope of seeing my son again.

The river made our traveling a little less vulnerable to nosey Serrones. We circumvented the towns and villages along the bank by wading up river, just off shore, in the darkness. I'm glad that I hadn't considered the ornery water creatures that might have been lurking in the river, as I might have had second thoughts about getting into it chest-deep. Other than picking up a few hitchhikers in the form of leech-like worms, nobody was the worse for the wear. All the while we kept a vigilant eye out for the fabled yellow arch, though nobody knew exactly what form it might take.

I was dislodging one of the aforementioned parasites when Jonesy called our attention to a faint yellow light ahead. We had just waded past a small village and were under the impression that all of its edifices were behind us. In the darkness we could barely discern the outline of a small dwelling. It was from there that a pinpoint of amber emanated. We inched closer to the building and caught a much better view of the yellow beacon that shone on the side of the house, about one square foot in size.

"You've got to be kidding me," I blurted in a loud whisper. Yet the more I thought about it, the more I understood it. It made perfect sense. If you wanted a symbol that nearly every inhabitant of Earth would recognize, and no Serrone could make heads or tails of, then why not this? Not one arch, but two—two golden arches. Even Ying recognized it.

"McDonalds!" she exclaimed. I had never seen her so animated.

"That *has* to be our signal," I said, after shushing Ying.

As certain as we were, we decided that one of us should check it out, and I volunteered for the job. I borrowed Ying's knife and crept up to the wall with the lighted sign. Beneath the arches was a small, unlit arrow that pointed toward the back of the building. There were no lights visible inside the structure—no signs of any activity whatsoever. I carefully made my way around the corner to the rear of the building with my gun at the ready. Moving cautiously against the back wall, I came to a door. Next to it was a small placard with the word "push" scribbled on it.

Below the placard was a button.

I considered returning to the others to report what I had seen, then decided that it would have accomplished nothing. The whole point was for one of us to take the risk without exposing the others, so I pressed the button. Within a few seconds, a small light above me turned on. I was being scrutinized. Shortly thereafter, the top half of the door slid open automatically, exposing a dimly-lit room behind it. The room appeared to be empty and I heard nothing. I wasn't sure what to do. Was I supposed to provide a password?

"Hello?" I murmured. "Um, Big Mac?... fries?... Filet-o-fish?" The bottom half of the door opened, and the light within the room brightened.

"Come on in," said a voice with an Australian accent. "You can lay that rifle on the floor."

"I'd rather not," I replied, as I slowly crept in. I wasn't a hundred percent convinced that it wasn't a trap, though it would have been a most peculiar trap, to say the least.

"You're safe here, mate," the voice said. "We don't want any accidents." His tone sounded genuine, so I relented and placed my rifle on the floor. I laid the knife next to it, following which the owner of the voice entered the room. He was a tall, fit man who appeared to be a few years older than myself. I was immediately drawn to his face, which was clean-shaven except for a neatly-trimmed brown mustache. I hadn't seen a closely-shaved face since arriving on the planet. He approached me with a grin and shook my hand in both of his.

"Welcome. The name's Will," he said warmly, as if I was his long-lost cousin. A second, much younger man entered the room. "And that's Jagger." Jagger nodded shyly to me. I surmised from his age and demeanor that he was a native-born human.

"I'm sure you've got a lot of questions—have a seat," continued Will. I was about to sit on a nearby couch when another door slid open and a Serrone walked in. We stared awkwardly for a moment, sizing each other up. He didn't seem frightened in the least—only curious.

"This is Johnson, or at least that's what we call him," said Will. "We can't pronounce his real name. This is his place." Will was beginning to remind me of Malcolm, albeit he was a slightly more chipper incarnation.

"He?"

"He, she—take your pick. It doesn't really work that way with them.

Anyway, Johnson's a friend. He just wants to say hello. We haven't had too many migrants lately," explained Will.

"Oh. Um, hello," I said to Johnson. I also bowed slightly, for reasons unknown.

"He can't understand you, mate. Use this." Will produced a small handheld device that resembled a smartphone. "Push this button and talk." As Will handed me the device, Johnson pulled out a small contraption from his pocket and placed it on his head. Part of it stuck into his tiny ear. I repeated my greeting. This time, Johnson reacted enthusiastically. My handheld device suddenly spoke to me in a computerized voice, similar to a sentroid's.

"Welcome," Johnson said via the device. No sounds emanated from his mouth. "We regret that you were taken from your homeland. We hope that you will find serenity in your new habitat." The device's choice of words made me feel a little like a zoo animal.

Although something might have been lost in translation, I appreciated the sentiment more than I could have imagined. As I write this now, I recognize the comicality of the moment, but at the time it just seemed surreal. I had never communicated directly with a Serrone in all those years on the planet, yet everything I was forced to do had been at their command. In an instant, Johnson's humble apology was nearly enough to rectify the whole ordeal—at least for a moment. I thanked Johnson again and he exited the room.

"As I was saying," said Will. "I'm sure you have questions, but I can't imagine that you came here alone."

I had completely forgotten about the others. I led Will to their hiding place, and he invited them to come inside. We crammed into the small room where Will briefed us on the remaining leg of our journey, assuring us that we would be entirely in their hands. "They" referred to Will and his team of volunteers who shepherd newcomers into Plymouth via their underground railroad.

We were to cross the river that night—as soon as possible. Jagger would pilot a small craft across the mile-wide stretch of water. On the other bank was a region known as Foronya, with a ruler sympathetic to the plight of humans—the patron Serrone of Plymouth. The sooner we could set foot there, the safer we (and Will, and Johnson) would be. Once ashore, we would camp for the remainder of the night then make our way southeast by truck until we reached a seaside port, several miles south of the estuary from whence we came. There we were to wait for a ship—of the marine variety. The boat would sail in a southeasterly direction until we arrived at the grail of our quest: the human settlement of Plymouth. We were instructed to keep our weapons—not that they would be needed during our journey, but because all citizens of Plymouth were encouraged to retain as many weapons as they desired. The security of the settlement was paramount, and thus the primary responsibility of everyone.

Our guides executed the trip without a hitch, as if they had performed the operation hundreds of times. We were detained at the seaside port for several days waiting for the ship to return from Plymouth. Our chaperone, Jagger, assured us that this was nothing out of the ordinary. The delay caused the accumulating anticipation and excitement among my fellow pilgrims to reach a fever pitch. I found it difficult to resist their contagious enthusiasm and finally surrendered to the notion that Plymouth was a genuine place.

My newfound exhilaration was dampened a bit when I asked Jagger if he knew anyone in Plymouth by the name of Nicholas, Tina, or Pablo, and he regrettably answered "no" to each. Nor could he recall ever meeting anyone fitting my detailed description of Monte, which no one would possibly forget. However, he qualified his response by noting that he was relatively new to the settlement and had spent most of his time working for Will outside of its boundaries. I confided to Ying that I couldn't bear the guilt of reaching Plymouth only to find that the others had died trying to do the same.

We woke one morning to see that our proverbial ship had come in during the night. We shook hands with Jagger and boarded the vessel, which was comparable to a giant floating hotdog. We soon discovered that it didn't float at all once it reached top speed, which was about fifty knots. At this velocity it managed to hover above the waves like a flying fish. I was more astonished to see that the entire crew of this avant-garde contraption, a captain and two mates, was human. The second mate was an amiable fellow who eagerly answered our questions. I decided against inquiring about my friends in order to spare myself the anguish of knowing. Bird asked what the population of Plymouth was.

"Including the ten of you," the second mate said, "that makes thirty-seven." He maintained a straight face for a moment then burst out laughing at his own joke. "Nah, I'm just playing with you. We've got nearly three thousand people now. Almost eight hundred are children."

At first, I was taken aback by the numbers. On second thought, they made sense. Abductions from Earth occurred over a period lasting more than twenty years. A lot of people can go missing without causing worldwide suspicion if handled discreetly, which seemed to be a forte of the Serrones. There could be thousands of humans on Serrone even before the number of native-born people was factored in.

It was what the second mate said next that floored me. He told us that we would be arriving in less than an hour. It turned out that the entire cruise only lasted four hours. I had been expecting it to take days—everything else had. Everybody seemed to be aware of this factoid but me. We pulled into the harbor shortly thereafter, leaving me very little time to mentally prepare for my arrival.

37

Plymouth, as seen from my vantage point on the pier, was not at all what I had imagined. I had long ago contrived a mental image of a primitive camp with a few log cabins interspersed with tents and campfires. That snapshot had remained frozen in my imagination over all those years, prevailing amid the denial of its existence. The waterfront I now saw before me represented a well-established settlement, reminding me of a prosperous frontier town in the Old West. The buildings were constructed of brick and neatly trimmed lumber, indicating the presence of competent saw mills and masonry ovens in the settlement. Betraying the Old West motif were the various self-propelled vehicles traversing the roads and paths near the dock.

I was equally awed by the size of the city. The shoreline stretched for hundreds of yards in both directions, and several piers jutted into the sea, to which clusters of tiny vessels were moored. From my position I could see up a main thoroughfare that ran from the waterfront into the city where it seemed to disappear on the horizon. Beyond the far edge of Plymouth lay the foot of a massive mountain range. These picturesque southern peaks were capped with the same violet-hued snow that colored the northern ranges in which I had lived. The town had the appearance of sustaining a population much larger than three thousand, as if its urban planners had prepared for droves of immigration. This impression made me feel welcome.

I also felt secure. Several tall watch towers rose above the buildings around the perimeter of the city. I could see large plasma cannons mounted in the two towers near the waterfront—possibly gifts from the citizens of Foronya, I wondered. The towers supplemented the imposing natural barriers of the mountains and the sea, placing the city in a well-defended position. The founders, whoever they were, chose well.

A small welcoming committee had gathered at the pier. Like our escorts on the underground railroad, these people had an established routine and had clearly processed hundreds of new migrants. Yet they still beamed with genuine exuberance, making us feel like honored guests, or long-lost relatives. They led the ten of us into a small pavilion near the dock and handed each of us a welcome package. The bag included a change of clothes, some peculiar fruits (or possibly vegetables) that I had never seen before, a hand-drawn map of the town, and a handful of freshly-minted coins. An older woman delivered the orientation.

She told us that the coins were forged from copper mined in the nearby mountains. A fixed amount of additional currency was placed into circulation as the population increased. We were also free to barter with goods, though like most newcomers, none of us possessed any. She described their form of government, as laid out in a constitution that we were encouraged to review. A council of eleven representatives was elected every two years. The council was chartered to run the city and make small decisions. A city commissioner was selected by the council to lead the small team of civil servants that provided basic services to the community. Weightier decisions were put to vote among all adult citizens. (I wondered how they determined who was an adult, as the exact age of many natives was uncertain.) She reviewed the map with us, highlighting points of interest, such as the general store, grocery, and hospital.

The woman, who served as the current city commissioner, wrapped up the orientation by telling us that we would have two days to decide if we wanted to stay. If so, we would be sworn to uphold the constitution of Plymouth. (As if we could go anywhere else.) We would be free to pursue any occupation or business, and all citizens were required to participate in the defense of the city, similar to a reserve army. She concluded by telling us that we could stay at the so-called "newbie barracks" at no charge for two weeks, following which we would have to find our own living quarters or begin paying a nominal rent. She opened the floor to questions before escorting us to the newbie barracks. Somebody asked about the threat of Serrone attacks.

"There has never been an attack on Plymouth," she assured us. She caveated the proclamation by telling us that mysterious sea and air ships had been sighted nearby—probably to "probe us." She then caveated the caveat by saying that they hadn't seen any airships in recent years.

I asked about the relationship with Foronya. She described how the Foroynans had set aside the land for Plymouth. They provided technological assistance in setting up a small power grid using a native source of energy (which still remains a mystery to me) and donated several vehicles. The commissioner told us that the Foroynans continued to provide security, though not within the city, and that their peacekeeping force was rarely seen. She then boldly predicted that Plymouth would soon outgrow its need for external security and become a formidable nation that was fully capable of defending itself.

"When we achieve a certain level of military capability, we will demand the release of all humans held in bondage on Serrone," she said proudly. That sounded like a pretty good cause to me—one for which my skills would fit nicely. I was very impressed by what I had heard and now it was finally time to see the town.

Each of us had been assigned a sponsor—a volunteer to help us adjust to life in freedom. Mine was a guy named Donald who grew up in Gulf Port, Mississippi. He greeted me with a warm Southern drawl following the orientation, and made me feel as if it was I who was doing him a favor. We spent a few minutes getting to know each other.

"Where ya coming from, Shaker?"

"Toghan. The northern region."

"You've come a long way."

"Tell me about it."

As we talked, I noticed that several other citizens had gathered to look over the newcomers. A small group of kids was among them, and one boy in particular immediately caught my eye. He had dark hair, a brown complexion, and would have been about twelve or thirteen years old. I politely interrupted Don's backstory at the first opportune moment.

"Don, who's that boy over there in the blue shirt?"

"That's Shawn. Do you know him?"

"No," I replied dejectedly. I decided just to ask him outright—just rip the bandage right off. "Is there a boy here, about that age, named Jasper?"

"That's Jasper standing right there next to Shawn," said Donald.

Yes! There he was. I don't know how I had failed to recognize him. He had his mother's eyes, and his posture reminded me of my father in a curious way. "Do you know Jasper?" Donald asked.

"If he's who I think he is, I'm his father." I sounded uncertain but I wasn't. There was no mistaking that he was *my* Jasper, and my heart began to pound, fueled by a mix of elation and trepidation.

"Really? I'll call him over," said Donald.

"Hold on." I needed to let it sink in. I briefly considered cleaning up and shaving first. In my current state I surely cut an imposing figure, and I didn't want his first impression to be one of intimidation. I called Ying over for her opinion, though I was really just stalling. Ying gave me the kick in the pants I needed.

"Why you ask me? Ask *him*," she said, pointing to the boy. I laid my rifle aside and asked Donald to call him over. What would I say to him?

Donald handled it perfectly. "Jasper, I'd like you to meet a friend of mine," he said, then handed it over to me.

"Hi Jasper. Do you live with a lady named Tina?"

"Yes sir. She takes care of me." He was very polite and well-spoken, unlike most of the native-born humans I had lived with in the slave camps.

"It looks like she does a really good job. What about a man named Nicholas—do you know him?"

"Uncle Nicholas?"

"Yeah, that's the guy," I chortled. "Did you come to Plymouth with him and Tina?"

"I think so. I can't remember."

"That's okay." I placed a hand on his shoulder. "Jasper, my name is Shaker. Do you know that name?"

"Yes sir."

"You don't have to call me sir. So… you know who I am?"

"Yes… they thought you were dead."

I playfully rubbed the top of his head. "Nah, never even came close."

"Where have you been?" he asked. It caught me a little by surprise.

"That's a very good question. I'll tell you all about it later—is that okay? Now let's go find Nicholas and Tina." Jasper studied me for a moment then hugged me. I did my best to wipe away my tears before I released him.

We set out on foot up the main thoroughfare—Donald, Ying, Ying's sponsor, Jasper, and myself. I kept my arm loosely around Jasper's shoulder as we walked. At one point he turned and looked up at me with a huge grin.

"Are you going to live with us?" he asked.

"I don't know, Jasper. I just got here. Let's see what Tina has to say about it."

We approached a handsome brick abode with a wide front porch at the end of a side street. Jasper took off running toward it.

"I'll go get her!" he shouted back to us. I was still about fifty feet from the porch when he emerged with her. The first thing I noticed was how she favored her right leg and walked with the aid of a cane. It drew my attention from her face. She froze as soon as she laid eyes upon me. I instinctively stopped and took a closer look. She appeared a bit older and it had done nothing to diminish her beauty. There was no mistaking her caramel skin, brown eyes, and long black braids. There was no mistaking my Leesheh. Nothing could have prepared me for seeing this spectral figure, returned from the dead.

"Shakespeare?" she murmured in disbelief.

"Yeah… it's me." That was all I could manage to say. I hurried toward her. She dropped her cane, rushed down the porch steps, and jumped into my arms. We remained in a speechless embrace for what seemed like several minutes. I gave up trying to hide my tears from my son.

"I can't believe you're alive," I told her.

"I can't believe that *you* are alive, Shakespeare. Where have you been?"

I realized how much I had missed the sound of her voice. I turned to Jasper. "I thought you said that you lived with Tina?"

"I do," replied Jasper. She lives with Mom and me." As if on cue, Tina emerged from the house to see the source of the commotion. She instantly recognized Ying and me, and bounded over to join the reunion with her arms flailing in the air. Leesheh dispatched Jasper to fetch our friends while the rest of us retreated into the house. Before long Nicholas arrived with Saba and their two young children.

"So… *you two*?" I said whimsically after we had spent a few minutes catching up. "When did *that* happen?"

"It started before we left Abasha City," said Nicholas. "You were just oblivious."

"Yeah, I guess so. I probably missed a lot of things in those days."

Their children, a seven-year-old boy and five-year-old girl, were as engaging and polite as Jasper. As would be expected, Nicholas was one of the resident scientists and inventors in Plymouth. His specialties were meteorology and timekeeping. He was one of the few citizens that interacted regularly with Serrones from Foronya to exchange ideas. Foronya was the first Serrone region to rise above the dark cloud of war that had enveloped the planet for decades. Foronyans were eager to rekindle the entrepreneurial spirit that enabled the wonderous scientific and technical achievements of earlier generations. They also recognized the potential of humans beyond physical labor and soldiering. As such, they welcomed collaboration with Nicholas and people of his ilk. His team had created a clock that measured seconds, minutes, hours, and days relative to Serrone. There were sixty seconds in a minute, sixty minutes in an hour, and twenty-four hours in a day. Although each was slightly longer than its counterpart on Earth, we couldn't tell the difference.

I was caught off guard once again when the celebration was placed into an awkward hold by the arrival of Pablo. I could see by the way he anxiously scanned the room that nobody had informed him about Susan. I took him into the kitchen and explained how she died while watching my back. I described how she saved my and Ying's lives. I told him that her death was my responsibility and asked him to accept my heartfelt apology.

"She knew what she was doing," he told me. "She made her own choices." I appreciated his kindness but I could see how much it hurt him to have his hopes revived so many years after coming to grips with her presumed death. He stayed at the house for a short while then quietly slipped out. I am glad to tell you that Pablo eventually found happiness with a woman who worked alongside him at a shop where they built and repaired furniture.

Monte made his appearance during dinner. It came as no surprise to hear that he was employed in the town's barbershop. During our time back in Abasha City, he was the only person I would trust to trim my beard. He and Ying shook hands, following which she shoved him playfully against the wall.

"How come you don't come get me?" she asked facetiously. "You here having fun while I out there fighting." Monte laughed and returned with a surprisingly witty answer—something akin to not wanting her around. It was clear that his command of the English language had surpassed his mentor's.

The party continued late into the night before the last guest, Monte, headed out. Leesheh and Tina insisted that Ying stay with us in the house until she could find a place of her own. Ying slept on a sofa in the living room while I retired upstairs with Leesheh. We were both too wired to sleep, so we decided to go outside and see the stars. She led me to the back of the house where a round, stumpy plant with oval-shaped, eggplant-colored leaves sat alone in the middle of the yard.

"Jasper and I found that outside the city and we transplanted it here," she said. We lay down underneath the plant where she proceeded to tell me her story, beginning with the day she was taken from me. I'll leave the details to her, in case she decides to write her own memoir one day, as I've encouraged her to do. I do feel compelled to mention the fate of her guardian, to whom, according to Leesheh, she owes her life. She described in detail how Mr. Swag stayed and protected her the night she lay near death in the jungle when the others ran off. She told me that he risked his own life to save her by surrendering to the Toghans. From there they embarked on a five-year odyssey, rich with trials and tribulations not unlike my own, before reaching Plymouth. Sadly, Mr. Swag died of an illness after spending only a year in freedom.

Since arriving in Plymouth, Leesheh had worked part-time as an attorney in a city with virtually no crime and very few civil cases. She found steady work drafting legal documents on behalf of the city council and sometimes volunteered at the daycare center.

On the following morning, Jasper headed to school and Leesheh showed me around the city. I suggested that we borrow a vehicle but she insisted on walking. She told me that her handicap looked worse than it felt. We found Luther behind the counter of the general store. He looked well for a man who surely was an octogenarian, though not even he could confirm his age. He told me how he was the owner of the store while the actual owner stood behind him shaking his head. I purchased a few sundry items at a price that supposedly included Luther's "personal discount," though once again the owner stood behind him and shook his head quietly.

From there, Leesheh took me to a building near the waterfront where Evelyn served as one of the four officers on the city's police force. We spent the better part of an hour swapping stories about the Battle of Abasha City. She recounted the journey that led them from Abasha City to Plymouth, and proudly noted that every one of the children with whom I had "flabbergasted" her that night at the tunnel was alive and prospering. All had found eager foster parents soon after arriving. Evelyn went out of her way to ensure that I met every one of the children during my first week in the city.

Tina and Saba both worked in the city's daycare facility. The term was a bit of a euphemism. The center went far beyond providing babysitting services for working parents. It also housed newly-arrived orphaned children while they awaited foster homes. Most of the children arrived under-nourished and under-educated. They required a lot of attention and care, which was happily provided by the dedicated men and women who worked there. A year after I arrived, Tina adopted two children from the center. They moved into their own house at the southern edge of town, just a short hike away from the foothills that lay at the base of the mountain range.

Ying found employment as a soldier in the small regular army that oversaw the coordination and training of the reserve defense force. She spent two weeks sleeping on our couch before renting a spare room in a house just down the street from ours. She eventually started a training and conditioning program for teens that she conducted in her spare time. Jasper was an active and eager participant. Leesheh and I were happy that Jasper was learning to defend himself, yet we dreaded the day that he might be called into real action.

I slowly transitioned into freedom and civilian life with the help of my family and friends. A few weeks after arriving, I accepted a position teaching English and creative writing to the high school students. Grammar was a necessity, but my heart was in creative writing. I wanted to foster a generation of writers who would become the foundation of Plymouth literature, and we were starting from scratch. Adults were welcome and encouraged to sit in on my classes, and many of the native-born former soldiers took advantage. I continued to write in my journal, though less about current experiences in favor of recapturing memories from pages that had been lost or destroyed over the years before they disappeared.

Epilogue

Last year, my wife and I attended the dedication of a memorial to all of the soldiers who lost their lives as slave warriors on Serrone. As we were walking home, she asked me about the journals I used to keep about my own experiences during those times. This inspired me to climb into our attic and rifle through the contents of an old locker I had stashed there more than thirty years ago. I came across stacks of handwritten pages describing the adventures of a man called Shaker. I sat on the wooden floor for hours reading the entire collection for the first time. Through a retrospective lens it wasn't difficult to see how the hero of the story was thwarted as much by his internal conflicts as by the villains who persecuted him. I could certainly relate to him, for I had walked in his boots. Yet I couldn't help but feel, once again, that I was reading about another man's experiences.

Shortly after arriving in Plymouth, I relinquished the names of Shaker and Shakespeare in favor of my Earth name. This was the custom of the former slaves—a symbolic way of denouncing and demarcating our years spent in servitude. We could never forget that horrific period of our lives, nor did we wish to. Reminders of the early years on Serrone were omnipresent. I only had to see my wife's impeded gait, or how she occasionally winced in pain, to recall them. Using our Earth names reinforced the notion that our current society strived to mirror those in which we had lived on our former planet.

It was Leesheh who encouraged me to aggregate the journals into a single narrative, to which I obviously agreed, and thus led you to this moment. I have spent many months bringing this character back to life—a labor of love that has brought me laughter and tears many times over. I am saddened to see that the end of the project is at my doorstep, yet I'm excited to undertake another literary challenge. Still, I feel compelled to prolong this one a bit more and bring you up to speed on the history of our determined and persevering society.

I am far too proud of my son to resist boasting about his accomplishments. Jasper inherited his mother's brains and just a touch of his father's stubbornness. He followed in Leesheh's footsteps, practicing law in the family firm before taking the helm upon her retirement. He presently splits his time among several endeavors. In addition to his law practice, he teaches at the college and serves on the city council. He still manages to find time for his wife and four children, though their grandparents are always eager and available to fill in when needed. My oldest grandchildren are blossoming into productive young adults in their own right. Their generation has never known wartime and will one day inherit a city of more than thirty thousand citizens.

Of my friends that survived their own personal journeys from cargo holds to Plymouth, all found happiness and success in some fashion or another, for there are many ways to measure them. The most prosperous were those who truly accepted, from the beginning, that they would never return to Earth, and embraced this city as their home. Some of my friends are still with us and others have passed on. Those who have died spent their final years living on their own terms in a free society.

This project has also rekindled memories of another friend, one whom I hadn't thought of in decades. I rarely venture far from Plymouth, and over the course of the few expeditions I've made, I have never come across a combot. Conventional wisdom suggests that the androids of my time have long since been recycled into modern versions designed for more peaceful purposes. It makes me sad to think that Dee is no longer alive—and yes, upon reading my journals, I'm convinced that he was a living being in his own right. If by some chance he's still out there in this world, I wonder if he ever thinks of me.

As the city commissioner predicted on the day I arrived, Plymouth eventually outgrew the protective shield of the Foronyan peacekeepers. Our burgeoning nation flexed its muscle to secure the peaceful release of all remaining human slaves, with support from Serrone regions that had grown weary of warlords and warfare. On Serrone, the monarchs, warlords, despots, and thugs gradually gave way to libertarian societies intent on reviving the scientific, technological, and artistic spirits of their ancestors. But the path ahead would be long and arduous. Diabolical forces powerful enough to reduce a great civilization to ashes are impossible to eradicate completely. Our greatest mistake would be to presume that such a downfall could never happen again.

I undertook this project to organize and document my experiences for personal reasons and to share them with my family. I soon realized that my story is a historical account of a period in Serrone, told from the perspective of a soldier serving in the rank and file of a slave army. I have made this narrative available so that future generations may understand the era of warlords from a single point of view. My story is just one of many, and I hope that my former comrades will document their own experiences. In fact, other historical records have preceded mine. We have enjoyed the advances of printing technologies in Plymouth for several years now, and have amassed a significant library of original work.

My more scientifically astute comrades assure me that the friends and relatives we left on Earth are long since deceased. The theory of relativity as applied to interstellar travel suggests that, from our perspective, far more time has elapsed on Earth than the decades we've lived away from it. My dream is that copies of this story might somehow find their way to Earth and enable the descendants of our families there to solve the puzzle of their ancestors' mysterious disappearances. You have likely noticed that this story is targeted for readers on Earth, which you may attribute to my fantastical notions (i.e., wishful thinking). I know that it cannot happen in my lifetime, but perhaps years from now, an envoy might return to my home world. There is an ongoing collaborative effort between humans and Serrones to renew interstellar space exploration. Surely there is a record—a roadmap of sorts, buried somewhere in the ruins of a great Serrone city—that describes Earth's location. Perhaps you are reading this on Earth?

Michael Taylor
Plymouth, Serrone Moon
The year 51 A.P.

ABOUT THE AUTHOR

C.C. Prestel is widely-considered to be the best author—in his home office. Following a career as a software engineer, executive, and small business owner in Maryland, he retired to Las Vegas, Nevada, where he decided to rekindle his passion for creative writing. In addition to novels, he dabbles in writing music and loves to jam on his guitar in the privacy of his bedroom. He also enjoys hiking and can sometimes be found at a Texas Hold'em no-limit poker table.

Made in the USA
Middletown, DE
10 May 2019